BOOK 3

On the

Road

to

Teman

By L. Nicodemus Lyons

Central Skagit Library District
110 West State Street
Sedro-Woolley, WA 98284
www.centralskagitlibrary.org

For a pronunciation guide, see the last page.

CastleLyons Books

Visit The Alliance website at:
theallianceseries.blogspot.com

Visit my author page at:
Amazon.com/author/nicodemuslyons

RYGIA

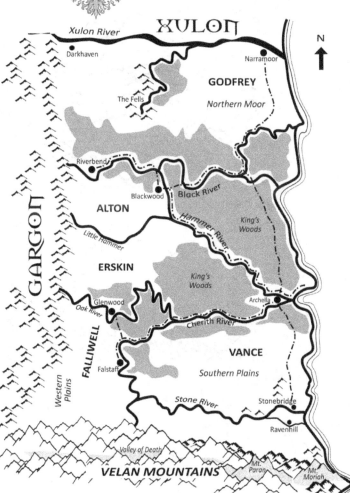

TEMAN

"You are going to have the light
just a little while longer.
Walk while you have the light,
before darkness overtakes you."

John 12:35

1
JUSTUS

1

Fourteen-year-old Justus Corden stepped into his uncle's shack, slamming the door behind himself. "I'm hungry."

"Git back out there and finish yer plowin'."

"It's done."

Milford leered up at him. Justus leered back, knowing he was already taller than his uncle by at least an inch and not afraid of him. He watched one of Milford's eyes squint. His uncle was beginning to fear him. These standoffs had become a frequent occurrence, and the tide was finally turning in Justus' direction.

Milford looked away first. "I ain't yer lackey. Find yer own grub. As if I ain't got enough to do without raising you all by myself."

Justus grumbled as he headed out, slamming the door again.

Milford yelled after him, "Git yourself a job while you're out there!"

Get a job? Justus ground his teeth in frustration. There was nothing he'd like better—a way to make his own money so he could leave this place for good. He'd been trying since he was twelve, but no jobs were to be had. Not in Darkhaven. Not for a Corden.

Seemed everyone in the village despised the Corden name. Outcasts and vagabonds themselves, they had made it clear that no one named Corden was welcome, even among their kind.

Justus had no idea why.

Creeping behind the miller's house, Justus inspected the

day's garbage. He knew the miller had just butchered a hog, and he hoped he might find some of the scraps. As he picked through the pile of garbage below the cottage window, the scent of rotting food curdled his stomach.

A breeze flowed in his direction, bringing a different scent. Inhaling deeply, he moaned in delight. Roast pork! *Oh, for a shank bone heavy with meat and dripping with juices!* He sidled closer to the window and put his nose by the crack between the wooden shutter and the window sill.

A man's voice met him. "Sure be a warm night. It's worse in here than outside, what with that pig roastin' there. Go open the shutter, woman!"

"As if you ain't got two good legs to walk over there and open it yourself, Arney!"

"Quit yer gripin', woman, and go open that shutter!"

Justus pressed himself to the house as the shutter slammed against the mud wall, barely missing his face.

"Blast that lazy, good-for-nothing..." The woman's voice trailed away as she stepped away from the window.

The next thing Justus heard was the front door opening.

"Where you goin'?" the woman hollered.

"Out for some air," Arney called from just outside the door.

Hearing no more, Justus wondered whether the matron had gone to join her husband. He peeked into the open window, eyes fixated on the hearth on the opposite wall.

The pig! Golden droplets of juice oozed from crackling brown flesh, dropping onto the fire and landing with a sizzle. Wisps of delectable aroma spiraled through the air, finding their way to Justus' nose. His eyes nearly filled with tears at the smell of it. He licked his parched lips.

The next thing he knew, his head was in the window and no one was in sight. For only a second he considered how easy it would be to jump through the window, pull a leg off the beast, then jump out and run. If there was one thing his long legs were good for, it was running like the wind.

His conscience pricked him. Unfortunately, his

conscience didn't scream as loudly as his empty stomach. He climbed in.

"What the—?" The matron stepped into the kitchen, grabbed an iron pot, and swung it toward him. Justus escaped through the window, but not before the matron yelled to her husband. "It's that Corden boy!"

Arney took pursuit, but Justus had already put a good distance between them.

Justus didn't return home until the next morning, when he found his uncle standing outside the door, fuming.

"What's the meaning of this? Stealing from the neighbors? You no good, thievin'—"

"I didn't steal nothing!"

"Arney Miller said you did. Said you made off with his dinner. He expects recompense."

A passing soldier pulled his horse to a stop and watched them.

"He's lying!" Justus shouted. "I didn't take nothing!"

"Did you or did you not break into his house?"

"Yes, but I didn't take nothing!"

"A likely story. What kind of thief breaks into a house and don't take nothing? I always knew you were good for nothing! You're no better than your mother!"

At those words, Justus hauled back and slammed his fist into his uncle's chin.

Milford fell sprawling to the ground. A string of curses flew from his lips. "Why, you—"

"Don't insult my mother!"

Milford rose. "I'll insult her if I want. She was just as good-for-nothing as you. Be thankful you never knew her, that lazy wench."

In a frenzy, Justus flew upon his uncle.

The soldier on horseback put his thumb and finger in his mouth and let out a shrill whistle.

Justus stopped mid-swing, nearly choking at the sight of

the soldier. Surely he was about to be arrested for stealing. Or fighting. Maybe both.

The soldier addressed his uncle. "How'd you like me ta take that there boy offa yer hands?"

"Oh yeah?" Milford pulled himself to his feet and brushed off his pants. "How much he worth to ya?"

"Give ya twenty silver pieces."

Milford snorted. "Forty."

The soldier's eyes moved up and down Justus as though determining his worth. Justus looked from the soldier to his uncle, not quite believing what was happening. "You... you'd *sell* me?"

"I shoulda got rid of you a long time ago." He turned to the soldier. "Forty silver pieces and he's yours."

"Awful steep for a boy of no training. I'll give you thirty, final offer." Without waiting for a reply, the soldier poured some coins from his pouch into his hand.

The jingling of silver convinced Milford, who approached the soldier and held out his hand. "You gotta keep a close eye on him."

"I can handle him." Silver coins dropped into greedy hands.

Milford smiled. "Pleasure doing business with you, Mister...?"

"Kelsie," the soldier said.

Justus stared agape at his new master.

"Cheer up, kid," Kelsie said. "You'll make a good squire. Bound ta be a better life than this."

With a sigh, Justus realized the soldier was right. At least as a squire under the care of a knight he'd have his meals and lodging taken care of. With one last look toward his uncle, who was already heading toward the tavern, Justus followed the soldier's horse down the road and all the way to Archella, the city of the king.

2

For the next three months, Justus learned what it was like to be a squire to Kelsie. Kelsie didn't own a home, so they lived in the castle barracks with other landless soldiers. Although Justus was little more than a servant—cleaning up after Kelsie, delivering messages, doing whatever was asked—he at least had food to eat and a place to sleep. Sure, it was just a mat on the floor, but it was Justus' mat, and it was away from Darkhaven.

Days weren't too bad. At least there was some training with wooden swords, and always there was wrestling with the other squires. Justus often took out his frustration on the others, which turned out to his advantage. Anger spurred him to fight hard and never accept defeat.

The youngest of the squires, Charles Iscuro, befriended him immediately. The two of them were the only fourteen-year-olds and the only first-year squires among those at the barracks. Charles helped Justus learn his way around the city and the castle, particularly the armory.

Since Charles had been a page for the past seven years, he knew a lot more than Justus did and taught him what he should do and how he should act around certain people, especially the barons when they were in town.

Despite the change in his life, things didn't move along as quickly as Justus would have liked. He kept thinking things were bound to get better. Surely some real weapons training would start soon. He spent every free moment in the armory, looking over the weapons, holding them, getting the feel of them, but as the days passed he began to doubt. It didn't seem as though Kelsie wanted to make a soldier out of him after all. He just wanted a man-slave.

Nights were the worst. Kelsie spent nearly every evening at the tavern, drinking himself into a stupor. Then Justus would have to drag him back to the barracks, put him to bed, and keep everyone else from making noise and waking him. The next morning, Kelsie would be in a sour mood and took it all out on Justus. It was Uncle Milford all over again.

Finally, at the end of his third month, Justus felt a glimmer of hope when Kelsie took him to the armory and said, "Go grab yerself a sword." Justus snatched up a wooden sword and happily headed toward the castle door.

Kelsie said, "King Arkelaus is gonna be watching all you squires today. Wants ta see how good ya are. Do me proud, boy."

"Yes, sir!"

As Justus emerged from the castle and stepped into the courtyard, he passed a tall, robust man with graying golden hair and a weathered, unshaven face. General Rolland Longsword, feared and admired among all Rygian soldiers, Justus included. He had seen Rolland watching him at training, and he had seen admiration on the general's face. Rolland's face was stoic as Justus passed by, but Justus thought he caught a glint in his eye.

"Mornin', Corden." Rolland gave a slight nod.

"Uh, m... mornin', General," Justus stuttered, stopping to stare up at him. That was the first time the general had ever addressed him directly.

Rolland said, "Do your best today. The king'll be watching."

As Rolland turned to enter the castle, Justus stared after him, watching the ornate silver sword emblem on his blue tunic fade down the corridor.

"Hey, Corden, what're ya waitin' fer?" Kelsie hollered from the center of the courtyard. Justus trotted to join his master and a couple dozen other squires and their masters. "Here, gimmie that." Kelsie took the wooden sword from

Justus and motioned toward the other boys.

Aside from Charles, all were older, between the ages of fifteen and eighteen. All had seven years of page training under their belts before they had even become squires. Many of them had a few years of squire training as well.

Despite the drawbacks, Justus was the tallest and knew how to use his height to his advantage.

"Start warmin' up, boys!" Kelsie shouted.

That was their cue to stretch their muscles through wrestling. Immediately four older boys approached Justus.

"Tired of the trouncing you got yesterday?" Justus teased. "Looking for revenge?"

He watched the leader of the boys motion to another, a stocky lad, who moved behind Justus. Justus kept his eyes on the leader and his ears on the crunching of footsteps behind him. When it sounded like the stocky one was right behind him, he spun around and grabbed him by the neck. Using him for balance, he kicked out a long leg and sent the leader sprawling. Tossing the stocky one aside, he gave a third boy a blow to the jaw.

A fourth rushed him. Justus grabbed his arms and swung him into the stocky lad, who had risen and was about to charge. Both boys rolled in the dust.

Huh, Justus thought, looking toward the castle door. *I thought the king was gonna be here. Too bad he ain't here to see that.*

After long minutes of sparring with several other squires and downing each one, Justus was called away by his master. Kelsie approached holding a three-foot steel broadsword. "Here, Corden. Give this a try."

When Kelsie tossed the sword, Justus caught it by the hilt. Finally! A real sword! It was heavier than it looked, and he found he had to spread his feet to steady himself. Imitating moves he'd seen the soldiers do, he sliced the air several times, back and forth, making figure eights.

"Ready?" Kelsie drew his own sword. Without warning, he swung the blade around and down.

Justus responded by instinct. His blade blocked Kelsie's and threw it back. But Kelsie was quick, repeating the attack from the opposite side. Again Justus parried the blow.

"Not bad," Kelsie said between strikes. "You been payin' attention."

"Yeah, I been watching the soldiers."

"Tell you what," Kelsie said amid the ring of steel. "Disarm me, and I'll buy you a pint."

Justus smiled. But again Kelsie was quick. This time he carved a tight arc around the blade and wrenched it from Justus' hand. The sword lifted into the air and landed with a thud in the dirt.

Soldiers chuckled. Squires laughed out loud. Kelsie said, "Next time, don't take a foolish bet. Be a few years before you can best your master."

Justus stared down at the sword. Although the laughter had subsided, it still rang in his ears. *A few years, huh?* He picked up the sword and shouted, "Kelsie!"

Kelsie faced him. With a surprised look and a shake of his head, he said, "Don't make no sense to humiliate yerself a second time."

"Maybe I got no sense, then. Have at me."

"Fine. I don't mind puttin' ya in yer place." Kelsie drew his sword and immediately swung.

Justus parried that blow and the next. Another parry to the left, one to the right, then he cleaved a tight arc around Kelsie's blade in the same manner he had seen it done. Kelsie's sword flipped from his hand and seemed to pause in the air before falling to the ground flat.

Soldiers and squires stared dumbstruck for a second then burst into cheers. Kelsie grumbled. Justus sidled up to him and said, "You owe me a pint."

The look on Kelsie's face took Justus aback. He saw something there he'd never seen before. Fear. Not a scared kind of fear, but the kind you might feel knowing you were about to be replaced. A hate-filled kind of fear.

A voice from atop the castle roof called down. "I say! Ho there, young Corden!"

Shading his eyes and looking upward, Justus squinted into the morning sun to see King Arkelaus standing with General Rolland at the parapet on the roof of the castle. The king's golden, shoulder-length hair gleamed in the sunlight almost as brightly as the jewel-studded crown on his head.

So that's where he was. I wonder how long he's been there. "Good day, Your Majesty!" Justus swept his arm out as he bowed at the waist.

"And a good day to you. I say, how long have you been practicing with a full-sized broadsword?"

"Why, it's my first time, Sire."

The king and General Rolland exchanged several quiet words, then the king turned and headed out of sight. No sooner had Justus begun to wonder if he'd made some offense, Rolland called down, "Stay there, lad. We're coming to you."

The soldiers and squires in the courtyard murmured as the minutes passed. Feeling certain he was about to be reprimanded, Justus asked Kelsie, "What's going on?"

Kelsie grumbled, "Don't know. And I don't like it none."

Finally the door opened and the general and king stepped out. King Arkelaus strode right up to Justus, who bowed.

"Look at me, boy," the king said.

Justus straightened and looked the king dead in the eyes, which he found to be very bright and full of wisdom.

"You were right, Rolland," the king said. "Fearless. Arrogant, perhaps?"

"Undoubtedly," Rolland said.

"I can't have that," the king said.

Justus braced for a rebuke.

"Where are you from, lad?" the king asked.

"Darkhaven, Sire."

"Darkhaven! Well, it's no wonder then. You must've grown up fighting."

"Yes, Sire."

King Arkelaus stared at Justus for several more moments, looking him up and down before calling to Kelsie.

Kelsie bowed. "Yes, Sire?"

"I want this boy placed under Rolland's tutelage."

Justus' eyebrows popped up, but not as high as Kelsie's did. "You what, Sire? You can't do that! I found him! He belongs to me!"

"Found him, did you? Rumor has it you *bought* the boy."

"Well, I, uh..."

"Did you or did you not exchange money for this lad?" The king's voice was demanding now.

Kelsie dropped his gaze. "I did, Sire." For a moment Justus wondered why Kelsie told the truth. Then he realized that he himself could verify the exchange of coin. Kelsie had no choice.

King Arkelaus said, "You know how I feel about the buying and selling of my subjects. Consider yourself fortunate that I don't strip your title and banish you from the city. Taking the squire from you is a light punishment. Corden, you belong to Rolland now."

As Kelsie stomped off, Justus peered up at Rolland, mouth agape.

"Shut your fly trap, boy," Rolland said without smiling. "Come with me."

"Where are we going?" Justus asked as he followed.

"My house."

"What for?"

"If you're gonna work for me, you oughta know where I live, don't you think?"

"Am I gonna live there too?"

"Yes. If you got any belongings, best get them now."

"I don't got nuthin."

"'Don't got nuthin'?"

"No, sir, not a thing."

"I'm not talking about your stuff, Corden, I'm talking about your speech. 'Don't got nuthin'. Hah! The king's highest commander won't have a squire who can't talk right. You're gonna be spending a lot of time in the castle now, serving the king and whatnot. Can't be talking like peasant-folk. Look, I know I don't always talk right, but at least I can talk respectable most times. I don't suppose you can read or write."

"No, sir." Justus found he had to hurry to keep up with the general's long strides. They had passed through the castle gatehouse and now headed south across the Cherith River bridge.

"Well, we'll get started on that," Rolland said. "Maybe some reading lessons will get you talking right."

Shortly after crossing the bridge, they took a road that led westward through the woods. Not far down the road, a small cottage sat in a glade, its thatched roof shadowed by tall oak trees. Behind the house, a wooden fence held two horses at pasture.

"This your house?" Justus asked.

"Don't be asking stupid questions. Of course it's my house." Rolland pushed open the door and stepped inside, Justus following.

The cottage was small—just one room with a small round table in the near corner, a bed in the far corner near the fireplace, and a couple of trunks for belongings. On second look, Justus spied a cot against the wall on the other side of the fireplace.

Rolland motioned toward the cot. "That's your bed."

"A bed? I get a bed?"

"You'll get a bed whenever we sleep here. Sometimes I stay in the castle. On those days, you'll take a mat in the barracks with the other squires."

Justus stood over the cot, looking down at it, saying nothing.

"Something wrong?" Rolland asked.

"No, nuthin's wrong. Ain't never had a bed before." Justus sat on it. "Why's this here, anyway? Did you know the king would give me to you?"

Rolland chuckled. "You're not the only squire I've ever had."

"Oh." For some reason, Justus felt a little jealous not being the only one. Despite Rolland's gruff manner, there was an underlying kindness to the man. Not to mention the fact that being squire to the highest officer in the realm was quite the step up.

"Why'd the king give me to you?" he asked.

"He wanted you brought up right."

"Brought up right? Whaddaya mean?"

Rolland sat at the small round table and motioned for Justus to join him. Taking the chair opposite the general, Justus looked straight into his steel-blue eyes.

Rolland said, "That's good, looking a man in the eyes like that. Not a lot of squires got that kind of pluck."

"Fearless?" Justus said, repeating the king's word proudly.

"Arrogant," Rolland said decisively. "Like Kelsie. King Arkelaus won't have that."

"I thought you said it was good. Plucky."

"It's good if it truly is fearlessness. But with you, I think it's arrogance. You stay with Kelsie and it truly will be. It's my job to drive it out of you."

"What if I don't want it driven out?"

Rolland leaned back in his chair, arms crossed. "Yup, it's arrogance."

"Arrogance, fearlessness... what's the difference? It keeps me on the winning edge."

"You think so, huh? Tell me, Corden, what does Kelsie do in the evenings?"

"He's at the tavern, usually."

"What's he do there?"

"Drinks, mostly. Ain't that what everyone does?"

"Drinks? Drowns in it, I'd say. Where does that leave you?"

"I take care of him after. Guess I don't see nuthin wrong with it."

"That's your problem right there. You don't see 'nuthin' wrong with it. Pretty soon it'll be *you* needing someone to drag you home to sleep it off."

"What's wrong with that?"

"To lots of folks, nothing. To King Arkelaus, it's everything. He's looking for good men. *Good* men, Corden, understand? Men who care more about loyalty and uprightness than anything else. Men who keep their wits about them at all times, not compromising themselves with too much drink. Men who care more about obedience and lawfulness—more than money, more than esteem, even more than this." With his last word, Rolland smacked his own forearm, grabbing at the thick muscle there.

"More than strength?" Justus asked.

"Don't be a wise-acre. Yes, more than strength, what else could I mean?"

Justus wondered if he was going to have to put up with Rolland's put-downs for the next seven years. Still, something within him stirred, as though a small spark of decency, dormant since birth, suddenly sprung to life. More than that, he felt as though he finally found someone he could look up to—literally.

Rolland rose and removed his sword belt. "Here, you can start by sharpening this. There's a whetstone on the hearth."

As Justus pulled the sword from its sheath, his mouth dropped open. "Whoa, this is beautiful!"

The silver blade was etched in ivy from the hilt all the way to the point—heart-shaped ivy leaves, each intricately filigreed. Just under the hilt, the ivy came to full bloom with a three-petaled flower. The length of the crossguard bore the wings of an eagle outstretched in both directions—white wings edged in gold.

But what really drew Justus' eyes were the gems—a ruby at one end of the crossguard and a sapphire at the other. A diamond sparkled in the pommel. "It's just like the sword on your cloak."

"What did you think it would look like?"

"I thought you carried a plain sword like everyone else. I thought your emblem was just, well, an emblem."

"No, it's my family emblem and my family sword. And it's old, so treat it with respect."

"How old is it?"

"I don't know. Been handed down for generations."

"How many generations?"

"If I knew that, I'd know how old it is, wouldn't I?"

Feeling a bit embarrassed for all his stupid questions, Justus turned back to gaze at the sword. On closer look, he could see tiny symbols filigreed in gold next to each jewel. "What's this?"

"Don't know," Rolland said.

"Are they symbols of some sort? They almost look like..."

"Letters. Yeah, I know. But I've never seen letters like that before. Don't know what they mean."

"Didn't anyone in your family know?" Justus asked.

"Maybe they did, long ago. But time has a way of losing things."

While Justus ran his fingers over the delicate filigree, Rolland asked, "What about *your* family?"

Justus stiffened, anger simmering in his belly. "What about 'em?"

"Who are they? What does your father do?"

"He's dead. Died before I was born. I never knew him."

"Sorry to hear that. How did he die?"

"He was murdered, all right? Anything else you want to know?" The rage began to come out in his voice.

"Do you know who did it?"

"Didn't ya hear me? It happened before I was born."

"Did your mother know who did it?"

"I dunno. She died when I was four. Been livin' with her brother ever since."

"Was he good to you?"

"Not ever." Justus knew his tone was sharp, but he couldn't help it. Nor could he help the cold shadow that he felt on his face. "Liked to remind me that my pa got himself killed. And he didn't never say nuthin' nice about my ma 'cause he didn't like that he had ta care for me."

"I'm sorry to hear that. Guess you got a lot of black marks to start you off in life. I'll have to start rectifying that right off."

Rectifying it? Justus wondered. Slowly a new feeling overcame him, pushing away the cold shadow and the anger. He almost didn't want to feel it, almost stuffed it back down inside, but then Rolland did something that made Justus nearly break down.

Opening a small box on a shelf on the mantle, Rolland pulled out a silver brooch shaped like a leaf of ivy with intricate filigree etching just like the ivy on his sword and his emblem. Just like the brooch Rolland wore at his own shoulder.

He set the brooch on the table in front of Justus. "Here you go. It's yours now, as long as you work for me."

Justus choked back the lump in his throat. He didn't like this kind of emotion washing over him, didn't want to show that kind of weakness, so he squelched it.

Rolland retook his seat. "I've been watching you, Corden. King Arkelaus and I've been talking. You got a lot of potential. But you also got a lot of anger bottled up inside. You gotta let go of it or it'll kill you."

"How do you know what's inside me?" Justus fingered the ivy-leaf brooch, embarrassed at the way his voice caught.

"Cuz I got it too."

Justus' mouth dropped open. "How'd you get rid of it?"

"I'll let you know when I do."

What? Rolland? Full of anger inside? He never showed it, at least not that Justus had seen. Sure, he was terse, his manner gruff, but he was also even-tempered. His eyes shone with intelligence, sometimes even compassion. How he managed to be that way while harboring anger from some unknown source, Justus couldn't fathom.

3

Justus spent the next four years as General Rolland's constant companion and servant. Soldier training started immediately, including horse riding. Justus trained on one of Rolland's two horses and learned quickly how to leap into the saddle without touching the stirrups and how to guide the horse by pressing with his knees, keeping his hands free for weapons.

Swordplay was constant, with a real steel broadsword, much to his delight. Holding a sword in his hand seemed such a natural thing, like he was born to it. He soon learned why Rolland was the highest officer of the land—his skills with a sword were unparalleled. And Justus had the honor of training with him. He couldn't believe the turn his life had taken.

Though Justus was now eighteen and the most skilled of all the squires, Rolland remained as gruff with him as ever, still making put-downs when appropriate. But Justus could see how Rolland's manner and methods had taught him to be stronger, smarter, quicker. Rolland would accept nothing but the best from him, which made all the difference in the world.

When not training, Justus sat with the other squires in the castle for lessons in reading, etiquette, even dancing, all taught by the castle scholar Demas, a thirty-something man with hair so golden it almost seemed unnatural. But Demas was a patient teacher, even with the roughneck squires.

The other squires grumbled more at the dancing than the reading, and at first it seemed as though there was no point to it for someone who wanted to be a soldier. But before long Justus could see how the dancing helped with his balance and with the ability to move quickly, turning and spinning without toppling over—traits that would serve him well on the battlefield.

Along with the training in weapons and scholastics, Justus was learning to serve—at the king's table, no less. The great hall in the palace of Rygia was a grand place to work, with a tiled floor, tapestries and heraldic shields on the walls, several tables and benches filling the huge room, and a long oak table on the dais. Chairs sat around three sides of the table, leaving one long side empty so servants could approach with platters of food and pitchers of drink.

The two chairs at the center were cushioned and canopied—thrones for the king and queen. The chair at the queen's right belonged to their nine-year-old son, Prince Medan. Above the thrones, a large shield on the wall bore the emblem of Rygia—a silver eagle on a blue field.

The rest of the chairs at the high table were reserved for special guests, especially the eight powerful barons of Rygia, who were often in the royal city for quarterly meetings and any other business that presented itself.

Serving the barons was at first nerve-wracking, but Justus soon learned that they took no notice of the squires, as though they were nothing more than ornaments flitting about the room. As long as plates and mugs were kept full, the squires were ignored. But should a baron find his mug empty, woe to the first squire he laid eyes on!

This behavior of the barons created a stark contrast to that of the king himself. King Arkelaus never failed to greet Justus personally and give kind words of thanks for his service, even in front of the barons. On quiet days, Justus often overheard Rolland giving the king reports on Justus' progress, as though Arkelaus himself had taken a special interest in him.

The king's wife, Queen Estrella, Justus found to be beautiful. Tall and stately, her long blonde hair always shimmered in the firelight, like silk ribbons. She was always smiling, which brightened any room she entered. She, too, greeted Justus personally, even inquiring to his health. Because of this, Justus made sure to take special care of her at the table, helping her to her seat and giving her the choicest morsels from the serving trays.

Though the queen was beautiful, she wasn't the most beautiful woman Justus had ever seen. That honor was reserved for someone special he had recently spotted in the marketplace. Unfortunately, his duties kept him so busy he rarely had time to go there. When he did, the chances of running into her were slim. So he always kept his eyes open for an opportunity to go to market, and when none came, he often created them.

One morning, while setting up the high table for breakfast, Justus kept close to his friend, Charles Iscuro. The moment King Arkelaus entered with General Rolland, Justus grabbed Charles by the tunic and plastered his fist into Charles' face.

"What the—!" Charles said, falling to the floor.

Justus lifted him and punched him again. Charles fell back against a table, arms flailing. His right hand slammed into a clay pot, smashing it. The sharp edge of a shard sliced through his fingers.

Justus leapt toward Charles yet again, but General Rolland grabbed him and pulled him off, shouting, "What's the matter with you?"

Struggling against Rolland's grasp, Justus pointed at Charles, yelling, "He called me a bastard!"

"I did not!" Charles shouted, gripping his bloodied hand.

King Arkelaus joined them, an angry look on his face. "Squire Corden, what is the meaning of this?"

Justus jumped to attention, putting an arm around Charles and smoothing his friend's tunic. "Nothing, Sire. Just a playful wrangle. Right, Charles?"

Charles grumbled, gripping his right hand.

"I thought you had a better hold on this squire, Rolland,"

the king said. "I'm surprised to see this kind of outburst. And bullying a man smaller than himself? What have you to say of this?"

"He can't help it, Sire, most boys are smaller than him."

King Arkelaus swept his arm out. "Look what you've done to the place, Corden. Clean up this mess, then out with you. You can clean the royal latrine for punishment."

"Yes, Sire!" Justus said with enthusiasm. As he trotted out, he heard the king yell at Charles, "Both of you!"

When Charles caught up with him, Justus grabbed him by the tunic and dashed out of the great hall. But instead of heading up to the king's chamber, he dragged Charles outside and through the castle courtyard.

"Why'd you have to do that, Cordo?" Charles whined, blood smearing both hands. "I never called you a bastard. I thought I was your friend."

"You are my friend, that's why you helped me get out of serving table just now."

"Yeah, but now we have to clean the latrine. Hey, where are you taking me?"

With his hand still on Charles' tunic, Justus pulled him through the open gate. "To the market."

"The market? What for?"

"You'll see."

Just beyond the gate were the lists—a flat area in front of the castle and between the two rivers, kept open for annual tournaments. Beyond the lists the city began, spreading from the Hammer River on the north to the Cherith River along the south and westward into the woods. Wattle-and-daub houses with thatched roofs lined dirt streets that followed no particular pattern.

At the very front of the city, a grassy field stood surrounded by streets on three sides and the lists on the eastern side. A well sat in the center of the field. One week each month, the field was jammed full of booths—vendors hawking wares, produce, and every imaginable good that Rygia offered. All kinds of people thronged amid the booths and tables, haggling over prices, corralling their children and their livestock.

Justus dragged Charles along the outskirts of the crowd, keeping near to the houses.

"Slow down!" Charles said, sticking out his bloodied hand. "Look what you did! I'll be scarred for life!"

"It's not a big deal," Justus said, unconcerned. "It's a badge of honor."

"It's my sword hand, for crying out loud! I'm bleeding all over."

"Charles Iscuro, you are such a baby. Here." Justus tore the edge of his tunic and handed the scrap to him. "Quit complaining."

Charles grumbled as he wound the scrap tightly around his hand. Justus didn't bother to see if Charles was finished before grabbing him again and yanking him into the shadows behind the tailor's shop.

"What's going on?" Charles asked.

"Shh, be quiet." With his body pressed hard against the mud wall of the shop, Justus slowly peered around the corner and whispered, "There she is!"

"Who?" Charles leaned around to see.

Justus pulled him back. "Be careful, she'll see you." With one arm pinning Charles to the wall, he peered around again.

A stunning young maiden was making her way through the crowd, approaching the tailor's shop. Her waist-length golden hair bounced with each step. Her bright blue eyes fairly sparkled, offsetting the natural pink glow in her cheeks.

Justus hadn't noticed that his hold on Charles had slackened until he felt Charles leaning around to see. "Wow," Charles said. "Who is she?"

"I don't know. I've only seen her a few times."

"Hey, wait a minute. Is that why you picked a fight with me? To get out of serving table? So you could gape at a girl?"

"Shh!" Justus clamped a hand over Charles' mouth.

Charles squirmed out of his grip. "Let me go! I can't believe this!"

"Shut up," Justus said through his teeth.

"I will not! Knocking me down and dragging me around all because of a girl. I oughta—"

Justus never heard what Charles thought he ought to do. Afraid the maiden would hear, all he could think of was how to shut Charles up. He tackled him, throwing him down and tumbling with him right into the street. As he leapt to his feet, he yanked Charles up with him and hauled back a fist, ready to strike.

He froze. There was the beautiful maiden standing before him, eyes wide, mouth agape.

Shame washed over Justus, quickly replaced by anger. This wasn't how he wanted her first sight of him to be— beating up on someone smaller than himself.

"This is all your fault." He slammed his fist into Charles' chin.

The next evening, after his chores were done, Justus found Charles sitting on a bench in the soldiers' barracks, furiously cleaning his master's helmet.

"Forget it, Cordo," Charles said without looking up. "I'm not doing anything for you anymore. Not after what you did to me yesterday."

"I said I was sorry. How's the hand?"

Charles held out his right hand to show Justus the ragged red line etched across his knuckles. "I'll be scarred for life!"

Justus pulled up a stool and sat on it. "C'mon, Charles, can't you just forget that? I promise I'll never hit you again. Just find out who she is and where she lives."

"Nothin' doin'. As far as I'm concerned, you can call our friendship off."

A dark tone colored Justus' voice as he said, "You don't mean that."

"I certainly do mean it."

Rising, Justus straightened himself to his full height.

"You oughta think about staying on my good side. You don't want me for an enemy."

"You're not so great as a friend, either!" Charles slammed the helmet on a table and squinted upward. "You think too much of yourself, Cordo. If you're so great, do your own spying. Or are you afraid to talk to a girl?"

"I'm not afraid of anything."

"Sure you are. I'm telling the other squires you were too scared to talk to a girl."

"Why, you—" Justus grabbed Charles and hefted him off the bench, but then checked himself. "I'll show you who's afraid." Dropping Charles, he headed for the door.

"Where are you going?" Charles called.

"To the market!"

An hour of standing in the market square produced no sight of the maiden. The sun was setting and the crowd had dispersed, leaving only a few stragglers while merchants began to pack up their wares.

Justus knew he couldn't stay much longer or Rolland would have his hide. At the sound of giggling, he spied a group of young maidens outside the tavern. Hoping *she'd* be among them, he headed in that direction.

No luck. Too bad he wasn't interested in any of those wenches, for any one of them would happily take his arm. But they weren't his type—much too brazen. One even beckoned to him with puckered lips.

No, that wasn't his kind of girl. He preferred the demure one, the unattainable one, the one he had to fight for. Giving the tavern a wider berth, he had just decided to head back when he heard a gentle voice.

"How much is this fine, white linen?"

It was *her*, standing at the tailor's booth, handling a sample of white cloth.

"Oh, that's expensive, my lady," the tailor said. "How much do you need?"

"Enough for one gown."

"That'll cost you a good month's wages. Are you prepared to pay for such a delicacy?" When the maiden didn't answer, the tailor ogled her up and down. "If you don't have the money, I'm sure we can work out some other arrangement."

"Money is no matter," she said quickly. Even from where he stood in the shadows, Justus could see redness creep into her cheeks. She pulled a leather pouch from her belt and dropped it on the table. "I intend to pay for my goods… with *money*."

The tailor cleared his throat and eyed the money bag greedily. "In that case, if you're looking for something special, take a look at this." He pulled a bolt of emerald-green fabric from underneath the others. "It comes from the far southeast, in Rhakos. A shipment just arrived from there last week. Here, feel it."

She gathered a generous portion of the cloth in her small white hands. "It's so soft."

"Yes, and warm too. Look how it shimmers. This is for someone very special. Someone as beautiful as you, perhaps?"

The redness returned to her cheeks. "It is quite lovely." As though struggling with her decision, she laid a hand on the white fabric she had previously inspected. "I, uh… I will take the green cloth."

"An excellent choice, my lady."

As the tailor measured and cut the fabric, the maiden counted out the money and laid it on the table. She tucked the fabric under one arm, picked up a parcel at her feet and headed down the street, back into the city.

Justus knew he'd lose her if he didn't make his move now. Trotting to catch up, he called, "Evening, my lady."

She hurried on her way without speaking or even looking at him.

He ambled alongside her. "Need help? Allow me." He reached for her bundle, but she quickened her step, still not acknowledging him. Undaunted, he bounded forward and stood in her way. "Excuse me, but I'm offering to help you."

She stopped abruptly and spoke in a cold, reserved tone, still not looking up. "No, thank you, sir."

"I daresay, any of those other maidens would jump at the chance to let me help them."

"Then please make your offer to them and leave me alone."

"Alone? You shouldn't be walking the streets alone carrying that kind of money. It's not safe."

Now she did look up, eyes wide in fear. "Is that what you're after?"

"No! I was only saying that you shouldn't—"

The fear in her eyes turned to indignation. "What I should or should not do is none of your business. One thing I will say—I should not be talking to a stranger."

"In that case, let me introduce myself. I am—"

"I know who you are."

"You do?"

"Everyone knows who you are, Squire Corden."

A big smile spread across Justus' face. "Well, then, we are not strangers."

"Do you know who *I* am?"

"No. But if you tell me your name, then—"

"Then we *are* strangers. Now please, let me pass."

Finding himself at a loss for both words and actions, he didn't move. They stood at an impasse for a few moments until she said, "Surely you don't intend to bully me like you did that poor squire yesterday, do you?"

So that's it. She thinks I'm a bully. "I would never do that. Please, don't be afraid of me."

The maiden studied his face. At first he smiled under her gaze, but as he looked into her beautiful blue eyes, he gave a start and lost his smile. Something he saw there unnerved him. At the same time, it intrigued him.

Something in those sapphire eyes drew him in. Something about this girl was very different from any other girl he'd ever seen. He had to know what it was.

"No," she said. "I'm not afraid of you."

"Then let me help you." He reached for her parcels.

She pulled to one side. "You can help me by letting me pass, thank you."

Without another word, she shoved past him and continued on her way, not once turning back to see the dejected look on his face.

4

The next morning as soon as he finished serving the king and queen at table, Justus pulled Rolland aside. "General, I wanna talk to you."

"You have to see the leather merchant and get fitted for a hauberk. Come on, I'll take you. You can talk on the way."

The two headed out toward the market, which slowly awakened in the cool of the morning. Merchants opened shutters and set wares out on tables. Farmers propped up their carts full of early summer vegetables. Boys pulled stubborn hogs along, yelling at girls who blocked the streets with their flocks of geese.

Not knowing where to begin, and wondering why he thought the gruff general could help him with his girl troubles, Justus hadn't formed a single word by the time they reached the leather merchant.

"Earnest!" Rolland called through the open door. "I got my squire here for that hauberk."

The leather merchant emerged, wiping his hands on a dirty apron and looking Justus up and down. "Sure is a tall one. Let's get him measured. Ethan! Bring a tape!"

The merchant's son, a young man slightly older than Justus, came out with a measuring tape in hand, giving a whistle when he spotted Justus. "Don't think we've ever made a hauberk quite so long, except for you, General. All right, lift your arm, Corden."

Rolland and Earnest began a conversation while Ethan measured Justus for his hauberk. Justus stared silently as

Ethan wrote down the measurements and handed them to his father.

"Good job, son. Now go see what the tanner's got for us today, there's a good lad."

As Ethan headed down the street, Justus noted how well the father and son worked together, one imparting skills to the other as a father should. Looking over at Rolland, Justus couldn't help but smile.

Rolland caught him. "What're you smiling about?"

"Nothing."

"What did you want to talk about?"

"Um, it's not that important, I guess."

Rolland began leading Justus back to the castle. "Come on, spit it out. Something's troubling you, I could see it on your face all through breakfast."

Taking a wide track around his real subject, Justus said, "People are afraid of me."

Rolland cuffed him on the shoulder. "Good! Keep it that way! No one'll ever bother you if they're afraid of you."

"But... they might think I'm a ruffian."

"You *are* a ruffian, that's what I've been telling you. Still working to smooth that edge out. You ready to adopt kinder, gentler ways, finally?"

"Well... there's a certain someone... I don't want... "

"Hah! This involves a woman, I'd wager."

Justus felt his cheeks flush. "All right, fine. Yes, it involves a woman. How do I impress her?"

"Impress her? You don't think she's impressed enough just looking at you? I've the seen the ladyfolk eyeing you, Corden. You've got nothing to worry about."

"Not with this one. She hardly notices me."

Rolland peered at Justus from the corner of his eye. "A rare bird, huh? Sounds like someone worth pursuing. Is she?"

"Is she what?"

"Worth pursuing! Good golly, man! Still with the stupid questions?"

"Well, how do I do it?"

When Rolland didn't respond, Justus repeated his question. But Rolland had stopped dead in his tracks, staring down the road that led into Archella from the north. A small entourage was coming across the Hammer River, horses' hooves clattering on the stone bridge.

At the front of the group, a large man rode a huge brown destrier. Cold blue eyes stared out from under bushy yellow eyebrows. A golden beard jutted straight out from his chin. Muscular arms bulged from a barrel torso. A large money bag jingled with every clomp of his horse's hooves. His green cloak boasted an image of a bear paw holding a spiked mace.

Baron Giles Godfrey, Justus thought. *Lard-bloated hedge pig.*

Justus personally had no reason to dislike Godfrey, but he knew Rolland despised him. He didn't know why but attributed it to the fact that Godfrey was often absent from council meetings, preferring to run his own little kingdom up on the northern moor.

When wars were afoot and soldiers needed, Godfrey always sent a fraction of the required number of consigned men. Yet when Rolland's help was needed on the northern border to stop the raids on Godfrey's land, he and Justus were there to help, risking their own lives.

"I didn't know there was a council meeting," Justus said.

"There's not."

"What's he doing here then?"

Again Rolland fell silent, glaring as Godfrey rode toward the market square and stopped in front of the tavern. A group of wenches giggled at him the way they had done at Justus, making Justus' skin crawl.

"How can they fawn on him like that?" Justus asked. "He's ugly as a boar."

"Ain't it obvious what they're after?"

Justus was surprised at Rolland's use of the word *ain't*. He only lapsed into peasant-speak, as he called it, when he was angry.

"What're they after?" Justus asked.

"Money! That's all a wench knows. Give her a drink, toss a few baubles in her path, and she'll eat out of your hand."

As Godfrey dismounted, Justus watched one of the wenches wrap her arm around one of his gargantuan biceps and walk with him into the tavern. "I thought he was married."

A growl escaped Rolland's throat. "Two or three times, maybe more. Drives his wives to their graves with his drunken brutality."

As Godfrey disappeared behind the tavern door, Justus could almost feel the rage that emanated from Rolland. All the anger he kept hidden now showed itself on his face. At the same time, Rolland absentmindedly pulled a small leather pouch from his vest pocket and dumped the contents into his hand.

Justus had seen that pouch before, but he had never seen what was in it. Whatever it was, Rolland held it in one hand, caressing it. From between Rolland's fingers, Justus caught the glitter of gold.

"What's that?"

Stirred from whatever thoughts plagued him, Rolland opened his hand to reveal half of a golden heart, intricately filigreed.

Justus said, "Hey, those markings. They're just like on your sword."

"I had it made special, to match."

"Sounds expensive. Where's the other half?" When Rolland didn't answer, Justus said, "You gave it to a woman, didn't you? Who was she? Where is she?"

"Her father gave her to someone else."

"Who?"

"Someone with more land and money than I had."

Justus stared at the tavern. "Godfrey?"

Rolland said nothing.

"Oh, man, how could she do it? Who would want to leave you for *him*?"

"Trust me, lad. Money talks louder than love."

"You still love her, I can tell," Justus said.

"I can't love her anymore. She's dead."

By the stars! So that's where his anger comes from. Justus could think of no words to say to console Rolland. But Rolland needed no consoling, for he quickly regained control of himself, dropped the charm back into its pouch, and headed to the castle without a word.

Released from his duties at midday, Justus again kept vigil at the market square, leaning against a shop wall, chewing a long blade of grass, hoping to see the mystery maiden, and mulling over what Rolland had said.

"Money talks louder than love."

Money. That was one thing he didn't have. By the way the maiden had been clothed, she obviously came from a merchant's family. Merchants made a lot more than soldiers.

But as squire to the highest officer in the realm, Justus had a promising future. Looking at the silver ivy-leaf brooch that held his plain brown cloak in place, he spit on it and buffed it with the heel of his hand. Maybe that would catch her attention.

Hearing a commotion at the tavern, he spied Godfrey emerging with one woman on each arm. He swayed, but they held him up and giggled.

Middle of the day, and he's already drunk. He'll not leave town fast enough for me.

As Justus stood there between buildings, eyeing Godfrey, a sound at his back made him turn to look. *By the stars, it's her!* The mystery maiden was making her way through the city but keeping behind the buildings, away from the market square.

Intrigued and enraptured, Justus followed but kept at a distance. Upon reaching the open expanse of the lists, the maiden paused to check the market area. Pulling a hood over her head, she hurried across the Hammer River bridge.

Justus ran to catch up. "Wait!"

With a look of fright, she turned, but seeing it was him, the fright left her face. However, she said nothing and continued down the half-mile road that led eastward to the harbor.

Justus trotted alongside her. "Excuse me, miss, but are you in trouble?"

"Please, leave me alone."

"What's the matter? Someone following you?"

"Go away, please."

"I can't go away. I want to talk to you. Listen, if I offended you yesterday, I apologize."

"You did not offend me. Now please, leave me alone." She quickened her step and hurried away.

Justus ducked into the woods to follow out of sight. She slowed as she reached the sandy harbor. He watched her take a deep breath, as though a great weight had just lifted. Finding a large rock that jut out from where the grass met the sand, she sat on it and watched the ships.

Two small wooden vessels, the *Allerion* and the *North Star*, bobbed as rolling waves passed under them. The ships' masts swayed like pendulums with each swell, tipping to the side, then righting themselves.

In deeper water beyond the two smaller craft lay four larger vessels, hardly affected by the waves. The heavy ships merely creaked against the pull of their anchor cables as the waves slapped their hulls.

Justus approached slowly, keeping his footsteps silent. The maiden was like a whole new creature—not the nervous bird that flitted through the city a moment ago. Now she sat serene, at peace. Taking a small black book from her belt, she opened it and began to read.

Not able to keep to himself any longer, Justus came up behind her, leaned toward her ear and whispered, "Hello."

She gasped and dropped the book. "Squire Corden!"

"Forgive me, I didn't mean to frighten you." He picked up the book and brushed the sand from it, but when he handed it to her, he pulled up short. Tear stains lined her cheeks.

"Oh, my lady! Whatever is the matter?"

She snatched a pink scarf from her belt with a fury that let Justus know exactly how she felt about his being there. "What do you want?"

"I just want to talk to you."

"Why?"

He opened his mouth but couldn't think of an answer. "Well... I... I don't have to have a reason. I should be able to talk to someone if I want."

Glaring, she ripped the book from his hand and resumed reading.

"Why won't you speak to me?"

"Why won't you leave me alone?" she said without looking up.

"I just want to know who you are."

"Hmpf."

"What are you doing here?" he asked.

She gave no response.

A sly smile crossed Justus' face. "Why, yes, I can see that you're reading, but what I meant was, what are you reading?"

Still no response.

"What's that you said? A book? Why imagine that. You're reading a book."

She continued to ignore him.

Justus began to add articulate gestures to his discourse. "Ah, but what kind of book, I ask her. But she gives me no answer. So I ask a different question. What are you doing here, I ask. Sitting, she replies. And I say, But why here? She smiles and answers, I like the sea. Ah, I say, I like the sea too. Have you ever been sailing? Oh no, never, she says."

He paused to glance at her. Her head was still down but her eyes were lifted toward him.

"Well, I have been sailing, I say to her. I've sailed the mighty kingship *Auberon*, and let me tell you, it's the most wonderful thing. The wind blows strong in your hair. You can smell the salt water. The spray tickles your face." He wiggled his fingers in front of his nose.

"Would you like to come with me sometime, I ask her. Oh yes, she says. I would go anywhere with you, Squire Corden. Oh, I say, but you can't, because..." He peered squarely at her, detecting a hint of a smile on her face.

"Because..." He put one hand beside her on the rock and leaned in closely. "Because we are still strangers since I don't even know your name."

They looked into one another's blue eyes for all-too-brief a moment before the maiden averted her gaze, melancholy resuming its grip on her.

Justus straightened himself and said, "Do you come here often? Because if you do, I will come here often too."

The maiden sat quietly for a moment, then she sighed the most beautiful sigh he had ever heard. "I do come here often," she whispered, drawing a smile from him. But his smile quickly faded as she added firmly, "Alone!"

"Alone? Why?" When she didn't answer, he asked again, "Why? What do you do here?"

Looking at the book in her hands, her cheeks flushed. "I..."

"Oh, of course, you come here to read. But why here? Surely it's much more comfortable at home. I would be happy to walk you there—"

"No! I mean... reading is not the only reason I come here."

"Really?" Justus said, enthralled that she was speaking to him. "What else do you do?"

"That's none of your business. Why do you want to know?"

"I just do. You're the most beautiful thing I've ever seen. I want to know all about you. Please, tell me. What else do you do here?"

The maiden blushed again. "You... you would laugh."

"No, I wouldn't. I give you my word."

Rage flashed in her eyes. "Your word? What good is your word? Who in Rygia ever keeps his word?"

Justus stood to his full height, dramatically placing one

hand on his heart, the other straight out to the side. He must have looked rather comical with his long arms and legs, for he could see her trying to stifle a smile. Standing in that fashion, he said, "On my honor as a squire—"

"And what sort of honor is that?" she said, angry again. "You squires are all the same. Roughneck bullies, picking fights with people weaker than yourselves. You're no better than highwaymen and robbers."

Her indignation took him aback, but there was more to it than that. That look again, in her eyes. What was it about her?

Hearing the sound of footsteps approaching, Justus spotted four squires coming from the direction of the castle.

"There he is!" one shouted.

"Hey, Corden, we've been looking all over for you."

"Go away," Justus said.

"Go away? General Rolland sends us to find you, and you tell us to go away. How d'ya like that?"

"I said, get lost." Justus looked the four boys over. Every one of them was smaller than him. He frowned.

One said, "C'mon guys, can'tcha see he's busy? Got himself a girl here. Let's just go back and tell the gen'ral that Corden's got more important things to do."

"Yeah," another said. "Rolland won't be happy to hear his squire's goin' soft for the girls."

Justus clenched his fist but restrained himself.

"Let's go guys," said the first. "Corden ain't coming."

Before Justus could breathe a sigh of relief, one of the boys approached the maiden. "Hey, get a look at this wench, guys. She's a real cute one."

"Leave her alone," Justus said.

"Yeah, she is," another said. "Hey, Corden, you sure know how to pick 'em."

The squire reached for her hair. "Say, honey, why not come with me down to— Whoa-a-a-a!"

Justus yanked the boy backward and threw him onto the sand. Ducking from the swing of a second boy, he grabbed a third and tossed him aside. As the second boy turned again on him, Justus landed a fist on his jaw.

The fourth squire jumped on Justus' back, but Justus threw him off like a sack of meal. The first boy recovered his feet, but Justus lunged toward him, sending them both rolling in the surf.

The two squires who were still on their feet rushed into the water after them. Justus hefted the first boy up, then laid him out into the shallow waves. With his fist still swinging, he knocked the next squire out. One of the other boys dragged the unconscious lad to the shore.

Water streaming from his hair, Justus reached back to punch the last of them, but this one was too fast. He sprang onto Justus, sending them both deeper into the water. As the two fell into the tide, Justus found his footing, pulled the squire out of the water, then shoved him back under.

The squire's arms flailed above his head, trying to pry loose from Justus' grasp. Finally Justus released the lad, who burst from the water, sputtering and gasping.

While the squire hacked and coughed at his side, Justus surveyed his work, pleased with himself. Sure, they were smaller than him, but there were four of them, after all, and he had just saved her from them.

Turning to look toward her, beaming with pride, his smile fled.

She was gone.

5

That evening Justus went about his castle duties in a sour mood. He maintained a code of silence to complement his frown while removing soiled platters and goblets from the tables in the great hall and taking them down to the scullery.

Charles followed his every step, whistling a cheerful tune. The sound only made Justus grumble.

"Hey, Cordo, slow down! You're making me run to keep up with you."

"I thought you called our friendship off."

"Oh, come on, you can forget about that, can't you? I've already forgotten about the thrashing you gave me. Besides, I have some information for you."

"You got nothing to say that I want to hear."

"Oh yes, I do. Believe me, you want to hear this."

Justus set a pile of plates on the table and glared at Charles. "Well?"

"Not here. We have to find a private place. As soon as we're done here, you come with me."

The two quickly finished their work—Justus glumly, Charles excitedly. The moment they were free, Charles dashed out the door.

Justus followed up a turret stairwell to the second level. "Where are you going?" His voice echoed up the spiral staircase.

"Somewhere private."

"There is no private place in a castle," Justus said.

"Oh yes, there is. The latrine!"

Great. How bad do I want to know what he has to say?

As he stood there thinking about it, Charles returned and grabbed him by the tunic. "Come on!" The two turned into a narrow opening set into the thick wall of the castle.

Justus put his hand over his nose. "Phew! Make this quick, Charles."

"It's about that maiden you like."

Now Justus was all ears. Plopping down over the hole in the bench, he said, "What do you know? Hurry, man, tell me!"

"Oh no. First swear your friendship to me."

"All right, all right, I swear!"

"You'll never hit me again?"

"Never! I swear! Now tell me... What's her name?"

Charles stood straight and tall, clearing his throat with a dramatic flair. He unrolled an imaginary document before himself and began speaking as though reciting newly proclaimed royal edicts. "Her name is Katrina Taylor."

Justus leaned back against the wall. "Katrina," he said dreamily. "Perfect."

Charles continued to read the invisible parchment. "She's the daughter of a seamstress whose husband died a few years ago."

"Katrina," Justus said again.

Charles peeked out from behind his imaginary document. "Hold on, Cordo, here comes the interesting part. She's betrothed to be married on her sixteenth birthday, which takes place shortly after Harvest Moon—"

"What?" Justus sat upright, his heart plummeting into the pit of his stomach.

"Just wait until you hear who the lucky man is."

Justus leaned forward, head in hands. "I don't want to hear it."

"Baron Giles Godfrey!"

"What!" Justus leapt up and grabbed Charles by the neck of his tunic. "That fat, drunken lout? It can't be! You're lying to me! Tell me it's a lie!"

"It's the truth." Charles reached around Justus' grapple-hold and pointed to invisible words on imaginary parchment. "It says so right here. He already paid the dowry. Quite a sum, I was told—"

Justus released his hold on Charles. "No! He can't have her! He's three times her age!"

"Not only that, he has a daughter Katrina's age too."

"He's a vicious brute! He can't possibly care about her! I won't let it happen."

"You won't let it? Just what do you think you can do about it? She's already paid for. He owns her. No one crosses Baron Godfrey."

Without explanation, Justus bolted from the room.

Dusk was settling as Justus ran through the streets of the city, watching the guild emblems above every door, looking for the home of a seamstress. Catching sight of a familiar figure ahead, he quickened his pace.

"Katrina!"

She turned around, surprised. "Squire Corden! How is it you've discovered my name?"

"Tell me it isn't true. Tell me you're not going to marry Baron Godfrey."

"I..." She shifted her gaze downward.

Justus' eyes followed hers until they rested on the expensive white wedding-gown fabric in her arms. "No! You can't do it!"

"What difference does it make to you? What's the matter with you, squire?"

Gazing into her sapphire eyes, Justus suddenly realized what he saw there. Purity. Innocence. Gentleness. *How can a woman like this even* think *of marrying such a man?*

"Do you *want* to marry him? I mean, in your heart?"

Katrina spoke as though reciting words put to memory. "What does my heart have to do with it? This is marriage. He's a rich man."

"So that's it. You want a rich man."

Her voice was almost inaudible. "No, that's not the kind of man I want."

"It's not? What kind of man *do* you want?"

"A faithful one."

"What do you mean?"

She frowned. "You see? Men in Rygia don't even know the meaning of the word."

"I know the meaning of the word. I was just wondering what *you* meant by it." At that moment, Justus knew that whatever this maiden desired, he would do for her. If faithfulness was what she wanted, he would promise it.

He reached toward her face. "Katrina, I—"

The pounding of horse's hooves made him pull up short. A horse and rider bore down on them, the large man in the saddle wearing an angry frown.

Katrina gasped. "Oh no! Hurry! You must run!"

"I will not." Justus took a stance in front of Katrina as Baron Godfrey loomed closer.

Katrina tugged at his sleeve. "Please, go away."

Justus stood firm, eyes glued to Godfrey. The large baron pulled hard on the reins, bringing his horse to a sliding halt, hooves digging up the dirt. He leapt from the saddle quickly for a man of his size, and the ground shook when his feet hit. As Godfrey stomped toward him, Justus realized just how big he really was.

Shoving Justus aside, Godfrey growled through his teeth, "Keep your hands off her! If you weren't Rolland's squire, I'd kill you right now."

He grabbed Katrina by the arm. "I've told you not to speak to any men. It's a good thing I came when I did, to put a stop to this foolishness." He began to drag her away.

Hot rage boiled over in Justus' soul. "Hey! Treat her a little more gently!"

"Gently?" Godfrey laughed. "She's a woman!"

"You treat your dogs better than that."

"And what if I do? She's my property." He tightened his grip, making Katrina cry out in pain.

Justus lunged and grabbed Godfrey's huge arm. Godfrey snapped his arm downward, out of Justus' grasp, and brought it back up again just as fast, catching Justus in the chin.

The immense power behind the movement sent Justus sailing through the air. He slammed against the wall of a cottage and slid to the ground, chinks of plaster raining on his head. He groaned in pain.

Before dragging Katrina off, Godfrey said, "If I catch you near her again, you're a dead man."

The next morning in Rolland's cottage, Justus worked slowly and stiffly, stopping now and then to rub a shoulder and wince or put a hand on his back and groan. His jaw throbbed but he didn't dare touch it, tender as it was.

"What happened to you?" Rolland asked.

"I got into a fight."

"I can see that. With whom?"

"Baron Godfrey."

Rolland exploded. "Godfrey! What on earth for? What would you two have to fight about?"

"Never mind." Justus plopped onto a bench, picked up Rolland's beautiful sword and clumsily began to clean it.

Rolland scratched the stubble on his chin. "Well, now you know what the other guy feels like. Hey, be careful with that."

"Sorry, General." Justus laid the sword on the table.

Rolland said, "You look like you could use a little swordplay to take your mind off things."

"Swordplay? I'm in no condition to—"

"That's the best time. This is what's it's like on the battlefield—cold night's sleep, aches all over, wounds crusting over, but you just gotta jump right back in."

"I know!" Justus said shortly. He'd already been in plenty of battles with the general, mostly along the northern border, in Godfrey's territory, warding off the Xulon raids.

Taking up his family sword, Rolland took a stance. "Draw your weapon!"

Justus responded reluctantly, nodding when he was ready. Rolland made a couple easy swings at him, and Justus blocked them half-heartedly. "I don't want to do this."

In reply, Rolland swung again. "Defeated already? You've never given up so easily! Now have at me!"

Again after a few feeble swings, Justus let the tip of his sword droop toward the ground. "I guess my heart ain't in it."

"What does your heart have to do with it? Fight! Your life is at stake!" Rolland's sword raced toward Justus.

Justus jumped back, barely avoiding getting his arm sliced off. Rolland's words brought Katrina's to his mind. *"What does my heart have to do with it?"*

She didn't love Godfrey. She didn't even want his money. All she wanted was faithfulness. And Justus knew Godfrey would never give it to her.

Angered, he started beating at Rolland's blade with his own, finding new strength in his rage.

Above the din, Rolland shouted, "You fight like a man possessed! What's gotten into you?"

"Nothing!" Justus said through his teeth, not missing a beat.

"Nothing?" Rolland gripped the hilt of his sword in both hands and swung left and right to keep Justus at bay. "If this is nothing, I'd like to see what happens when it's something!"

The two continued awhile longer until Rolland permitted Justus to rest. Justus plopped onto a stool, then rolled off it and lay on the floor, groaning in pain.

Rolland said, "You're letting your anger take control. Can't let that happen."

"My anger makes me strong," Justus said.

"Sure it makes you strong, but it makes you blind too. And stupid. You keep feeding it and it'll grow into something you don't recognize anymore. Gotta put a stop to that right now, before it gets out of control."

Justus leaned on one elbow and peered up at him. "Is

that what happened to you? Did your anger get out of control?"

Rolland stared back, saying nothing for a long time. When he did answer, all he said was, "Yeah."

"What happened?"

"I don't reopen old wounds, Corden. Let it go."

"But you still feel wounded, I can tell. I know the anger's still there—I saw it yesterday. How do you control it? How do you make it work for you?"

"I'll tell you how *not* to do it. You don't wait until it's too late, when the anger's all you have and you let it swallow you up in a drunken stupor and you start doing stupid things that get you into trouble with the law until you're looking down the blade of someone better than you and you wind up sucking mud and blood in a ditch somewhere with nothing left to live for. That's how you *don't* do it."

"How'd you get out?"

"King Arkelaus. He found me, brought me out, gave me a second chance when I didn't deserve it."

That was all Rolland would say about that, but he added, "There's nothing I wouldn't do for that man. But that's how he is—always looking for the good in people, which is hard to do, let me tell you. Good souls are rare. If someone's got one, it's usually destroyed early in age. People livin' only for themselves and what they can get. Strong taking from the weak. No one looking out for anyone else. Nope, there aren't too many good souls in Rygia, that's a fact."

That's it, Justus realized. That's what he had seen in Katrina's eyes. *She has a good soul.* But the moment he realized it, he felt the anger again. *Godfrey's gonna kill it in her.*

"Get up," Rolland said. "The leather merchant wants to take another measurement."

"No, thanks."

"Come on." Rolland gave Justus a light kick in the boots. "A trip to town'll do you good. How about stopping at the bath house, soak in some hot water?"

"Not interested."

"Why not?"

"Godfrey's still in town."

"What, can't bring yourself to face him again?"

Justus grumbled before asking, "Have you ever fought him?"

"Me? Fight Godfrey? I guess so, once or twice. But that was in the tournaments. And it was a long time ago."

"Ever take him down?"

"Sometimes."

Justus pulled himself to his feet. Looking Rolland squarely in the eye, he brandished his sword and said, "Show me."

Rolland narrowed his eyes. "What?"

"Show me how I can take down Godfrey."

"Are you possessed? No one crosses Baron Godfrey, least of all a sassy squire." Rolland scratched his chin. "What do you expect from a fight with him? Revenge? Because he laid you out?"

"He threatened me."

"Did he now? Well, you can bet if Godfrey makes a threat, he means to make good on it."

Justus took a few swings in the air. "I mean to be ready. What do I need to know?"

With a determined glint in his eye, Rolland set upon Justus with all his strength, holding nothing back. In only a few short strokes, Justus was disarmed.

"Come on," Rolland said. "Do it again."

Justus attacked again. Again he was disarmed.

"Come on, boy!" Rolland shouted.

Once again, Justus picked up his weapon and fell upon Rolland. The hilts of their swords locked—their faces only inches apart. Rolland narrowed his eyes. With a great heave he shoved Justus backward, sending him crashing into the furniture.

"Why'd you have to do that?" Justus said, groaning.

Rolland stood over him, sword pointing at his face. "The

day you can beat me… that's the day you can go against Baron Godfrey." He helped Justus to his feet.

Justus put a hand to his sore head. "I have to, General. At least I have to try."

Rolland sheathed his sword. "Trust me, the taste of revenge is not that sweet. I won't put you at that kind of risk."

"I can do it, General."

"You overestimate yourself. Overconfidence is a foe, not a friend. Conquer it."

"Yes, sir."

"What has you so fired up against Godfrey? Judging from the way you fought me just now, I would say you could possibly stand a chance… maybe, in time. But you're still fighting with anger, like it's all you know. It'll get you into trouble someday."

He crossed his arms. "It's already gotten you into trouble. With Godfrey. What do you suppose would happen if you challenged him? Do you think his men-at-arms would just stand idly by? They'd be all over you the moment you turned your head."

"But if I could fight him one-on-one…"

"Where will you find that kind of opportunity?"

"In the tournament."

"The tournament!" Rolland threw his hands up in exasperation. "Now I know you're possessed!"

"I can do it, General. If you show me how, I know I can do it. Give me a chance."

"Have you forgotten you're a squire? Squires can't fight knights in the tournament."

"Is it against the rules?"

"Why, no, I don't think there's a written rule. But you won't find a knight who'd lower himself to fight a squire. He'll either come off looking like a bully or be horribly shamed if he lost."

"Would I be disqualified?"

"Disqualified? You won't even be allowed on the lists!"

Knowing Rolland had his own qualms against Godfrey,

Justus felt he just needed to find the right angle. "What if no one knew who I was?"

"What? A disguise?" Rolland scratched his chin more vigorously. "A mystery knight? King Arkelaus loves a mystery." He stuck a finger in Justus' face. "You're not yet skilled enough with a lance."

"I can learn enough to unhorse him. Then I can engage him in hand-to-hand combat."

"Hmm. I would enjoy seeing Godfrey humiliated." Rolland shook himself. "What am I thinking? You've tricked me with your demonic guile! Get out of here before it comes upon me as well!"

Justus smiled as he turned to leave. He knew Rolland was hooked.

6

Justus dove into his training in earnest, quickly advancing through the finer points of swordplay, learning tricks that had been handed down through Rolland's family that no other Rygian had quite mastered or was brave enough to try.

He learned he could grab his own blade in his left hand to "shorten" the sword and thrust with more power.

He learned how to grab his opponent's blade with his bare hand, pull it up and over his opponent's head, then slide his own blade along it to cut off the opponent's head in a scissors-style stroke.

He learned how, when unarmed, to avoid a thrust and grab the opponent's blade, again bare-handed, take away the sword and turn the attack around.

But the move he mastered the quickest, and which became his favorite and most used, was to tuck his wrist tightly inward while meeting the opponent's blade with the backside of his own. In that position, he could step forward and wrench his blade around his opponent's. At its worst, this succeeded in pushing his opponent's blade away. At its best, he could wrench the sword from his opponent's grip and fling it out of reach.

One morning, Rolland threw a strange-looking helmet toward Justus. "Here, try this on."

Justus looked it over. It was different from typical

Rygian helmets, with the front coming all the way down beyond the forehead to cover the eyes. A slit allowed the wearer to see out.

"Where'd you get this?" he asked.

"I had it made special, to keep you from being recognized at the tournament. But it will impede your vision. Try it out."

Justus put it on. "I can see all right."

"Good. Now try fighting in it."

Justus and Rolland exchanged blows for a quarter hour. Under the helmet, drops of sweat ran off Justus' forehead and into his eyes. He blinked hard, but the second's delay caused him to miss a stroke.

Rolland said, "That mistake will lose the battle for you. Don't get distracted."

"Yes, sir." Justus swung and missed again.

"The tournament's only a month away," Rolland said amid thrusts. "You've a long way to go, Corden."

"I can do it."

"Not yet you can't."

As Justus raised his sword, Rolland's left hand flew up to grab him by the wrist and hold his sword at bay. "If you intend to fight Godfrey, you *have* to win. If you lose, you lose more than just a contest. You lose your honor." In a quieter voice, he added, "I lose my honor too."

Justus whipped the helmet off. "Hey, this is *my* fight, not yours. I know you lost your woman to him. Why didn't you ever fight him for her?"

Rolland said angrily, "Because *she* left *me*. It was her choice. She obviously didn't love me anymore."

Justus wondered how that could be possible. Who would choose Godfrey over Rolland? He couldn't think long, though, for Rolland renewed the attack, giving Justus no time to replace the helmet. Again and again the general's sword fell. Again and again Justus parried.

"You're tiring!" Rolland yelled.

"I am not!"

"Yes, you are! Remember this—at the tournament you'll have to prove yourself. You'll have to take on other knights and beat them before a man like Godfrey will accept your challenge. Otherwise he'll take your challenge as a joke and have you hauled off. You'll be tired by the time you face him."

"How many do I have to take?"

"Two or three."

"I can do it."

"Hah!" Rolland threw Justus against the wall—again.

Justus was often sent to work with the other squires so he could adapt to different fighting techniques. Despite the fact that Justus and the older squires had been trained with steel swords, Rolland insisted they use wooden ones, afraid someone might lose an arm courtesy of Corden.

But during one session, as Justus' repeatedly *thwacked* his wooden sword against another, he heard a shout behind him.

"Hey, Cordo!"

Wheeling about, he spied Charles Iscuro holding a steel sword. Charles fell upon him quickly, not giving him a moment to change out his wooden sword. But Justus wasn't deterred or even slowed. Dropping the wooden weapon, he spun and stepped backward, close to Charles, wrapped an arm around Charles' weapon and snatched the blade from him, saying, "I'll take that."

But Charles had some knowledge of what Justus was capable of and was prepared. From the sidelines, another squire tossed him a second steel sword, which he slammed into Justus' blade. When Justus countered, Charles ducked and came up with a dagger from his belt.

Again Justus dropped his sword. Leaning to avoid the strike, he grabbed at Charles' dagger wrist with one hand and his sword wrist with the other. Being taller, he easily twisted Charles' arms around and held him in a headlock of his own arms.

"You got smarts, Iscuro, I'll give you that," Justus said. "You're probably smarter than any other squire I know. But you'll never beat me. Know why?"

"Why?" Charles rasped.

"Cuz your heart ain't in it. You got no reason to do better. Your life ain't on the line."

"Neither's yours."

"Yes, it is. It always is."

"What're you talking about?"

"Even when I'm just training, I know my life depends on it. You learn that lesson and maybe you'll beat me one day."

As he released his hold, he slid both weapons from Charles' hands and kept them for himself. At the same time, he felt a hand on his shoulder. Startled, he wheeled about, swinging both blades.

Rolland ducked. "Ho, Corden, watch out!"

"Sorry, General."

"Thought you'd be tuckered out by now. Looks like you've still got some fight in you."

"Sure, I got some fight in me yet."

"Have at me, then." Rolland pulled his sword. Justus cut downward. As Rolland swung up to meet it, he yelled, "Not like that! You're getting used to fighting squires. When you fight a man the size of Godfrey, you gotta put more of your weight into it."

At the mention of Godfrey, Justus struck harder.

Amid strokes, Rolland said, "I feel anger in your every stroke."

Justus grit his teeth and pressed even harder.

Rolland said, "Learn something from Iscuro. Fight with your head, not your gut."

Justus heard the words but ignored them, lashing at Rolland with renewed strength.

"Whoa, Corden! Hold on! Have you forgotten the tournament is a *mock* battle? All you have to do is get his helmet off, then you'll have your revenge and it'll be over."

Justus hesitated. *Mock battle? That'll never do.*

With the tournament still three weeks away, Rolland set Justus to work on the jousting. Wearing his new leather hauberk covered with steel chainmail, Justus rode with Rolland through the woods, toward the seashore far to the south of Archella, away from curious eyes.

On the way there, Rolland said, "Your swordplay's good, Corden, maybe even good enough to give you a chance. But before you take up swords, you have to unhorse him. That'll be the hard part."

He rattled Justus' chainmail. "This is a good defense against the sword, but it's not lance-proof."

"But we'll be using blunt lances in the tournament."

"At that speed, a blunt lance can be as deadly as a pointed one, if it strikes true. Your shield's gonna be your best defense."

Emerging from the woods, Rolland brought Justus to a wide strip of sandy beach. "This oughta soften your falls a bit. Now remember, Godfrey's not as tall as me, but he's every bit as heavy. He'll be hard to unhorse. But once you do that, you'll have the advantage. He can't rise quickly with all that weight."

"I understand." Pulling his special helmet on, Justus set to work.

Rolland insisted on spending that night in the castle, expressing concern that some of the squires might notice them gone too often and catch on to what they were doing. He was right. By the time Justus plopped onto a mat, Charles was already there, eyeing him suspiciously. Other squires were there too, but many had already fallen asleep.

Charles asked, "Where you been all day? We don't see much of you anymore."

Distracted by his thoughts, Justus pulled out the sword he'd been using and inspected it, searching every inch for nicks or cracks.

Charles nudged him. "Hey, I'm talking to you, Cordo. What's up?"

"Huh? Oh, nothing."

"All the guys think you're spending your time with some pretty maiden. It wouldn't be that Taylor girl, would it?"

Justus glared at Charles from the corner of his eye. "I've been with General Rolland. Ask him."

"I'm glad to hear it, cuz I didn't know what to say to the other squires. They keep asking about you."

"What did you tell them?"

"Nothing. Do you think I would tell them you've been going after Godfrey's woman?"

Justus grabbed Charles by the neck of his tunic. "Never mention that name around me, understand?"

"Sure... sure, Cordo. Take it easy." As Justus released his grip, Charles smoothed his shirt. "You still riled up about him? I thought you'd forgotten that already."

Justus leaned back against the wall and sighed. "I can't, Iscuro. I can't forget about *her*."

"Oh, so it *is* that Taylor girl! Forget it, Cordo, she's not for you. You can have any other girl you want."

"I don't want any other girl. I want Katrina."

"That'll be the day."

"What do you mean by that?" Justus asked sharply.

"She belongs to someone else. Don't you know what that means? That means you can't do anything about it."

"Oh yes, I can." Justus resumed his study of the blade. "I intend to win her."

"Win her? What do you mean?"

"Huh? Oh nothing. I mean, uh... I intend to win her heart."

Charles raised his eyebrows. "With a sword? You think you'll win her heart with a..." His eyes became quite large. "Oh, no! I know what you're thinking!"

"Keep quiet, Iscuro."

"You're crazy!"

"I said, keep quiet."

Charles grabbed Justus by the sleeve and whispered harshly, "You're crazy. Do you have a death wish?"

"I'm not gonna die."

"Oh yeah? Just last week Godfrey killed a man for looking at her. Didn't you hear about that?"

"It's only a rumor. Godfrey denies it."

"You're still a fool. How do you intend to do it?"

"That's none of your business. And it's none of anyone else's business either, understand?"

"Of course, I understand you. Hey, why would I want to tell anyone? I'm sure all the guys would be happy that you're about to get yourself killed. All the less competition for them."

"I'm gonna win this, Iscuro."

"Oh sure, have it your way. Wait a minute. Does she *want* you to do this?"

"She doesn't know."

"Doesn't know? What makes you think she'll appreciate it?"

"Why wouldn't she?"

"Godfrey's rich. You've got nothing."

"She despises Godfrey, I can tell."

"Everyone despises Godfrey, but it don't keep the ladies from him. Why would she choose a poor squire over a rich baron?"

"If I win her, she'd *have* to marry me."

"Oh, I get it. You don't really want to win her *heart*. You just want to win her *hand*."

Justus' thoughts took an abrupt turn. Charles had a point.

"Listen, Cordo, I know you won't like what I'm about to say, but hear me out before you beat me up, all right? Let's say you win. All you'd be doing is making her go from one forced marriage to another and take a big step *down* on the way. She'll despise you more than she ever despised Godfrey."

Charles imitated Justus' voice. "'Uh, excuse me, miss, I

just won your hand, so if you don't mind, I'll take you to my home now. Of course, I don't have a home because I don't have any money. But if you'll just get on my horse... Oh, I forgot, I don't own a horse either. Come to think of it, even my sword is borrowed—'"

"Shut up!"

Charles stopped short and winced, bracing for a blow. When none came, he opened one eye. "Aren't you going to hit me?"

"No."

"Why not?"

"I made a promise, didn't I? I said I wouldn't hit you anymore, and I won't go back on my word."

Justus sat quietly for a long time. Charles was right. Katrina hadn't shown any inclination she liked him, much less wanted him. A couple of times he had thought he caught a glimpse of attraction in her eyes, but he could have imagined it.

Finally he said, "You're right, Charles, I can't make her love me by forcing her to marry me."

Charles patted him on the shoulder. "I'm glad you can still see reason. I'd hate to see a good friend die because of a stupid fight over a girl."

One side of Justus' lip curled up in a smug smile. *Oh no, Charles, I still intend to win her. I'll win her hand and her heart.*

Settling down onto the mat, he mumbled, "Thanks for the advice."

7

The day of the tournament finally arrived. Justus, Charles, and the other squires rode at their masters' sides, carrying their masters' armor. Justus' own chainmail lay hidden in a bundle behind his saddle. As the knights approached the castle, they were joined by many lords, ladies, peasant-folk, and merchants, every one of them with the fair complexion, blond hair, and blue eyes of a true Rygian.

The clearing in front of the castle had taken on a whole new appearance. Wooden platforms decked with colorful banners encircled the lists. Brightly colored pavilions dotted the outskirts. People from far and near crowded the platforms, vying for the best seats.

As Justus and Rolland approached their own blue and white pavilion, Justus scanned the crowd. Spotting Baron Godfrey, he narrowed his eyes and scowled. The lord of the northern moor had one of the best seats—directly opposite the king's own chair on the other side of the fighting field. Justus and Rolland dismounted, but Justus kept one eye on Godfrey.

"Here, put this up." Rolland handed Justus a wooden shield painted blue with the emblem of his ornate family sword.

Justus took the shield to the rail where all the eligible contenders' shields hung, taking special note of the location of Godfrey's green shield, boasting a golden bear paw holding a mace, set upon a green field. Next to it hung Kelsie's shield, blue with a hand emblem.

As he returned to join Rolland at their pavilion, he caught sight of Katrina and her mother climbing into the stands, heading straight to where Godfrey sat. Justus frowned.

Rolland said, "Save it, Corden. Don't spend your strength in anger before you even begin."

A blaring of trumpets signified the entrance of the king. Everyone rose as King Arkelaus, Queen Estrella, and nine-year-old Medan entered the lists, flanked by several soldiers in blue cloaks bearing a silver eagle—the King's Guard, headed by the gray-haired Captain Tybalt. After parading the entire length of the fighting area, the royal family took their seats on the platform opposite Baron Godfrey.

A herald stepped out to the center of the lists and called in a loud voice, "Hear now the rules of the tournament! Broadswords and lances may be used, but lances must be blunt. Battle axes are not permitted. Points will be deducted for missing a stroke, wounding a rival's horse, hitting beneath the belt or when a rival's back is turned, and striking with the shaft of the lance instead of the point. A winner will be declared when he has torn his opponent's helmet off. Let the games begin!"

A hearty cheer rose from the crowd.

Rolland said, "Help me into my armor. I'm sure to meet my share of challenges today."

"What about Godfrey?" Justus asked, pointing to the stands. "Why isn't he getting ready?"

"No one challenges Godfrey anymore, not after he killed three knights in a melee. Ever wonder why King Arkelaus banned the melee? That was why. He said it wasn't worth the loss of good men. Remember this, Corden... When you go up against Godfrey, he'll be fresh. You'll be tired."

"But his shield's hanging—"

"That's just for show."

Inside the pavilion, Justus helped Rolland into a heavy, padded tunic. Over that, he pulled on his chainmail and topped it all off with his blue tunic bearing his family sword.

But instead of putting the ornate family sword into his sheath, Rolland laid it on a table and took his second sword instead.

Justus asked, "Aren't you using your best sword?"

"No, you are."

"What?"

Rolland handed the ornate sword, jewels gleaming, to Justus. "You'll need all the help you can get. This sword might be old, but it's been well cared for. I've had to replace the binding on the grip a couple times, but it's the strongest blade I've yet to see."

Justus didn't know what to say.

"Now you keep out of sight so no one will miss you later on," Rolland said.

"What if you take a fall? I should be there to help."

"I'm not going to fall, trust me."

As Rolland headed off, Justus found a secluded place under the scaffolding of the king's platform where he could watch the proceedings and gaze occasionally across the lists at Katrina.

The tournament began.

A young soldier spurred his mount toward the center of the lists. Justus knew him—Hector Broadfield. He'd been knighted only the previous summer and was an arrogant young man who boasted often but couldn't always make good on his claims. Justus figured he hurried out first to try to earn favor with the king, assuming he performed well.

But Justus knew the tournament was unpredictable in that regard. Although the fights created a perfect opportunity for young men to show their might and perhaps move up in rank, it didn't often happen that way. Older, seasoned veterans, while lacking the speed and zeal of the young men, hadn't lived so long without learning a few tricks.

Broadfield brought his horse to face the royal family, saluted the king and queen, then turned about to make his challenge. Pulling his lance from its pouch, he tapped Kelsie's shield with the butt.

From above him, Justus heard King Arkelaus call out, "A friendly challenge to Kelsie!"

Striking an opponent's shield with the butt of the lance, as opposed to the point, signified the challenger's desire to engage in friendly combat—merely a contest to prove who was the stronger. This was the only type of challenge King Arkelaus approved.

Kelsie rode onto the lists to face the challenger. At a signal from a trumpeter, the two spurred their horses to charge full speed toward one another, lances aimed directly at each other's shields.

Kelsie's lance impacted Broadfield's shield with a loud crack, sending the man to the ground. In an instant, Kelsie turned his horse and bore down on Broadfield, who had barely regained his feet.

From under the royal platform, Justus could hear the conversation between King Arkelaus and the queen.

"That Kelsie is a quick one," Arkelaus said.

"He is cruel and relentless," Queen Estrella said.

"I am aware of his qualities, good as well as bad," the king said. "I was merely commenting on his quickness."

"I'm amazed he shows regard for tournament rules," Estrella said.

"If he didn't, he'd be disqualified."

That set Justus to thinking. Disqualification could ruin his plans. Being a squire challenging a knight wasn't the only rule he planned on breaking. Oh well, he couldn't change anything now.

As Kelsie galloped down the lists, Broadfield reached for his sword but wasn't fast enough. Kelsie snatched the helmet off his before a sword was drawn.

Only a feeble cheer rose from the stands. People had come to see some real battles, not this type of easy win. Leaning against the wooden supports of the platform, arms crossed, Justus thought, *I could've taken him, easy.*

The next fights proved more entertaining as more evenly matched opponents took to the lists. General Rolland was occasionally challenged by younger men, but he easily dealt with them. The older soldiers refrained from engaging the general—they knew better.

Throughout the morning, Justus noticed that Kelsie didn't make any challenges of his own. That is, not until Rolland had completed his third fight. At that time, Kelsie rode up to Rolland's shield and tapped it with his sword.

King Arkelaus called out, "A swordplay challenge to General Rolland!"

Justus suppressed a laugh. Every year Kelsie tried to impress the king by putting up a good fight against the mighty Rolland Longsword, but never until the general had tired after a few battles.

As Rolland and Kelsie engaged in swordplay, Justus could see Rolland was holding back. *What's he doing? Trying to give Kelsie a fair shot? Unless he's saving his strength. But for what?*

Finally Rolland made his move. At the next clash of their swords, he tucked his wrist in tightly and met Kelsie's sword with the back of his own. A quick flip of the wrist and he enveloped Kelsie's blade, wrenching it from his hand.

Before the blade hit the ground, Rolland shoved Kelsie backward with his shield. Kelsie landed on his back in the dust, Rolland's foot on his chest.

"Take your helmet off, Kelsie," Rolland said.

Kelsie did as he was bidden.

The crowd cheered, seeming to like the fact that Rolland showed courtesy by letting Kelsie take his own helmet off. Justus wondered if he would have been so magnanimous, had it been him.

Two older knights took to the lists. Disinterested in the battle, Justus watched Katrina throughout the fight. She spent most of her time fanning the air between herself and Godfrey and making conversation with her mother.

As squires helped two wounded combatants off the field,

Justus watched General Rolland ride past him, out to the center of the field, where he stopped to salute the king.

Justus had never seen Rolland make his own challenge at any tournament in the past. He was always too busy taking on everyone else's challenges and wouldn't risk tiring or injuring himself by adding to his fights.

Curious, Justus leaned forward, keeping his face barely inside the scaffolding, watching Rolland head straight to Godfrey's shield and tap it with the butt of his lance.

What, by the stars, is he doing?

Godfrey rose from his seat with a scowl so deep that Justus could see it from where he stood. The big baron's boots stomped loudly on the platform as he headed toward his pavilion to make ready.

Justus remembered accusing Rolland of not fighting for the woman he'd lost to Godfrey. *Is that what he's doing? Trying to get back at Godfrey after all this time?* No, that couldn't be it. Rolland never let personal grudges cloud his reason.

Maybe he just wants to tire him for my sake. That has to be it. Well, don't worry about me, General. I can do this.

When Godfrey was ready, emerging from his pavilion wearing a green tunic over his chainmail, he mounted and faced off with Rolland on the opposite end of the lists. At a blast from a horn, the horses burst into a gallop. Both lances struck their targets squarely with a loud crash. Both men managed to keep their seats.

At their second charge, both lances aimed true. A loud *crack* of lances against shields sent both men to the ground. They rose and drew their swords, the scraping of steel loud in Justus' ears.

Justus glanced at Katrina, who seemed quite interested in this fight. "Just you wait, Katrina," he whispered. "I'll give you a fight to remember."

A cry from the field brought Justus' attention back to the lists. Rolland was bent over, gripping his right hand, blood streaming down his sword.

He's wounded! Justus rebuked himself for not watching. Godfrey, now with the advantage, raised his sword to strike again.

Rolland gave a great roar. Rising to his full height, he cut upward with his blade. The force of the clash threw Godfrey off balance. Rolland threw his shield aside and gripped the bloody hilt of his sword with both hands. He began slashing left and right, driving Godfrey backward.

They came near to where Justus stood under the platform. Rolland gave one last, great heave, but Godfrey refused to fall. The hilts of their swords locked. At this distance, Justus could see that the hilt of Rolland's sword had broken and was hooked onto Godfrey's blade. Nothing Godfrey did could pull it free.

Godfrey pressed his weight into Rolland's sword, right against Rolland's wounded hand. Rolland tried to brace against it with his left arm, but Justus could see his wounded right hand shaking.

Just as Justus thought it was over for Rolland, Rolland released his left-hand grip on the sword, holding it only with his wounded right hand. Now all the force of Godfrey's weight was at Rolland's weak point.

What're you doing, General?

Rolland reached up with his left hand to grasp Godfrey's helmet.

Godfrey must have seen what was happening, for he tried to push Rolland away. But as he did, Rolland let go of the sword and stepped to the side. As Godfrey lunged, Rolland was no longer there to press against.

Godfrey fell to his hands and knees in the dust. Rolland faced the stands, Godfrey's helmet in his hand. The crowd roared.

Justus ran onto the lists to see to Rolland.

"I'm all right," Rolland said, panting. "Get my things." After Justus retrieved the shield and sword, Rolland said, "The hilt broke. Crosspiece was driven right into my hand."

"How did he manage that?"

"You didn't see it?"

"No, I missed it."

Rolland cuffed him in the back of the head. "You should've been watching. What'd you think I was doing this for?"

Inside their tent, while Justus bound the wound, Rolland said, "Maybe this isn't such a good idea."

"I'm not giving up."

"He's put on weight since I fought him last."

"That's his problem."

"It's *your* problem now!"

"You can't let all our hard work be for nothing!"

Rolland's composure softened. "Well, if ambition earns you any points, you'll come out the winner. All right, get ready then. Take down your first challengers quickly. Don't give Godfrey too much time to regain his wind. And watch out for that backhand stroke of his."

8

As another joust began on the field, Rolland walked stiffly along the platform to take a seat next to the king. Wounded as he was, he would not be expected to participate in any more fights.

He glanced toward his pavilion, seeing Justus emerge from the back, wearing his chainmail but no tunic, and the helmet that covered his eyes. Justus took the reins of his horse and joined the waiting knights at one end of the lists. Rolland could see them talking to him and to each other, but he couldn't hear them.

He had advised Justus not to speak lest his voice give him away. Seeing one of the knights knock on Justus' helmet made Rolland chuckle and let him know that Justus was keeping his silence.

When the battle on the lists subsided and the combatants were led away, one of the waiting knights shouted, "Sire! We have a stranger in our midst! A silent one!"

King Arkelaus leaned forward. "A stranger? A silent knight? Come forth, Sir Knight!"

Justus mounted and approached the platform.

The king said, "Look at this, Rolland. A knight with no distinctive markings. What make you of this?"

"Why not ask him yourself, Sire?" Rolland said.

"Sir Knight!" the king called. "What is your name? Where are you from?"

The undistinguished knight made no reply.

"You will answer me, Sir Knight, or answer to my men-at-arms!" Arkelaus motioned toward the King's Guard, and Captain Tybalt made a move toward the platform stairs.

To stop him, Rolland called out loudly so many could hear, "Sire! Perhaps this knight has reason to keep his identity hidden. Surely that is permissible. If he gives us a good show, perhaps we should humor him."

"Is that so, Sir Knight?" King Arkelaus asked. The strange knight nodded. "Very well, you may keep your identity to yourself as long as you please this court." Sitting back in his chair, he said to Rolland, "This ought to be good."

"I'm certain of it, Highness," Rolland said through his teeth.

As a newcomer, the man who quickly became known as the Silent Knight was allowed to make the next challenge. He directed his horse toward the shield of Baron Falliwell, per Rolland's suggestion.

In his early forties, Falliwell was not too old to be considered an unworthy challenge, and his skills were well developed, but he was of slight build and would be more easily unsaddled. Not only that, the crest on Falliwell's helmet would allow Justus to make a move that Rolland had taught him.

The opponents took their places and lowered their lances. At the signal, their horses took off like arrows released from the bow. The lance of the Silent Knight slammed right on the mark, in the center of Falliwell's shield, sending Falliwell to the ground. Since Justus had not been unhorsed, he was allowed to remain in the saddle if he chose, which he did.

The Silent Knight dropped his lance and drew his sword. Falliwell rose and also drew his sword. Bearing down on Falliwell, the Silent Knight sliced the air with his blade, meeting Falliwell's with a loud clang.

Immediately the Silent Knight's sword flew up and around, catching his opponent's again, this time with a backhand stroke. Falliwell's sword dropped to the ground.

As Falliwell stooped to retrieve his sword, the Silent

Knight brought his horse to an abrupt turn, dropped his shield and guided the horse to pass on Falliwell's left.

After picking up his sword, Falliwell rose ready to meet his opponent right hand to right hand. But the Silent Knight was bearing down upon his left side. Falliwell's momentary hesitation betrayed his surprise at the move.

Rolland knew this was a risky move, for it exposed Justus' unshielded side to Falliwell. If Falliwell kept his sword high enough, a wide sweep could wound Justus without harming the horse—a perfectly legal move.

But Justus seemed ready for that. As Falliwell swung his blade around, Justus leaned forward to evade the stroke while reaching out with his left arm. Grasping the crest of Falliwell's helmet, he jerked it off and threw it aside. The horse continued on its charge while Falliwell's blade sliced the empty air.

The crowd cheered.

King Arkelaus called, "Good move, Sir Knight!"

Queen Estrella sighed. "Mercy, we have another Kelsie on our hands."

General Rolland mumbled, "Show off."

The king said, "I say, Rolland, that move reminds me of something you used to do."

Rolland only cleared his throat.

While Falliwell was assisted off the field, Rolland watched Justus make his next challenge, striking the shield of Hector Broadfield, the young arrogant knight who had challenged Kelsie at the outset of the tournament.

Since Broadfield had won every other match after that first loss to Kelsie, Rolland thought a win against him ought to help Justus prove that he was adept enough to challenge more worthy foes, like Godfrey. And he believed Justus had more than a fair chance to beat Broadfield.

Broadfield was unhorsed first, and once again Justus set upon him from atop his own mount. He kept his horse circling Broadfield while cutting toward Broadfield's head with his sword over and over again. Broadfield fended off the blows, but when his arms began to tire and fall, Justus struck him in the helmet. He crumpled and landed face down in the dirt.

Rolland was relieved to see Broadfield rise to his feet with the help of his squire. Turning to face the Silent Knight, Broadfield removed his own helmet.

Cheers rose from the people. Rolland could sense their intrigue with this Silent Knight, even overheard some of the King's Guard whisper words of admiration.

Rolland smiled to himself, beginning to think that Justus might do well against Godfrey after all. Godfrey would be the next man he'd challenge, now that he had proved himself against smaller prizes.

But no sooner had Justus returned to the center of the lists, ready to salute the king and make his final challenge, when Kelsie rode out onto the field. Kelsie drew his lance and tapped the plain shield Justus was holding.

Rolland stifled a curse. This wasn't the plan, but Justus was compelled to respond. The knights took their places and the signal sounded.

With a thunder of hooves, Kelsie's lance slammed hard into Justus' shield. To Rolland's relief, Justus' lance also met its mark. But the force of the jolt wrenched Justus' right shoulder backward and propelled him off his horse. With his lance still in the crook of his arm, Justus landed heavily on his right side.

When Justus sprang up, Rolland could see he was wounded. Justus unsheathed his sword and immediately wrenched in pain, favoring his right elbow.

The king and queen seemed oblivious to the Silent Knight's plight. Queen Estrella said, "He's a quick one."

"The people are enthralled with him!" King Arkelaus said happily. "He is giving us a good show indeed. What say you, Rolland?"

Rolland didn't answer, eyes glued to the fight, hands gripping his chair.

The king looked down at Rolland's whitened knuckles. "I say, Rolland, you look rather pale."

Rolland leaned forward in his seat, watching Kelsie wheel his horse around for a second charge, sword in hand. Seeing Justus drop his shield and slide his own sword back into its sheath, he muttered, "What's he doing? The fool!"

Justus picked his lance up from the ground, supporting his right arm with his left hand, and aimed it at Kelsie's unshielded side.

No, no, idiot! Too dangerous! Rolland thought. From his lower vantage point, Justus' lance could easily strike the horse instead of the rider, instantly disqualifying him. But if his aim was true, Kelsie would be impaled.

Kelsie must have seen it, for he leaned sharply to his left, swinging his sword arm up over his head to avoid collision with the lance. The movement sent him off balance. As the horse reached the end of the lists and prepared to make a sharp turn, Kelsie lost control and fell.

"Good move, Sir Knight!" King Arkelaus called. "Wouldn't you agree, General?"

Rolland let his breath out in a great *whoosh*. "Yes, Sire, it was a great move."

Justus dropped the lance, took up his sword and shield and ran toward Kelsie. But the distance between them gave Kelsie enough time to regain his feet. He easily blocked Justus' first stroke and took the upper hand.

Rolland knew what Kelsie's strength was like. He could see Justus faltering with each strike of the blade. He could see how Justus was favoring that right elbow. He knew that Justus had to act fast or he'd have no strength left to deal with Godfrey. He also knew that there was little Justus could do in his state.

Once again Rolland watched Justus throw off his shield. He grasped the sword with both hands, putting his left hand in the dominant position. Before Kelsie could react, Justus made the twist with his left hand rather than his right, enveloping Kelsie's sword and wrenching it from his grip.

Queen Estrella jumped to her feet. "Good sword!"

Kelsie dove for his sword. Justus stomped on the blade to keep him from it. As Kelsie remained on his knees, hand on the hilt in the dust, Justus tapped Kelsie's helmet with his own blade, indicating that he could remove it himself.

But Kelsie only sneered. Lashing out with his left arm, he knocked the sword out of Justus' hand.

"Big mistake, Kelsie," Rolland said out loud. Now that Justus' hands were both free, he did exactly what Rolland expected—grabbed Kelsie's helmet in both hands and yanked it off.

Rolland sprang to his feet, hollering a whoop of victory. The people in the stands cheered loudly, men throwing their hats and ladies waving their scarves.

Rolland's victory cry faded quickly from his lips as he watched Justus limp over to his horse and weakly pull himself into the saddle. *Don't do it, Corden. There's still time to pull out. Forget the revenge. You've given us a show, now put an end to it.*

But Justus faced the king and saluted.

King Arkelaus said, "Do you believe this, General? The man intends to continue fighting."

Rolland only grumbled.

Justus turned to face the opposite stands, placing one hand over his heart and holding the other straight out to the side. The people cheered all the louder, as though he had just made a salute to them.

But Rolland saw something different. The young maiden sitting next to Godfrey's empty chair leaned closer in, mouth agape. Whatever it was that Justus had done made her recognize him.

Justus' horse reared as it pivoted and galloped straight to the railing full of shields. As he came to a halt, Justus stretched his lance forward and struck Baron Godfrey's shield with the *point*.

"Nooo!" Rolland roared, bounding to his feet.

Justus had just challenged Godfrey to a fight to the death.

9

As Justus drew to one end of the field, he could hear Rolland yelling to the king, "A fight to the death is not allowed! Tell him it's not allowed!" But the king only responded with a shrug and a shake of his head.

Justus knew he couldn't be stopped—he had checked the books himself. He knew King Arkelaus didn't particularly like the Joust of Death, but he also discovered that the rules had not yet been changed. The challenge was legal.

Watching Baron Godfrey take his place at the opposite end, Justus felt his entire right arm throbbing and knew he couldn't handle the lance properly. His arm shook so violently he struggled to keep hold of the heavy weapon. But there was nothing he could do about it—the signal sounded and both horses exploded from their places.

As the horses closed the distance, Justus saw instantly that Godfrey's lance wasn't directed toward his shield but toward his *head*. He ducked. His own lance struck Godfrey's shield off center and shattered. The impact threw him from the saddle.

Now Justus was unhorsed and Godfrey wasn't. This was not the plan. Hoping to use his lance again as he had against Kelsie, he looked for it but saw only splinters of it everywhere. He drew his sword, knowing that a three-foot blade was no match for a nine-foot lance.

The pain in his arm screamed in his head. He grasped his sword tightly, feeling the strain all the way to his shoulder. With his left arm, he tucked his shield closely to himself.

The pounding of hooves echoed between his ears. He

watched the tip of Godfrey's lance point straight toward his chest, looming closer. A hush fell over the stands.

"So long, stranger!" Godfrey yelled.

Seeing but one course open, Justus leapt away from the oncoming lance, right into the path of the charging horse. The battle-trained destrier would have continued its charge, but Justus swung his blade across its line of vision. The glint of the sword so close to its face caused the horse to rise on its hind legs.

Godfrey couldn't react fast enough. His great weight had already begun to shift and there was no stopping it. He slid to the ground.

Justus also couldn't react quick enough. As the horse descended, a hoof struck Justus' shield, knocking him to the ground.

Pain shot through his arm. His head spun. Somehow he managed to roll with the fall and scramble to his feet. He tottered momentarily. The ground swayed. The stands spun around him.

The delay was all Godfrey needed to regain his feet, looking unaffected by the fall. He drew his sword, shouting, "I'll have your head on a pike!"

Justus took the full force of Godfrey's strike with his shield on his left arm. Godfrey struck again and again, Justus meeting it each time with only his shield, Rolland's ornate sword hanging useless in his right hand. Step by agonizing step, he was driven backward. Soon he stood directly in front of Katrina's seat.

With a surge of strength, Justus tightened his grip on the hilt and cut upward. But Godfrey countered with a powerful backhand stroke, catching Justus in the right side. The steel blade smashed through his chainmail and his new hauberk.

Justus crumpled to the ground. As Godfrey raised his sword for the murder-stroke, Justus could hear Rolland's voice bellowing, "Get up! On your feet, knave!"

But a different voice called even more urgently to him. "Get up! Get up, Sir Knight!"

It was Katrina's voice. *Hers. She* called him to rise. Slowly and painfully, he rolled onto his hands and knees, jagged edges of broken chainmail digging into his torn flesh.

Lifting his head, he could see Godfrey standing over him, sword raised, but staring into the stands instead of at him.

Again Katrina called out, "Get up! Get up, Sir Knight!"

A growl rose from Godfrey's throat. "You're next, little canary."

"Nooo!" Justus yelled, swinging Rolland's sword in his left hand. With his right he gripped the pommel.

Blades clashed, steel ringing again and again. Left and right, Justus relentlessly swung, the superior metal in Rolland's sword holding its own against Godfrey's. Inch by inch, Godfrey was driven backward.

Justus no longer felt pain, no longer felt weariness. All he saw was Rolland's blade gleaming, jewels sparkling, as though it had come to life in his hands, as though it belonged there.

With a final lunge, he caught Godfrey's blade in his own hilt. As Godfrey tried to pull away, Justus hooked a long leg around Godfrey's and tripped the giant. Godfrey swayed momentarily, then fell flat on his back.

Justus placed the tip of his blade in the crook of Godfrey's neck, holding that position for what seemed like the longest minutes of his life. His chest heaved with each labored breath. The crowd fell silent.

"What are you waiting for?" Godfrey growled.

Justus rasped, "Your life is forfeit to me. Are you prepared to redeem yourself?"

"What do you want? My horse? Armor? Money?"

"I want none of those things."

"What then? Name your price!"

Keeping his sword on its target, Justus raised his right hand to point toward the stands. "Katrina Taylor!"

"What!" Godfrey attempted to rise.

Justus pressed his sword further into Godfrey's neck. "Katrina or your life. Which will you give me?"

Godfrey spat to the side. "If you take my life, you would have her anyway."

"Precisely."

"Take her then!"

"And the dowry."

"What!"

"And the dowry!"

"All right, all right, the dowry, too!"

With one last great sigh, Justus took a step backward. As his weight shifted to his wounded side, he doubled in pain and hit the ground. Through the slit in his helmet, he could barely see Rolland vault over the platform rail and run toward him. Soon many other knights and squires surrounded him.

"Get back!" Rolland yelled. "Give him some room! Bring me a pallet!"

"No!" Justus said hoarsely. "Help me to my feet."

"You shouldn't stand."

Justus grit his teeth. "I intend to walk off the lists."

"Idiot." Rolland helped Justus to his feet and began to lead him toward the pavilion.

Godfrey was on his feet as well. "Hold! I would know my conqueror!"

Rolland and Justus ignored him and continued on their way.

King Arkelaus' voice brought them to a stop. "Rolland! Bring that man here!"

"Here it comes," Rolland said quietly. "You ready for this?"

Justus nodded and the two turned to face King Arkelaus, who stood at the platform rail.

The king said, "Sir Godfrey has the right to know his conqueror. Enough of games. Let us see who this great warrior is, so we may honor him aright."

The Silent Knight removed his helmet, shook his golden bangs from his eyes, and lifted his eyes to the king.

"Squire Corden!" the king exclaimed.

Amid the rising murmur of the crowd, Rolland turned Justus away to get him to the pavilion. After removing the chainmail and padding, he helped Justus lay on the table and started pulling pieces of metal from his wound.

Justus yelled, "Ow! Hey, be careful!"

"Careful, my eye! I ought to bash your head in. A girl! This was about a girl! You said it was because Godfrey threatened you."

"He *did* threaten me."

Rolland roughly yanked another piece of metal from Justus' skin. "If I'd have known what this was really about, I never would've allowed it. Mangy cur. You tricked me!"

"I thought you'd be glad we humiliated Godfrey."

Rolland shook a bloody metal ring at Justus. "This victory'll come back to haunt you, mark my words."

Godfrey's voice hollered from outside the tent. "Rolland! A word with you!"

"Just a minute," Rolland said curtly.

Godfrey stormed in. "That boy is only a squire!"

Rolland squared shoulders with him. "So?"

"He can't fight in the tournament. He should be disqualified."

King Arkelaus stepped in, followed by Demas, who held an open book. "I think not, Sir Godfrey. We've checked the books. There is no rule denying squires the right to—"

Godfrey interrupted, "The Joust of Death is illegal! This whole match was illegal! I demand a rematch!"

The king said, "There will be no rematch, Godfrey. The Joust of Death has been in disuse at my preference, but it's never been removed from the books. Squire Corden won fairly."

"But, Sire—" Godfrey began.

Rolland shoved him. "Get outta my tent, Godfrey!"

Glaring around Rolland's tall frame, Godfrey said, "I'll get you for this disgrace, Corden," and stomped out.

Justus let out the breath he'd been holding through the entire altercation. Now King Arkelaus approached him and looked down at him, saying nothing, just looking deep into his eyes with that gaze of wisdom.

Finally a smile broke out on the king's face. "Well done, lad. Well done. When you've finished your training, I'll have a special position reserved for you, if you want it."

Justus smiled. "Thank you, Sire."

10

A week passed. Justus spent the time recuperating at Rolland's cottage, not allowing any visitors. He wanted the time to think deeply about what he had to do next, for it was a very difficult thing for him. More so, he felt, than the tournament.

By the time the week was out, he was anxious to be out of the confines of the small cottage and get some fresh air. But first he summoned a boy to deliver a message. That done, he waited another excruciatingly long hour before heading to Katrina's house.

Standing at her doorstep, he could hear a woman's angry voice coming from the other side of the door.

"What are you doing with that dowry money? That money is mine!"

"No, Mother, it belongs to Squire Corden now," Katrina said in a quieter voice.

"And just what do you think you'll do now? Marry the squire? Can he afford to keep you? With Godfrey all your needs would be provided. And mine!"

"Your needs? Is that all you can think about? I couldn't bear being with a man like Godfrey. So vulgar, so boorish…"

"So rich!"

"So unfaithful!"

"Bite your tongue, Katrina! Godfrey's a good man."

"No, he isn't, Mother. Squire Corden's a good man."

Justus smiled at that.

The mother said, "A good man? He's a boy! He doesn't own land to stand on! Where will you live? What will you do?

Do you suppose your seamstress skills can support the two of you?"

Those words helped Justus force his smile away. He rapped on the door.

Katrina opened it and flushed when she saw him. "G... good day, Squire Corden."

"Good day, Katrina." He tried to keep his voice on an even keel, not give anything away. *This has to be her choice, not mine.*

They stood on either side of the doorway in silence until Katrina found herself and said, "Won't you come in?"

Justus stooped to clear his head of the doorframe.

"How are you feeling?" Katrina asked.

"Much better, thank you." To the mother, he said, "How are you this fine day?"

She turned her back to him with a snort.

Katrina stepped between the two, diverting Justus' attention to some items on the table. "I've gathered everything together, just as your messenger said. This is the dowry money." She placed a large money bag in his hands, then pointed to a smaller moneybag on the table. "That was to be used for new clothes. All I've bought with it is this," she showed him some emerald-green fabric, "and this."

Justus watched her lift a piece of beautiful white fabric, covered with floral stitching in white thread.

"This was for my, um... my wedding dress. I haven't finished it, as you can see."

He fingered the white cloth, dozens of thoughts swirling in his head, all of them about her. He wanted her so badly, wanted to see her in that wedding dress, standing next to him. But he couldn't force it, couldn't *make* it happen.

Steeling his resolve, he nodded toward the smaller moneybag and the fabric on the table. "Keep those for yourself." When Katrina's mother turned to see what was going on, he plopped the dowry moneybag into her hands and said, "With this, I redeem Katrina from her obligations. She is free to marry whomever she chooses."

With that, he left the cottage and headed straight for the harbor to find his friend Lemuel, son and first-mate to Lamar, the captain of Rygia's seafaring fleet.

He didn't have to look long, for the moment Lemuel caught sight of him, he trotted up to him and shook his hand heartily. "Why, Corden, you're on your feet again! Good to see you!"

Justus grit his teeth to hold back the pain that lingered in his elbow and shoulder.

Lemuel said, "Quite a show you gave us, quite a show! When you took that contraption of a helmet off and I realized who had just taken Godfrey down, I nearly split my sides laughing. What a sword!"

"Thank you, Lemuel."

"Course I always knew you had a good sword. I seen you fight alongside General Rolland. Weren't it just a year ago that we met the Xuloners across the river? Why, you saved my life then. Ain't never gonna forget it. Gave those Xuloners a whooping, didn't we? And that Godfrey—he didn't give us a word of thanks. I nearly lost my life up there, and what did he give us? Nothing but complaints about coming late. Who does he think we are, gods of the wind?"

"Lemuel, I have a favor to—"

"How's your wound, anyway? I'm surprised to see you up and about. What brings you down here?"

"Actually, I came to ask a favor."

"Did you now? Well, bless me! What can I do for you?"

After presenting his request, Justus said to himself, *All right, Iscuro, this is your idea. If it doesn't work, you'll answer to me.* The only thing left to do was wait. Finding the same rock he'd once seen her on, he sat.

And waited.

Finally he heard her voice behind him, saying, "I thought I'd find you here."

He turned to see her standing there looking at him, although he still could hardly believe it. "How'd you know where to look?"

"You promised you'd come here often."

"You remembered," he said, letting his smile show only in his eyes.

"I remember every word you ever said to me."

Those words gave him a surge of hope, but he kept it from showing on his face. They stared at each other in silence for some time until she said, "What if I hadn't come?"

"Then I'd be waiting a long time."

Again, silence. She seemed uncertain, but he wasn't going to encourage her one way or the other. He didn't even break a smile. *She* had to make the first move.

She took a step closer. Her long hair glimmered like golden silk ribbons, her blue eyes gazed at his with curiosity and indecision. "May I... ask you... a question?" she faltered.

"Please."

"I don't... I don't understand your intentions."

"I have no intentions."

"But... what about the dowry... and... the tournament, and... Well, you *did* win me from Baron Godfrey. Do I not belong to you now?"

Justus had to turn away to hide the shadow that crossed his face. "No, Katrina, you don't belong to me. I've set you free."

"Forgive me for asking but... why would you do that? Don't you want me?"

Of course he wanted her! Couldn't she tell? Every fiber of his being longed to hold her in his arms and claim her as his own. He couldn't stand the thought that she might fly away and someday become someone else's prize. But her choosing him of her own free will would be worth the agony he put himself through.

Finally he said, "I won't lay claim to your heart by *buying* you, Katrina."

"Oh," she said in a very small voice.

Lemuel's voice from across the water interrupted their quiet gazes. "Hey, Corden! You coming or what?"

"Where are you going?" she asked.

"Sailing. Want to come along?"

Katrina smiled slyly as she spoke the very words he had said to her on this very spot two months earlier. "Why, yes. I would go anywhere with you, Squire Corden, especially since we are... no longer strangers."

Justus could no longer hold back the broad smile that had fought against ever since she arrived. Taking her hand, he led her to a small skiff and rowed her to the *Allerion*, where Lemuel stood waiting to hoist anchor.

Small swells sent the *Allerion* bobbing gracefully up and down, giving rhythm to the racing of Justus' heart. He stood with Katrina at the bulwark, watching the harbor grow dim on the horizon.

"It's wonderful!" she said above the flapping of the sail and the splash of the waves.

"Yes," he said, his eyes not leaving her face. She remained looking outward, wind whipping her golden ribbons of hair.

She said, "It's just like I imagined it would be."

"Me too."

She looked at him in surprise, as though just now realizing what he meant. Flushed, she turned away, but he put his fingers to her cheek and turned her back. With her face so close to his, her lips glistening, he could hold it in no longer. He closed his eyes and touched his lips gently to hers.

The *Allerion* rose and dipped again, but he barely noticed. All sounds, all movement, all seemed far away. All he saw was her, gazing at him.

Finally he asked, "What do you want of me, Katrina? I'll be anything you ask me to be, do anything you want me to do. Just say the word. What do you want me to be?"

"Faithful, Justus. That's all I ask. Would you be faithful to me? Would you love me until the day I die?"

"No," he said without hesitation. Seeing her face fall, he laid a hand on her cheek and said, "To love you until the day you die means there would come a time when I stop loving you. I'll never stop loving you. Not until the day *I* die."

11

Throughout the next months, whenever Justus could escape his squirely duties, he spent the time with Katrina. The only sad time came when her mother fell seriously ill. He helped Katrina care for her while still fulfilling his duties at the palace. Her mother held out through the winter, but the coming of spring saw no improvement, and one day she quietly passed away.

The dowry money dwindled to almost nothing, paying for doctors, medicines, rent, and food. Since Justus was still a squire and not yet on the king's payroll, he couldn't help pay the expenses, and Katrina's seamstress work alone could not cover them. A debt had already amassed, and upon the death of her mother, she had to move out.

So Justus decided to ask the king for that promised position, even though he was only nineteen years old. As soon as Katrina's mother was buried, he went to the palace.

"Come in, Squire Corden," King Arkelaus called from the high table. "What can I do for you?"

Justus bowed. "I have a request, Your Majesty."

Before Justus could speak, a courier burst into the great hall with General Rolland on his heels. "Your Majesty! The Gargons have attacked Baron Falliwell's lands and burned entire villages to the ground!"

"Gargons!" King Arkelaus said. "My lands, will they ever cease?"

Rolland said, "Sire, I've already called for the troops to assemble. I suggest you dispatch us immediately to—"

"By all means, Rolland, make haste! Do not delay!"

Rolland said to Justus, "Come on, Corden, no time to drag your feet."

"But I—"

King Arkelaus said, "I am sorry, squire, your request will have to wait. Now go."

As Justus followed Rolland out of the great hall, he said, "Let me at least tell Katrina."

"First get my things ready, and yours. Then go, but be quick about it."

Justus flew through his work before rushing to Katrina's house. Bursting in the door, breathless, he caught sight of her reading from a small black book.

She gasped when he burst in, and, spying the chainmail he wore, said, "Oh, no."

"Gargons again. Rolland says this could be a long one."

When his gaze rested on the book she held, she said, "It gives me great comfort when I'm alone. And when you're fighting your many battles."

He touched her face. "Don't be afraid, Katrina."

"I see fear on your face."

"I'm not concerned for myself but for you. I hate to leave you alone."

"I'll be all right."

"You ought to find a matron to stay with you."

"I'll be all right, Justus."

"No, I insist. Do you know of anyone?"

"Well... I do know of someone, but... "

"But what?"

"You should know she's the one who gave me this book. She... she's a believer in the, um..." She cleared her throat. "The God of Teman."

"Teman? You mean... Teman?" He pointed south.

"Yes, Teman."

"I didn't know there were any Temanites in Rygia."

"She's not Temanite, she's Rygian."

"Well then, how...?"

"I don't know how it started, but her whole family have been believers for generations."

"Have they met any Temanites? Have *you* met any Temanites?"

"No, have you?" she asked.

"No." All Justus knew was that the elusive neighbors to the south were alleged to have brown eyes and hair, but no one really knew for sure. And no one really cared. Rygians had heard so many rumors about the people and their haunted mountains that they stayed away. As long as Teman didn't bother Rygia, Rygia didn't bother Teman.

Katrina said, "You won't tell anyone, will you?"

"Tell anyone what?"

"That her family are believers."

He shrugged. "Why would I do that? Is it something I should worry about?"

"Not at all."

"Fine, then." He kissed her on the forehead. "If that's the companion you want, I don't care, as long as you're not alone."

With one last hurried kiss, he left the cottage.

Justus and the king's army emerged from the western woods at dusk, the fertile valley of the Cherith River stretching before them. Beyond the valley, a ridge of low, bare mountains separated Rygia's lands from the Gargon plains.

Ahead, he could see Baron Falliwell's castle sitting in the midst of freshly plowed land. Some distance beyond that, a wall of black smoke rose against the twilight sky—the only evidence that Rygian cottages once stood there.

Rolland sent a contingent to report his arrival to the lord of the land. Soon Baron Falliwell arrived accompanied by many men-at-arms.

"General Rolland!" Falliwell called as he neared. "I'm relieved to see you!"

"Give me a report, Falliwell."

Falliwell stared off toward the smoke. "This is no ordinary raid. They used to be satisfied to carry off food and supplies and perhaps a woman or two. Now they're attacking entire settlements, burning them to the ground. They come at night and in small numbers. By the time we discover where they are, it's too late."

Rolland spat on the ground. "Cowards!"

"Maybe so, but they're deadly cowards. When my men-at-arms go out to battle them in the morning, they meet us in full force."

"Full force? What do you mean?"

"Thousands of them."

"All together?"

Falliwell nodded.

"That's not typical Gargon behavior."

"That's what I thought," Falliwell said. "I've never known their tribes to unite like that."

"What's their method of attack?" Rolland asked.

"They come in waves on horses that never seem to slow. They pelt us with arrows coming down like rain. They're not accurate shots, but the arrows fall thick, leaving my men nowhere to go."

"What of your defense?"

Falliwell shrugged. "We try to counter attack, but they retreat out of range as quickly as they come. My men are more than a little frustrated—"

"They don't use their sabers?"

"They carry them, but we have yet to come near enough to engage them. If we could, we would've seen some success by now. But those horses of theirs! I've never seen such swift ones! When they retreat, they easily outrun us."

Rolland rubbed his chin. "Must be a new desert breed. Well, cheer up, my man! Once those Gargons get a look at the force we've brought, they'll lose heart. Gargons are easily discouraged. I've yet to see them stay the course of a good battle."

Falliwell seemed skeptical, but he led the king's army to

his castle where he provided refreshment. When they finished, Justus followed Falliwell and Rolland outside as they discussed their plans.

"My men are camping near the settlement over there." Falliwell motioned with his arm toward the recently destroyed cottages to the south. "You can join them there at daybreak."

"How long have these attacks been taking place?" Justus asked.

"Nearly a week. Almost every night they find a new settlement to destroy. Their arrows have killed many, wounded even more, yet we've not managed to inflict much damage on them."

Rolland gave Justus a cuff in the shoulder. "Until tomorrow morning, eh, lad? We'll teach those Gargons to get off our land and stay off for good!"

Just after sunrise, Justus followed Rolland toward the blackened settlement. In the distance, he could see Falliwell's forces already under attack by a mass of Gargon warriors.

At a signal from Rolland, the trumpeter sounded a battle cry. The Rygian army charged across the valley.

The Gargons beat a swift retreat toward the plains. By the time Rolland and the king's army arrived, not one Gargon was left. All had retreated as quickly as Falliwell had described.

"Who's in charge here?" Rolland asked.

A mail-clad soldier trotted up. "I am. Name's Parrin."

"Ho, Parrin!" Rolland said. "I see we've frightened them off! Like cats and mice, eh?"

Parrin shook his head. "It's happened before. They'll be back. You'll see."

"We'll wait," Rolland said. "But they'll think twice before attacking now that I've arrived."

And wait they did. Throughout the morning the men waited and watched. They passed the time by learning the details of what had happened in Falliwell's territory over the past week.

As midday came and went, the men began to complain of hunger. Throughout the hours of the morning, Rolland had not allowed them to eat, but as the afternoon wore on he had to concede.

Shortly after they finished their meal, a cry arose from the sentries.

"Here we go again," Parrin said. "Looks like they've increased their numbers, too."

Rolland said, "Bah! And we with full stomachs. Come on, men!"

Justus and the army followed Rolland, riding at full speed. But soon they learned what Falliwell's forces had been dealing with. Heavy showers of arrows came at them so thick no one could complete the advance.

Those in the front lines were hit heavily, men and horses alike falling. As one flurry subsided, another shower fell, then another.

Finally the barrage ceased. When the men dared to peer out from behind their shields, the Gargons were already on their way back across the valley.

Some Rygians began to pursue, but Rolland commanded the trumpeter to recall them. "No use wasting ourselves in vain chasings," he said.

Upon returning to camp, Parrin took a hard look at Justus. "Aren't you just a squire? You should've stayed at camp with the rest of them."

Rolland laid a hand on Justus' shoulder. "Not this one. He fights at my side. And it looks like we'll need every available hand for this."

Parrin nodded. "You see what I mean. We're exhausting ourselves without one dead Gargon to show for it. After too much of that, the men get angry and turn on each other."

"Can't allow that." Rolland looked out toward the plains. "I wonder what's brought so many of them together? Usually they'd rather fight with their neighbors than join them."

Justus said, "All it takes is one man. The right sort of man."

"You could be right. Let's keep an eye out for whoever's in charge. He'll be our main target."

Justus squinted into the distance, studying the area to which the Gargons had retreated. He imprinted the location onto his memory, then joined the others as they prepared to bed down.

During the night, Justus awoke to a sentry hailing Rolland. In the distance, he could see an orange glow. Another group of cottages was burning.

Rolland grumbled as he got up. "North, huh? We'll have to move camp now if we hope to save any lives over there."

Parrin had also been awakened and joined them. "It's always like this. Every night they pick a new location. Keeps us on the move. And we have to move, or they start massacring the people. But we never know where they'll strike next, so we move in the middle of the night. The men are tired come morning."

"This is no way to run a war," Rolland said.

"What else can we do?"

"I'll let you know as soon as I figure it out."

Throughout the next battles, Justus watched for a leader among the barbaric people, but Rolland said the leader might be keeping well back to avoid being spotted.

For two days and nights the Rygian army pursued the Gargons from place to place across the valley. Even the reinforcements grew frustrated, feeling just as weary from chasing as they would have from battle, with little to show for it.

Each time the Gargons retreated, Justus took note of which direction they headed. In the afternoon of the third day, he pulled the general aside.

"General, I have an idea. I think I can figure out a way to—"

He was interrupted by the warning signal of the trumpeter.

"Save it for later," Rolland said.

Justus followed Rolland into battle once again. The two took the lead as the Gargons repeated the scenes from the previous days.

Suddenly Rolland gave a shout. "That's him! The leader!" He charged right into the thickest downfall of arrows. Justus followed, keeping his shield overhead.

Rolland suddenly gave a cry of pain, but he spurred his horse and charged again. Justus directed his horse through the mass of horses and arrows. Finally catching up, he could see an arrow sticking out from Rolland's thigh.

"Get back, General! Get out!"

"I've got him in my sights." Rolland continued to press forward.

But the Gargons had begun their retreat and were well out of reach. Their swift horses quickly increased the span between armies.

Turning to head back to camp, Rolland tugged on the arrow in his thigh. Instantly he stiffened. "That ain't coming out easy. Point's barbed." He shook a fist in the air. "When I get an arrow I would take it from a worthy foe, not you, you fat son of a jackal!"

"You get a good look at their leader?"

"Leader? Hah! He's a coward like the rest of them! They shoot and run instead of meeting their enemy face to face!"

Rolland fell silent after that, and soon his horse began to lag behind. When Justus turned to look, Rolland's head drooped forward and he leaned to the side.

"General!" Justus shouted.

Rolland slid sideways off his horse and landed on his side with a thud, one foot dangling in the stirrup. Justus rushed to his side while others came running.

He's feverish," Justus said. "Arrow musta been poisoned. Carry him back to camp. Hurry."

For the next hour, Justus and Parrin worked at removing the barbed arrow. Rolland had lost consciousness and they were glad for it. The wound was deep and ragged, removal of the head laborious.

Not until dusk did they finish. A poultice was applied to draw out the poison, and the wound was bound tightly. Justus roused the general and made him eat a bit of stew. That finished, Rolland lay back on his mat and groaned.

"What do we do now?" Parrin asked.

Justus knelt beside Rolland. "Listen, General, can you hear me?"

Rolland cursed. "Of course I can hear you, stop shouting in my ear."

"Did you hear what Parrin said?"

"By the stars! My leg is wounded, not my ears!"

"I told you earlier I had an idea. I think it'll work."

Rolland lay quiet for a moment, then said, "Very well. Bring me my sword."

"Your sword?"

"Yes, my sword! What's the matter with you? Am I speaking gibberish?"

When Justus placed the sword in Rolland's hand, Rolland rolled onto his left side, supporting himself on his elbow.

"Kneel, Corden," he said.

"What?"

"I said kneel!"

As Justus lowered himself to one knee, General Rolland laid the flat of his blade on Justus' right shoulder, then his left, saying, "I now dub you as a fully-fledged knight of the realm of Rygia."

He threw his sword down and punched Justus in the arm. "You're in charge. Now leave me alone." He flopped onto his back and closed his eyes.

Justus rose, confused, surprised, and a bit dazed. He'd just been knighted. It wasn't exactly how he had pictured it, but the honor was the same. Actually, it was a great honor since he was only nineteen.

An encouraging look from Parrin assured him the men were ready to follow his command. "All right, men, follow me."

12

Darkness began to overtake the land as Justus peered across the sky. "We need to try a whole new tactic. Take them by surprise before they attack again. Give them a dose of their own poison."

He pointed toward a low, shadow-covered mountain in the distance. "Every time they retreat, they head in that same direction. It must be where their camp is. Who's scheduled for the night watch?"

"Captain Arnet's men," Parrin said.

Justus called for Arnet. "Instead of keeping watch here tonight, I want you to take your men over there." He pointed across the valley, toward the mountain. "Don't approach the Gargon camp. Just keep to the side of the mountain until morning."

"Travel all night? My men ain't cats. We don't see in the dark."

"There's just enough moonlight. Be sure to keep well enough away so they don't hear your horses."

"Then what?" Arnet asked.

"The rest of us will stay here and wait for them to attack in the morning."

"Wait?" Parrin asked. "While they destroy another settlement?"

"We can't help that," Justus said. "There's no way to know which settlement they'll strike. We just keep wasting our energies on chasing from one to the next. Well, we're not going to meet them on their terms anymore. While their forces are over here, we'll head over to *their* side."

Parrin nodded. "Take the attack to their camp."

"Exactly. If the Gargons follow their same tactics, they'll hit a settlement in the morning. So Arnet, when morning comes, you head right into their camp and burn their tents. When they see the smoke rising, they'll retreat."

"What're yer men gonna do?" Arnet asked.

"Hem them in. We'll take positions over there." Justus pointed toward the valley. "Right behind that low rise where we can stay out of sight. Once the Gargons pass by, we'll come up behind them. Your men can charge them straight on. We'll have them pinned."

Arnet said, "Sounds good to me."

"Me too," Parrin said.

"Then get going. Arnet, take your men and head out immediately. You can catch some rest once you've crossed the valley. Parrin, you and your men get some rest. We'll take positions just before daybreak."

By late afternoon the next day, Justus' men returned amid whoops of victory. "Corden the Conqueror!" they shouted. "Corden the Conqueror!"

"What's all the ruckus?" Rolland shouted as he lay on his mat. "Someone give me a decent report. Parrin!"

Parrin shouted, "He did it, General. Your squire did it! Uh, I mean... guess you ain't a squire no more, Corden. Well, he did it. Once we had those Gargons penned down, we were finally able to take to swords. We lost some men, but they lost more."

"Good for you, Corden," Rolland said. "What about their leader?"

"He got away," Justus said.

Rolland spat. "Got away, huh? I suppose we'll hear from him again."

"Not for awhile, I'm sure," Parrin said. "We cut his forces in half!"

When Arnet's men returned to camp, Justus could hear more hoots and hollers. Rolland asked, "Now what?"

Arnet came to report. "My men was just tellin' Parrin's men about our little bonfire. Those tents went up like kindling!"

One of his men said, "You shoulda heard them women and children screaming!"

"What!" Justus shouted. "What women and children?"

Parrin said, "Gargons always travel with their entire tribe—women, children, everything. What of it?"

"I didn't mean to kill women and children," Justus said.

Arnet said, "Well if we didn't, we'd have lost the battle. Is that what you wanted?"

"No, I just... There had to be another way."

"There weren't no other way," Arnet said. "We did exactly like you told us, and it worked. Now buck up!"

Justus looked to Rolland, who said, "Arnet's right. That was a good plan you had. Don't start second-guessing it."

"But innocent lives—"

"Innocent! Do you think there weren't Rygian women and children in the cottages they destroyed? That's innocence! Those Gargons deserved whatever you did to them, and more. Personally, I would've slain any Gargon child I came across if it meant saving the lives of my own people. Now get off your high horse and praise the men for their good work, else you'll lose their respect. Understand?"

"Yes, sir."

Days later, Justus finally returned to Archella, where he slipped wearily from his horse and went straight to Katrina's house. She bounded to him and threw her arms around his neck when he entered.

"I heard the army return some hours ago. I heard them hailing your name. What took you so long? Where were you?"

When he didn't answer, she pulled away. "What is it? What's wrong?"

"I did a horrible thing." He plopped into a chair near the table. She came to stand near and let him wrap an arm around her. "I didn't mean to kill women and children. I didn't know."

"I'm so sorry," she whispered.

"All I could think of was you," he said. "What if something like that happened to you? I can't imagine how I'd feel if... if you were..." He cleared his throat. "If anything ever happened to you, I don't think I could bear it."

She crawled into his lap and held him in silence for a long time.

Finally he said, "Well, one good thing comes of this."

"What's that?"

"Not another day will go by before I marry you."

"What? But what about...? How can you...?"

"Don't worry. Rolland knighted me on the field of battle. I went to see the king as soon as we returned. He's going to give me some land, and next year when Captain Tybalt retires, he'll make me captain of the King's Guard."

The next afternoon they were married. King Arkelaus married them within the castle, and afterward a banquet and dance were held for them and for the victorious army.

Late into the evening, after much celebrating and dancing, Justus took Katrina back to her cottage. They lived there for another month, until he finished building a new place on the plot of land he had chosen. It was a quiet location, three miles south of Archella and only a half-mile walk through the woods to the sea.

The first time Justus had seen this place, he knew it was made for them. Katrina could spend plenty of time at the beach reading her book. With the period of peace that followed the Gargon battle, he was able to complete the cottage and plow a garden for her.

Just before Katrina moved in, her house servant Bett added the finishing touches, then went to stay with her own grown children until Katrina should call for her services again.

13

Late in the summer of the following year, Justus burst through the door of his cottage. The short woman hovering over a kettle let out a gasp and dropped a wooden spoon. She picked it up and shook it at him. "Master Corden, you startled me!"

"Sorry, Bett."

"What's the hurry? Something important happening at the castle?"

"No, things are pretty dull. So dull, in fact, that I've been dismissed for a couple weeks. Where's Katrina?"

Bett pointed the spoon toward the door. "At the seashore, as usual."

As Justus headed out, he spied the dwindling wood pile against the side of the cottage. Grabbing a wheelbarrow and axe, he whistled on his way down the path toward the sea.

The path ended and the woods gave way to grass, which sloped gently downward into a sandy beach. Here and there, rocks jutted out from under the grass. Katrina sat on one of these.

She looked up when he approached. "You're home early."

"I couldn't wait to be with you, so I told the king to find someone else to protect him."

"You told him no such thing."

Justus kissed her. "And then I told him I wouldn't be back for a long..." he kissed her again, "long..." and again, "time."

"How long?" She closed her eyes for another kiss.

He put a hand on her protruding stomach. "Long enough to help our son into this world."

"Son?"

"He'll be a strapping lad. And he'll look just like his father."

"What if it's a girl?"

"I don't think she'd be so pretty if she looked like her father."

Katrina giggled. "I'm glad winter's coming."

"Glad? They say it's gonna be a harsh one."

"Good. That means no battles. You'll be home long enough to give our baby a good start in this world."

"Speaking of winter, the wood pile's getting low." Justus pulled his tunic off, found a dead tree and began to chop away at the trunk. Katrina opened her book and continued reading.

An hour passed before Justus split the final piece of wood in half. He tossed it onto the pile in the wheelbarrow and fell to the sand at Katrina's feet. "Read to me."

Katrina read, "'For I have chosen him, so that he will keep the way of Eloah by doing justice.'"

Justus hooked his hands behind his head and stared at her. "You are so beautiful."

She prodded his bare side with her foot. "I won't read to you if you won't listen."

"Sorry. Read it again."

Katrina repeated the verse. When she finished, he just continued to gaze at her as before.

She said emphatically, "By doing *justice*."

"I guess I'm more well known than I thought."

"Interesting you should say that. I've read this portion over and over again, and every time I get this feeling like…"

"Like what?"

"Like it really is talking about *you*. As though Eloah has his hand on you. I can feel it."

"What, exactly, do you feel?"

"That you've been chosen for some great task."

"What kind of task?"

"I don't know."

He raised himself onto one elbow. "So this God… Eloah… He's the God of the Temanites, right?"

"Yes."

"Well, if the Temanites need a god, let them have one. They're strange people anyway."

"How can you say that if you've never met one?"

"Everyone says so. I've heard stories."

"Stories from whom? People who've seen Temanites?" She had a sly look on her face as she asked it, like she knew that he knew that no one in Rygia had ever seen a Temanite—at least not that they admitted.

"Well, no…" he said.

"If no one's seen a Temanite, where do the stories come from?"

He shrugged. "I don't know. Maybe the same place that book came from."

"But what do you really know about Temanites?" she asked.

"Nothing, I guess. But who cares? If they want me to know about them, they should come out from behind their mountains and introduce themselves." He jumped up and grabbed the axe. "I'd like to meet them in battle!"

"Whatever for?" Katrina asked.

"Just to see how they fight. How do people like that fight?"

"People like what?"

"People who hide behind mountains. People who believe in an unseen God." He made a few swings with the axe. "Do you know what I believe in?"

She closed the book and leaned toward him. "What do you believe in?"

He flexed an arm. "I believe in the strength of a man. And in a sword and a good horse. These are things you can see and feel. Put your faith in that, Katrina. And in me."

"Surely you believe in more than that. Look around you."

She swept her arm to take in the sand and sea. "You must realize there is more to this world than what one can see with his eyes."

"You're right." Justus sat beside her on the rock. "There's loyalty to one's country. I believe in that. There's no higher calling for a man than to give fealty to his king." He gazed at her. "And to a beautiful woman."

Katrina shook her head. "One's highest duty and loyalty must be to Eloah, for it is he who builds the kingdoms to which all men belong and swear allegiance. It is Eloah who sets kings on thrones. Through him a kingdom is torn from the hand of one and given to another."

"So this Eloah is a God of war. Now the story becomes more interesting."

"Oh no! He's a God of peace and love."

"That's not the picture you painted just now."

"Oh dear. I'm going about this all wrong."

Finding a splinter of wood stuck in his pants, Justus pulled it out and chewed on it. When he looked up, Katrina was staring at him with an odd expression. "What is it?" he asked.

"I just realized something. I've often wondered about your life, how you wound up here, working for Rolland, why you're so good at what you do, and why you have such a good heart. Now I know. Eloah made you that way for a reason. He's destined you for something."

"Now you're speaking nonsense. Chosen, destined... I don't believe in Teman's God, so why would he want anything to do with me?"

"That can only remain to be seen."

The next eight weeks passed all too quickly. The days grew shorter and the wind grew stronger, stripping the Rygian woods of its autumn glory and leaving a stark bareness in its place. Icy rain beat incessantly against the roof of the little cottage—a forewarning of worse days to come.

Inside, Justus paid no heed to the banging of the shutters or the howling of the wind. He paced back and forth in the kitchen, pausing at each sound that came from the bedroom. Each time he heard Katrina's labored breathing or her gasps of pain, he darted toward her door. But then he'd stop. Bett was in there with her. This was women's business.

Hours passed. Much too long, he thought. Something was wrong. Something was horribly wrong.

Finally all was quiet. He listened for the cry of a newborn infant but didn't hear a thing. Soon Bett emerged for more water.

"What is it, Bett? Is everything all right? Has the baby been born?"

Concern and fatigue lined her face. "No, Master Corden. The baby is stubborn."

"What about Katrina?"

"She's asleep, but not for long, I'll wager."

"How can I help? What can I do?"

"Ain't nothing you can do but pray."

"What do you mean? Is Katrina all right? Will she be all right?"

Bett shook her head. "I've seen this before, Master Corden. It don't look good."

"I'm going in." He started for the door.

"No! Do not go in until you have prayed. And prepared yourself for the worst." Entering the room, she shut the door behind herself.

Justus stood horror-stricken. The worst? Surely that couldn't mean... No, it couldn't. Katrina was all right. She *had* to be all right. What did Bett mean?

Powerless, Justus had no idea what to do. No sword, no lance, no suit of armor could help him now.

"Do not go in until you have prayed," Bett had said. But pray to whom? To Katrina's God?

With nowhere else to turn, he cried out to the thin air, "Please, Eloah! Help her!"

A shriek pierced the cottage. "Jus — tus!"

He burst into the room, then stiffened.

No battlefield experience could prepare him for what he saw. Katrina lay pale as death, sticky blood covering the bed and blankets. Bett was trying desperately to coax a little head out from the womb. Sweat soaked Katrina's face and hair. Her eyes, usually bright like the sky, now seemed dim and glazed.

Justus' own blood drained from his face. The room began to sway. Another scream from Katrina, and the baby issued forth amid a stream of fresh blood. Then all was quiet.

Bett cleaned the baby's face, clearing away the residue that clogged her nose and mouth. With a sharp gasp, the baby let out a wail. Bett wrapped the child in a soft, white blanket.

But Justus saw only Katrina, her life slipping away before his eyes.

At the baby's cry, Katrina feebly extended her arms. Bett gently placed the child into the crook of the mother's arm and whispered, "She is a beautiful girl."

Katrina lifted weary eyes and whispered, "Look at her, Justus. Look at our little Anna."

His lips formed the question, "Anna?" but he was unable to find his voice.

"It means *merciful*," Katrina said, "because Eloah will be merciful to you. He told me so."

She reached a trembling hand to him. The moment her hand touched his, she closed her eyes and took her last breath. The pale, white hand slipped from his grasp.

"No... No... Katrina." He stepped backward and stumbled over a stool. *No... This can't be happening.*

Bett took little Anna from her mother and held her toward him. "I'm so sorry, Master Corden, but your daughter needs you now."

Justus didn't hear. With Katrina's screams still echoing in his ears, he ran out of the cottage.

~~~

General Rolland paced back and forth before King Arkelaus.

"I've seen to the burial of Corden's wife," the king said. "Have you heard anything from your men?"

"No, nothing, Your Majesty. No one's seen him."

The king shook his head sadly. "It's as though he, too, has died. I've sent messengers all over the realm, even as far as Darkhaven, but no word yet."

"What about the baby?" Rolland asked.

"The housekeeper took her. She'll care for her well."

Rolland's pacing never slowed until the king put a hand on his shoulder and said, "We've done all we can. I'm so sorry, my friend."

Winter passed, then summer with no word from Justus Corden. Rolland busied himself with the new squires and the king's army. King Arkelaus kept occupied with matters of the realm. But neither of them could last a day without giving a thought to the great soldier who had seemed to come from nowhere, graced their city for a short time, then disappeared.

Yet another winter brought its bleak starkness to Rygia, and another summer came again to warm and refresh the land. Still no word came from Rygia's mighty warrior.

14

An old cart creaked noisily as it traveled the dark trails of the northern Rygian woods. The cloaked figure upon it sat hunched forward, appearing as weary as the bony mare who strained under the weight of its load.

The gray, overcast sky lent no sunlight through the bare branches of the trees overhead. Dried leaves swirled in the breeze, falling to the road only to crunch beneath the cart's wheels.

As he entered the town of Darkhaven, the cloaked traveler heard a clamor in the direction of the town square. Heading there, he found a great crowd had gathered. Men, women, and children filled the open plaza. Boos and cackles and shouts of "Murderer! Kill him! Kill the murderer!" rang out.

With a tug to his hood to completely shadow his face, the traveler pushed his way through the throng. In the center of the plaza, he spied a wooden platform with a noose hanging from a crossbeam.

A man stood on the platform, hands bound behind him and a black hood over his head. Two guards stood on either side of him. A hangman brought the noose around the man's neck and took his place by the lever that would release the floor hatch and send the doomed man to his death.

The traveler accosted the nearest villager. "Where can I find the town constable?"

"Over there." The villager pointed to another platform on the opposite side of the square.

As the traveler eased his way among the mass, he began

to notice more than shouts of "Kill the murderer." Many women appeared to be crying, dabbing at their eyes. Were they crying for the victims, or was it something else?

Upon reaching the second platform and finding several leading citizens seated there, the traveler said, "I am looking for the town constable."

"I am he." A portly man rose and called out to the prisoner, "Do you have any last words, Nakar?"

One of the prisoner's guards called back, "He says, get on with it."

The traveler pulled a rolled document from his cloak. "I have an order from the—"

"Very well," the constable said, ignoring the traveler. "Let it be known that for the crime of murder, on this twenty-ninth day of October, this man's life will be taken from him. Hangman, you may proceed."

The hangman grasped the lever. Men cheered. Women wailed. Children hid their faces in their mother's skirts.

The traveler shouted with a voice of authority, "Stay your hand, executioner!"

The hangman paused.

"You will proceed, hangman!" the constable said.

The hangman began to pull the lever. The floor of the gallows gave a jerk. The prisoner's feet slipped.

"Stop!" the traveler shouted.

The hangman froze. The prisoner struggled to regain his footing on the partly open floor.

The traveler shouted in a loud voice for all the people to hear. "I have an order from King Arkelaus for a stay of execution of this criminal!"

A gasp went up from the crowd. The hangman removed his hands from the lever.

The constable scowled, snatched the document from the traveler's hand, broke the wax seal and scanned the parchment. "The king cannot do this! The crime of murder is punishable by death. It's the law."

"Do you have proof of his guilt?" the traveler asked.

"He made a confession! Several of us witnessed it." The constable peered down his nose at the cloaked traveler. "King Arkelaus is not above the law. This execution will go forth. Hangman!"

The hangman stood with a heavy case of indecision. The prisoner strained to keep his footing on the crooked hatch.

The traveler said, "The king has granted a stay of execution, as is his right."

"Why would the king stay the execution of a confessed murderer?" the constable asked.

The traveler said, "I wish to question the prisoner. When I am through, we shall see what is to be done."

"And just who are you?"

"An official of the royal palace."

"You expect me to delay fulfillment of the law?"

"There is no harm in delaying."

"There is great harm! He killed a man! Restitution must be made. A life for a life!"

"I will argue no more with you," the traveler said with an air of authority. "Hangman, return this prisoner to confinement."

"You will do no such thing!" the constable yelled.

A woman emerged from the crowd and took hold of the traveler's cloak. "Please, sir. This man is innocent. Please, don't let them—"

"Silence, woman!" the constable said. "He is guilty! He has confessed to the crime!"

"Then let him make his confession to me," the traveler said.

The hangman obeyed the traveler and led the prisoner off the gallows.

The traveler did not go immediately to question the prisoner. Instead he found a tavern and sat down to a mug of ale. As patrons of the tavern filtered in, he hoped to catch enough of their conversation to hear what they might say about the prisoner.

But the people of Darkhaven did not take well to

strangers, so they warily kept their distance. The traveler could hear their muffled conversations and knew they were talking about him and about the prisoner, but he could not catch enough to understand what they were saying.

A young, unkempt woman stepped into the tavern, her tattered shawl and dress betraying her poor status.

The tavern keeper yelled at her. "Hey! We don't serve women here!"

The woman ignored him and made straight for the traveler. "Please, m'lord, a word?" This was not the same woman who had approached him in the town square, but the traveler saw same imploring look on her face.

The tavern keeper took hold of the woman's arm and hustled her out. "We don't serve women here."

"Please, m'lord!" the woman called over her shoulder.

The traveler rose, tossed a coin to the tavern keeper, and left. Finding the woman outside, he said, "What is it you wish of me?"

"Please don't let them kill Nakar. He be innocent."

"They say he has confessed."

The woman hung her head.

"Be honest with me, woman. Is he guilty of murder?"

"If he be murderin' anyone, it be only thieves and murderers demselves."

"What can you tell me about this Nakar?"

"Not much. He be keepin' to himself and ain't often seen. At first, people thought he be a passing highwayman. We be gettin' a lot of those here."

The traveler said, "I am aware of Darkhaven's reputation. It is Nakar I am interested in. What can you tell me about him?"

"All I know is that Darkhaven be a better place these two years past, ever since Nakar be around."

"Two years, you say?"

She nodded. "If he be executed, it only be provin' the authorities right. It prove they be the stronger and can do whate'er they please."

"Why are you defending a confessed criminal?"

At first the woman didn't answer, but when the traveler repeated his question, she said, "He only be a criminal if it be a crime to do what be right."

"What right has he done?"

"I told you. He be riddin' the town of thieves and murderers."

"By killing them?"

She didn't answer.

"Tell me, woman. Is it right to take the law into your own hands?"

"If laws be unheeded by them what oversee 'em, what else can we do? The constable himself be the cause of much trouble."

"It is unwise to speak ill of the town's leading citizen," the traveler said.

"I only speak what be true. Them that cheat and steal do so with the blessing of the constable, for he be taking part of their gain for turnin' a blind eye. He don't defend them that're stolen from, for they be poor and can't pay him. And he never defend a woman. He speak kindly to them, as though he'll defend them, but then he be using them instead, leaving them worse off than if they never come to him."

"Is that what happened to you?" the traveler asked.

The woman turned her face away.

"Woman, you have nothing to fear from me. I, on the other hand, hold the future of this Nakar in my hand. If you wish to help him, you must speak to me."

"All right, I will say dis. My story ain't much different from other women in this town. We be seen as chattel, or less. Our children be treated like vermin. While the men spend their earnin's on drink and carousing, our children be going hungry."

"That does not answer my question. What is it Nakar has done for you that you would take up his cause so bravely?" When the woman again hesitated, he said, "I promise you, I will not condemn you."

The woman peered up into his eyes. He looked down on her with compassion, and that seemed to give her courage. But she spoke haltingly, as though her confession came with difficulty.

"My father… he have his way with me… ever since I be a little girl. When I be old enough, I go to the constable for justice. He take me in and… after he hear my case, he… he take me to another room. He said he help me if I…"

Tears slipped down and her voice caught. "He kep' me for several weeks while he be usin' me. All that time he make me think he be dealin' with my case. When I finally demand that he do what he promise, he be very angry. He said he find my father innocent and hand me back over to him."

A shadow of anger passed over the traveler's face.

"So I run away. But I be caught by the shire-reeve." She sniffed and wiped her cheek. "Do you know who the shire-reeve of Darkhaven be?"

The traveler shook his head.

"The constable's son." At this, she broke into sobs. "He be worse to me than any other. He said it be my punishment."

The traveler laid a hand on the woman's shoulder. "Tell me exactly what this Nakar did for you."

The woman said defiantly, "I never be afeared of my father or the constable's son again."

The traveler understood. "I am sorry things are this way in Rygia. Perhaps someday things will change. Tell me, woman, why do you stay in Darkhaven?"

"I ain't got nowhere to go, m'lord."

"Very well, I shall do something for you, if you will allow me. I know the lord of a city south of here. He is a good man. If you wait until I have finished my business, I will take you to him and see that he gives you a decent employ."

"Why you be doing that for me?"

"Because there's something I want you to do for me. If I were to place the constable under arrest, would you testify to his ill-repute? And could you find others to do the same?"

The woman smiled broadly. "I would and could, m'lord!"

Near the end of the day, the traveler finally made his way to the bread house, which had been converted into a prison after falling into disuse. Of late it had fallen into disuse as a prison as well, for the only people who were actually arrested in Darkhaven were those who crossed the constable. People who dared were few and far between.

Producing the king's document, the traveler was allowed to enter the bread house. Several empty rooms stood in a row in an underground chamber. Upon reaching a closed door, the guard unlocked it and allowed the traveler to enter.

Benches lined three sides of the wooden chamber. The prisoner lay on his back on one of them, staring at the wooden ceiling. His long golden hair fell past his shoulders, and a trim yellow moustache and beard framed his face.

"Leave us alone, please," the traveler said. The guard closed the door and left.

The prisoner did not take his gaze from the ceiling as he asked, "Who are you?"

"I was going to ask you the same thing."

"Apparently you already know who I am, according to that document you carry." The prisoner pointed to the traveler's parchment but did not move his gaze from the ceiling.

"I may know your name, Nakar, but I do not know who you are."

The prisoner said nothing.

"King Arkelaus has granted me the power to pardon you if I deem it right. You would do well to speak to me."

"Why should the king care what happens to me?"

"From the time your story reached his ears, you have intrigued him. You are somewhat of a mystery. Where do you come from? Why do you do the things you do?"

Again the prisoner said nothing.

The traveler said, "You are a criminal yourself, yet you do not abide other criminals. This is a ponderance."

"Go ponder it someplace else."

"You are belligerent indeed," the traveler said. "What has filled you with such bitterness?"

"That's none of your business."

"Most people who have their execution stayed are very willing to make their lives my business."

"You had no business staying my execution. I killed those men. I deserve death."

"Those men? I believe the charges involve the death of only one man."

"Apparently I killed the wrong man," Nakar said.

"Indeed. The constable did not look too kindly on the murder of his son."

"Yeah, that, and the fact that he was next on my list."

"No wonder he was so anxious to finish your execution."

A long silence ensued. The prisoner finally said, "Is there anything else you wanted?"

"Yes," the traveler said. "I want you to help me find something."

"What is that?"

"Yourself."

"What?"

"Your grief and anger have blinded you to who you really are. You have been through more in your young life than others who have lived three times as long. And now you have returned to your childhood home in an attempt to hide from your grief, but you find you cannot rid yourself of it. Instead, you've let it grow into an anger you can't control. You justify the anger by taking it out on wicked men, but you find no solace in it. You only succeed in falling deeper into the dark pit where bitterness dwells, and so you have estranged yourself from who you truly are."

Nakar slowly sat up, peering into the shadows that hid the traveler's face. "Who are you?"

"The question is, who are you? Do you even know?"

The prisoner swallowed hard.

"I believe you have lost something of yourself," the traveler said. "I, too, have lost something."

"What is that?"

"I have lost my captain of the Guard and have come to find him. I wonder... is he still alive... somewhere in there?"

Trembling, the prisoner rose. "Who are you?" he asked again in a whisper.

The traveler pulled the hood from his face.

The prisoner's mouth fell open. He managed to croak, "Your Majesty!" and fell to his knees.

King Arkelaus laid his hand on the prisoner's shoulder, feeling him shake with sobs.

"Why did you come?" the prisoner asked at last.

"I wanted to see for myself if the things I had heard about this Nakar were true, and if this Nakar was who I believed him to be. I wanted to judge for myself whether you deserve to return to my employ. I believe that you do. Will you come to resume your place in my service, Justus Corden?"

Justus' voice cracked. "I don't deserve mercy by your hand."

"And what would this world be like if we all got what we deserved? Nevertheless, mercy is what you shall have, if you are strong enough to accept it."

"But I've spilled Rygian blood. I must atone for the things I've done."

"The things you have done spring from your deeply ingrained sense of right and wrong," King Arkelaus said. "You have a good soul, Justus, but it's trapped behind walls of grief and bitterness. Your anger has misguided you for a time, but you can put this part of your life behind you."

"How?"

"To atone for your crimes, you shall serve the people of Rygia in the manner that suits you best. I charge you with the duty of protecting the land of Rygia and the royal line of Arkelaus for the remainder of your days."

King Arkelaus reached out his hand. "Rise, Justus. It's time for you to come home."

2

ARELI

15

King James Eliada of Teman strolled briskly through the halls of his palace. To his right marched the captain of the King's Guard, Benjamin Elkanah, wearing a red cloak with a golden elk. To his left marched a golden-cloaked young member of the Guard, Kyle, who doubled his steps to keep pace.

"What's the matter, Kyle?" James asked. "Too fast for you?"

"No, Your Majesty, I just didn't realize there was cause for such haste."

Captain Benjamin said, "Trust me, Kyle, there is always cause for haste when an Eliada is involved."

"Yes, Captain," Kyle said.

James halted in front of two huge, ornately carved wooden doors with images of plants, flowers, and animals carved from edge to edge. In the center was the emblem of Teman—a four-pointed compass set within an oval, with flames of fire reaching out from the inner corners of the compass points.

With a sly smile toward Benjamin, James grasped the two handles.

Benjamin pointed to the scars on the stone walls on either side of the doors and said, "Your Majesty, is this really necessary? You need not do such a thing to get the room's attention. By mere position—"

"Thank you, Benjamin, for your counsel. I shall take it into consideration." With that, the king yanked the doors open and they slammed against the walls, sending chinks of stone clattering to the floor.

Every head in the council room turned with a gasp, followed by a *whoosh* of relief. A short man with white hair, slightly balding, and a trim white beard approached. "Your Majesty, please, you must not tax the doors so. All you need do is raise your hand and you will have the attention of the entire room."

"I do not want the *room's* attention, Sospater. I seek the attention of my most worthy subjects, and I shall gain it in any manner I choose."

"Of course, Majesty. But as your chief advisor, I—"

"Thank you, Sospater, for your advice. Now if you will take your seat, please."

As Sospater joined six other black-robed elders at a large, horseshoe-shaped table in the center of the room, he said quietly, "Why did Eloah give the royal line such wills of iron?"

"So we can deal with stubborn elders," the king said with a smile. "Yes, I heard you, Sospater."

Sospater turned red.

James scanned the room. "Areli has not arrived?"

"No, Sire," Sospater said.

"Until he gets here, let me just say that I have brought you together to share the most excellent news..."

Sospater cleared his throat loudly.

"What is it now?" the king asked.

"Forgive me, Your Majesty, but there is one small item I think you should attend first."

"What is that?"

Sospater nodded toward the wall behind the king. "*That* small item."

James turned to see a boy of seven sitting on a bench against the wall. "Josephus! What are you doing here?"

The prince jumped to his feet. "I was told you wanted me."

"Who told you that?"

"Mari!" The prince fumed and darted out the door.

James said, "Kyle, go with him. See that he's where he's supposed to be."

~~~

Josephus raced through the hall, burst into the armory, and lunged at his sister. "You weasel! Make me miss sword practice! I'm gonna—"

Eleven-year-old princess Mariya pointed a sword in his direction, making little circles in the air, the blade's tip just inches from Josephus' stomach. "You're going to what?"

"What're you doing?"

"Practicing my swordsmanship. Not bad, huh? Look at this." Mari swooped the sword in large figure-eights, punctuating each swoop with a thrust and a "Hah!" Finished, she said, "Azel says I'm doing better than most boys my age."

Josephus looked from Mari to the sword master, Azel, who had a rather sheepish look on his face. "How long've you been doing this?"

"About three months now." Mari jabbed the point at Josephus, who jumped back.

Azel said, "Your Highness, please, say no more. You could get me into a great deal of trouble with your father."

Josephus' eyebrows raised. "Father don't know?"

"You won't tell him, will you?" Mari said.

"Oh yes, I will!" He turned around and ran into Kyle.

"No, no, Little Highness. Your father's in the midst of a very important forum. You are not to interrupt him."

Mari said, "Please, Jose, don't tell."

"Don't call me Jose! And you!" He turned to Kyle. "Don't call me Little Highness!"

"Forgive me, Your Highness."

Mari grabbed Josephus' sleeve. "Please don't tell."

He crossed his arms. "I'll make a trade."

She looked suspicious. "What kind of trade?"

Leading her away from the adults, Josephus said quietly,

"Next time we're at Silver Meadows..."

"Not the silver mine thing again! I told you, if you try to sneak off like that again, I *will* tell Father!"

"Then I'll tell about this." Josephus waved his hand toward her sword.

"This is different. You can't go exploring a silver mine alone. You're only seven."

"Stephen was with me."

"He's only seven too."

"And you're only a girl!"

"I don't care if you do tell Father on me, I won't let you do such a stupid thing."

"Fine." Josephus headed off with Kyle right behind.

~~~

Mari tossed her sword onto a table. "Little brothers are such a nuisance."

Azel gave a sad shake of his head. "This will surely spell the end of your lessons. And you were such a good student."

He picked up a smaller blade and said, "Then again, dagger throwing is always fun."

~~~

King Eliada heard it first, then the elders, and a hush fell upon them as they listened. The *tap, tap* of a cane preceded the entrance of a tall, shrouded figure, his features concealed by his hooded cloak, his slow, stiff stride betraying his great age. The king and elders waited in patient silence, for he was Areli Beth-Birei, the prophet of Teman.

"Come, Areli, let me assist you." The king reached a hand toward him.

The prophet waved his free hand. "No, James." Aside from Queen Bernice, Prophet Areli was the only person in the land with the freedom to use the king's given name, which the prophet did with a mixture of reverence and affection.

"Thank you, no," Areli said. "I can still carry my own frame. There is precious little else I can do for myself. Grant me that, at least." Reaching the table, Areli hooked his gnarled cane over his arm and lowered himself to a chair.

James said quietly to Sospater, "After today's meeting, move that chair closer to the door."

Areli said, "My hearing is still quite keen, I assure you."

Embarrassed, James cleared his throat and addressed the elders. "Now that Areli has arrived, we may begin. Our prophet has a wonderful announcement for us. Areli, if you will."

Areli said, "I bring news from Mount Eben-Ezer. A child has been born to the Areli line—a daughter. My great-great-granddaughter, Areli Beth-Aven."

Happy murmurings spread among the elders. "A house of strength," one said. "A house of trouble," another said.

Elder Nathaniel nodded. "The name means both."

Areli said, "She was born a week ago, on the first of May. My great-grandson says she is a healthy and beautiful child."

"But does she have the mark?" Elder Reuben said.

The king frowned. "Elder Reuben, as you well know, this matter takes time. Be patient."

"Forgive me, Your Majesty, but it's been so long since a prophet was born in Teman. Not since Areli Beth-Birei was born one hundred years ago has the mark of Eloah been seen on one of his descendants."

"Areli—the light and vision of God," Elder Nathaniel said. "Since those days this realm has waited eagerly for a word or vision from Eloah. Some say perhaps the lamp of Areli is dying or has gone out altogether."

Prophet Areli said, "I am afraid your words are true, Nathaniel. Indeed, I have often felt as though the light is gone from my own eyes. I have seen the passing of three generations of Eliada on the throne, yet I have not been given a word from Eloah since the days of your father's father's father."

King James nodded. "Your last prophecy was during the

reign of my great-grandfather. I shudder to think it might have been the last. If we lose the light of Areli, this realm will not stand."

Head Elder Sospater said, "Foreboding words but true, for Eloah appointed both the lines of Eliada and Areli to lead this realm. Should one of the lines fail, the people would begin to lose faith. And we all know what a blow that would be to the Elyon race. It has happened before, it can happen again."

Elder Reuben could keep patient no longer. "But we do not yet know whether this child will bear the mark. It will take months before the infant blue color in her eyes turns to brown."

"Perhaps even a year or two," Sospater said.

"What do we do in the meantime?" Reuben asked.

"In the meantime, we wait." Areli leveled a gaze at Reuben as he added, "Patiently."

King James dismissed the elders and headed to the throne room, the hand of the old prophet on his arm for support.

Areli said, "There was more in the letter from my great-grandson. A word for you, my friend."

"For me?"

"Yes. It seems my family has found a way to extract the juices of the Skotos plant without the use of heat. They hope this new method will allow the juice to retain more of the plant's healing properties. A stronger medicine for your wife, perhaps."

"That is good news. When will they have some ready?"

"Very soon. I plan to travel to the Kolan Mountains to see the child. You have been invited to come also. They will have the medicine ready for you to bring home."

"Excellent! I shall make arrangements immediately."

Areli said, "May I also suggest that you bring your son, the crown prince. He has seen seven summers already. It is time he visited the holy mountain."

"It shall be done," the king said.

16

With Captain Benjamin standing at his side, King Eliada sat on his throne under the vaulted ceiling of Teman's throne room, having second thoughts about a trip to Mount Eben-Ezer.

His wife, Queen Bernice, sat on the throne beside his, her curly brown hair drawn up in numerous braids woven around a circlet of gold. Her beauty was only slightly marred by the pale tone of her skin, but the stern look on her face brought a flush of hot pink to her cheeks.

"I will hear no more of your nonsense," she said. "You will go to Mount Eben-Ezer, and that will be the end of that. Do not be concerned for my well being. Do I not have the finest physicians in the land looking to my every need?"

"But what if you were to take another spell like last month? I do not wish to be away when you need me most."

"And what do you think you can do for me that our physicians cannot?" She laid a hand on his. "Go to the mountain, James. See the new daughter of the Areli line. Bring back the new medicine for me. All will be well, I promise."

The creaking of the doors quieted their conversation. Prophet Areli entered and slowly approached the throne. He did not bow when he arrived, for his position was equal to that of the king's. He stood before the dais, leaning on his cane, studying the king.

"What is it, Areli?" James asked.

"You have a look of concern about you."

"I was concerned about leaving Queen Bernice alone."

"That was not your only concern."

"How well you read me, Areli," James said. "You're right. Ever since the council meeting, I've been thinking about the possibility of Teman being left without a prophet. It would destroy us."

Areli continued his study of the king's face before saying, "This realm has endured much since the time of creation. The Kaion race rising in power, the loss of the Volon race, even the fall of the Elyon themselves. But from the time that Eloah placed the line of Eliada on the throne and gave the gift of prophecy to the line of Areli, we have stood firm. We have not faltered in our faith or our service to Eloah since that day."

"But what if the line of Areli was lost to us? What would happen to Teman then? Is it possible? Could we truly fall, like we did long ago?"

"Eloah is with you, James. He will not let you fall."

King James sighed. "I feel as impatient as Elder Reuben to see whether your new great-great-granddaughter will bear the mark of a prophet."

"Ah, but you must be patient, James. All will work according to Eloah's good plan."

"Tell me again the prophecy you made over my great-grandfather, Areli. Refresh my memory. It was so long ago, it's easy to forget."

"To me, it was only yesterday." Areli closed his eyes and whispered the words. "'Then will all the shining lights of the heavens become as darkness. The hearts of many will be troubled. Yet take courage! For when love and faithfulness meet together, when righteousness and peace kiss each other, then shall faithfulness spring forth from the earth, and righteousness look down from heaven.'"

"Words of mystery and yet words of hope," the king said.

"That is the thing with prophecy. One never understands the full meaning until it comes to pass."

"Then we know this prophecy has yet to be fulfilled, since we do not understand it."

"That is correct." Areli furrowed his wrinkled brow, making the lines deeper still. "Why such a long face, James?"

"Only one word from Eloah in over eighty years. Why has Eloah been silent? Surely he has not left us."

"I hear doubt in your words."

James knew Areli was right, but he didn't have long to think about it, for the creaking of the door again interrupted him.

Soldier Kyle strode in and bowed on one knee. "Forgive me, Your Majesty, but I'm afraid the prince will wait no longer. He has held his patience as long as he can."

"Very well, Kyle, let him in."

The moment Kyle motioned toward the door, Prince Josephus bounded through the room, stopping abruptly at the foot of the dais, as though he had almost forgotten his place. With a bow of his head, he said, "Permission to approach the throne?"

"Granted," James said.

Queen Bernice beamed, reaching a hand out to him. "You play your role well, my son. You make me so proud."

Taking her hand, the prince kissed it. "How are you today, Mother?"

"Better, now that you are here."

King James said, "Tell me, son, have you set things straight with your sister?"

"Uh..." Josephus hesitated, looking from his father to his mother.

"You came here to tattle on her, didn't you?" James said.

Josephus flushed. A quick glance to the old prophet made him turn away, but his eyes returned to meet those of Areli and became fixated.

"It's different in front of Areli, isn't it, son?" James said. "He does that to me as well. He—"

When James caught the intense stare down between the prince and the prophet, he nearly gave a gasp. To his surprise, Areli's eyes seemed brighter than ever, as though a half century had been erased from his age.

Areli slowly stretched out his hand, laying it on the prince's head. His voice was faint, as though far away, as he repeated the words of the prophecy. "'For when love and faithfulness meet together, when righteousness and peace kiss each other...'" As his words trailed off into silence, he closed his eyes and took a deep breath.

Released from captivity, the prince's eyes darted away. "What does it mean, Father?"

"I know not. Areli, what does it mean?"

The old man shook his head. "Forgive me, but I too know not."

"You don't know? Surely you have some inkling. At least you must have *felt* something."

The old prophet shuddered. "Do not ask me what I felt. It is too strong for words."

"I must know, Areli. What was it?"

Again Areli returned to his study of the king's face. After some time, he said, "Come with me, James. Let us walk the gardens."

With Areli leaning on his arm, King James headed out of the castle and down the embankment, into the moonlit gardens along the inner slopes of the coastal mountains. Footpaths wound back and forth amid flowers and herbs, their fragrances released as the prophet's robe brushed against them.

Areli came to a halt and turned to look back at Castle Mountain. "Look at your castle, James."

James gazed at the white stone walls and tall, slender turrets gleaming in the blue light of the moon. A small group of soldiers made their way up the switchback trail toward the castle entrance. From behind Castle Mountain, ocean waves crashed against the rocky coast.

He watched and listened until he could be patient no longer. "What am I supposed to see?"

"You tell me."

"I see the castle and the mountains. I hear the crashing

of the waves. It is as it always has been, ever since this castle was built."

"A stout castle, a symbol of our strength, is it not?"

James didn't answer, preparing himself for the real question he knew was about to come.

"I have a question for you, James," Areli said.

"I knew it."

Areli was unruffled. "Look at your castle, James, and tell me... In what do you place your trust?"

"My trust is in Eloah," James said without hesitation.

"Hmm." Areli never looked at James, giving nothing away in his demeanor. "Tell me, James, what are the mandates laid upon our people by Eloah?"

"The mandates of Teman are but three." James spoke the lines as though reciting a grade-school lesson. "To keep faith in the Lord, to protect and maintain the royal line of Eliada, and to always live in the land Eloah gave to us—the land of our creation."

When Areli said nothing, James said, "Why ask me this? Are you testing me?"

"Testing you? I suppose. I am reminded of the words in our Book of Light: 'The Lord left him to test him, to know all that was in his heart.'"

A sharp pain gripped the king's heart. "Left him? What are you saying, Areli? Eloah will not leave me, will he? Surely he knows my innermost thoughts and has no need of a test!"

"Do not tax yourself so, James, I am only asking a question. Posing a fantasy, if you will."

"I do not wish to entertain your fantasies, Areli."

"Be patient. Hear me out. What if the Lord did leave you? What would you have left? In what would you place your trust?"

"That is a fantasy I *certainly* will not entertain."

"Humor me. Answer the question. Speak from the heart. If he did leave you, where would you place your trust?"

James shook himself, the thought of being cut off from Eloah too much to bear. But as his eyes fell to the mountains that surrounded them, and as his ears were tuned to the waves that crashed relentlessly and yet found no ingress, he knew the answer.

"The land. I trust this land that Eloah has given us, for my life as sovereign is tied to the heart of it."

"Well spoken. Now look at your land and tell me what you see."

"In the darkness all I can see are the snow-capped peaks of the mountains."

"Mountains, yes," Areli said. "A bastion of strength. An impassible defense. True?"

"Yes, your words are true, Areli. These mountains have always been our best defense against enemies."

In the darkness, James heard Areli sigh and felt the slumping of his shoulders. "What's the matter, Areli?"

"It is as I have feared."

"What? What did you fear?"

"Tell me again what you just said."

"These mountains have always been…" The king's voice trailed off into near silence as he finished, "…our best defense."

"Yes, exactly as I have feared. By your own confession you place a great deal more trust in your land than in your Lord. Is it not so, James?"

The king slunk to his knees. "My God, forgive me. I've been a fool."

"No, James, you are no different from your forefathers." Areli helped the king to his feet. "It was the same with your father and with his father ever since I can remember."

"You reveal things within me that even I cannot see."

"It is only natural for a man to trust that which he can see and feel."

"But what does it mean? What is this test you spoke of? Surely Teman does not require a great calamity to befall it just to prove where I place my trust. Must the Lord leave me so more distressing truths about myself can be laid bare before the world?"

"I do not have an answer for you, James, but I do have advice."

"I value your wisdom above any man's."

"You must venture beyond these mountains to find your answer."

"Venture beyond the mountains? What do you mean?"

"You must learn to trust Eloah in a place where your mountains are not."

"No king has ever left the land appointed to him by Eloah."

"Why not?" Areli asked.

"This land is our mandate. The life of a sovereign is intricately bound with this land that speaks witness of Eloah."

"Speaks witness to whom?"

"To us, his people."

"Why do those who already believe need a witness?"

"What... what do you mean?"

"This land of Teman was not created by Eloah solely for our benefit," Areli said. "All within this great land—from the three rivers that flow into one, to the narrow path and the solitary gate leading into the castle of the ancients—all speak of Eloah's nature. But not just for us—for the whole world to see. We have vast knowledge. We have vast strength. Yet we keep it all locked away behind these mountain walls."

The king shook his head. "In times long past, many Temanites had left this land to bring the knowledge of Eloah to nearby realms—Xulon, Gargon, even as far as Rhakos. Many never returned. Some did return, but always destitute. The other realms do not receive us kindly."

He looked southward. "Those who left Teman to start a new realm in Petros fell prey to an enemy hand." He pointed northward. "Even Rygia, our closest neighbor, spurns us. They shut themselves off from us and persecute any Temanites who dare go there."

"Do these facts cause you fear?"

"Not just me but all of Teman. No one wants to risk their

lives anymore. We've tried and failed."

"And so we have shut ourselves away and begun to trust our mountains more than we trust our Lord. All while the other nations die without the knowledge of Eloah."

"They have no desire to know him! Their only quest is war and dominance. They would seek to subdue us for the riches this land holds. And..."

"And what?" Areli asked.

"And my own people would turn away. They would mix with unbelievers and lose faith."

"You believe that to be true?"

"I *know* it to be true! It happened long ages ago right here in Teman. In more recent history it happened again, in Petros."

"And you fear it would happen again?"

"Isn't that why we have the mandate, Areli? Isn't that why we're supposed to keep to this land... so we don't fall away?"

Areli sighed. "How complacent we've become, so secure in our surroundings. You're wrong, James. Our faith is not weakened when faced with difficulty or when challenged by controversy. Such things only serve to *reveal* where our faith truly lies. No, James, our faith will not wane when we have the courage to venture beyond the mountains. I believe the opposite is true—that it grows weak when we stay here in complacency."

"I don't think I understand you."

"It's been a long time since we've been tried... since we've had nothing to rely on but Eloah himself. This is not true faith—sitting here at peace and rest with security all around. True faith is revealed only in difficult times and circumstances."

Thinking on the prophet's words, King James couldn't help but see the truth in them. "Do you think there will come a time when Eloah will test our faith?"

"I know there will."

"You *know* it? Why? Did you have a vision? Did Eloah

speak to you? Was it back there in the throne room, when Josephus was there? What happened between you and him?"

"I will not mislead you, James. The words I have spoken to you out here in the garden are my own. I did not have a vision."

"But something happened in the throne room."

"Yes, that cannot be denied. Neither can it be explained. I did not have a vision. I had... a memory."

"A memory?"

"I was but a lad when I spoke that prophecy before the courts of your great-grandfather, but I have never forgotten it. The words came to me like a great wind, and then... darkness."

"Darkness?"

"That was all, just darkness. In my youth and inexperience I thought the darkness signified the end of the vision."

"Did it?"

"No. And I have never forgotten the feeling that accompanied the darkness."

"What was it?"

"Emptiness... despair... fear. All of those."

"What did it mean?"

"At the time I thought it meant nothing. I thought perhaps my fear stemmed from the unfamiliarity of the gift and the overpowering presence of Eloah's spirit. Now, at last, I am beginning to think otherwise."

Seeing the prophet fall into deep thought, King James decided against asking another of his many questions.

Finally Areli said, "In the throne room, when I looked into the eyes of your son, the words of the prophecy came rushing into my mind. And then it came again—the darkness, the emptiness, the despair. Now I believe it was all part of the vision itself."

James felt a shiver rush up his spine. "I do not like what you are saying, especially in regards to my son."

"The crown prince is as much a part of the future of

Teman as you, James. Even more so. Do not hold him from his destiny."

"What destiny?"

"Only Eloah knows. But this I believe—an answer may be found for you, and for him, on the holy mountain of Eben-Ezer. Be patient."

17

Prince Josephus sat in the royal carriage as it lumbered steadily along the foot of Teman's coastal mountains. Across from him Prophet Areli dozed, his head nodding with the rocking of the carriage.

His father, King James, peered out from between the curtains of the window, his golden crown bearing rubies and amethysts. He was a handsome man, usually with a carefree look and smiles to spare. A trim beard and moustache always framed his smile, and laughing brown eyes peered out from the shadow of his dark-brown bangs.

But there had been no laughter the last few days, and smiles were rare. Ever since that day in the throne room, he'd been carrying a look of concern and had been quieter than usual.

Josephus kept his eyes on Prophet Areli. Having always felt a measure of discomfort around the old man, his feelings were not lessened simply because Areli was asleep. Despite the prophet's closed eyes and occasional heavy breathing, Josephus couldn't help but feel uneasy seated this close to him.

"What are you thinking about?" His father's voice startled him. He hadn't even noticed when his father had turned away from the window.

"Oh, uh... nothing."

"You were quite deep in thought, I'd say."

Josephus wasn't sure he wanted to say what he was really thinking. But it had been on his mind ever since that day in the throne room. His father wasn't the only one disturbed by things that had happened that day.

With a glance to the old prophet to make sure he was still asleep, Josephus said, "That day in the throne room, when Areli looked at me like that." He stopped there, finding it difficult to express himself.

"I know what you mean," James said. "It bothered me too. Probably not as much as it bothered you, I can see that. Tell me, son, what did you feel when Areli looked at you like that? When he said the words of the prophecy. What did you feel?"

After a moment of thought, Josephus said, "Lost."

"Lost?"

"And alone. Alone in the dark."

"Were you frightened?"

Josephus nodded.

"I'm sorry, son."

"What did it mean?" Josephus asked.

"I don't know."

"Does it have something to do with me?"

"I hope not. But don't dwell on it, son. You have your whole life ahead of you. Don't spend it worrying."

Josephus wasn't sure he'd stop worrying, but at least he could try to think of something else. He pulled the window curtain aside and gazed out. The carriage was heading south, toward the Kolan Mountains, on a road that ran along the foot of the coastal mountains. Josephus' window faced the west, overlooking rolling green hills that all looked the same after awhile.

Pulling himself halfway out the window, he looked forward. "Hey! The Kolan Mountains don't look any closer than they were this morning!"

From a seat on the top of the carriage, Captain Benjamin Elkanah peered down. "Can I help you, Your Highness?"

"We've been traveling for three days. Why aren't we there yet? Are you sure we're on the right road?"

Benjamin chuckled. To the soldier next to him, he said, "What do you think, Kyle? Are we on the right road?"

Kyle chortled. "I'm not sure. Perhaps we took a wrong turn. Let's ask Uriah. Hey, Uriah!" he called toward a red-cloaked soldier who rode on horseback in front of the carriage. "Are you sure we're on the right road?"

Uriah turned in the saddle and frowned. "Are you serious?"

Kyle pointed toward Josephus. "His Highness wants to know."

When Uriah turned back toward the front, Josephus was sure he heard him grumble. Plopping back onto his seat, he felt his cheeks flush.

His father said, "Don't worry about it, son. When you're older, you'll have more patience for long journeys like this."

"When I'm older, I'm riding a horse, not this rickety old carriage."

"This is the finest carriage in the land!"

"I'm still riding a horse. It's faster."

"Yes, you could get there in half the time, but riding would be much too hard on you at this age."

"I could do it," Josephus said confidently.

"Just like you thought you could hike off to a silver mine all by yourself?"

Josephus held back a smile. In order to keep his sister from telling on him, he had told his father himself about trying to sneak off with Stephen. His father had responded with a bit of horror at the thought and a smattering of pride for his son's honesty and courage to come forward.

James said, "The silver mines aren't all that interesting anyway. Nothing but rock and such. But there's something in the Kolan Mountains much more wonderful than any silver mine."

"What's that?"

"The cavern gardens of Mount Eben-Ezer."

"A garden? What's so great about that?"

"Not just any garden... a *cavern* garden. Think of it, a garden inside a cave. No light at all, yet the most magnificent plant grows there."

"How can a plant grow with no light?" Josephus asked, skeptical.

"The Skotos plant is very special. The name means *darkness*."

"Is the plant dark?"

James laughed. "No, quite the contrary. It's named after the darkness where it lives, for it grows only in the caves of Mount Eben-Ezer. But the plant itself is the whitest white you've ever seen."

"A white plant in a dark cave?"

"Yes, but you can't see it's true color inside the cave. Lantern light doesn't do it justice. You must take it outside, under the light of the sun. But you must be quick, for once exposed to the sun, the color fades almost immediately."

"Huh." Josephus tried to sound interested, but he really wasn't.

"The Skotos plant isn't the only white thing in the cave," James said. "Many creatures live there, all of them white."

"Like bats? White bats?"

"No, no bats. Fish, salamanders, crabs..."

"Oh," Josephus said, still uninterested. "I've seen those."

The king spoke in a whisper, as though trying to make his words seem all the more wondrous. "Not only are these creatures white, they are all completely blind. They have no eyes."

"No eyes? How did that happen?"

"It didn't just happen, Eloah created them so. They live in darkness and have no need of sight. Eloah does not give someone something he does not need."

"He gave me a sister," Josephus said with a groan.

"That will be enough of that," the king said sternly. "By the way, I wonder how her dagger practice is coming."

Josephus' eyebrows crawled up his forehead.

"Yes, son, I know about it. Just before we left, she confessed to me that she had taken some sword instruction. While I was disappointed in her hiding it from me, I respected her coming clean just as I had with you. And since she had switched to a dagger, I allowed her to continue. A dagger is more suited for a woman, don't you think?"

"She's not a woman, she's just a girl."

"All the better, then."

That evening, the carriage arrived at the city of Tetra, which sat at the foot of the Kolan Mountains. Situated on a high plain, the large city was divided in half by a steep river gorge. Two tall stone bridges, supported by great arches, connected the two halves.

As the carriage rolled over one of the bridges, King James ordered it to stop and brought Josephus out to look. Excited for the first time on this trip, Josephus leapt out from the carriage and leaned on the bridge's rail. Far below him, so far it made him dizzy, a river stormed past.

"Is that the River Tria?" he asked.

"Good for you! You've been paying attention at lessons."

"It's so strong."

"Yes, by the time it reaches Tetra, it's been joined by many other rivers. Back on the north side of Teman, all the rivers are slow enough for boat traffic. But not here."

Captain Benjamin joined them. "Sire, Lord Sebastian is ready to receive you. The whole town is awaiting your arrival."

"Yes, let's be on our way."

Eager to stretch their legs, Josephus and his father walked the remaining distance to the manor of the lord governor of the city. There a great feast awaited them in an open square, and afterward they spent the night in Lord Sebastian's home.

The next morning, Josephus joined his father and Lord Sebastian in the governor's stables, watching servants load bundles onto four mountain ponies.

"Do we get to ride now, Father?" he asked.

"No, the ponies are for our supplies, and some extra supplies for the Areli family. We'll be walking the rest of the way."

"Walk?" Josephus whined. "Why must we walk?"

"Patience, my son. We're walking for Prophet Areli's sake. He finds it easier than riding horseback on steep mountains."

As they began the trek out of the city and up the Kolan Mountains, Josephus noticed that of all the King's Guard who had accompanied them, only Kyle and Captain Benjamin were with them, leading the four ponies.

Josephus asked, "How come the rest of the guards aren't coming?"

"The Areli family is not equipped to host so many people at once. The five of us alone will tax their resources, I'm sure."

This being Josephus' first trip up the Kolan Mountains, he craned his neck all around, taking in the sights. The foothills they climbed were green and lush, blanketed in grass, with patches of early summer flowers brightening their path. Here and there, a stand of poplar or pine trees lent shade, and an occasional boulder made a nice chair for resting on. Beyond the foothills, the Kolan Mountains rose up gray and steep, with snow-capped peaks.

The path along the foothills began easily enough, winding its way upward, but the higher they ascended, the steeper the path became. Feeling his legs giving out with each step, Josephus continually looked back at the ponies, wishing he was riding one of them.

"How long till we reach the top?" he asked.

"We'll reach Mount Avalee before the sun sets," James said.

"Mount Avalee? When will we reach Mount Eben-Ezer?"

"Tomorrow morning."

That sparked Josephus' excitement. "Are we going to camp out like the soldiers do?"

"No, we'll spend the night with the sisters of Avalee."

"Sisters? Oh, no! Why does it have to be sisters?"

Prophet Areli said, "Has the prince not yet learned of the sisterhood?"

"No, Areli," James said. "Why not tell him yourself?"

Areli said, "On Mount Avalee live three sisters who devote their lives to the study of medicinal arts, much like what my family does on Mount Eben-Ezer. But whereas my family cultivates only one very special plant, the sisters grow an abundance of herbs that are used in the healing of many ailments."

James said, "Do you remember when you were ill and we gave you a potion to drink?"

Josephus crinkled his nose. "Yes."

"It came from the sisters."

"Is that what they'll feed us tonight?"

James laughed. "No, son, they eat normal food like we do."

Areli added, "They raise their own chickens and goats, and they keep a garden of vegetables and tend a fruit orchard. It's quite a remarkable place."

"How can three girls take care of all that?"

Areli said, "They are not alone, for you see, orphan girls are brought there to live and study. That way they can learn the medicinal arts and live productive and useful lives when they are grown."

"Only girls?" Josephus asked. "What happens to orphan boys?"

King James said, "If they have no other family to take them in, they become soldiers. No orphans are left to themselves in Teman. We give them a life and a reason to live and serve others. Not only are they given sustenance but a paying future as well."

The trek went more easily with the conversation and with several stops along mountain streams to refresh themselves and refill waterskins. By the time the sun began to set, they had reached the crest of Mount Avalee, the last foothill before the Kolan Mountains.

Despite the fact that he didn't care to spend the night with a houseful of girls, Josephus was very glad to have arrived for he was quite tired and hungry. Even before he could see the cabin, a wonderful aroma touched his nose.

"That smells like chicken soup!"

"Indeed it does," Areli said.

The path emerged from a stand of pines and opened onto a treeless crest. On the opposite end stood a large wood cabin with a covered porch and a stone chimney. Nearby was a large barn. Two women came out to meet them, bowed before the king, introduced themselves as Luan and Loruah, and invited them all inside.

Josephus barely took the time to greet the women, for the moment he heard the words, "Dinner is waiting," he could think of little else. Eagerly stepping inside the cabin, he closed his eyes and sniffed deeply of freshly baked bread.

When he opened his eyes, he found he was standing in the cabin's great room, with a fireplace on the wall opposite him. To his left was a hall that led to bedrooms. To his right, another hall with more bedrooms. Next to the fireplace an entryway led to the kitchen, which was where the two women led him.

The kitchen was quite large, its walls covered with cabinets, and dried herbs hung everywhere. A very large table sat in the middle of the room, with a meal already laid out—bowls of hot soup and plates of dried fruit. Several young girls set tin mugs of goat milk by every plate. The third sister, Lissa, pulled a tray of freshly baked bread from a brick oven built into the stone chimney, above the fireplace.

When the king and his party were seated, Areli gave the blessing, and Josephus heartily dove in. Between bites he studied the three sisters, who had joined them at the table. Luan was the oldest, her brown hair showing the beginnings of gray. Lissa was next, then Loruah. They looked similar, as sisters should, although Luan was taller than the others.

While the adults engaged in conversation using words too big for Josephus to understand, he turned his attention to the girls who served them. The youngest was no older than himself, her brown hair neatly tied back in a braid, and her large, doe-like eyes flitting nervously from one guest to another.

"Don't be scared," Josephus said, his mouth full of hot bread.

The youngest of the three sisters, Loruah, said, "They've been quite nervous all week, knowing you were coming."

"Me?" Josephus said.

"Well, you and your father. This is their first time serving royalty."

"Doesn't Lord Sebastian ever come up here?" Josephus asked.

"Oh, yes, on occasion. But he's not quite as foreboding as the Eliada family."

Josephus could hardly take his eyes from the girls, who served them silently and adeptly, casting glances toward him now and then.

Luan said, "They are quite lovely, are they not?"

"Huh? Oh, I guess so, for girls."

Loruah chuckled. "You will come to appreciate them soon enough, Your Highness. One of these young ladies may very well save your life some day."

"I don't need any girl to save my life."

"She means with their medicinal talents," Lissa said. "Everyone in Teman, whether noble or peasant, will need the services of these girls sooner or later."

"Why can't we just grow our own plants on our own mountains?" Josephus asked.

Luan said, "I am certain the royal gardens contain a great many healing herbs, all of which had their beginnings here on this mountain. Here the climate is perfect for cultivating medicinal herbs—just enough rain, just enough sunshine, and very healthy soil. The Kolan Mountains are like a nursery, where the healthiest of plants grow and perpetuate. Sometimes, in the northern climes, an entire crop of herbs can die off. Then the people come here to gather rootings and reestablish their crop."

"So they *do* grow their own herbs in the rest of Teman."

"Of course, that's only wise," Luan said. "But to learn the art of caring for them and extracting their healing powers, that takes a special kind of skill, learned only here. Once these girls have completed their studies, they'll be given homes in cities and villages throughout Teman, where they can ply their trade and earn a living by helping others."

His bowl empty, Josephus let out a big yawn. King James said, "It's been a long day. Will you show us to our quarters?"

Luan nodded toward the doe-eyed girl who had served Josephus. "Abigail will show His Highness to his room."

Josephus followed Abigail to one of the bedrooms, where a straw-filled mattress covered with thick quilts awaited him. A plain straw mat lay nearby for the soldier Kyle.

"Is that the best you can do for my guard?" Josephus asked.

"We don't have much," Abigail said. "Everyone had to give up something."

"What did you give up?"

Abigail made a quick glance toward the bed.

"I'm sorry," Josephus said. "Where will you sleep?"

"I'll share with someone. Good night, Your Highness."

"Good night, my lady."

Abigail paused, eyes wide, probably never having been called "my lady" before, especially by a prince. Blushing, she hurried out.

Mount Avalee

18

The next morning, Josephus was awakened by Abigail's voice. "Master Areli calls for you, Your Highness."

Groggy, Josephus dragged himself into the great room, feeling new aches from yesterday's uphill hike. Prophet Areli stood near the fireplace leaning on his gnarled cane.

"It's awful early, Areli," Josephus said.

"It's the best time of all to see this mountain. Come with me." Areli headed for the door.

"What about breakfast?"

"Breakfast will be awhile. The girls are still milking the goats."

"You mean the girls are already up and working?"

"Of course. You'll find no lackadaisies here."

"I'm not a lackadaisy! I had a long, hard day yesterday." Even as Josephus said the words, he realized that Areli had made the very same mountain hike and seemed none the worse for it. In fact, the mountain air seemed to have invigorated him.

"All right, let me get dressed." By the time Josephus was ready, Kyle had also risen and joined them.

Areli led them along the northern side of Mount Avalee, between large beds of spring blooms—yellow daffodils, white and yellow narcissus, purple crocuses, and irises in a rainbow of color. The sweet smell of the irises rose on a breeze to meet them.

As the mountain began to slope away, Josephus found it covered with more and more beds of flowers and herbs trailing all the way down toward the valley. The plants were quite young, it being late May, but it was an awesome sight nonetheless.

To his left, a long row of trellises were covered with grapevines, budding in speckles of light green. Beyond that, pine trees created a dark backdrop.

"It's so big," Josephus said.

"Just wait, Your Highness." Areli took Josephus back across the crest to the opposite side of the mountain, the southern side. A great apple orchard spread before them, covering the entire southern slope with white blossoms.

Areli said, "This mountain is named for these apple orchards. The word Avalee means apple."

"I thought it meant bird," Josephus said.

"It does. You will find that many ancient words have dual meanings."

"Why don't we speak the ancient language anymore?" Josephus asked.

"It is a holy language, not meant for common use. In the beginning, Eloah created three races of mankind. All spoke the same language, for Eloah meant for them to live and work together and to share their gifts. The holy language was reserved for communion with Eloah himself."

"What happened to the other races?"

"They moved away. Only the Elyon remained in this land, for it was Eloah's command that they do so."

"The Kaion came back to war with us."

"Ah, you have been paying attention in your studies. Do you remember the names of the wars we had with the Kaion?"

"Um... Kaiandrian?"

"Calandrian," Areli said. "Those of the Kaion race who warred against us came from a realm they called Calandria."

"Why did they war against us?"

"No one knows for certain, except that they had turned away from Eloah to serve a god of darkness. That's why the Elyon are afraid to leave this land, you know."

"Because they might run into the Kaion?"

"No, because they fear that leaving this land will cause them to turn away from Eloah, as it did with the Kaion and the Volon."

"You mean the Kaion and the Volon used to live here too?"

"Yes, they did. In fact, I'll let you in on a secret."

"A secret?"

"Well, perhaps not so much a secret, but a bit of little-known fact. These mountains we're standing on, what are they called?"

"The Kolan Mountains."

"And what does the name mean?"

"Strength," Josephus said.

"What is the name of the western mountain range?" Areli asked.

"The Elan Mountains. That word means strength too. And the Velan Mountains in the north mean strength."

"Very good, Your Highness. Now, do you remember what I said about the ancient words often having dual meanings?"

"Yes."

"Well, these mountains are called the Kolan Mountains because the Kaion race used to live over there," he pointed southward, "on the other side of this range."

"Really?"

"Yes. At the dawn of creation, that is where Eloah placed them and where they cultivated the gifts that Eloah gave them. The word Kolan means 'strength of the Kaion.'"

Areli pointed north. "The Volon race used to live on the other side of the northern mountains, so those mountains were named Velan."

"Strength of the Volon?"

"Yes," Areli said. "And the Elan Mountains?"

"Strength of the Elyon?" Josephus said.

"Exactly. When Eloah created them, he gave each race specific gifts. Their gifts were their strengths."

"What's our gift?"

"The gift he gave to the Elyon was flora and fauna. We

understood how to work the land to bring forth plants for food and for healing. We domesticated the animals. The Elyon were the wisest of all the races, so Eloah also gave us the gift of humility, so that we would not lord it over the other races."

"The wisest," Josephus said, a bit proudly.

"And the humblest," Areli said in a tone that reminded Josephus of his schoolmasters. "And Eloah commanded the Elyon to be the keepers of knowledge. That is why we have such a vast library. Everything we learn, we write down."

Josephus said gloomily, "And we have to study."

Areli laughed. ""Study is good. You are studying right now."

"It doesn't feel like studying," Josephus said. "What gifts did the other races get?"

"Of that we know only a little. Our oldest records were destroyed during our Dark Time. But the names of the races shed a little light on their gifts."

"The word Elyon means people of the most high," Josephus said.

"Very good. Do you know what the word Kaion means?"

Josephus shook his head.

"It means, people of the burning light."

"Burning light? What does that mean? What was their gift?"

"It had something to do with fire, I remember that much. Now the Volon, that is the most interesting of all. Their name means people of the wind."

"People of the wind?" Josephus said excitedly. "You mean they could fly? Like birds?"

Areli laughed. "I really don't think so. But one of our books says their gifts were wind and water."

"Wind and water. What does that mean?"

"I'm afraid I'll have to brush up on my reading before I can answer that."

"What did the Volon look like?"

"That's another mystery lost over the ages. No one

remembers anymore what either of the races looked like. Most Temanites have never even heard the words Volon or Kaion."

"But we know a little about the Kaion."

"Yes, we know a little, but only because they had returned to war against us. All Temanites are taught about the Calandrian Wars so that they learn to trust in Eloah, who saved us."

Josephus said, "It was after the Calandrian Wars that the line of Eliada was put on the throne."

Areli's gray eyebrows rose on his wrinkled forehead. "You really do pay attention at your studies. You are right. But what you may not know is that the Eliada line was the line of the very first kings of the Elyon, from the dawn of creation."

"Really?"

"Yes, but their name was different back then. It was Eliána."

"That sounds a lot like Eliada."

"Indeed, for one comes from the other. During the Dark Time, your ancestors were in danger of losing their lives, since they were of the line of kings. So the firstborn son of the king changed his name to Eliada and left the royal city in order to carry on the line."

"Huh," Josephus said. Looking at the sun, he said, "Are we going to be late? Father wanted to reach the Areli home yet this morning."

"We still have time. Come." Areli led Josephus through the apple orchard to more orchards—pear, cherry, and peach. From there they went down the south side of Mount Avalee and up the next slope, climbing higher and higher.

"Areli, you're going to tire me out before we hike up Mount Eben-Ezer," Josephus complained.

"We can stop here. Look that way." Areli pointed eastward with his cane, toward the sea.

"It's foggy over the sea," Josephus said.

"Not fog, Your Highness. Those are clouds."

"Wow! We must be really high!"

"Not as high as we will yet be. Look over there." He pointed west, toward a tall mountain. "That is our destination. Mount Eben-Ezer, the highest mountain in all of Teman."

"Are we going all the way to the top?"

"No, not all the way. My family lives along the northern slope, about there." Once more he pointed.

"Do they live there all alone?"

"Yes, but they have plenty of visitors, and they visit the sisters often. They spend their winters in Tetra with Lord Sebastian. And of course, there's the hermit of the southern slope."

"The hermit of the southern slope?"

Areli nodded. "On the opposite side of Mount Eben-Ezer lives a hermit, a very strange man. He does not speak much, nor does he ever descend to the city. He comes to my family or to the sisters when he is ill or when he needs supplies, but they may be the only humans he ever sees."

"Can we visit him?"

"If you wish, I will take you to him. He does seem to enjoy one or two people as company now and then. But as a rule, he does not care for the ways of men."

A growling in Josephus' stomach put an end to the studies. By the time they returned to the cabin, a simple meal of cheese, bread, milk, and honey was laid out and waiting for them. Josephus finished quickly, anxious to be on his way.

19

By midday they reached their destination. Josephus plopped down on the cool grass of Mount Eben-Ezer's northern slope, glad to finally stop walking uphill. He closed his eyes against the sun, but soon the sun seemed to darken. When he opened his eyes, he was staring into the face of a strange man whose shadow covered him. The man had all the characteristics of a Temanite except for one thing—a shock of pure white hair on his forehead. Josephus couldn't take his eyes from it.

"Looks like this one has had too much traveling," the man said with a chuckle.

Josephus heard his father's voice from a short distance away. "I don't think he'll want to do much traveling for a long time."

The strange man bent over and reached his hand out. "We have a meal prepared for you. Would you like to join us?"

Accepting the offered hand, Josephus rose, eyes still pasted to the anomaly in the man's hair.

"My name is Aviur," the man said.

"Areli Beth-Aviur?" Josephus asked.

"That's right. I'm the prophet's great-grandson."

"But you're not a prophet." Josephus said it more as a question.

"No, I'm afraid Eloah has not seen fit to bestow that office upon me. Nor upon my father or my grandfather. The gift often skips a generation or two... or three."

Josephus followed Aviur to a very strange house built

right into the side of the mountain. He could see a front wall with two big glass windows, but there were no other walls. A chimney rose out from the side of the mountain just beyond the front wall.

At first he thought the inside must be awfully dreary. But when he entered, he found that the windows let in plenty of light. He also caught the sweet, piney fragrance of rosemary, which made the place smell clean and fresh. The front door opened to a great room with several cushioned chairs. To the right was a kitchen and table. No wall separated the kitchen from the great room for they shared the same windows.

All of this the prince took in at a glance, for no sooner had he entered the room than something else took his attention. In the far corner sat a beautiful woman with long, straight hair. Josephus' eyes went past the woman to what she was holding—a tiny baby, the most beautiful baby he had ever seen. He tiptoed up to her.

The mother pulled the blanket away from the baby's face and whispered, "Your Highness, meet our little Aven."

The moment his gaze fell upon her face, Josephus realized he didn't feel alone anymore. The lostness, the darkness, the fear that had fallen on him since that day in the throne room evaporated, gone simply because *she* was there. Such a peace came upon his heart that he didn't even realize he was smiling very brightly.

Until his father came up behind him and said, "She has quite an effect on you, I see."

Josephus cleared his throat, embarrassed.

"What is it you're feeling?" James whispered, laying a hand on Josephus' shoulder.

"I feel happy."

"Interesting," James said. "We don't even know yet whether she'll be a prophet."

"It doesn't matter. She just makes me feel happy."

Aviur had been quietly laying a meal on the table and now beckoned them to come. The woman laid the baby in a wicker basket and joined them. Aviur said, "This is my wife, Eshana."

"My lady," Josephus said in response.

"Such manners for one so young," Eshana said. "You've been well groomed, Your Highness."

Josephus blushed.

Aviur took a seat across the table from Josephus, which made Josephus stare all the more at the shock of white hair. Throughout the meal he couldn't take his eyes from it. Images of white plants, white salamanders, and white crabs danced in his mind.

So wrapped up in his thoughts, he didn't realize he was interrupting a conversation when he asked, "Do you get that from the cave?"

The men hushed and stared at him, then broke into laughter.

Prophet Areli said, "Oh no, young prince, that's a birthmark. It appears among the Areli line now and then. I, myself, had such a mark in my younger days." He touched the gray hair at his temple.

Aviur appeared surprised. "Birthmark? I thought it was a sign of wisdom."

The men laughed again, the noise evoking a cry from the wicker basket. Josephus leapt up and ran to the baby. Kneeling, he leaned his face over hers, which was all scrunched up as if she was preparing to let out a holler.

"Shush, little Aven. Don't cry."

She opened her eyes and looked toward the sound.

"There you go, that's better." He touched her cheek, and her arms shot up and waved about.

"What do you think of her, Your Highness?" Eshana asked.

"I like her, but her eyes are so blue."

"That will change."

"When?"

"Oh, maybe just a few months, maybe more. In our family it sometimes takes three years."

"I don't think I can wait that long."

"Wait for what?" Eshana asked.

"To see if she has the mark."

Eshana laughed. "You will just have to be patient, Your Highness."

Aviur came to stand behind him. "Your father and I are heading to the cave, Your Highness. Would you like to join us, or are you too tired?"

"I'm not too tired. Can I go, Father?"

"As long as Kyle stays with you."

Aviur led Josephus and the others along a worn-out path that ran westward from the house, along the northern slope, until they reached a large hole in the side of the mountain.

"That's it?" Josephus asked, unimpressed. "Just a hole in the ground?"

Aviur held a lantern over the opening. "Look again, Your Highness."

As the hole was large enough for a man to sit in, Josephus was able to take the lantern and lean inside. The lantern light bounced off glossy walls that led deeply downward into blackness.

"How far down does it go?"

"Pretty far."

"How do you get down there?"

"Look under your chin."

The prince drew the lantern under his face and looked. A series of steps had been carved from the stone and made their way downward at a dizzying slope.

"Wow! Can we go in?"

King James said, "You and I will go in, but Areli will stay here to visit with his great-great-granddaughter. Kyle, stay close to Josephus."

"Yes, Sire," the young soldier said.

Aviur entered the cavern hole first, carrying the lantern. Josephus watched as he held onto iron rungs driven into the rock for support. When he reached the bottom, he lit several more lanterns hanging from the walls.

His voice echoed upward, "All right, you can come down now."

Kyle went first, then Josephus, followed by King James and Captain Benjamin. When all had reached the bottom, each were given a lantern.

"Excuse me, Aviur," Kyle asked, "but why don't you make that hole any bigger? It wouldn't take too much work."

Aviur said, "We must keep the cavern climate as close to its natural state as possible. The Skotos plant is extremely delicate. If we upset the balance of nature here, we could lose the only source of the plant we have."

Aviur headed down a narrow passageway. As Josephus followed the others, a clammy chill crawled up his spine. Just as he was beginning to think he did not like caves, the passageway opened out into a room of tremendous proportion. All he could do was turn in circles, holding his lantern out and gazing at the immensity of it.

On the far side of the large cavern, three passageways led in different directions. All were much larger than the first passage they had traveled, enabling men to walk side by side, even with laden arms.

"This is better than the entrance," he said.

"Oh yes," Aviur said. "Only the entrance is so narrow. The rest of the cavern is more like this."

"The rest?"

"This cavern stretches for miles in every direction. A person could really get lost if he didn't know his way around. After awhile all the walls start to look the same."

Josephus' mind wandered. "If this big hole is miles long, what holds the mountain up?"

"Faith!" Aviur said with a laugh.

The passageway opened to another room, not as large as the first but quite spacious. The walls here looked different from the rest, whiter and with an odd texture.

Aviur put his hand to the wall. "This is where the Skotos plant grows. See?"

Josephus looked harder, holding his lantern close. When he touched the wall, it felt soft and spongy.

"The plant grows tight against the walls," Aviur said. "Try to pull one off."

Josephus grasped a piece of the spongy material and pulled. Bits of the leaves broke off in his hand, but most of the plant stayed firmly embedded.

Aviur said, "It's not easy to get the entire plant out from the wall, but since most of the healing qualities are in the roots, that's what we must do. We've been working over here, see?"

Following the light from Aviur's lantern, Josephus saw where the wall had been chipped away. "You have to take out chunks of the wall to get the plant out?"

"Exactly."

"No wonder you need faith to hold the mountain up."

Aviur chuckled.

"Is this all there is?" Josephus asked.

"Oh, no." Aviur held his lantern high, illuminating the room and revealing more tunnels. "The growth continues down those passageways. There's more than we can access in a lifetime, I think."

"How do you get the juice out?" Josephus asked.

"Once we remove all the bits of stone from the roots, we put the entire plant in boiling water, here." Aviur showed Josephus a hearth and kettle. Above it, a fist-sized hole led to the surface, directing the smoke outward.

"Do you do all the work yourself?"

"Oh, no. People come up from Tetra and help out. We appreciate it, especially when it comes to removing the plant from the rock. Sometimes whole sections break off and the rubble pours on your head."

King James asked, "Are you sure it's safe? I wouldn't want anything to happen to you."

"We've had some carpenters shore up the walls for support, and some stone masons came to study the situation. They assure me that all is well."

Before leaving the cavern, Aviur went to a table filled with tools. Underneath the table was a wooden box full of empty crystal vials. One full vial sat on the table. Aviur handed it to King James. "This was refined a few days ago. Give it to Her Majesty the Queen with our best wishes and prayers."

"Thank you, Aviur," the king said, tucking the vial into his belt.

"One last thing." Aviur pulled a piece of the plant from the wall and gave it to Josephus. "Put this inside your tunic to keep it in the dark. When you get outside, let your eyes adjust to the light, then pull it out."

Josephus was the first one out of the cavern, pulling himself up by the iron rings as he climbed the stone steps. When his eyes had adjusted, he pulled the plant out and gasped. "It's so bright! It almost sparkles!"

But almost as soon as he said it, the plant faded to a yellow color, then shriveled into a dry brown mass.

"But what about the juice?" Josephus asked.

King Eliada pulled the vial from his belt and looked at it.

Aviur said, "It'll stay clear for about a fortnight. But the moment you see a tint of yellow in it, throw it out."

"I will," the king said.

Josephus ran ahead of the others, bounding into the Areli house and straight to baby Aven. As he leaned over her and cooed at her, she grasped at his nose. Her little tongue went out and in as she made gurgling noises. Josephus moved his tongue in and out until she squealed in delight.

"She likes you," Eshana said.

"I like her too." From the corner of his vision, Josephus watched his father and Prophet Areli come close and watch the two of them.

James said, "I know he is only seven, but I have never seen him enjoy a girl before."

"This is no ordinary girl," Areli said.

James scratched his beard and sighed. "Maybe it's just wishful thinking, but as I watch them, I think perhaps this is the answer to my questions."

"How so?" the prophet asked.

"Think of it. Think of their names. Areli Beth-Aven—love and peace. Josephus Eliada—righteousness and faithfulness. What strength that pair would give to this nation."

When Areli didn't respond, Josephus looked up and found the prophet staring silently down at the two of them.

"Interesting," Areli said.

"What's interesting?" Josephus asked.

But all the prophet said was, "Only time will reveal the truth."

20

Early the next morning, Josephus was informed they would be leaving later in the day.

"Leaving already? We only just got here!"

"I am sorry, son, but it's because of this medicine. We must bring it to your mother as soon as possible."

"But Areli was going to take me to visit the hermit."

"Hermit?" the king asked.

"He lives on the southern slope. Areli said he would take me there."

"What's this about, Areli?"

"If you think we can spare the time, James, I believe it would be good for the prince."

"Well, I suppose so, if you can be back by midday. We'll have the ponies ready by then."

"Leave your guards behind, Your Highness," Areli said. "Two visitors is about all the hermit can handle at one time."

Josephus followed Areli up and around the mountain, along a narrow trail that circled the slope. On the southern side of Mount Eben-Ezer the trail ended. The ground leveled out into a grassy field before falling away steeply.

Areli took Josephus across the field, seeming to head straight toward a mountain wall. But as they neared, Josephus could see a cave, its opening shaded with pines. A very strange-looking man emerged.

"Is that him?" Josephus asked, staring at the man's long, wild hair, unkempt beard, and roughly sewn leather clothing. In one hand he held a bow, and a quiver of arrows was slung over one shoulder.

"Yes, that's him. Good day, Beale. Do you remember me?"

"Relly," the hermit said in a rough voice.

"Yes, Areli," the prophet said. "This is Prince Josephus."

Beale stared hard at Josephus, keeping silent.

"What's he doing?" Josephus asked.

"Studying you. Deciding if he likes you."

"Does he understand what we say?"

"A little."

"He's awfully rude. Doesn't he know who I am?"

"He understands nothing about kings and prophets. To him, all men are the same."

When the hermit turned and walked toward his cave, Areli followed.

"Are you sure it's all right?" Josephus asked.

"It's perfectly fine. If he did not want us to be here, he would stand defensively and stare at us until we left. The fact that he turned his back on us shows he trusts us."

Josephus whispered, "You told me he was strange, but... wow."

The hermit turned and stared at him again.

Josephus froze. "Did he hear me?"

"He can hear a baby bird a mile away," Areli said.

"Did he understand me?"

"He may not understand all of your words, but I am sure he understood your tone."

"Now what do I do?"

"Nothing. Let him decide what you should do."

After a brief stare, the hermit turned again to go into his home.

"Come," Areli said.

Josephus remained glued to his spot, hardly daring to breathe.

"It's all right," the prophet said. "He has accepted you."

Josephus let his breath out and followed through the wide opening of the cave.

The place was nice, for a cave. The stone walls were white, and a bearskin lay on the floor. Along one side of the wall, a bed had been carved into the rock and was laden with animal skins of all kinds. A hearth was carved into the opposite wall, with a hole leading up and out, much like in Aviur's cavern.

"This isn't so bad," he said. "Actually, it's rather cozy."

Areli sat down on the bearskin and motioned for Josephus to do the same. The hermit dipped a wooden bowl into a pot on the hearth and handed it to Areli.

Holding the bowl in both hands, Areli took a sip. "Mmm, fruit soup." He handed the bowl to Josephus.

"Fruit soup?" Josephus peered inside. The mixture was thick and purplish with a sweet scent. He shrugged his shoulders and tried some. "Mmm, blueberries and cream! Delicious!"

The hermit grunted.

"He likes you," Areli said.

"I'm glad. I like him too."

"You should. He is quite a remarkable man."

"How so?"

"As you have already discovered, his hearing is quite keen. So also his sight. He is an excellent hunter." The prophet motioned toward the hermit's bow and quiver. "He mimics the calls of the animals with perfection. And he seems to be able to feel what is happening with the earth."

"What do you mean?"

"He always knows what kind of weather to expect. Just before any harsh winter storm hits these mountains, he has gone to warn my family so they can leave quickly for the city. It's too bad he cannot teach that skill to others. It would be quite beneficial."

"Does he go to the city during the winter, like Aviur and Eshana?"

"Oh no, he does not care for large groups of people nor for the ways of men."

"But doesn't the winter weather get too harsh?"

"Somehow he is able to survive up here. He probably follows the animals to the lowlands further south of here."

"Follows the animals? Areli, you jest."

"Believe what you will. I only know what I have seen and heard. And if the hunting is good on the other side of the mountains, he has been known to stay there for years."

"Has he lived alone all his life?"

"As much as anyone can tell."

"But he visits your family from time to time?"

"Only on great occasion, when something important is happening."

"Like the weather?"

"Or if he is ill."

"Does he know about the baby?"

"Let's ask him. Beale, have you seen the baby yet?"

"Bay-bay?" the hermit asked.

Josephus said, "Beth-Aven. Do you know Beth-Aven?"

The hermit smiled. "Bethen!"

"Beth-Aven," Josephus said slowly, with great enunciation.

"Bethen," the hermit said.

Areli said, "Apparently he has met her. See how he lights up when he thinks of her."

"He wouldn't hurt her, would he?"

"You have no need to fear him. He would not hurt anyone. But come, we must be on our way if we are to return to your father by midday."

The trip back to Temana seemed just as long as the trip to Mount Eben-Ezer, but Josephus' thoughts were full of Beth-Aven. Once home, he went with his father to the royal bedchamber to tell his mother all about the little baby.

While there, his father gave the Skotos medicine to his mother. She took only a drop, and within a short time, the color returned to her cheeks.

When Josephus and his father left the bedroom, he asked, "Why is Mother sick all the time?"

King James had Josephus sit at a table in the

antechamber and spoke in quiet tones. "I suppose it's time you knew. She's been ill ever since giving birth to you. Actually, it started after giving birth to Mari. It was just too much of a drain on her. After you were born, she was much worse. The doctors say something might have been damaged inside her."

"But why doesn't it heal?"

James shrugged. "There are some things we may never know, but one thing we can always count on. Eloah knows best, and he keeps everything in his care."

21

Over the next two years, King James received eight more vials of the expensive medicine. Queen Bernice showed much improvement with each dose, but when there was none, especially during the winters, her health declined. Yet she remained cheerful and did her best to appear strong before her people.

On a morning in early April, nearly three years after the birth of Areli Beth-Aven, James thought his wife looked better than she had in years. As he sat with her in their private antechamber, a low fire warming the room, he said, "It does my heart well to see you so improved, my love. Perhaps as time goes by we'll see a complete recovery."

"That remains in the hands of Eloah." Bernice laid a hand over his. "I have had such a wonderful husband to see me through all of it."

"Speaking of husbands, have you talked to Princess Mari yet?"

"Oh, dear. I guess I had forgotten."

"Bernice! How can you forget such an important thing?"

"I meant to tell her yesterday, but then I did not have the heart. Are you sure it would not be wise for you to tell her? You have such a special relationship with her, she may take the news a little better."

"No, that would not do. This kind of thing ought to be done between mother and daughter. Her fourteenth birthday is only a few months away. She'll need time to get used to the idea. Tell her by the end of the week."

"It will be done."

At a knock on the door, James called, "Enter."

A guard stepped in and said, "Prophet Areli is here, Sire."

"Show him in."

The tapping of the prophet's cane came more quickly than usual, it seemed. "Why, Areli, what potion has given you this vigor?" the king asked.

"Not a potion but the news I bear brings life to these old bones."

"What news?"

Areli pulled a rolled parchment from his cloak and handed it to the king. "Read for yourself."

James scanned the document. "By Elán!" Dropping the parchment onto the queen's lap, he bolted out the door. "Call the council! Immediately! Come, Areli, what's taking you so long?"

Less than thirty minutes passed before all seven elders had gathered in the council chamber, but the king felt as though hours had gone by. As each elder entered, he ushered him to his seat as though no one was moving fast enough. Head Elder Sospater was the last to arrive. The king nearly dragged him to his seat.

Sospater said, "Please, Your Majesty, what is the cause for such haste? Why are you acting in this manner? The people will think you insane."

James said, "Esteemed elders, no longer will the people of Teman say visions are a thing of the past. It's my privilege to inform you a prophetess has arisen in Teman!"

"What!" Sospater exclaimed amid the rising chatter of the council. "What do you mean?"

"We have just received word that the child Areli Beth-Aven does indeed bear the mark of Eloah!"

Elder Reuben leaned forward. "You mean she bears the green star? In her eyes?" He pointed to his own eyes as he said it. "Have you seen it, Areli?"

Areli said, "We have only just received word, Reuben."

Reuben stood. "But she does bear the mark? You are certain?"

The king said, "Reuben, Reuben, please return to your seat. Yes, the letter is quite clear. I will prepare to leave immediately to see this wonder for myself. This is a day of great rejoicing! A prophet has returned to our land!"

"She should be brought here, to the castle." Reuben jabbed a finger on the table for emphasis.

Sospater said, "Reuben is right, Your Majesty. A child of this importance should not be raised so far from the royal city and the protection of the castle. The Kolan Mountains are a treacherous place to live. Bring her down that she may be reared in a manner befitting her position."

"Of course, of course, all will be done. I believe arrangements are already being made, are they not, Areli?"

"They are," Areli said. "The letter from her father says she will be brought down from the mountains as soon as she is weaned."

"When will that be?" Sospater asked.

"A few months," Areli said.

"A few months?" Reuben said. "Your Majesty, you cannot wait that long. She must be brought here immediately!"

The king said, "Now, Reuben, have a heart. She will be allowed to stay with her parents a few months longer. Not another word about it."

~~~

When Prince Josephus heard the news about little Aven, he could not contain his excitement. Over the three years since he had seen her, he had forgotten all about that day in the throne room, when Areli had looked deep into his eyes, said the words of the prophecy, and brought fear to his heart. Now, knowing that a new prophet had arisen—*his* prophet—he felt that all would be well in Teman and there was nothing to fear.

His request to come along on the journey delighted his

father. After a hasty preparation and fond farewells to Queen Bernice and Princess Mari, they were on their way.

This journey seemed much quicker to Josephus than the last time he had traveled this route, but still not quite fast enough.

James said, "Why, son, you're like a pot ready to boil over."

"Sorry, Father. I'm really trying to act my age."

"Act your age? You're only nine, Josephus. Don't try to grow up too fast."

"I'm nearly ten, Father."

"Oh, of course. And ten is so much older than nine."

Josephus frowned.

"Tell me, son, what in particular are you so excited about? Do you wish to see the caves again?"

Josephus shrugged. One trip in the caves was enough.

"How about the hermit?"

"I suppose I'd like to see him again."

"But that doesn't seem to excite you. Hmm." The king scratched his trim beard. "Could it be the little girl? Are you excited to see her?"

Josephus felt his cheeks flush. But he managed to say, "Who wouldn't be excited? A prophetess! I've never seen the green star in a prophet's eyes."

"Few have, my son, this is a great privilege. But I had hoped you were excited just to see Aven, regardless of the mark."

Cheeks burning, Josephus pretended to look out the carriage window.

"I'm sorry, son, I have played with you long enough. I just hope your sister shows that kind of excitement when she gets the news."

"What news?"

"By tomorrow night, your mother will have informed her that it's time for her to be betrothed."

Josephus felt a little sorry for her. "Betrothed? To who?"

"To *whom*. That I cannot tell you. It would not be right for you to know before she does."

"You mean she doesn't know yet?"

"Actually, we have not yet made a firm decision. But we have someone in mind."

22

"Mother, how *could* you?" Princess Mariya said. "How can I be thinking of marriage? I'm only thirteen!"

"But, my dear, you won't be marrying him on your birthday. It's only a betrothal ceremony."

"But I want to devote my life to Eloah, not to a husband!"

"This is the way you are ordained to serve Eloah, by bearing descendants to the Eliada line. It is the country's mandate and your personal responsibility."

"But I'm not ready!"

"Look, Mari. After your betrothal on your fourteenth birthday, you'll have four years to get to know him. By the time you're eighteen, you will be more than ready."

"Get to know who? Don't I get to choose my own husband?"

"Not entirely. Choosing the right man for the princess of Teman is a great responsibility. Should anything happen to your brother, you and your husband would inherit the thrones. It's best if he is of some distant relation to the Eliada line."

"A relative? Whom do you mean?"

"Your father and I were thinking of Aaron Elkanah."

Mari opened her mouth to object, then realized she didn't know who Aaron Elkanah was.

Bernice said, "He's a nephew to Benjamin Elkanah. He's from the city of Teruma, but he's stationed here in Temana now. He was recently promoted to captain of the bowmen in General Garth's unit."

"A captain! He must be terribly old."

"He is only twenty-two."

"But, Mother, that's so ancient!"

"When you are eighteen and he is twenty-seven, it will not seem like so many years. Your own father is eleven years older than me, you know."

"But Mother..."

"Your father and I believe he is the best choice possible. Trust me, we're keeping your feelings in mind. Captain Elkanah was the youngest of those we considered eligible. And he is quite handsome."

"Says who?"

The look on her mother's face told Mari just how frustrated her mother was getting. She felt a little bad for that.

Bernice said, "Aaron's loyalty to the house of Eliada is unparalleled. As are his skills. He's the best bowman in all of Teman."

"Does he know you've chosen him?"

"Yes."

"What!"

"We felt it only right to speak to him before making any plans. After all, if he wasn't interested, then you and I wouldn't be having this conversation. Of course, he knows you will be allowed to make the final decision."

"I... I can make the final decision?"

"Oh, Mari, we would never make you marry against your wishes. But I will be honest with you, we did not expect quite this much remonstration."

Mari cast her gaze downward. "I'm sorry, Mother."

"You still have some time to get used to the idea," Bernice said. "It is six months until your birthday. By then you might see things differently."

"Does the decision have to be made by then?"

"Well, I... I don't know. Tradition always places the princess' betrothal on her fourteenth birthday."

"But is it a law?"

"No, it's not a law, it's tradition."

"Maybe we could wait another year or two."

Bernice gave a sigh of exasperation. "You will have to speak to your father about that."

Leaving the throne room, Mari walked slowly through the castle corridors, a heavy weight pressing on her heart. *Marriage? I'm not ready for that. I'm not ready to even* think *about it!*

At times like this, she knew exactly what could cheer her up—a good battle story from General Garth. She exited the castle and headed toward the soldier's barracks.

Seeing a group of soldiers standing outside the stablehouse, she pulled up short. *I wonder if* he's *there. Aaron.* But she had no way of knowing since she didn't know what Aaron looked like.

He was a captain, so he'd have a red cloak, she knew. Only officers and members of the King's Guard wore red cloaks. *Elkanah.* The Elkanah family bore a golden elk on their cloaks. Each individual had a variation on the emblem, but all would have the standing elk with a crown around its neck, like Captain Benjamin.

Sidling up to the stablehouse, she peered around to have a closer look. A couple of the soldiers wore red cloaks, but she couldn't see their emblems.

A gruff voice behind her made her jump. "What might the princess be doing here?"

She spun around and looked up into the weathered face of General Garth. "Oh, General, it's you," she said, a hand to her racing heart.

"What are you doing here, and all alone?"

"Just looking."

"Looking for what? A handsome young man?"

"No, thank you," she said, chagrined.

"Why, what's the matter, Your Highness? You don't seem to be yourself."

"I'm just a little distressed, General."

"Why?"

"I'd rather not say."

"Perhaps Her Highness would like some cheering up."

"Oh yes! Would you tell me a story?"

"What kind of story?"

"A battle story."

"You are the strangest girl, Your Highness. I know of no other maiden who is cheered by war stories."

"Please, General, it would make me feel so much better."

"All right, all right. Where would you like to go?"

"Right here in the stables would be fine. I want to visit Dorcas."

Stepping into the stables, she was met by the earthy smell of hay and horses. She loved that smell. Finding the stall of her own wheat-colored pony, she stroked its nose. "Hello, Dorcas. How are you today?"

The pony nickered.

Garth brought two stools and sat on one. "You know, you've already heard all the stories I can tell you. We don't get many battles in Teman."

She sat down. "Tell me one over again."

"Which one would you like? How about the story of the Rhakosian attack, when all their ships smashed to pieces on the rocks? You always liked that one."

"No, tell me about when the Gargons tried to cross the Elan Mountains on burros, and the Temanite army routed them in a day."

"Ah, yes, that was in the days of your grandfather, King Joram. He was a brilliant warrior. Of course, so is your father. He's not yet tried in battle, but I daresay he'll be a mighty force to reckon with if it does happen. But, enough of that. you wanted a story."

An hour later when Garth reached the end of his tale, Mari had a smile on her face.

Garth slapped his knee. "I daresay, those Gargons will

think twice before crossing the Temanite army! Well, my princess, did that cheer you up some?"

"Yes, a little."

"Only a little? What else can I do for you?"

"Would you take me riding?"

"Riding? I'm afraid I don't have time for that right now. But I'm sure any other soldier would be willing to escort you."

"All right. Please have someone tell Mother where I am."

"Of course. Now I must be off."

As the general headed out, Mari watched his red cloak and castle tower emblem disappear through the entry. The thought of going riding with anyone but General Garth wasn't appealing.

She peeked outside the stable door and found Garth nowhere in sight, but the soldiers were still standing there, talking and laughing. *No, this won't do at all.*

"I guess we won't be going out today, Dorcas," she said as she returned to her pony. "I'm sorry."

She scratched the pony's forehead. "Do you know what just happened to me? No, I suppose you don't." Leaning close to the pony's ear, she whispered, "I'm supposed to get married."

The pony's ear flicked at the feel of her breath.

"Oh, not right away, but it's being arranged. And you know what? They're trying to match me with a man I don't even know. Yes, you heard me right. He's a *man.* I'm only a girl. What do you think of that?"

She found a brush and ran it over the pony's neck and side. "I really don't want to be married. I don't want to spend my days making tapestries or hosting social events. You know what I'd rather do? I'd rather hold a dagger than a sewing needle. That's the way to best serve Eloah—by defending our land, not by keeping house."

She sighed. "I'm not really rebellious, am I, Dorcas? Not deep in my heart. I just want to do something great for Eloah. That's not wrong, is it? If I were married, I'd have to see to the needs of my husband and children. Where's the greatness in that?"

She took a comb and began to untangle the pony's cream-colored mane. "The Book of Light says an unmarried person is concerned about the Lord's affairs, but a married person is concerned about the affairs of this world. I don't want to be concerned with the affairs of this world."

Looking right and left and seeing no one, she said in a quieter voice, "Do you know what I really want? I want to travel. To bring Eloah's glory to the nations. But don't tell the elders, Dorcas, they wouldn't approve."

She paused from her work, absentmindedly winding her fingers through the pony's forelock. "You know, if I tell my parents I don't want to marry that captain, they'll only find another candidate. What if I don't give them a decision by the time my birthday comes? What if I say I'm still thinking about it? I can tell them I just want more time to get to know him better. Then they may not push me so hard. What do you think of that, Dorcas?"

She smiled to herself as she resumed her work, picking snarls from the creamy mane. The place became quiet, interrupted only by an occasional snort from a horse or the shuffling of hooves in the straw.

A voice behind her made her jump. "Excuse me."

She gasped and dropped the comb. Seeing a soldier in a red cloak standing behind her, she wondered how long he'd been there and whether he had heard her talking to herself.

"Excuse yourself!" she said, infuriated.

"Forgive me. Frightening you is the last thing I wanted to do. I thought perhaps you had heard me approach."

"No, I did not hear you. I was busy."

"You shouldn't be doing that work. Let me call a stablehand for you."

"I am doing this because I like to do it."

"I'm afraid I've gotten off to a bad start," he said. "Would you forgive me and let me start over?"

Is he apologizing or just being arrogant? She didn't answer him, hoping he'd go away.

He did not. "I was just passing by, and when I saw you here I thought perhaps you'd like to go riding but were lacking an escort. I'd be happy to take you."

"I wouldn't ride with you. I don't even know who you are, soldier."

"Again I plead your forgiveness. My name is Aaron. Aaron Elkanah."

Her mouth dropped open. She turned quickly toward her pony so he wouldn't see the shock on her face. As she picked the pony's comb off the floor and resumed her grooming, she realized he did resemble her brother's friend Stephen, son of Benjamin Elkanah. The resemblance was close enough that he could be mistaken for Stephen's older brother.

"Are you all right, Princess Mari?"

"My name is Mariya," she said firmly. "Only my family may call me Mari. My immediate family."

"I... I'm sorry. Would... would you like to go riding?" he stammered, seeming to have lost his confidence.

She kept her face toward her pony. "I guess I don't really feel much like riding."

"Perhaps another time then." As she gave no response, Aaron quietly headed out.

Mari studied him more closely as he walked away. Sure enough, there was the golden elk on his red cloak—an elk with a crown around its neck, only Aaron's elk also had an arrow in its mouth.

She sighed. He *was* good-looking, like her mother said. Chiseled face, big puppy-dog eyes, hair a light shade of brown, like the color of hazelnuts. She certainly couldn't argue with her parents' choice by virtue of his looks. And he seemed nice enough.

That cinched it. Aaron was someone she could at least tolerate. By telling her parents she would take the time to get to know him and perhaps consider him for matrimony, she determined to put off the dreaded betrothal ceremony as long as she could, even past her fourteenth birthday if at all possible. At least it would keep her parents from finding someone who might be less tolerable.

As Aaron reached the stable entryway, he glanced back and caught her looking at him. He smiled as he stepped out.

Steaming and fully embarrassed, Mari turned away. *I hope he didn't think I was watching him because I* like *him!*

23

The air atop Mount Eben-Ezer was quite chilly for April, Josephus found. The snows were still receding, melting into rivulets that ran everywhere, muddying his boots. He pulled the hood of his cloak over his head to guard against the wind. By the time he could see the Areli home just ahead, he was exhausted and ready to drop.

A little girl nearly three years old came running out of the house, her straight brown hair bouncing as she ran. She giggled and clapped her hands when the pack ponies stopped before her.

Seeing her took all Josephus' weariness away. She was still fascinating to watch, though he didn't know why. *She's just a baby*, he told himself.

He heard his father behind him. "Looks like she still has the same effect on you."

He blushed and turned away.

"That's all right, son, nothing to be embarrassed about."

"Is that Aven, the prophetess?" Josephus asked. He knew she must be, but she was so different from the last time he was there.

Eshana rushed out from the house and took Aven by the hand, panting. "Yes, this is Aven, although some days I would like to think she is not."

"What do you mean?" Josephus asked.

"I mean, for a prophetess, she's just like any other girl. I do have to chase after her a lot, to keep her from danger. Sometimes I think she has no fear."

"What's there to be afraid of up here?" Josephus asked.

"Heights, mostly. I wouldn't want her learning about heights by tumbling down them."

While Aviur helped the king's guards unload the ponies, Josephus followed Eshana and Aven inside. He stayed very close to Aven, trying to look into her eyes at every chance, but she kept turning her head this way and that, not letting him.

"She won't look at me. It's like she's shy."

Eshana paused. "That's unusual for her." When Aviur and the others entered, Eshana said, "Look at this, Aviur. Why would Aven be shy toward the prince? She's so outgoing with everyone else."

"That is strange," Aviur said.

Josephus put his hands on her cheeks to hold her face still and look into her eyes. "I don't see any green star."

Aviur said, "It's very faint, only visible by the light of the sun. And the sun has to hit her eyes just right. Not even a lantern will bring it out."

"How do you know the sun isn't playing tricks on you?" Josephus asked.

Prophet Areli said, "You'll be certain. Once you see the star, you'll be certain."

"But the star can fade, right? Yours faded."

"Yes, mine has faded, but that is only because I am old. As other parts of your body wear out, so do the eyes."

"Will she grow to be as old as you?"

"Who can say? Only Eloah knows the times set for a man. Some are made to grace this earth for but a short time."

"But she's a prophetess. Surely Eloah will let us keep her for a long time."

His father said, "Let you keep her? You sound as if you own her."

"I didn't mean it like that. But... well, she's supposed to be *my* prophetess, isn't she?"

"If you mean she's to stand beside you as you rule, yes. That's the way it's been for over two thousand years—king and prophet together."

Eshana said, "Your Highness, would you mind taking Aven outside to play while we prepare your meal?"

"Sure!" Josephus hoped to get a glimpse of that star while the sun was still out. Reaching for Aven's hand, he said, "Want to go outside?"

Aven stared at him.

"Can she talk yet?" he asked.

Eshana chuckled. "Believe me, she does her share of talking. Just give her some time to get used to you."

"Get used to me? Don't you remember me, Aven? No, I suppose you don't. If I'd seen you any place besides here, I wouldn't know who you were either."

Eshana ushered Aven toward the door. "Go on, Aven, the prince will play with you."

Aven looked at the prince's offered hand once more, then she grasped it and followed him outside.

~~~

When the two children had left, King James noticed a strange look on Aviur's face. "What is that gleam in your eye, Aviur? You look like a man with a secret."

"Indeed," Aviur said. "A wonderful surprise."

"What could be more wonderful than the birth of a prophetess?" James said.

"Oh, it's not quite as wonderful as that, but it is most wonderful nonetheless. The Skotos plant has budded."

"Is that a good thing? What does it mean?"

Aviur said, "I'm not sure myself, but it must be a blessing from Eloah. Nowhere in the Areli family records is there a word about a flower on the Skotos plant. I think the buds will bloom any day now."

He took a seat at the table. "Imagine it! Maybe the flower will produce a stronger medicine. Stronger, even, than the roots. Or maybe the flower will make seeds. Seeds can be powerful sources of medicine."

"That does sound promising," James said. "A flower on

the plant of darkness. I would like to see this wonder for myself."

"Oh, um... I'd rather you didn't," Aviur said.

"What's the matter?"

"Remember that crumbling in the walls, from chipping the plant away? Well, we've had to shore up the walls a lot more than before. There's been too much crumbling."

"Too much? How much?"

"Large parts of the cave walls are falling in."

"By Elán! Are you in danger down there?"

"It's fine, we have it under control. Some carpenters from Tetra will be coming up soon to help us build better supports."

"Maybe you should stay away from the cave until they come."

"I can't slow the work now, not with the plant about to flower. Don't you realize what this could mean for the queen?"

"What?"

"Maybe it'll be a complete cure for her. Maybe even fruit! Can you imagine that?"

"Still, you shouldn't be down there without help."

"As I said, some men are coming soon. Everything will be fine."

"As long as you're careful," James said.

Aviur waved it off. "I'm sure there's no real danger. At any rate, this medicine is well worth it. But I don't want you going down there, Your Majesty. You are much too valuable to the country."

James placed his hand on Aviur's shoulder. "*You* are valuable to the country. And to my family."

~~~

Josephus tried to get Aven to hold still so he could turn her toward the sun and look into her eyes. But she was full of energy and ran squealing up and down the mountainside.

She particularly enjoyed it when he chased her.

Finally he caught her. "Got you! Now come closer."

"Lemme go!"

"Oh no, not until you show me your eyes."

"I don wanna."

"Come on, just one little look."

"No!" She tried to pull away.

"I'll tickle you."

"No!"

"Yes!"

He wrapped his arms around her and dug his fingers into her sides. She screamed and squealed, kicking her legs and struggling to break free.

Still holding her, Josephus plopped to the ground and rolled until he had her pinned underneath him. He looked into her eyes, but his own head cast a shadow on her face. "Drat!"

She smiled and touched his cheek with her soft little hand.

He said, "Mmm, you smell like rosemary. That's my favorite."

"What you name?" Aven asked.

"Josephus."

She squinted her eyes.

"Josephus," he said. "Can you say that?"

"Jose?"

"No, no. Jo-see-fus."

"Jose!" she said. "Jose, Jose, Jose!"

"Stop it, Aven! Say Jo-see-fus, Jo-see-fus."

"Jose!"

"Arrgghh! You're just like my sister. You know, Aven, I don't know if I like you or if you just bother me."

He let her free, but she didn't run away this time. She lay on the grass next to him, watching him. Seeing that she was looking at him, he pretended not to be interested.

After a few moments with no attention, Aven rolled over and bumped into him. He ignored her. She stood up and looked down at him. Still he ignored her. She threw herself onto his belly.

"Oof!" Next he found himself being tickled by tiny little hands all over his belly and sides. "Hey, stop it!" he laughed, more from the silliness of it than anything.

She continued to torment him, her high-pitched giggle echoing across the mountaintops. Finally, worn out, she stopped. They both lay on the grass, panting.

When he had caught his breath, Josephus again looked into her face.

"No look my eyes!" she said, sticking her lip out in a pout. The sight nearly made him laugh. As he leaned over her, his medallion fell out from under his shirt.

She reached for it. "What this?"

"My medallion. Want to see it?"

She smiled and nodded.

He pulled the red ribbon from around his neck and dangled the golden disk over her outstretched hand. "First let me look at your eyes."

Aven's smile faded and her bottom lip stuck out again.

Josephus swung the medallion before her. "Want to see this? Show me your eyes."

Aven's eyes went from the medallion to the prince.

"Here, look," Josephus said. He showed her the image on the front of the disk. "This is a lion, my family symbol."

He turned it over. "This is called the Elaad. It's the symbol of Teman. The points stand for the four points of the world—north, south, east, west. It means that Eloah is everywhere. And see this circle? It means that Eloah is the God of the whole world. When you put the compass inside the circle, it's like an eye—the all-seeing eye of Eloah."

She touched the image and said, "Eye."

"That's right, an eye. Now can I look at your eyes?"

She touched one of her eyes. "You can look my eyes. See?"

"No, not here. Over there." He took her hand and led her to a sunny patch. With his hands on her shoulders, he turned her to face right into the sun. He peered closely, frowned, squinted, and looked harder.

There it was—the green star. A faint outline of many green points within the brown of her iris.

"Boy, you really have to be looking to see it, don't you?"

"You no like my eyes?" Aven stuck her lip out again.

He tried to keep himself from laughing. "Sure, I like your eyes, don't pout. Here, you can have my medallion now." He laid the golden disk in her hand.

Her little hand was barely big enough to hold it. "I have it?"

"No, you can't. It's mine."

"I wan it."

"Sorry, Aven, only a crown prince can wear that. But I'll let you play with it when you come to live in the castle." He took the medallion and drew the red ribbon around his neck, tucking the disk under his shirt. "You'll be coming soon. We'll play together then, all right?"

"All right, Jose!"

When they returned to the house and joined the others for dinner, King James said, "Well, son, what do you think of her?"

"I like her. She's a lot of fun."

"A lot of fun? She's a prophetess."

"She's a little baby girl, Father," Josephus answered as though everyone ought to know it.

"What did you think of the mark?"

"I guess I was expecting more."

Prophet Areli said, "And so you should, for the mark used to be much brighter. It has faded a little with each generation, but not so much as to make it indistinguishable.

"I'd like to see it for myself," the king said.

Josephus chuckled. "First you have to catch her."

24

Early the next morning, when Aviur prepared to go into the cavern to prepare a vial of medicine for the king, Areli invited Josephus to join him in visiting the hermit.

Eshana said, "Do you mind keeping Aven with you? I'm going down with Aviur, and she tends to get underfoot down there."

"You take her in the cavern with you?" Josephus asked.

"Of course, what else can I do? She loves it in there, but she does sometimes get in the way. And she really would enjoy seeing her friend Beale again."

Eshana gave them a basket of bread to take to the hermit, Josephus took Aven's hand, and they were on their way.

While they walked, Josephus said, "Why does this guy choose to live as a hermit, anyway?"

"It's the only life he knows," Areli said. "And Beale is not the only one. There are several hermits who live in the southern mountains. Not together, mind you. They are scattered far and wide, all the way to the western mountains and beyond."

"Seems an awfully strange life."

"Indeed. But what if I were to tell you that my family line began as hermits?"

"What? That's hard to believe."

"It's true. You see, during our Dark Time, when we began destroying our writings, there were those who knew such a thing was wrong. They knew they had to preserve the writings somehow, so they took as many scrolls as they could, what hadn't already been destroyed, and left the cities, moving deep into the mountains, away from civilization. They lived as hermits to protect the scrolls and to keep themselves away from the darkness that had come to Teman."

"Did we ever get those scrolls back?" Josephus asked.

Areli shook his head. "Not many. It's been over two thousand years since the Dark Time. The descendants of those who first took the scrolls to the mountains no longer know about them. They continued to live as hermits with each passing generation. These people are uneducated, you see. Many don't even talk, much less read."

"But your line came back?"

"Yes, my line came back. You see, my line could still read and hadn't forgotten the particular scrolls that they had hid. My ancestors had been studying the scrolls, generation after generation."

"When did they come back?"

"It was during the Second Calandrian War, when it looked like Teman would be destroyed by the Kaion race. A hermit named Areli came out from the mountains with some of the scrolls.

"Now, there wasn't a king on the throne at that time, for Teman had been in darkness for a thousand years, warring with itself, living in wickedness. But this Areli knew the name of the royal line, since that name was in his scrolls—Eliána."

"Hey, that's *my* ancestors' name—Eliána."

"Yes, that was the name of the original line of the kings of this realm, appointed by Eloah himself. When Teman had fallen into its Dark Time, people set out to destroy the royal line of Eliána, so your ancestors changed their name to Eliada and moved away from the royal city. That city and its castle were destroyed."

"Did your ancestor find my ancestor?"

"Yes, he did. He found a man named Eliada and saw that he was a good man, trying to avoid the evil and darkness all around him. Eliada produced the symbol of his royal name—

the medallion you now wear—to prove to Areli that he was the true descendant of the Eliána line."

"I didn't know this medallion was that old."

"Your particular medallion isn't old. Copies have been made over the years."

"So what happened when Areli found Eliada?"

"He gave him the scrolls and showed him how the people used to live in harmony with Eloah, in righteousness and faithfulness, in peace and love. He explained that the Kaion were overpowering the Elyon because the Elyon had turned away from Eloah. Eliada and Areli tried to take that message to the people, tried to get them to turn from their wicked ways. They had help from Eliada's younger brother, a man named Elkanah."

"Like Stephen Elkanah?"

"Yes, exactly. That is how the Elkanah line is related to your line."

"What happened next? Did the people turn back to Eloah?"

"Not all of them, but a large number did. They gathered together to call out to Eloah to rescue them from the Kaion."

"Oh!" Josephus exclaimed, remembering his lessons. "That's when the Great Wave of Elán came and destroyed all the Kaion who had set foot on our land!"

"Yes, you are correct. The wave also destroyed many of the Elyon, but it did not destroy those who had joined with Eliada and Areli for they had gathered on the western mountains to pray. The Great Wave did not reach that far, but it did cover a third of our land.

"After the Kaion had been destroyed, Eloah placed Eliada on his rightful throne and gave him the Three Mandates, bidding all the people to bind themselves to those mandates so such a disaster would not befall them again.

"And to reward the Areli who had brought the scrolls, Eloah gave him the gift of prophecy and ordained that an Areli should always rule alongside an Eliada—king and prophet together."

Josephus asked, "When Areli brought the scrolls back, that wasn't all of them, was it?"

"No, not nearly. It was only the few that my family had saved. Those that were taken by other families are still lost, I'm afraid."

"Hasn't anyone ever gone looking for them?"

Areli laughed. "What a daunting task that would be! These mountains stretch for a hundred miles or more. Where would you even start? Even with a thousand armies, I doubt you could find them. They were kept hidden, after all. And now it's been so long, I can't imagine that any have survived. Parchments do not keep well after a couple thousand years."

"What about the ones Areli brought back? Do we still have those?"

"We do. They are kept in a special archive, deep inside Castle Mountain."

"Why inside the mountain?"

"That is the best place to preserve parchment. Exposure to light or air or changing temperatures would ruin them. So they remain safe until the day they are needed again."

Aven let out a squeal, stopping their conversation. She released Josephus' hand and darted toward the hermit's cave, just ahead.

Josephus said, "She seems excited to go there."

"Her mother tells me they have developed quite a friendship."

Beale came out from the cave wearing a black bear skin draped over his shoulders. He gave a nod toward Josephus.

"Hey, it's like he remembers me."

"I'm sure he does," Areli said.

As Aven ran up to him, the hermit broke into a big smile. "Bethen!"

"Beth-Aven," Josephus said.

The hermit nodded. "Bethen."

Josephus followed the hermit into his cave and sat on the floor. He watched curiously as the hermit and little Aven interacted. The hermit even said a few words.

"Here, Bethen, set table." He handed Aven a bowl of figs.

"Look at that," Josephus said. "He's talking."

"Eshana told me that Aven is teaching him," Areli said.

Aven scrunched her nose as she set the figs on the table next to the basket of bread.

Josephus said, "Why would he want to learn now, after all these years?"

"Perhaps it's for Aven's sake, so he can communicate with her."

"He really likes her, huh?"

"It seems she likes him as well."

Josephus took a fig. "Hey, these are fresh. How can he get fresh figs in the spring?"

Areli said, "Aviur tells me that some of the fig plants in the southern valleys produce a small crop in the spring. Enjoy it while you can. Even a king doesn't often get fresh figs on his table."

Josephus bit off a piece. "Mmm, so sweet."

Areli said, "Have you ever heard the saying, 'like looking for flowers on a fig tree'?"

"Yup," he answered, mouth full. "It's because there aren't any flowers on a fig tree, right?"

"Wrong."

Josephus slipped the last bit into his mouth. "Wrong? What do you mean?"

"The flowers on a fig tree are hidden." Areli cut a fig open. "See, the flowers are on the inside."

"Wow, that's neat." Seeing that Aven was watching them intently, Josephus held the cut fruit out to her. "Look at that, Aven. Flowers on the inside."

A sour look came across her face.

"Here, Aven, want a fig?" he asked.

"No!" she said emphatically.

"You can have it, it's all right. Here."

"No!"

"What's the matter? These are very good."

"I don like it."

"You don't like figs? I thought everyone liked figs, especially fresh ones. Try it."

"No! I don like it!"

"All right, all right, you don't like figs."

Too soon it was time to bid the hermit good-bye. They left the basket of bread there, and Beale gave them the bowl of figs to take to Aven's family.

That evening at the dinner table, Josephus took a fig from the bowl and tried again. "Here, Aven, want a fig?"

"No, no, no!" she said.

He chuckled at the angry look in her eyes. "Come on, just one."

"No!"

"Stop it, son," his father said.

"But look at this. Who doesn't like figs?" Josephus again held the fruit out to her and again she turned her nose at it.

"Don't torment her so. That behavior does not become a prince."

Josephus flushed, but Eshana came to his rescue. "It is odd, but she never did like them. I don't understand why."

Prophet Areli said, "There's always something different about everyone, and there's always a reason."

"Even not liking figs? Seems like a small thing," Josephus said.

"One may never know the reason," Areli said.

Josephus said, "I'm sorry, Aven, I won't tease you anymore."

Aven jumped down from the table and bounded toward the door. "Come play wi' me, Jose!"

He chased after her. "Don't call me Jose!"

As the carriage finally rolled northward toward home, Josephus listened to his father and the old prophet lay plans for the prophetess' arrival at the castle.

James said, "Aviur said he would bring her to the palace on the summer solstice."

"That will be about eight weeks from now," Areli said.

"Yes. I believe the elders are already preparing her quarters."

"She must receive the proper training," Areli said.

"Of course. And she will be raised with the prince. The two will grow up together, study together, play together, and become the best of friends."

Josephus said, "And then I'm going to marry her!"

King and prophet fell silent.

"You what?" James asked at last.

"I'm going to marry the prophetess."

"Why do you say that, son?"

"I don't know. I guess it's because when I look at her, I feel real good inside. Happy, you know? Like everything's going to be all right."

James and Areli smiled.

~~~

Standing on a balcony of a tall turret, Princess Mariya felt terrible inside. *Marriage.* The thought had haunted her since the day her mother had brought it up—the very day she had met Aaron Elkanah. It's not that she didn't like him. He was very nice. Probably make a great husband.

But it's not what I want. Her highest goal in life was to bring the light of Eloah to those less fortunate, to those in the neighboring realms—Gargon, Rygia, Rhakos, and Xulon.

How will they ever learn to serve Eloah if we stay locked up here behind our mountains?

She knew why her people were so reclusive. Occasionally Temanites would venture out, never to be heard from again. Rygia especially was known for swallowing Temanites. For some reason unknown to her, Rygians had a particular hatred of her people.

Maybe things would be different if we weren't so secretive, she thought.

A gull called to her. She looked up and watched it float effortlessly on the breeze. Flying away. Sailing away. Calling her to join it. Venture out. See other lands.

The waves crashed on the rocks below. As they pulled back, she imagined being on a ship and pulling away from these shores.

Is it wrong of me? she wondered. Her people were tied to this land. That was one of the Three Mandates—to keep this land as a witness to Eloah. *But a witness to whom? Shouldn't we invite others to share the glory of this land with us? Eloah, forgive me if I'm wrong, but I believe you put this desire within me.*

The door opened behind her, giving her a start. Captain Aaron Elkanah stepped out bearing a handsome smile and a cheery greeting. "Good morning, Princess."

She resumed her vigil over the sea. "Good morning."

"Do you mind if I join you?"

"I suppose not."

He stood beside her at the parapet, leaning over it, resting his arms on the brick wall. She said nothing, and neither did he for a long time.

"I've been talking with your mother," he said at last.

"You have?" She tried not to show concern in her voice.

"Yes. She said you'd consider me as a husband."

Mari gulped back her apprehension at having misled her mother only to keep her parents from finding someone else and having to go through this all over again.

"She said you just wanted some time to get to know me better."

Silence followed.

Aaron said, "So I thought perhaps we could do something together. Get to know each other."

"What... what did you have in mind?"

"Nothing specific, I wanted you to choose. What would you like to do?"

Mari took a deep breath and let it out slowly. "I want to travel."

"Travel? You mean you want to go riding?"

"Not just riding… *travel*. I want to see the world."

"The world? Why would you want to see that? It's a wicked place."

"Surely good people live in places other than Teman."

"Perhaps, but they'd be few. And they wouldn't believe in Eloah."

"Why is that?"

Aaron had no response.

Mari said, "Because no one's told them of Eloah, that's why."

Aaron drummed his fingers on the parapet. "You know, the city of Teruma, where I come from, is one of the most beautiful places in Teman. It sits at the junction of the three great rivers, right where they join to become the River Tria. Perhaps you'd like to travel there someday. I think that once we're betrothed, your parents wouldn't object to our taking a trip there. You could meet my parents."

Mari's stomach tied into a knot. "Do those lands look much different from these?"

"Oh, yes. The River Tria is so wide in that spot, they had to build the biggest bridge in all of Teman. It's quite a marvel."

"I've seen bridges before. Want to know what a marvel is? I've read that the people of Rhakos can make a cloth that feels like water on your skin. That's a marvel. And they can make a curved glass that will let you see things that are miles away as if they are close up. That's a marvel."

"Teman's full of its own marvels," Aaron said.

"But I know about all of those. I want to know more."

"The library is full of books about other lands."

"The library? I don't want to *read* about other lands. I want to *see* them. How much do we really know about them, anyway? Wouldn't our library be better served if someone were to go to those places and write about them?"

"I don't think you should entertain such thoughts, Princess. It's ordained for the Eliada family to rule from the city of Temana, not travel to other lands."

"Would we not make better rulers if we knew more about other lands?"

Leaning on the parapet, he looked out over the sea. "The elders would disapprove of the things you're saying."

"Disapprove?" Mari chuckled. "They would be aghast!"

"You ought to keep your fantasies in check, Highness. You don't want to earn their ire."

Mari stared at Aaron, now realizing beyond a doubt that he was not for her. Yes, he was nice and even handsome, but if he didn't share her dreams, she would be miserable.

She also realized that what she really wanted more than anything, more even than travel, was a man who wasn't afraid to stand against the elders from time to time.

"I do not fear the ire of the elders," she said. "The royal family of Eliada is not beholden to them."

Aaron shook his head. "You're still very young. Perhaps when you grow up you'll adopt a more mature outlook on things. Good day, Your Highness."

As Mari watched him disappear into the turret, she thought, *This is no good, I can't keep up this charade.* The whole betrothal issue kept her heart in gloom. She had to face the truth and tell her parents.

25

A few days after the king and his party left the mountain, the hermit Beale gathered up his hunting bow and arrows to follow a herd of elk that had passed by. He descended the slope and headed toward the woods.

He stopped. Something was wrong. He stood still for the longest time, trying to understand what the earth was saying to him.

Then he felt it—a tremor in the ground. The elk? The tremor came again, this time more pronounced. The mountain!

He dropped his bow and ran back to his cave, but as he neared it, the mountain shook violently. A chunk of rock split off the upper side of the cave and crashed down, blocking the entrance.

"Bethen!" He ran along the path leading to Aven's house.

The mountain shook again. He stumbled and slipped downward. Rocks tumbled around him. He scrambled back up and ran.

The Areli's house was in ruins, the front wooden wall smashed to bits, rubble blocking it.

"Bethen!"

Hearing a muffled voice, he headed toward the sound, toward the cavern. The entrance was impassible, for a boulder had fallen over the opening, blocking most of it.

A voice called from inside. "Help us! By Elán, help us!"

"Bethen!" the hermit called.

"Thank heaven, someone's out there."

Beale heard stones showering the inside of the cavern. He heard a child crying.

Voices said, "Get Aven out! Hurry!"

"Here, you take her. I'll help you up."

"Bethen!" Beale called.

A little hand appeared through the narrow opening. He grasped it tightly. The ground shook again. The child cried more loudly.

"Bethen, come, Bethen!" He took both her hands in both of his and pulled.

The ground gave a tremendous lurch. Rocks and gravel tumbled down the mountainside. The whole earth seemed to sway.

"No! Eloah! No!" the voices called.

Then all was silent.

~~~

Prince Josephus stood on the stone courtyard of the castle, looking out toward the city. A rider approached, horse's hooves tearing up the ground. He never slowed, not even for wagons, plowing right past them, scattering people, geese, and even soldiers. Reaching the foot of Castle Mountain, he flew from his horse and ran up the switchback trail.

Josephus rushed to the throne room, passing Areli on the way. Bursting in, he arrived in time to see the courier drop to one knee before the king.

King James rose. "What's the meaning of this, courier? Your news must be either urgent or grave for you to behave so."

The courier panted heavily, straining for breath. "It's both, my king. I've ridden night and day to... to... "

James called to a servant, "Bring refreshment! This man is overcome with exhaustion." The servant ran out.

Prophet Areli entered. "What news is this?"

The king said, "I have yet to hear the message myself.

Our courier is overcome with fatigue."

Josephus watched the courier shake his head. "Nay, Sire, it is not fatigue that overcomes me, but grief."

"Grief? Then tell us quickly."

"Great disturbances have shaken the holy mountain, Mount Eben-Ezer. When the carpenters arrived at the Areli home, they found..." He gasped for breath.

Josephus felt panic grip him. He drew closer to hear better.

"Found what, man?" the king said.

"It is so terrible I cannot say."

The king grasped the shoulders of the messenger and lifted him to his feet. "Speak! What of the Areli family?"

"They're gone, Sire."

"Gone? What do you mean, gone?"

"Their home was in ruins and the entrance to the cave is blocked. No sign of life was found."

Josephus' mind went numb.

The courier said, "Miners from Tetra are working to remove the rubble, but from the looks of it—"

King Eliada shouted to a servant, "You! Summon General Garth! Send him to the holy mountain without delay! Tell him to take a garrison of soldiers and miners and dig through the ruins. Make haste!"

"What of Aven?" Josephus asked in a small voice.

When the messenger turned to look at him, he did not need to say anything. Josephus could understand merely by the look on his face.

He shivered. His stomach lurched. He felt his father's hands on his shoulders, but he took no comfort from the touch.

The king asked, "How many bodies have been found?"

"Not a one," the messenger said.

"Then we may yet hope."

When Areli spoke, his voice sounded much older than usual, Josephus thought. "No, James. If they were still alive, they would have contacted someone."

"But they could be alive, trapped inside that infernal cavern!"

Areli asked the courier, "When did this happen?"

"The ruins were found four days ago."

"No one could survive that long," the prophet said.

"Do not give up so easily, Areli!" the king shouted. "Perhaps they've already been found and another messenger is on his way here."

But the eyes of the messenger told Josephus what he had seen.

Areli's voice seeped in grief. "They are gone, James. I can feel it, here." He laid his hand over his heart.

King Eliada stared at Areli for a long time before saying, "I must tell Bernice."

~~~

When King Eliada told his wife, she took the news hard. The blood drained from her face. Her knees buckled. As she fell, he caught her and helped her to her bed. She lay there silently, staring at the canopy.

The king's gaze fell to an unopened vial on the table. He handed it to her. "You've not taken this since I returned. It will keep only another week."

"I thought there might be a day when I had greater need of it."

"Like now?"

When she turned her eyes to him, he could see they were full of tears. She said, "What was the price of that medicine, James? The lives of the Areli family? The total loss of the Areli line?"

"Total loss? By Elán!" He hadn't yet thought of that. The loss of the line of prophets. No more prophets to rule beside the king. "Oh, great Eloah. Josephus!"

The thought of his son being the first Eliada to rule without a prophet brought James to his knees at his wife's bedside.

~~~

Mari knocked gently on the door to her parents' bedchamber. At her father's call she quietly pushed the door open and entered. Her mother lay sleeping on the canopied bed. Her father knelt beside her, his head bare. The crown sat on a bedside table. She rarely saw him without that crown. He looked rather forlorn.

"What's going on?" she asked. "What's the matter with Mother?"

He spoke very softly. "The news upset her so much, it seems to have worsened her condition."

"What news?"

"You've not heard?"

She shook her head.

"The holy mountain has swallowed the Areli family. They're gone." His voice choked at his last words.

Mari gasped, hands over her mouth. "Not the prophetess!"

Her father nodded grimly.

Mari felt her body grow heavy. She managed to make her way to the bed and knelt opposite her father. Suddenly her own demands seemed petty and selfish.

After a long time of silence, he asked, "What is it you wanted?"

She looked into his eyes, usually so filled with mirth. But now those eyes seemed dark, as if an emptiness had settled on his heart.

"What did you want, Mari?" he asked again.

"I'm sorry, Father. I came to complain about my betrothal, but now..." She swallowed hard. "Now it seems so petty. I feel I must put my destiny in the hands of Eloah and accept it with faith. Whatever you decide for me, I will trust in you and in Eloah."

He managed a smile and reached his hand out. "Come here."

She moved to his side of the bed and knelt beside him.

He ran a finger through her hair. "Your hair is just like your mother's, thick and wavy. I love that about her."

She nodded.

"You're so much like she was at your age. So full of adventure and faith. So independent."

He squeezed her hand. "I would never put you through a betrothal that doesn't make you happy. We certainly don't need any more unhappiness in this castle, not after this. If you're not ready yet, we can wait. We can wait as long as you want. I'm sure Aaron would understand, given the tragedy that's befallen us."

The heaviness in her heart lifted, just a little. "Thank you, Father."

"Just remember this... You can always trust your fate to Eloah, even in the darkest moments. He knows best. He is in control."

She looked at her sleeping mother. "Even in this?"

"Even in this."

~~~

That night Prince Josephus tossed and turned in his bed. In his dream he stood on a mountainside, but the mountain trembled beneath his feet.

"Aven!" He ran around the side of the mountain amid rolling, bouncing stones. "Aven!"

A tiny hand reached toward him. He grabbed it. "I got you!"

The mountain lurched beneath him. The little hand slipped from his grasp.

"Aven!"

He bolted upright in bed, panting. For a moment, he thought it was just a dream. Then he remembered that it was true. It was all true. The prophetess Areli Beth-Aven really was gone.

He looked at his empty hands, seeing several teardrops fall onto them.

Teman had lost the line of Areli—the line that was to rule side by side with an Eliada. He would be the first king of Teman without a prophet at his side. But for him it was worse than that, much worse. He had lost the little girl that he loved.

A sharp pain stabbed at his chest, as though a great hole ripped through his spirit. Then came the feelings of lostness, loneliness, and darkness—all the fears that had come with Areli's vision.

He remembered words his father had said. "There are some things we may never know, but one thing we can always count on. Eloah knows best, and he keeps everything in his care."

Eloah, Josephus prayed, *I need you. I need you more than ever.*

~~~

King Eliada refused to hold a memorial service for the Areli family until he received definite word from General Garth. That word did not come for another month, when Garth returned with his men.

The news he brought was grave. His men had managed to clear both the Areli house and the hermit's house, but nothing was found in either place. At the site of the cavern, however, the mountain's instability prevented much work. After having dug far enough to find some human remains, another cave-in buried their previous, painstaking efforts.

The king commended Garth on his decision not to risk the lives of his men. What the general did find was considered enough evidence to confirm the deaths of the Areli family members.

The very next thing King Eliada did was ban anyone from ever setting foot on the accursed Mount Eben-Ezer.

After a solemn and heart-rending memorial service, the king escorted the elder Areli through the castle corridors. It seemed as though the prophet had grown years older in just

206 | *The Alliance, Book 3*

a few weeks. His every step was an effort, each breath a struggle.

"My son," the king said. "Josephus. He'll be the first king to rule without a prophet. What darkness is this, Areli? Why would Eloah let this happen?"

"His ways are beyond understanding."

"But to leave us without a prophet? Without the Areli line? How could that happen in Teman? Do we not serve Eloah faithfully? Why has he done this?"

"Your doubts are resurfacing, James."

"How can I not have doubts in the face of this? This is the worst disaster to befall this land in two thousand years! It was Eloah who ordained that this realm be ruled through both lines. A king cannot govern without the wisdom of the prophets. Why would Eloah not preserve the Areli line? Why would he leave us alone?"

"He has not left you, James. He wishes to teach you something."

"To teach *me* something? Do you mean this happened because of *me*?"

"Not just you. All the people of Teman."

"I cannot believe that. What could he possibly want to teach us that takes this kind of tragedy?"

"One never knows what the lesson is until they reach the end of it."

"The end of it? The light of Areli is all but snuffed out. How can there be more of an end than that?" The king's voice became softer, quieter, more foreboding. "We are on the eve of a great darkness, and you, Areli Beth-Birei, are the last prophet."

Areli's eyes pierced the king's. "Then as the last prophet, let my words to you be these. You are right, James. We *are* on the eve of a great darkness. The light is snuffed out, but only because it has been kept hidden under a bushel too long. From now on, if it is light you seek, you must venture beyond."

Those words caused the king to stop in his tracks.

Areli continued on his way to his chamber where he spent the next weeks in mournful seclusion.

A few weeks after the memorial service for the Areli family, Queen Bernice's heart simply gave out. She was buried on a hillside surrounded by maple trees, alongside others of the Eliada line.

3
ROLLAND

26

Late one afternoon in September, nearly six years after the death of Justus Corden's wife, General Rolland Longsword stepped into the armory of the Rygian castle. Long-handled torches hung in sconces on the stone walls. All manner of battle axes stood in barrels in the corners. Iron and wooden swords filled more barrels. Bows and quivers full of arrows hung on the walls.

A door on one side of the room led to a storage room with shelves built into recessed walls—shelves filled with helmets, breastplates, and other pieces of armor. A store room at the other side of the armory held shields—mostly wooden ones, but some were iron-plated.

Two squires busied themselves at a long table, inspecting chainmail tunics for damage. Rolland pulled a bench out from the only other table in the room and sat down. Slipping his family sword from its sheath, he ran a finger up and down the finely crafted blade, eyeing the intricate carvings.

For years he'd studied this sword, from the little seed at the tip of the blade to the vine of ivy that curled all the way up, intertwined about itself, until it came to full bloom just under the hilt, a flower with three petals.

Along the crossguard stretched the wings of an eagle— white wings edged in gold. Gems in the crosspiece and pommel were bordered by strange markings resembling letters. But whether the markings meant anything or if they were just intricate filigree, he had no idea.

He found a rag and buffed the blade until it gleamed.

Holding the sword up to the light from a window, gazing down the length of it from tip to hilt, he gave a start.

"What in the world...?"

He brought the point closer to his eyes, keeping the blade horizontal. At this vantage point, he could see images hidden among the vines—images that looked very similar to the letters around the gems.

"Hmm," he muttered. Although the letters were similar in style, they were clearly different from those around the gems. If they truly were letters, and possibly even words, the words were different in each place.

"But what does it say? What does it mean?" he wondered aloud.

"What's that?" Justus Corden's voice at the doorway did little to distract Rolland.

"Nothing." Rolland's eyes didn't leave his sword as he studied how the markings on the blade were only visible when the blade was held horizontally at eye level.

Soon he began to hear the scraping of stone against metal. Justus sat across from him at the table, sharpening his sword. The rasping sound seemed sharper than usual, the *thwisk, thwisk* of the stone almost projecting anger. Looking up, Rolland could see fury in Justus' movements.

When Justus had returned to Archella four years earlier, he'd been reinstated as captain of the King's Guard. He wore the cloak of the King's Guard—blue with a silver eagle, its wings outstretched. He executed his duties in exemplary fashion, his skills at fighting and at leading better than any other soldier Rolland knew.

Yet he was a somber figure, speaking little and smiling less. He wasn't the same man that Rolland had known before. Several times Rolland had tried to get him to talk about the things that pained him—his wife's death, his two years' absence. But Justus usually responded by telling Rolland to mind his own blasted business.

Rolland looked to his sword and back at Justus. While Justus was still his squire, Rolland had considered bequeathing the sword to him. After all, he had no heirs of his own. In fact, he hadn't even taken another squire after Justus for he'd never found another young man of the same caliber.

But after Corden's wife died and Justus had become so bitter, Rolland thought perhaps the sword shouldn't go to him. There was something too special about this sword to put it in the hands of just anyone. It had to be the right sort of person, with the right heart.

"What're you staring at?" Justus asked.

Rolland laid the sword on the table. "You, Corden. I'm staring at you. Why are you still around? I sent you home hours ago."

"I have things to do." Justus made another swipe along his blade.

"You should leave that kind of work to the squires."

"When it comes to my sword, I like to take care of it myself."

"That's all well and good, but you can do it at home," Rolland said.

"I can do it here too."

"Don't you have a daughter at home? How old is she now?"

The whetstone stopped mid-stroke as Justus paused to say, "Six next month."

"Wouldn't she like her papa home?"

Justus slammed the stone on the table. "Why are you so concerned about my daughter?"

"Hey, I was just asking."

After a short stare-down, Justus snatched the stone and returned to his work.

Rolland asked, "So who takes care of her?"

"My housekeeper, Bett."

Again silence fell upon the two, the only sound the scraping of stone on metal.

"I never see her around," Rolland said. "You should bring her out to the market now and then."

"Who, Bett?" Justus snapped.

Rolland chuckled. "No, your daughter." But the look on Justus' face caused his smile to fade.

With a scrap of linen, Justus rubbed the blade up and down. "What's the matter with you, anyway?"

"Me? I was wondering the same about you."

"Wondering? Sticking your nose in where it doesn't belong is what I call it."

"I'm concerned about you, Corden."

Justus held his sword up and studied it under the light from the window. "Oh, yeah? Why is that?"

"You keep to yourself too much. You don't spend much time at home. It seems all you like to do is fight. And when you're at battle..."

Justus narrowed his eyes. "What about it?"

"You become a madman."

"That's just what the other soldiers say."

"They say it because it's true. I've seen you. You seem to lose all your senses."

Justus placed the tip of his sword into its scabbard and slammed the weapon into place. "And what if I do? I win, don't I?"

"Sure you win, so far. But one of these days you'll get yourself killed with your foolhardy heroics. I don't wish to see that happen." Rolland's eyes locked with Justus'. "You have really changed."

"*I've* changed? What about you? Whatever happened to the big, bellowing general we used to hear all over the castle? You've gotten soft, Rolland."

"Well, I guess that comes with age. I am fifty-eight, after all."

"That's no excuse."

Rolland said, "Maybe I haven't changed so much. Maybe you just think I'm soft because you've become so hard. Do you ever think about that? What kind of a man are you at home? What does your daughter see?"

"Do you have anything important to say, or do you just want to bother me about my personal life?"

"Now that you mention it, there is something I've been wanting to tell you." Hesitating, Rolland almost thought better of what he was about to say, but he dove in headfirst. "I think it's time you let Katrina rest."

"How dare you!" Justus pointed to a small leather pouch hanging from Rolland's belt. "You still carry around a charm to remind you of someone you lost eighteen years ago!"

"At least I don't make everyone around me suffer for it." The silence that followed told Rolland that Justus accepted his words, though he didn't say so.

Rolland rose. "Before I go, the king wanted me to give you a message."

"What is it?"

"He's leaving on a visit to Baron Vance's tomorrow."

"Tomorrow? That's short notice."

"He wants to make this journey quickly, before winter sets in. Queen Estrella's going as well."

"I'll be ready."

Rolland ran a hand through his gray hair. "Well, that's the thing. They'd rather you stayed here."

"Why? I'm captain of the King's Guard, I go where the king goes."

"Your loyalty to King Arkelaus is unsurpassed, I know. But you're responsible for the entire royal family, not just him. Since Prince Medan is staying here, the king would like you to keep watch over him. I'll be accompanying the king, so there's really no need for you to be there."

"Well, if you're going, I suppose that'll do."

"You're also in charge of the king's army while I'm gone. If anything happens, it's up to you to defend the realm."

"Up to me? You're only going to Vance's. If anything happens, I'll send for you."

Rolland pursed his lips. "You may not be able to reach me in time. I'm sure you can handle it fine without me."

Justus nodded. "I'll take care of everything."

Rolland put a hand on Justus' shoulder. "I know you will. That's why I asked you."

27

Leaving the armory, Rolland headed up to the king's antechamber where he found the king on a chair at a table and Chamberlain Demas standing next to the king. Several small pieces of paper lay on the table before the king.

King Arkelaus looked up when Rolland stepped in. "Ah, General Rolland, have you done what I asked?"

"Yes, Your Majesty, Captain Corden will take care of everything while we're gone. And I did manage to find some good men to accompany us."

"Excellent. Close the door, Rolland, I'd like us to talk in private."

When Rolland complied, the king motioned for him to come closer. "I've perused these documents the chamberlain gave me, and I—"

He stopped abruptly, peering at the top of Demas' head. "I say, Demas, you must apply your lotions to your hair once again. The brown is beginning to show."

Demas' wide blue eyes flit from the king to Rolland. "I, uh... I..."

"Don't you worry, Demas. Rolland knows of your Temanite heritage. Aside from me, he's the only one."

Demas swallowed hard, a worried look on his face.

"You can trust Rolland, Demas," the king said. "I trust him with all my confidences."

"Yes, Sire," Demas said with a bit of a tremble in his voice.

The king waved toward the papers on the table. "Now, as to these documents. Where did you say you got them?"

"I, um..." Demas cleared his throat, again glancing to Rolland.

Rolland said, "I've already read them, Chamberlain, and I know they came from Teman, originally. But how did they come into your care?"

When Demas didn't answer right away, King Arkelaus said, "Have no fear, Demas. No one in Rygia will know that these came from you."

"Forgive me, Your Majesty, I just... well, most Rygians would just as soon kill me as see me with anything belonging to Teman." He looked straight at Rolland when he said it.

Arkelaus leaned back in his chair. "Why is that, do you suppose?"

"Why is what, Your Majesty?" Demas asked.

"Why do men of Rygia disdain Teman so?"

"Why shouldn't we?" Demas said. "Most have never seen a Temanite. We imagine what they must look like, we make up stories about them. I've heard some rather wild tales, myself."

"What wild tales? What have you heard?"

"That the Temanites are a race of powerful spirit beings who call upon an unseen god to fight their battles. Ships mysteriously vanish in their waters. Entire armies have been lost to the mountains that open up and swallow men whole. Even the foothills on Rygia's side of the mountains are said to be haunted."

"Hmm." Arkelaus stroked his golden beard. "If no one's ever seen a Temanite, where did these wild tales come from?"

"They've been told in taverns for generations," Demas said. "Where and how they started, who can say?"

Again King Arkelaus peered at Demas' hair. Rolland followed his gaze and noticed the brown roots amid the unnaturally golden locks.

The king said, "Your own mother was a Temanite, Demas. Surely *you* don't believe them to be spirit beings."

"It was my *grandmother*, Sire. She died before I was

born, so I never knew her. But no, I don't believe them to be spirit beings."

"Whatever happened to your grandmother?"

"Poisoned. Her only son—my father—was already grown, and he had blonde hair and blue eyes, so he felt he was safe. It wasn't until his wife gave birth to me that his fears resurfaced."

"Your brown hair," the king said.

Demas nodded. "One day he never came home. My mother took my brother and me into hiding after that. Eventually she found a way to lighten my hair with herbs and juices. When I reached adulthood, I knew that if I ever had children, my true heritage could be discovered. I mean, what if a child of mine was born with brown eyes? It's one thing to color your hair, but there's no hiding the eyes. So I became a eunuch."

King Arkelaus nodded. "I understand. It's no wonder the Temanites haven't come out to meet us. When they do, things like this happen—poisoning, hiding, fear. We Rygians have been abusive to them, even murderous. But why? Why do our people hate them so?"

"I know not, Sire," Demas said.

Arkelaus took the papers from the table and sorted them all together. "This was all you had?"

"Yes, Your Majesty."

"Where did you get them?"

"They were part of a book that my grandmother had brought from Teman. There's nothing else left of the book. My father destroyed it, afraid someone might find it and kill him for having it."

"Why didn't he destroy these pages?"

"They were loose and had fallen out. I found them and hid them under my bed. He never knew I had them."

Arkelaus sighed. "This small bit of text is like a morsel that whets the appetite, don't you agree, Rolland?"

"Indeed, Your Majesty," Rolland said.

The king said, "I wish to learn more, Demas. I wish I

could meet a Temanite. Other than you, I mean. Didn't you say you had a brother?"

"Yes, Sire."

"Does he look like you?"

"If you mean does he have brown hair, no. He looks fully Rygian."

"Does he have any children?"

"He, uh… He remained childless for many years. Now he is too old to bear children."

Rolland noticed a distinct hesitation in Demas' words but said nothing about it.

"Hmm. That is too bad," the king said.

"What do you mean?"

"I see a quality in you that is not found in men of Rygia. I've come to the conclusion that you, Demas, are different because of your Temanite heritage. These writings you gave me confirm it. We in Rygia live right next door to them, and what kind of people are we? Decadent, argumentative, quick to fight even among ourselves."

"Oh, but Sire, you are not that kind of person. Nor General Rolland."

"Oh, a few are noble, like Rolland here. But men like him are very hard to find. I thought I had found another noble soul in Captain Corden, but since the death of his wife, I'm not so certain anymore."

The king fell silent for a time. As he appeared to be in deep thought, Rolland and Demas waited.

Finally the king said, "I'm concerned, Demas. I'm concerned for the realm. It seems to grow worse every year."

Demas said, "Forgive me, Your Majesty, but you've been saying that ever since you returned from Darkhaven, when you found Captain Corden."

"Yes, Darkhaven. That was the first time I had ever been there, and hopefully the last. Yet I fear the rest of the realm may one day become as Darkhaven is. We certainly seem headed that way. I've tried to change things by enacting new laws, but I've made little headway."

He shook his head ruefully. "The lords and officials of our land find ways around my laws. They govern only to sate their own lusts. Isn't that true, Rolland?"

"Yes, Sire, that's been my observance as well."

Demas said, "Such a dark picture you paint."

"Dark, yes. Dark. That's exactly it." Arkelaus grew pensive. "Rolland, do you remember my father?"

"Yes, Sire, I was a young man during his reign."

"In my father's day, our ships would sail around the continent, trading with Xulon and Rhakos, even with Gargon on occasion."

"Those were glorious days," Rolland said.

"But they didn't last long. One day, one of our ships never returned. My father went searching for it himself, on the kingship Arkelia."

"Did he find it?"

"No, he never did. But I remember the day he returned from his journey. He was a changed man. He became much more reclusive and forbade the rest of our ships from sailing beyond our own waters."

Rolland nodded. "I remember that, the day the edict was announced. It seemed an odd thing. I think most people were flabbergasted. Your father never gave an explanation."

King Arkelaus said, "Not publicly. But privately, to me, he did."

"What did he say?" Rolland asked.

"He told me there were dark powers on the sea. Great powers, vastly beyond our own. He said we were fortunate they took no notice of us. That we would be best off if we did not get in their way."

Rolland said, "The fleet captain was quite upset over the moratorium."

"Yes, he certainly was. Men like him are born to sail. This current generation of sailors has seen little of the seas beyond Rygia, fortunately. They do not miss what they do not know."

The king fell silent, stroking his beard, thinking. "Ever

since my father told me about these dark powers on the seas, I have had dreams."

"What kind of dreams?" Demas asked.

"Disturbing dreams. Dreams I do not care to remember. I dream about a darkness approaching our land. I see a door, and behind that door is the darkest night you have ever seen. No moonlight, not even a star, just a thick and dreadful darkness. Only that door can keep the darkness out. But then a man comes and opens the door. The darkness spills onto the land and swallows everything it touches. And then... then I see who it was that opened the door." He shivered, as though a shadow had passed over him.

Demas asked in a whisper, "Who was it, Sire?"

"It... it was *Rygia*."

"Rygia? What do you mean?"

"It is we ourselves who let the darkness in. We could keep it out but instead we chose to let it in. It's as if my people welcome the darkness." He pulled his cloak more tightly around his shoulders. "As I dreamed this dream, I began to understand what the darkness wanted."

"What did it want?"

"The darkness seeks the hearts of men. It devours them... feeds on them... yet it is never satisfied."

"But it was just a dream, Sire."

"No! No dream has ever left me feeling this way. It was too real, too close, too... consuming. And I've had this dream over and over again. Now I know I must seek a solution or there will be no hope."

"But what cure is there for darkness?"

"Light, Demas! Light!" The king shoved the parchments at Demas' chest. "And now I know where to find it."

As Demas clutched clumsily at the parchments, a few fluttered to the floor. "Where, Your Majesty?"

"In Teman, of course! I've already begun to discuss this with Rolland. I plan to visit our southerly neighbors immediately."

"*You*, Sire?" Demas asked.

"Yes, me. And you are going to help me."

"*Me*, Sire?"

"Rolland has already gathered a small number of soldiers for me—a party of men whose hearts will not fail them for fear of entering Teman. Men whom I can trust to keep a confidence. Which, I daresay, was a difficult thing, was it not, General?"

"Indeed," Rolland said. "I did manage to find three—Geoffrey Ironfist, Charles Iscuro, and a new young recruit named Arlen Brody."

Demas said, "You're not taking Captain Corden?"

"Not this time," the king said. "He's the only one I'd entrust the realm to in my absence."

"But only three," Demas said. "Is that enough?"

The king said, "Four counting Rolland is plenty. The smaller the party, the less chance of word getting out. I don't want anyone to know what I'm doing, at least not until I've returned. That way, if for any reason this trip proves unsuccessful, no one will be the wiser. If, on the other hand, I accomplish what I have set out to do, I will discuss the matter with the council."

"What are you expecting from me, Your Majesty?" Demas said.

"You're to cover for me while I'm away. As far as anyone else is concerned, I am visiting Baron Vance. He will corroborate the story. And you will be in charge of the castle. I appoint you as castellan in my absence."

"Oh, but Sire—"

Arkelaus held up a hand. "No objections, Demas, it is already done. You are to handle all the affairs while I am gone. And if anyone asks about me, I am at Baron Vance's manor in Stonebridge."

At the look of concern on Demas' face, he added, "Do not worry, Chamberlain... er, Castellan. I promise not to be gone long. It's a two-day journey to Teman, then a few days in that country, and another two days back. I ought to complete the trip in a fortnight. That is a fair amount of time to be gone visiting one of Rygia's barons, is it not? Rolland has taken care of the details. We leave tomorrow."

"Tomorrow? But, Your Majesty, what about the queen? What about the prince? What about—?"

"Hush your fears, my friend. Queen Estrella will accompany me. Her presence will make a social call to Vance's more believable, and she is anxious to make acquaintance with our Temanite neighbors. Prince Medan, now that is another story. I am putting him in Captain Corden's charge."

"Does Corden know where you're going?" Demas asked.

"No, and neither does the prince. Let it remain so for now. Oh, there is one more item. Prince Medan is eighteen years old now. It's time we chose a suitable bride for him. The queen and I have already begun making betrothal arrangements."

Demas' face brightened. "That is good news, Sire."

"I have already sent the proposal to the lady's father, but I will leave all future correspondence in your hands. You must see to it that the arrangements are agreeable to both parties. The wedding is to take place on Medan's twentieth birthday."

"Whom do you have in mind?"

"I have chosen a young lady whose father is quite wealthy. He owns a great deal of land in this country, has a large number of men in his command, and wields much respect and influence. By betrothing his daughter to the prince, I will be securing his fealty for life and strengthening the country as well."

"Excellent, Your Majesty, I am so happy for you and your son. So tell me... what is the name of the lucky family?"

Arkelaus smiled. "Godfrey."

"Godfrey!" Demas exclaimed.

"Yes," the king said. "And you, Demas, will deliver this news to the prince first thing tomorrow morning."

28

The next day, after the king had left, Captain Justus Corden stood in the courtyard of the Rygian castle, trading sword strikes with eighteen-year-old Prince Medan.

"No, no, no, Your Highness, don't slap at me with your blade. If you want to pierce chainmail, thrust, like so." He demonstrated.

"Like this?" Medan responded with an obvious lack of enthusiasm.

At eighteen years of age, Medan's steel-blue eyes lacked the luster and wisdom of his father's, Justus thought. He didn't have the same drive and purpose, the sense of responsibility that King Arkelaus embodied.

Medan was a good-looking young man, with silky golden hair that hung straight down to his shoulders then curled inward slightly. His loose white shirt was gathered at the waist by a wide brown belt. Brown leggings and boots hugged his slender legs.

Justus faced off with the prince once again, but then he stopped, feeling a chill crawl up the back of his neck. Turning, he spotted one of the councilmen standing nearby, watching them intently.

The councilman's once-golden hair, now mostly gray, was oiled to a shine and hung down to his shoulders. A gray moustache and pointy beard offset the pale blue eyes. Around his silvery-gray tunic he wore a black leather belt that held a Rygian broadsword. Under the tunic he wore black leggings and boots. He looked much the same as any other Rygian lord, only colder.

"Good day, Captain Corden," the man said.

Justus turned away, muttering, "Good day, Baron Alton."

"I see you've been put in charge of the prince."

Ignoring him, Justus said to Medan, "Come on now, have at me."

The prince made only a half-hearted attempt. Justus was about to correct him when Alton shouted, "Well done, Your Highness!"

Justus shot him a glare. "Do you mind?"

"Don't take that tone with me, Captain." To the prince, he said, "Such a good sword! I've seen my own squires working with my men-at-arms, and they are not as quick as you."

Justus said, "Then why not go back to your castle and give your own squires some tips?"

"Are you finished working with the prince, Captain?" Alton asked, ignoring his comment.

"Why?"

"I'd like you and the prince to join me at table. I believe the meal is prepared."

Justus slipped his sword into its sheath. "Not today, sorry."

"Oh dear." Alton almost seemed disappointed. "I had hoped to hear about your latest conquests. I've been away for so many months now."

Justus looked the councilman over. The many jeweled rings on his fingers told of the success he had found in another of his trading ventures overseas. Alton was known for returning with a shipload of goods from other realms that he then sold to merchants who, in turn, sold them to the people throughout the realm.

The wealth this brought Alton was unparalleled in Rygia. Justus knew that Alton had found a way around the sailing restrictions put in place by the former king. Mostly he traveled by land to Xulon, where he could commission a ship to just about anywhere.

Justus said curtly, "Like I said, not today, Alton."

"*Lord* Alton," he said with a sneer.

"Excuse me!" Justus snipped without correcting himself. "Perhaps some other time."

The strained conversation came to an abrupt halt when a courier charged through the gate. "Your Highness!" He leapt off his horse and headed straight for the prince.

"Yes, what is it?" Prince Medan asked.

"It's the Gargons again. They're devouring the countryside along the western border."

Medan said to a servant, "Get the castellan." Then he looked toward Justus.

Justus said, "I'll gather the men and send word to the lords of the outer territories. We might need their help." He trotted toward the barracks to prepare.

When all was ready and Justus returned to report to the prince, he found Medan in a close and quiet conversation with Baron Alton. He slowed to listen as he approached.

Alton said, "Did you not know the women of Rygia are considered the most beautiful in the world?"

"Really?" Medan asked.

"Oh, yes. Men of other lands have been known to pay quite a sum for a Rygian wife."

"Pay?" Medan asked, alarmed. "You mean our women are being sold?"

"No, no, not at all. I merely meant they *would* pay quite a sum. It's a shame that the man who would be king over such beautiful women would have to settle for less than the best."

"It wasn't my choice," Medan said. "I mean, Lady Godfrey, of all people! What's my father trying to do, curse me? And to send me the news through a chamberlain! How could he do such a thing to me?" He stopped his rant abruptly. "Oh, Captain Corden, there you are."

Alton turned sharply and gave Justus a look that showed he didn't appreciate the interruption.

"Everything's ready, Your Highness," Justus said.

"Good. Go in the name of Rygia, Captain, and give those Gargons the scourging they deserve."

Justus asked, "What about you, Highness? Who'll protect you while I'm gone?

Alton said, "I was just about to discuss that with the prince myself. Why not come to my manor, Your Highness? My walls will protect you well." In a quieter voice, he added, "While there, we can peruse those other, um, *options* I mentioned."

"Thank you, Alton, I believe I'll do that."

Justus said, "But, Your Highness, don't you think you ought to stay here in your father's absence?"

Alton said, "You know, Captain, I've been concerned about that very thing."

"What very thing?"

"The absence of the king. Where is King Arkelaus?"

"He's visiting Baron Vance, you know that."

"Quite a long way to travel with just four guards, don't you think?"

Justus waved it off. "General Rolland was with them. The king's in good hands."

"Oh, I suppose. It all just seemed so secretive to me."

"Look, I don't have all day to stand around and talk about this," Justus said.

Prince Medan said, "Of course, Captain, be on your way. I'll be fine at Alton's manor in Blackwood. Off you go."

Justus bowed his head. "Yes, Your Highness."

29

Shadows of evening spread across the northern border of Rygia, draping the city of Narramoor in twilight. Inside Baron Giles Godfrey's castle, long tables in the great hall overflowed with men and women of high standing in his territory.

But the bright colors, happy conversations, loud laughter, and merry clinking of mugs were all lost on the guest of honor—Giles' daughter, Rolanda. A gloominess settled in her heart, deepening with the coming of night.

Yet she maintained a resolute face, as was her habit. Long ago she had mastered the technique of keeping her expression aloof, even stone-cold sometimes.

A glance toward her cousin Gregor told her that he had not yet adopted her skills. He wore his emotions openly—on his face but never on his lips. No one in her father's territory knew what the two of them shared.

Giles Godfrey stood and held a mug aloft. "A toast to my daughter, the new queen of Rygia!"

"Hail!" the guests shouted.

Rolanda murmured, "The future queen, you mean."

"As you say, my dear." Godfrey downed his mug in one swallow and wiped his scraggly yellow beard with his sleeve. "My acceptance letter has been sent, and pending the dowry arrangements, all has been settled. In two years, when both my daughter and the prince turn twenty years of age, they will be married! And I, Baron Godfrey of Narramoor, will be father to a queen!"

A messenger burst in and ran toward the high table. "My

lord! The Gargons are attacking the western border! Captain Corden has requested our assistance."

Godfrey slammed his mug on the table. "How dare you interrupt my celebration with the name of that bastard bride-stealer! How dare he ask me for help!"

Gregor stood. "Uncle, I'll assist, if you allow it. I'll take my own men and—"

"I do *not* allow it! Corden will receive no help from us. Mark my words... once my daughter is queen, I'll rid this land of that scoundrel of a captain."

As Rolanda watched Gregor return to his seat, she caught his gaze again—a gaze filled with unspoken feelings.

Finally the meal ended, to Rolanda's relief. While Godfrey remained in the great hall to help his guests finish off a cask of ale, Rolanda snuck out a back door and went straight to her room. She sat alone for some time, anxiously awaiting the sound of a familiar knock at her door.

Nearly an hour later it came. "Who goes there?" she asked.

"Gregor, my lady."

She let him in, closed and locked the door behind him. "Are you sure no one saw you?"

"Course not. They're all too drunk to notice me."

Scanning his stocky frame, she said, "A man like you not be noticed?"

He laughed, but his laughter was hollow and quickly subsided. "Two more years. Two years and you'll be gone, given to that selfish... childish... infantile... prince!"

She might have laughed at his angry flailing and the redness that grew in his cheeks, if she had felt like laughing at all. But laughter was far from her this day.

"Maybe it's for the best," Gregor said in a sad tone.

"How can that possibly be?" she said sarcastically.

"You're my cousin. I can't ever hope to have you." He reached to touch her hair, then thought better of it. "Blast it all. I love you, Rolanda. More every year. I can't help it."

She managed to smile at him. Gregor was a large man,

like his uncle, but very different. Especially his eyes. Gregor's bright blue eyes bore a gentleness she had never seen in Giles. His thick blonde hair and trim golden beard did little to hide the emotion he wore so openly on his face.

"I love you too, Gregor." She said the words, but they seemed bitter, in a way. Unrequited love truly was a terrible thing, she was learning. At eighteen she should be experiencing the joys of love, of being with someone who warmed her heart. No one had ever done that for her like Gregor.

She had to tell him. Reveal to him her secret. Now, with this impending marriage to Prince Medan, she had to let him in on it. But it wouldn't be easy.

She began to pace, wringing her hands. "Gregor, there's... there's something I must tell you. Something very important. Please don't be angry with me for not telling you sooner. I would have, but I feared your uncle's wrath. Yet now with this betrothal, I cannot wait another moment."

"Nothing you do or say would ever anger me."

His voice was soft, gentle. She halted in front of him. "You are so different from your uncle."

"That's a good thing, right?"

"That's a very good thing," she said.

Again his hand reached out, and this time he didn't stop it. His thick fingers ran gently down her golden hair and played with the ends. "Well, maybe it's because I have something he never had."

"What's that?"

"Your love."

She sighed.

"All those years growing up," he said. "Can't imagine what I'd be if you hadn't been here."

She took his hand in hers. "Oh, to be children again, when we could laugh and play without a care. Now I feel as though the weight of the world is upon me."

They fell silent for a moment, gazing at each other, his fingers entwined in her hair, until he said, "You had something to tell me, you said."

"I do, but I... oh, I don't know if I can. But I must. You have to know, Gregor. You have to know what I've known for several years now. Don't be angry with me for not telling you sooner."

"What is it?"

In a very quiet voice, Rolanda said, "Giles Godfrey is not my father."

She watched for his reaction. At first he stood silently, staring blankly. Then his eyes grew large. "You toy with me."

"No, it's true. Mother told me on her death bed." She pulled a chain from around her neck and showed him the pendant—half of a golden heart, etched with intricate filigree.

She said, "This was my mother's. She wore it all the time, never took it off, until the day she died. When she handed it to me, she said, 'This was given to me by the only man I ever loved... your true father.'"

"Who is he?"

Rolanda shook her head. "I don't know. At first I thought she was going to tell me, but she seemed afraid to. I'm sure she feared Godfrey's wrath. Then she died, and I never learned the truth." She looked up into Gregor's face. "You're not angry with me?"

"Angry?" A great smile spread. "How can I be angry? You're not my cousin. Now I can marry you! We have to tell Uncle Giles immediately." He headed for the door and reached for the handle. "We'll put a stop to the betrothal and—"

Rolanda lunged to stop him, but he had already stopped himself.

"Drat! We can't ever tell Uncle Giles."

"No, we can't," Rolanda said. "If he knew, he'd kill me."

"He would, that." Gregor swore under his breath. "But, blast it all, Rolanda, he wants you to marry the prince!"

"And as long as I must call him my father, I dare not refuse his wishes."

Gregor's great shoulders drooped. "Do you *want* to marry the prince?"

"No, I want to marry you."

"But how can we?"

"We cannot, not as long as Godfrey lives. But how much longer can that be? He's nearly sixty years old. When he dies and you inherit his manor, the whole world can know I was never his daughter."

"What can we do until then? What about the betrothal?"

"I've tried to reason it through ever since hearing of it. There's nothing we can do. I have to go through with the marriage."

"My heart had soared only to plummet."

"I know, dear Gregor, mine as well. But hear me out, I have a plan. After I marry Prince Medan and satisfy Godfrey's desires, I'll do all I can to find legitimate reason to leave the prince. If I do, Godfrey cannot argue my leaving."

"How can you be sure? Won't he seek retribution against the prince?"

"Perhaps, perhaps not, it depends on the reason for my leaving. But trust me, Gregor, I will dissolve the marriage as speedily as possible. Then I can come home to you."

He kissed her on the forehead. "And then, no more hiding. I'll be free to love you."

"No, not totally free. Not while your uncle lives."

"Secretly then. But in the meantime, I pledge myself to you as your champion. I'll stay by your side in Archella so you won't be alone."

"You'd do that for me?"

"I'd do anything for you."

She felt his arms wrap around her. He kissed her on the lips, more passionately than ever before.

"How I've longed for this," he said. "All these years, watching you, being with you, never able to have you. Keeping my thoughts and desires to myself."

She clutched at him a little more tightly. "And each time you kissed me I longed to tell you but dared not."

"You're a wise woman." He kissed her again, pulling her body close to his.

"No, Gregor, we mustn't."

"I want to have you before that prince gets his hands on you."

"No, I must remain unspoiled, lest the prince be displeased."

"Let him be displeased. Then he'll send you home to me."

"No, Gregor, stop!" Rolanda pushed him away. "My leaving must be *his* fault in order for Giles to take me back."

Both Rolanda and Gregor tried to catch their breath.

"You're right," Gregor said, panting. "You're always right." He reached for the half-heart pendant hanging around her neck. "Whoever your father was, he must've been wise. You must've gotten all that wisdom from him."

"I'd like to think so."

~~~

Rolland rode alongside the king's carriage as they headed down the road that led southward through Rygia. Geoffrey Ironfist and Arlen Brody sat above the carriage, and the last soldier, Charles Iscuro, rode to the rear.

As they emerged from the King's Woods, a vast plain stretched before them. Beyond it, the mountains of Teman were but a thin line of gray along the horizon.

The sun was near to setting by the time they reached the city of Stonebridge, where Baron Vance resided. The city lay on flat, fertile ground halfway between Rygia's wooded lands and the mountains of Teman.

Walls two hundred years old circled the city. Rolland remembered a conversation he had once overheard between Baron Vance and King Arkelaus—that those walls had been built at a time when Rygia feared the Temanites might emerge from their mountains and attack.

But no attack ever came, and the fears morphed into wild tales that kept Rygians from ever venturing over those

234|<i>The Alliance, Book 3</i>

mountains. *Why are we so afraid of them? What happened two hundred years ago?*

Before entering the city, Rolland bade the soldiers to let their horses drink at the Stone River. Oak trees along the banks were just starting to turn to their autumn reds. Although the day had been warm, a nightly chill was already settling around them.

Rolland peered over the walls to the gray mountains in the distance. He had to admit, he felt a bit apprehensive about this journey. What lay beyond the mountains? What were the Temanites like? What gave rise to the fears that built those great walls?

"You have really gotten soft," Corden had said. Looking at those mountains, feeling a quivering in his gut, Rolland thought maybe Corden was right.

Perhaps it was because he was getting old. Perhaps it was because there had been no major battles for several years, no reason to maintain the bravado. Perhaps it was the influence of King Arkelaus' steady and gentle spirit. Or perhaps it was because he had spent the last four years trying to counter-balance the angry young Captain Corden.

Whatever the reason, Rolland knew he had changed. Now that there was someone like Corden to step into his shoes, he found he could turn his mind to other things, like what to do with the rest of his life.

He pulled the broken heart pendant from his pouch and touched it to his lips. *If only things had been different. If only she had stayed.* How different his life would have been if he had not let her slip away.

The gate of the city wall opened. It was time to go.

30

Across the mountains, in the land of Teman, King Eliada sat alone in the throne room, gazing at the empty throne where Queen Bernice used to sit. It had been four years since her death, but he still missed her.

At least he had Mari and Josephus. Mari, especially, did much to fill his empty heart. She was now seventeen and quite the young lady, even taking to fulfilling social obligations that were normally expected of the queen. James appreciated it so much that he never again brought up the question of marriage. He knew she would cross that bridge when she felt ready.

Somehow Mari had become stronger, it seemed, since her mother died. More independent and self-assured. Then again, James realized that was the way Mari always had been. Taking on her mother's role only offered the opportunity for her true character to manifest.

The tapping of a cane in the corridor told him Areli was approaching. When the old prophet entered the throne room, James thought he looked every bit his one hundred and six years.

"Yes, Areli, did you need to see me?"

"I did. I want to talk to you about your daughter's birthday celebration."

"Everything's arranged. We're planning a large banquet and—"

"I did not come all this way to check on banquet arrangements."

"What is it, then? I sense a rebuke coming."

"She is turning eighteen. It should be a wedding ceremony, not a birthday celebration."

"Don't start with me, Areli. Mari's free to make her own choice."

"I think you wouldn't mind if she chooses not to marry at all. I think you've become more dependent on her than you like to admit."

"Perhaps," the king said.

"Perhaps if she were married and gave you grandchildren, you would find your heart lightened."

"I think Mari's misery would overshadow any of my own happiness."

"This is not a matter of her feelings," Areli said. "It is a matter of ensuring succession to the throne."

"As Mari oft reminds me, that is Josephus' responsibility, not hers, so that the Eliada name will continue as well as the line."

"He is but fourteen. It will be awhile before he can fulfill his duties in that area. Princess Mari must do her part. I need not remind you that it is unwise to place all your eggs in the same basket."

"And I need not remind you that there is no fury like a woman's scorn."

Areli managed a smile. "I know how the princess feels, and I understand your dilemma, but having a sure successor to the royal line is not mere duty—it is a mandate from Eloah. To fail to fulfill our mandates is to invite tragedy."

"Don't you think I know that? Every night I pray that something worse won't befall us. I see dark times ahead, Areli. Without the light of the Areli line, what darkness might we plunge into?"

"So it is light you seek?"

"Of course. The Areli line is the light of this realm, and once you're gone, that light will be gone as well."

"Indeed," Areli said. "Tell me, have you given any more thought to what we discussed last week?"

"I have, Areli, and I must admit my heart is torn."

"Is it your heart that is torn, or is it your mind? I think your heart is the same as mine on this matter, but your mind is slow to follow."

"You're right, old friend. What you propose has become the greatest desire of my heart. But I do have fear."

"What is it you fear?"

"The council. I spoke with them just yesterday about it. They do not approve."

"The council is not the governing authority in this land," Areli said, "Do not forget, their existence is not by Eloah's ordination. They are merely, shall I say, assistants. They exist to advise the king, not command him."

"I know, Areli, but for a king to act against the advice of the council is still a serious matter."

"No member of the council would disapprove of any action that has a prophet's sanction," Areli said.

"Yes, I know. But without you at my side, they would not be convinced. They need to hear it from your lips, Areli."

"Then I shall speak with them today."

"Are you up to it? I mean, I know how hard it is for you to be out."

"A matter of this importance is of greater value than my health. I will attend the council with you this evening, and they will agree to our proposal."

"But a journey to Rygia?" the king said. "Ever since the days of the first Rygian king, that country has been hostile to us. It's been a very long time since a member of the royal family has crossed the mountain pass, and he was killed for it. That's why the elders are so adamantly opposed."

"They misinterpret the mandates," Areli said. "They take them to mean that it is the king's place to stay behind the mountains. But you think differently, do you not?"

"Yes, I do now," James said. "You've tried to make me think differently for a long time. Unfortunately, it took the loss of your family to make me see it—to help me understand what Eloah wished to show me."

"And what is that?"

"That I've become too complacent, too secure behind these mountains. That I need to trust in Eloah alone—not in the mountains, not in this land or its people, not even in..." James looked into the prophet's eyes.

"In what?" Areli asked. "Do not be afraid to say it."

"In you," the king said. "In the Areli line. Knowing that your line will no longer be with us has opened my heart to new visions. Eloah is teaching me something."

"What is he teaching you?"

"To reach out. To bring our light out from under the bushel so it can shine more brightly."

"Even in darkness, you can still hold a candle," Areli said. "You have done well, James."

The king rose and took Areli's elbow, leading him down the carpet and into the corridor. "I do feel as though the future of Teman lies in this venture to Rygia, but I do not understand why."

"The why is not always ours to know. Sometimes we have only the dream to guide us, not the understanding."

"The dream," James said with a sigh. "The council doesn't share it. Do you know what they told me yesterday? They said the people are beginning to show fear. Doubts. Lack of faith. With the loss of your line, they wonder whether Eloah is displeased with us. That perhaps he has withdrawn his presence from us."

"That is disturbing," Areli said. "Do not believe that for one moment."

"I shall try." The king paused from their slow walk. "Do you remember that day—has it been seven years ago already—when you asked me to consider what it was in which I place my trust?"

"I may be old, but my memory has never failed me."

"You said perhaps I needed a test to reveal all that is in my heart."

"Yes, I remember."

"At the time I was afraid Eloah would leave me in order to test me. Now I see it was partly true. Once you are gone it will be as though a part of Eloah has left me. I will be alone, in a sense. Alone to face the council. Alone to face... the unknown. And yet I believe Eloah would have me face the unknown in order to prove my faith is truly in him and not in any tangible thing."

Areli put his weathered hand on the king's shoulder. "Do not fear the unknown. There is no place you can go where Eloah is not."

"Oh, but there is a place where Eloah does not exist," the king said.

Areli looked surprised. "What kind of place could that be?"

James wrapped his arms around himself, feeling a sudden chill. "Eloah is light and in him is no darkness at all. But in a heart that is filled with darkness—that is a place where Eloah is not."

Areli stared long and hard at his friend. "So, the king becomes a prophet."

The king suppressed a laugh. "No, my friend, I am not a prophet. I am only... how can I say this? For the last four years, since the holy mountain swallowed the last of the Areli line, I've had dreams."

"Dreams?"

"Not dreams like you have when you sleep, but dreams that possess your every waking moment. Dreams that oppress you and possess you until you'll do everything within your power to see them fulfilled."

"And what are those dreams, James?"

"To do as you have challenged me. To venture beyond. To take what light we have left and spread it around so it may grow once again. That is what my heart beckons me to do."

"But your mind is yet disobedient."

"My mind tends to listen to the council."

"Then let your mind listen tonight when I speak to the council. They will not refuse you when I give my sanction.

Heed my words, James. Once the council assents, you must go there expediently."

"Why such haste?"

Areli touched his chest. "I feel a burden in my heart, as though a door has opened briefly and will soon shut. This opportunity may not last forever. You must take it before it flits away."

"Very well."

31

Leaving the carriage in Stonebridge, General Rolland led the king's small entourage on horseback. After riding throughout the morning, they reached the foothills of the mountains of Teman. A misty fog shrouded the mountains, making them seem quite ghostly, Rolland thought.

King Arkelaus pulled his mount alongside Rolland's. "I see no way through this fog. How can we find a pass?"

"If a pass even exists," Rolland said. "Didn't you review the archives? Were there any records of a crossing into Teman?"

"No. If any Rygians ever went to Teman, it was not recorded. I had no idea it would be so difficult to get there."

"Perhaps we'll find something further westward."

"Very well, lead on."

Rolland directed his horse toward the west, King Arkelaus and Queen Estrella at his sides. Charles Iscuro and the other two soldiers followed quietly behind.

Rolland turned in the saddle to peer at them briefly. Their wide eyes and long stares toward the wooded foothills made it obvious they were already wondering what they had gotten themselves into. He could hear them murmuring but could only make out the words "enchanted" and "spirits."

He had to admit, he understood a little of what they were feeling. Demas' stories had run through his mind more than once upon arriving. Spirit beings. Haunted forests. Mountains swallowing people whole. He didn't realize quite how nervous he was until a shout rang out and his heart nearly stopped.

Turning his mount eastward toward the sound, he spied a score of strange-looking warriors emerging from the mist. All wore bright golden breastplates and held tall lances. Most wore golden cloaks, but the three that rode front and center wore red.

Rolland heard Charles Iscuro mutter something under his breath. Although he couldn't hear what was said, he heard the apprehension in his tone.

"Enough of that," Rolland said. With a command to his horse, he trotted right up to the strangers. King Arkelaus followed, leaving Queen Estrella behind with the three soldiers.

The three Temanites with the red cloaks came forward. As they drew near, Rolland could see the emblems on their tunics. The man in the center wore a white tunic bearing a red lion. He also wore a gold crown with rubies and amethysts. To his left rode an older man with a silver castle tower on his red tunic. The man to the right of the king wore a standing golden elk, also on a red tunic.

The closer they came, the more Rolland could see of them. Every one of them had brown hair, just like the stories.

The one with the crown said, "Greetings. I am King James Eliada of Teman."

Rolland was about to speak, but King Arkelaus passed him by and spoke first. "I am King Magnus Arkelaus of Rygia. I've come to make your acquaintance."

The Temanite king looked surprised. "And I have come to make yours. Welcome, Your Majesty. We meet at last."

If traveling through the mountain pass seemed a bit eerie to Rolland, with the mist hanging low and obscuring all but the shadows of tall mountains close at their sides, entering Teman made up for it. As they emerged from the mountain barrier, the mist dissolved and the sun shone in rays through the clouds, revealing a grand realm.

Before him and to his right, rolling green hills stretched

far off toward the horizon. Many hills were covered with orchards, all wearing autumn colors. To his left, he could hear ocean waves crashing against the rugged black mountains that hugged the coastline. Behind them, the barrier mountains rose up sharp and gray, like the teeth of a great dragon, stretching far off toward the west and disappearing into the distance.

"We call them the Velan Mountains."

Surprised at the strange, gruff voice, Rolland quickly straightened in his saddle, feeling a bit embarrassed for having been caught gaping at the scenery. The man who had spoken was General Garth, who wore the castle tower on his red tunic. Up until that moment, neither Rolland nor Garth had spoken, both preoccupied with watching their kings.

As it turned out, there was no need for apprehension where the two kings were concerned. They rode side by side, along with Queen Estrella, talking incessantly, as though they'd been friends for years. Only once was their conversation interrupted when King Eliada sent two soldiers ahead to inform the palace that there would be guests for dinner.

King Arkelaus was just as enamored with the countryside as Rolland. The bits of conversation that Rolland could overhear were Arkelaus' questions about the land and its people, and King Eliada's patient answers. Rolland also noticed that neither king spoke about the reasons behind their chance encounter. No doubt they wished to keep the conversation light, saving the hard points for later.

Just as Rolland was beginning to think the land of Teman couldn't be any grander, they entered the city of Temana and approached the castle. "By the stars!" he said under his breath.

The city streets were cobbled and clean, with two-storied homes arranged in straight lines. Golden thatched roofs shaded white-washed walls. Many windows were shuttered, due to the lateness of the season, but even the shutters were welcoming, with detailed carvings in the wood.

One main road led from north to south, separating the city from the castle, where Rolland's eyes had riveted. The entire Rygian party pulled their horses to a halt and stared at it, rather awestruck.

The castle sat on an outcropping of one of the coastal mountains. A long, switchback trail led up to the door within a round gatehouse. Seven tall towers reached toward the sky, each with a red conical roof. A stone patio lay between a many storied palatial building and a smaller building made of white stone and housing windows of colored glass.

"It's even nicer inside."

Again General Garth had spoken, drawing Rolland's attention away from the sight. He found that the Temanites had all dismounted, their horses being turned over to stablehands who led them away toward a long stablehouse that was, unsurprisingly, very clean. Rolland and the other Rygians dismounted and followed their Temanite hosts up the switchback trail.

Entering the castle, Rolland found Garth's words to have been an understatement. The corridors were clean and bright, with white-washed walls, many covered in tapestries or paintings. Every oaken door they passed was filled with intricate carvings. Even the sconces that held torches to the walls were fancier than what he'd seen in the Rygian palace, their black iron molded into graceful swirls and floral patterns.

He followed the two kings into the throne room, which was quite large and taller than any room he'd ever seen. He and the other Rygian soldiers craned their necks to look upward at the high arched ceiling. Several pillars stood in the room to support the ceiling. A red carpet led down to the dais, where two intricately carved wooden thrones sat, each with red and gold cushions.

On the wall behind the thrones hung a golden emblem— a circle containing an image with four points. Coming out from the inner corners of the four points were what appeared to be flames of fire. Standing on either side of the emblem, as though they were holding it, were two gilded lions.

"It's called the Elaad," King Eliada said.

Rolland hadn't noticed that the Temanite king was standing near to him. King Eliada was a handsome man, with dark brown hair and a trim beard and moustache.

"It's our symbol for the eternal God," the king said. "The four points of the compass set within an all-seeing eye. The lion is the Eliada family symbol."

Queen Estrella said, "It's beautiful. This whole place is beautiful."

"Thank you. Speaking of beautiful, here is my lovely daughter, Princess Mariya."

A young woman entered wearing a white gown and lavender robe. A thin circlet of gold adorned her head. Her dark brown hair was gathered into many braids that entwined around the crown, looped down to her shoulders and back up again.

She carried herself in a stately fashion, like a queen. Her brown eyes seemed to sparkle when they lit on Queen Estrella. She curtseyed. "It's a pleasure to make your acquaintance, Your Majesties."

"And I yours," Queen Estrella said. "My, but you are a beautiful young lady."

"I was just thinking the same about you," the Temanite princess said.

King Eliada said, "My daughter will be celebrating her eighteenth birthday in three days. I do hope you can stay for the celebration."

"Please do," the princess said. "Your presence will make the day even more special."

"We'd be delighted," King Arkelaus said.

King Eliada said, "And now, may I introduce my son, Prince Josephus James Eliada."

A boy of fourteen approached, wearing a thin gold band atop his head of curly dark brown hair. He wore a white tunic with a red lion, like his father's, and around his neck was a gold medallion hanging by a red cord.

Another boy entered with the prince. He was about the same age, but his hair was a lighter shade of brown, like hazelnuts, with bangs falling into his wide-open eyes that darted from one Rygian to another.

King Eliada said, "This is Squire Stephen Elkanah, son of Captain Benjamin, whom you've already met."

As Stephen walked past Rolland, he stared open-mouthed at Rolland's blue eyes and golden-gray hair. Rolland stared back, right into the boy's large brown eyes. Stephen flushed and looked away.

The prince seemed humored by his friend's behavior, but he remembered his manners as he approached King Arkelaus and Queen Estrella, bowing and saying, "Welcome to Teman."

King Eliada said, "Now that you've met my family, I'll have my servants take you to the guest rooms. There's plenty of time to freshen up before dinner."

None of the Rygians were prepared for the elegance of the feast held in their honor. When he was led to the banquet hall, Rolland had to stop in the doorway to take in the sight. Many long tables were covered with white linen and set with plates of pewter. The goblets were plated with gold and the spoons and eating knives were decorated with gold filigree.

The high table sat along one wall. King Eliada invited King Arkelaus and Queen Estrella to join him there. He said to Estrella, "Would you allow my daughter to sit beside you?"

"I'd be delighted," the queen said.

Rolland and his men were led to one of the other tables, which stood perpendicular to the high table. Rolland sat at the end closest to the high table, with General Garth sitting at his side. Prince Josephus and Squire Stephen joined them as well.

The three Rygian soldiers, Charles, Geoffrey, and Arlen, sat across from Rolland and Garth, along with Captain Benjamin Elkanah, Stephen's father. The remaining tables became filled with Temanite soldiers and ranking citizens of the city of Temana, as well as seven older men who wore black robes.

The Rygian soldiers began their meal in silence, all a bit overwhelmed. A small band played lively music from a balcony, which helped fill the conversational void on the soldiers' table.

But on the high table, the two kings, the queen, and the princess engaged in friendly chatter. From where he sat, Rolland could hear much of what was said.

"I must say, King Arkelaus..." King Eliada began.

"Please, call me Magnus."

"Magnus, then. You may call me James. I must say, Magnus, you do not seem at all like I imagined Rygians to be."

"And how did you imagine us?"

"Forgive me but... well, barbaric... decadent."

Rolland heard one of his soldiers make some sort of scoffing sound under his breath. He glared at all of them, not sure which had done it. When they each had caught his eye, he twirled his eating knife in his fingers as a silent warning. They returned their eyes to their plates, warning taken.

King Arkelaus chuckled. "You're not far off, James. Not far off at all."

"But you're not barbaric at all," King Eliada said. "One look at your beautiful wife and your noble warriors," he paused deliberately, "is enough to change anyone's mind."

Redness flared in the soldiers' cheeks. Rolland wondered if the Temanite king had heard the scoff and was either toying with them or politely dismissing their impropriety. Either way, it made him smile.

"Why, thank you, James." King Arkelaus said. "And I must say that your people are nothing like we imagined them."

"And how is that?"

"Ghosts. Spirit beings."

King Eliada laughed loudly. "I assure you, we are but flesh and blood."

"I can see that. Although I daresay that the sight of you emerging from the mountain mist would cause many of my people to quake in fear."

King Eliada said, "And I wonder, if my people were to encounter yours, they might think they had seen the face of an angel."

At that, Rolland nearly choked on a bite of meat. When he looked up, he saw all three of his men scowling at him. He rolled his eyes and shook his head.

General Garth said, "Relax, General Longsword. You and your men aren't the only ones feeling uncomfortable." He pointed to Squire Stephen, sitting at his other side.

Mouth hanging open, Stephen's eyes were riveted on the Rygian who sat directly across from him—Charles Iscuro. Stephen's eating knife hovered halfway between his plate and his mouth, where it had stalled for the last several minutes.

Rolland heard Prince Josephus say, "Shut your mouth, Stephen."

The squire's mouth clamped shut, but his eyes stayed wide and his knife remained aloft.

Captain Benjamin said, "Please forgive my son's curiosity. He has never seen people who look different from himself, and he is naturally curious."

"Curious?" General Garth said. "Gobsmacked, I should say."

The Temanite officers laughed, and Stephen turned a bright shade of red.

Rolland could see that Charles was quite uncomfortable under Squire Stephen's intense stare, especially when Charles reached for a goblet and Stephen blurted, "By Elán! What happened to your hand?"

"Stephen!" Benjamin scolded.

Stephen flushed again.

Charles quickly tried to hide his right hand by putting it

on his lap and taking up his goblet in his left hand. But Rolland knew what the squire had seen—a thick, dark scar that stretched across all four of his knuckles.

Rolland said, "Now there's an interesting story. I was there. I saw it."

Charles plunked his goblet down and glared at Rolland.

"Is it a battle wound?" Stephen asked.

Charles hadn't stopped glaring at Rolland. Obviously he didn't think the story was worth telling.

Rolland had no qualms about it. "No, not a battle wound. Came from a friend of his. Nearly sliced his fingers off."

"Some friend," Stephen said.

Rolland said, "Not the kind of guy you want to cross."

"Who is he?"

Geoffrey Ironfist said, "Captain Corden, the mightiest Rygian warrior that ever lived. Next to General Rolland, anyway. We call him Corden the Conqueror."

Stephen leaned back in his chair and crossed his arms. "Really? What makes him so great?"

As Geoffrey told the story of how nineteen-year-old Corden led the Rygians to victory against the Gargons eight years earlier, Rolland was glad to see that at least one of his men was beginning to warm toward the Temanites.

"The Gargons?" Stephen said. "A nineteen-year old? That's some feat!"

A maiden's voice from the high table drew everyone's attention. "Please, good sir, tell us more." It was the Temanite princess, who apparently had been listening in.

Garth said to Rolland, "I'm sure she'd enjoy hearing some new war stories. I'll bet you have a few."

"That I do," Rolland said. "But about Corden—he's like a crazy man with a sword in his hand."

Garth said, "Not a good combination. I'd hate to face a sword like that."

Rolland said, "You know what? Me too."

Garth jabbed his knife toward the west. "The Gargons give us trouble too, way over on the Elan Mountains."

Prince Josephus said, "But they never get close enough to be a real threat. Usually they lose a lot of men and horses when they try to cross the ravines."

"Why go to all that trouble?" Geoffrey asked. "What do Gargons want in Teman?"

Squire Stephen shrugged. "They're Gargons. Do they have to want something? I think they fight just to fight."

Rolland said, "Yeah, Corden is like that sometimes."

"I'll bet my father could take him!" Stephen said. When his father glowered at him from across the table, Stephen slouched in his chair, saying, "Well, you could."

When the meal ended, Rolland and his three men were invited to join the Temanite soldiers outside and share some hot spiced wine. They followed General Garth to the soldiers' barracks—a long building on the castle side of the city, set up against the coastal mountains. In front of the building a fire blazed.

Several soldiers had already gathered, talking, laughing, and sharing stories. They quieted when the Rygians arrived, staring at them apprehensively. Introductions were made and mugs of wine passed to the guests.

Several Temanites got up from a long bench and offered the seat to the Rygians. As Rolland joined his men there, he noticed the Temanites keeping their distance, eyeing them warily. Some were amiable enough, but most remained reserved.

General Garth lightened the mood by opening a conversation. "General Longsword's told me that they've had some run-ins with the Gargons. Up close and personal, he says. I'm sure we'd like to hear the story, wouldn't we?"

Several Temanites murmured their interest, so Rolland obliged, being sure to include the part about how a squire named Corden was knighted at the age of nineteen and led the men to victory. By the time he had finished, most of the Temanites seemed to have relaxed.

During the conversation, his gaze frequently wandered to the sword hanging from Garth's belt. The sheath was wood and leather, but the ornamental gold filigree that adorned it was quite beautiful. The entire hilt of the sword gleamed with gold. He said, "That's a fine sword you have there, General Garth. May I see it?"

Garth pulled his sword from its sheath and handed it to Rolland. "Call me Jed. Short for Jedidiah."

"It's magnificent. Iron blade?"

"Steel. The blending of iron and carbon creates a much stronger blade."

"This hilt... is it pure gold?"

"No, it's an alloy created for strength, like the blade."

"Remarkable. And beautiful." Rolland returned the sword to its owner, then pulled his own family sword from its scabbard and handed it proudly to Garth. "What do you think of this one, Jed?"

Garth studied the weapon for several moments. "I have never seen its equal. This is fine workmanship, General Longsword."

"Call me Rolland. It's been passed down through my family."

Garth ran a finger along the flowering vine carved on the blade, then touched the markings by the jewels in the pommel and hilt. "These are interesting markings. Are they words?"

"I don't know. If they are, I don't know what they say."

"You've been left with a mystery, then." Garth looked more closely at the markings. "You know, there might be someone here who can help with your mystery."

"Who's that?"

"A very, very old man. Perhaps you'll meet him while you're here. Or, if he's up to it, I'll take you to him." Garth tested the Rygian sword in the air. "This would take some getting used to. It takes a strong arm to handle such a heavy weapon."

Rolland retrieved his sword from Garth and slid it back into its scabbard. "That it does. I think you'd find Rygian soldiers to be quite a challenge."

Garth eyed the three sitting on the bench. "No doubt there."

Rolland did his own study of the Temanite soldiers. "I wonder who would come out the winner."

Garth shook his head. "I hope never to see that day." He stepped over to a soldier in a red cloak sitting on one end of the bench. On the ground next to the soldier was a bow and a quiver of arrows. Garth said, "This is Aaron Elkanah, nephew to Benjamin. He's captain over my bowmen and one of the best archers in Teman."

"*The* best," Aaron said without a smile.

"That's probably true," Garth said. "Aaron, give me one of your arrows."

Aaron drew an arrow from his quiver and handed it to him.

Garth said, "In Teman it's considered a gesture of peace to hand over a weapon to an enemy. By doing so, we show that we don't wish to make battle with them. It's also a sign of absolute trust in our God, for it is he who defends us, not these weapons."

He handed the arrow to Rolland. "Accept this as a sign of peace between you and me."

Rolland accepted the Temanite arrow with reverence. "I'm honored. Thank you."

32

On the second evening of their visit, King Arkelaus walked alongside King Eliada through the corridors of the Temanite palace, with Queen Estrella and Princess Mariya following behind. Their conversation remained light, as it had throughout the day. The Temanite king pointed out varying pieces of artwork on the walls, particularly small statues that stood in recessed areas—images of former kings.

Upon reaching the end of a corridor, King Eliada took them up a tall spire. As he opened a door that led out to a balcony, he said, "I think you'll like the view from here."

Arkelaus stepped out, wind catching his face and taking his breath away. The balcony faced westward, overlooking the city. A full moon had arisen amid a starry sky, casting a blue glow over the night landscape. Yellow light from lanterns and fireplaces shone through glass windows in many houses.

"Your city is beautiful," he said.

"Thank you."

Though King Eliada's words were few, King Arkelaus detected a solemnity that hadn't existed in previous conversations. He also noted that King Eliada's smile had faded. "What's on your mind, James?" Arkelaus asked.

King Eliada said, "I must confess to you, Magnus, that my reasons for bringing you here are more than just social. I sought you for a purpose."

"*You* sought *me?*" Arkelaus shook his head. "I was the one seeking you. I did come all the way to the mountains, after all, hoping to find you."

"Is that so? Why would the king of Rygia seek to enter Teman?"

"I'm looking for something."

"Indeed?"

Arkelaus gazed up at the night sky. A thin blue-gray cloud floated across the expanse, gradually obscuring the moon from view. He shuddered.

"What troubles you, my friend?" King Eliada asked.

Arkelaus said, "I've been burdened for some years now. My heart is heavy over the state of my realm. I came here hoping to find something that might help my people."

"What is it you seek?"

"Light."

"Light?"

Arkelaus nodded. "You see, I've had dreams... very disturbing dreams... about a darkness gripping my country. I fear it has already entered and is beginning to swallow us. I feel I must seek a light that will dispel the darkness from my land."

"What kind of darkness?"

Arkelaus shook his head. "I don't fully understand it. All I know is that it is there, and it seeks to devour my realm. The mere thought of it fills me with fear, and I am not the kind of man who is prone to fear."

"I can see that. Tell me, Magnus, why did you think you could find your answer here?"

"I came across some writings from Teman."

"You did? What were they called?"

"Called? I wouldn't know. I had but a few pages."

"How big were they?"

"About like so." Arkelaus motioned with his hands.

"Oh." The momentary excitement in King Eliada's eyes left as quickly as it had come.

"Why do you ask?" Arkelaus said.

"I was hoping you might have found the answer to a mystery."

"What mystery?"

King Eliada said, "About two hundred years ago, during the reign of the first king of Rygia, my people came to your people with a gift. It was called the Golden Leaves of Light. This was no simple gift, mind you. It was the most treasured possession of my people, very old and very dear to us."

"And you gave it to *my* people?"

"Yes, to your first king, King Malchus Arkelaus. We told him that the gift contained the knowledge that leads to eternal life. My people left the gift with King Malchus to see what he would do with it. One year later, a prince of Teman went to Rygia to learn what had been done with the gift, but he and his party were killed."

"Great stars! I'm surprised your people didn't retaliate."

"We would have. But a surviving soldier from the prince's party returned to say it was the prince's dying wish that we not retaliate. He said that if we did, Rygia would never find the light within the gift. So we remained behind our mountains, hoping that one day Rygia would come to us. And here you are, two hundred years later."

"Two hundred years?" Arkelaus said. "That's the age of the walls around Baron Vance's city. That must be why they were built. The people were afraid Teman would attack after the death of their prince. But why did my people kill your prince in the first place?"

"I thought perhaps you could tell me," Eliada said.

"How could I? It is your story after all."

"Not that part of it. We never did learn why Rygia turned against us without provocation. And we never learned what had happened with our gift."

"The Golden Leaves of Light, you say?" Arkelaus asked.

King Eliada nodded. "Have you heard of it? Is there anything in your annals about it?"

"I will have to look into that," Arkelaus said.

"Yes, do, and get back to me. Needless to say, we are very curious about what happened. It's been a two hundred year old mystery to us."

"Such a shame. Your people tried to bring us light so long ago and we spurned it."

"And yet you came across some writings," Eliada said. "What did the writings say?"

"They spoke of light—a light in which there is no shadow. It said, 'The people walking in darkness have seen a great light. On those living in the land of the shadow of death a light has dawned.'"

"You're quoting from our Book of Light," King Eliada said.

"Book of Light? So you do know the light of which I seek."

"I do. I also know the darkness you spoke of. The darkness is that which exists in men's hearts when all they live for is themselves. They become consumed by the darkness until they are blinded to all that is good and right."

"Your words are true," Arkelaus said. "I've seen it among my own people. What light will dispel this darkness?"

"The light is Eloah, the God who created this world. He himself is the light you seek. But if you would have his light, there is a price to pay."

"Tell me, what is that price? I am willing to pay it."

"You cannot buy Eloah's light with silver or gold. A man must first of all recognize that his heart is dark and needs the light. Then he must be willing to exchange darkness for light, death for life. He must want to live in the light instead of the darkness. The price, then, is to lay down your life and take up the life of Eloah. Only in that way can you let his light into the darkness of your heart."

"What man would choose to keep darkness if light is offered to him? What man would choose death over life?"

"Many men prefer darkness, my friend."

Arkelaus recalled his trip to Darkhaven and the overwhelming darkness he felt there. "You're right. I fear this darkness will one day destroy us. How can I prevent that from happening? How can I show my people their need for light?"

"You cannot force it upon your people. They must choose for themselves. But if you first have the light within yourself, they will see it in you and perhaps desire it."

"Would the God of light stoop so low as to live in the dark heart of a Rygian such as myself?"

"Eloah lives in any heart that is humble and admits its need. You cannot make yourself worthy to receive him. Leave it to him to dispel the darkness."

Queen Estrella said, "I would like to know more about this God of light."

King Eliada smiled. "Mari, would you take the king and queen to the chapel and tell them the story?"

"Of course, Father."

King Arkelaus and his wife followed the Temanite princess down several flights of stairs, out onto a stone courtyard under the moonlight. On the opposite side of the courtyard was the white stone building with colored glass windows they had seen when they first arrived in the city.

As they entered a door under one of the windows, Arkelaus heard his wife gasp. And no wonder—the room was exquisite, with a carpeted floor and wooden shelves under the windows holding many candles, all lit. The firelight danced off the painted glass, spraying color in all directions. The windows themselves were each as tall as a man. It seemed as though the images on the glass told a story.

Queen Estrella said, "It's so beautiful."

King Eliada said, "We have a servant whose one job is to keep these candles lit every day and every night."

On the floor in the center of the room stood a rectangular stone object. Estrella pointed to it and asked, "What is that?"

"That is the altar," Princess Mariya said.

"What's an altar?"

"It's a place where you come to meet with Eloah, to lay down your will for his." The princess stood under the first of the five windows, the sparkling colors of light dancing off her thin gold crown.

Motioning toward the window, she said, "Eloah is the God who created all the universe. He created three great races of mankind and set them on this world to live." She pointed to the second window. "The land of Teman was created to bear witness to his glory, and he chose one of the races to be caretakers of that land."

The third window was different from the rest as it pictured a more gruesome scene. "But his chosen race proved themselves no different from the other races, for they fell away from the path of righteousness and forgot their creator and his ways. Because they had fallen away, they were nearly destroyed."

She moved to stand under the fourth window. "Therefore Eloah came down to reveal himself to them in a new way. At that time, he returned the line of Eliada to the throne, to rule the land in righteousness and faithfulness. He also ordained that the line of Areli should stand beside the king and rule in love and peace. He did this because it was an Eliada and an Areli who brought the light of Eloah back to the realm and led us out of our Dark Time."

Motioning toward the fifth and final picture, Mari said, "Eloah gave the people Three Mandates and promised that as long as we hold to these mandates, He would always protect us. From then on, we have obeyed his commands and followed in his ways, and he has never failed us."

Arkelaus moved closer to the first window. "These three races you spoke of—the images are vague. Who were they?"

King Eliada said, "We are of the Elyon race. The other races were called Kaion and Volon, but the last we had seen of them was just after our Dark Time. We have no records of who they were or what they looked like. In fact, we have very few records of those early days of history, except that the Volon were eventually wiped out by the Kaion. The Kaion tried to wipe us out as well, in what we call the Calandrian Wars."

"That's very sad," King Arkelaus said, noticing how intently King Eliada was looking at him. "You don't... you don't think *my* people are these Kaion, do you?"

Eliada shrugged. "You're not Elyon, that's for certain. What do your archives tell you about your past?"

"Our archives are only as old as Rygia is, about twelve hundred years. I don't know anything about the time before my people came to this land."

For the first time since arriving, King Arkelaus felt a little uncomfortable, hating the thought that his race might have once tried to eliminate another race. Fortunately, Queen Estrella changed the subject.

Drawing near to the fourth window and looking up at it, she asked, "How does the light of Eloah come to people who are in darkness?"

The princess said, "First, you must die. Not a physical death, though. It's like when you plant a seed in the ground—it must first die before it can live again a hundredfold. After our Dark Time, the people of Teman learned this lesson. Now we live our lives devoted to him."

Disappointment tinted Estrella's voice. "So Eloah has chosen the Temanite people in which to shed his light?"

King Eliada said, "Not as you are thinking. The Temanite people were the first, but only because they were the last to have fallen away from him and the first to have returned to call upon him once again, after their Dark Time. But anyone may do the same."

"Anyone?"

King Eliada nodded.

Queen Estrella approached the stone altar, gathered her long pink gown into her hands, and knelt.

King Arkelaus joined her.

33

The next day at the Temanite palace proved quite a busy one for King Eliada. While the castle servants prepared for Princess Mariya's birthday celebration—decorating the corridors and banquet hall, creating culinary masterpieces in the kitchens—the king spent many hours before the elders in the council hall, defending his dream.

"King Arkelaus of Rygia has come into Teman for one reason—to help his people escape the darkness that comes when one has no god. He and I are of the same mind on this. We wish to create an alliance between our countries to—"

"We make no alliances with unbelievers," Elder Eleazar interrupted.

"The king of Rygia is a believer as of last night," the king said.

The elders murmured among themselves. Eleazar said, "He is only one. What about the rest of his country? Will they be so easily turned?"

"That is hard to say, but I do know this. If we do not make an effort, they will surely fall to the darkness that is to come."

"If darkness comes to Rygia, what business is that of ours?" Elder Laban said.

"Laban, I'm surprised at you," the king said. "Do you not care what happens to our neighbors?"

"As long as it doesn't happen in this country. Our job is to keep ourselves and our land pure."

Eleazar said, "Laban is right. Imagine what mingling with unbelievers might do to our own people."

"It would lead us straight to destruction," Laban said.

Elder Nathaniel said, "You don't know that. Perhaps it would lead to the salvation of the Rygians."

Elder Reuben said with a tinge of anger, "Why are we even talking about this? The Rygians are the Kaion race!"

"Oh, pshaw, the Kaion," Nathaniel said. "They are no such thing."

"They are!" Reuben said. "When they first settled here, they had come from across the sea on large ships, as did the Kaion from eons ago. They do nothing but fight among themselves."

Nathaniel said, "At least they aren't fighting with us. If they were the Kaion, they'd be trying to destroy us."

"Perhaps they yet will," Reuben said. "And we're just letting them in. The Kaion had vowed to destroy us as they had destroyed the Volon. Since the Rygians are obviously not Elyon, they must be Kaion. Mark my words, one day they'll turn their weapons against us. We must do everything in our power to keep them out of Teman."

"Elders, please," King Eliada said. "I thought I would have more support than this. Sospater, you've been silent all this time. What is your opinion?"

Sospater said, "My opinion is to learn the will of Eloah in this matter. Without Areli here to speak for him, we have no way of knowing it."

"But when Areli last stood before this council, he did reveal Eloah's words to you," the king said.

"That was regarding allowing you to speak with the king of Rygia. Making alliance with Rygia is quite another matter."

Elder Reuben said, "Sospater is right. We need to hear from Areli before we can entertain any notion of alliance with an unbelieving nation. This is a highly irregular proposal, one requiring extreme caution and sure direction."

King Eliada threw his hands in the air. "All right, I will go to Areli. Perhaps he will find the strength to come to you himself."

~~~

If Rolland had thought the previous dinners were elaborate, he discovered he had only seen a sampling of Teman's propensity for grandness. Princess Mariya's birthday gala on the evening of September twenty-seven brought out more wondrous foods, more colorfully dressed people, and more bright decorations than before seen.

Banners of all colors lined the banquet hall, each boasting the emblem of a notable family line. Rolland recognized the king's golden lion, Garth's castle tower, and Captain Elkanah's golden elk, but there were so many more, including a black horse, a green star, and a golden ram's head.

As he stood looking up at the banners, he was interrupted by a bard with a lute. Instantly the bard made up a song about him.

"The general is large, and yes, he is quite tall. But even he must crane his neck to look upon the walls!"

Rolland felt heat rise in his cheeks as the people chuckled. Fortunately, General Garth ushered him to a table before another song could be composed. The other Rygians followed, making sure to give the bard a wide berth.

When Prince Josephus entered, his friend Stephen beside him, the bard approached. But Josephus gave him a stern look and said, "Get away from me." Stephen snickered while the bard moved to the high table to create a song for Princess Mariya.

As the two boys sat down, Rolland heard Prince Josephus say to Stephen, "I hope Father doesn't make me kiss her for her birthday."

With an announcement from a trumpet, two doors at the back of the room opened, and several servants emerged single file, each carrying a tray laden with food. Merry conversations were accompanied by the clinking of dinnerware as trays were passed from table to table.

General Garth said, "Rolland, you know that man I said might help you with your sword? He—"

"He what?" Rolland looked up from his plate to see that Garth was staring wide-eyed toward the main doors. From where Rolland sat, he could see the Temanite king at the high table also staring wide-eyed and open-mouthed toward the door, just as Garth was. The king's knife fell from his hand and clattered onto his plate. The entire room hushed.

Rolland looked to see why everyone was so awestruck. To his surprise, it was nothing more than a very old man, rather feeble looking at that. He wore a long brown robe with the hood down, revealing long gray hair, a long beard, and a weathered face. His gnarled wooden cane tapped the floor as he strode between tables and approached the dais.

The old man kept his gaze on the high table. The looks on the faces of the Temanites, especially King Eliada, was of utter astonishment. By the looks on the faces of King Arkelaus and Queen Estrella, Rolland would have thought they were staring at the face of a god. Charles Iscuro and the other Rygian soldiers, however, held looks more of fear.

He wasn't surprised, for even though the man appeared ordinary, something about him set Rolland on edge. So much so that he gave a start when he heard Garth whisper, "By Elán, that's him."

Rolland swallowed a lump in his throat. "*He's* the one who can tell me what the sword says? Never mind, I don't want to know."

~~~

Princess Mariya watched the old prophet with a trembling in her heart. His gaze was fixed on *her*. He strode up to her and looked down on her, right into her eyes.

She gasped. The mark of Eloah shone brightly in his brown irises—a thin green line in the shape of a star. It was the first time she had ever seen it.

Areli leaned his gnarled cane against the table and

placed both hands on her head. She heard him take a deep breath, and then he spoke.

"He hath broken down the middle wall of partition between us. Now shall two be made one, thus making peace, that both may be reconciled unto God." As if every last ounce of his strength had left him, Areli closed his eyes and let his shoulders slump. Picking up his cane, he slowly headed back toward the door.

Mari heaved a great sigh, having not taken a breath during the entire intense experience.

"Wait!" her father called. "Areli, come back!"

But the prophet continued on his way, the sound of his cane growing ever fainter.

Feeling a hot flush in her face, Mari put her hands to her cheeks. She could hear her father's voice, but it seemed like an echo from far away.

"There, elders, you see? Eloah has spoken and we must obey. The wall of partition will be broken and two shall be made one, thus making peace. That sounds like an alliance to me."

The next voice she heard was that of Sospater, but his voice, too, seemed far away and echo-like, as though he was inside a cave. "That may be, Your Majesty, but there is much left unclear."

Her father said, "Why else do you suppose the message was spoken in the presence of foreigners? If the message were meant for Teman alone, it would have been given to Teman alone."

"That is true, Sospater," Nathaniel said.

"Very well," Sospater said. "We will draw up terms for alliance first thing in the morning."

By this time, Mari's hot flash was running through her veins.

"Are you all right?" Queen Estrella asked.

"I need some air. Please excuse me." She pushed away from the table and headed outside.

A cool breeze touched the autumn evening. She walked

slowly amid the terraced gardens on the inner slopes of the coastal mountains. Her hot flash gone, it left a chill in its wake. Shivering, she wrapped her arms about herself.

"Mari," said a gravelly voice behind her.

She spun about, finding herself face to face with the prophet. "Areli, you startled me."

"Forgive me," he said with a slight incline of his head. In his hands was a cloak, which he placed on her shoulders.

"Thank you. What are you doing here? You don't look strong enough to be out."

"You have many questions, Princess. I came to answer them."

She shivered again and pulled the cloak more tightly around her neck. "I don't understand the prophecy, Areli. Was it about the alliance, as my father believes?"

"The others were meant to understand it in regards to alliance."

"Then why was it given over me?"

"Because it was meant for you."

"I still don't understand. If the prophecy was meant for me, why was it given in the presence of so many people, including foreigners and unbelievers?"

"It was given to Teman in the presence of foreigners so they will continue their plans for alliance. It was given to unbelievers so when it comes to pass, they will know that Eloah is God. It was given to you for it contained a message only for you. Many times in prophecy there is a nearer meaning and a distant meaning. Yours is the distant meaning."

"Then what am I to do with the message?"

"Carry it in your heart alone, until the fulfillment. Only then may you speak of it, for anything you may say before then is mere speculation. His ways are not our ways. Trust his ways."

"Why are the ways of Eloah so mysterious? Why must it always be a matter of trusting without fully understanding?"

"To fully understand is to have no need of trust."

"But if Eloah would explain it to us now, it would be so much easier for men to believe."

"Oh no, Princess, the opposite is true. If men were given too much of an explanation, they begin to see what they think is the prophecy's fulfillment in every little thing that happens. Or worse—they try to make it happen themselves. People tend to fulfill what they *believe* will happen for they make decisions based on their perception of the future. That perception is usually incorrect. Then, when things do not work out according to their expectations, they blame Eloah for not keeping his word."

"What should I do?"

"Just do whatever Eloah sets before you to do. Nothing more, but no less. Let that be an instruction to you." He stood silently for a moment. "May I say one thing more?"

"Please."

"Perhaps your father was right in not forcing you to marry too soon. Forgive me for having doubted."

She looked at him quizzically, but he said no more.

~~~

The banquet over, General Rolland and Charles Iscuro headed down the corridor toward the guest chambers.

"So, what do you think?" Rolland said.

"About what?"

"About making an alliance with Teman."

"I'm not paid to think, especially about something like that. But that prophet..." Charles shivered. "Sends a chill up my spine."

"Mine too. What do you think about the people?"

"They're all right, I guess. A bit reserved."

Rolland chuckled. "They probably think we're the reserved ones. You've hardly said a word since we got here."

"I don't have anything to say. I will say this—that prince and his friend are something else."

"Yeah, they are, aren't they? I like them. I..." He halted.

"Great stars, there he is." The cloaked old man was heading straight for them. Rolland shuddered.

"Like I said," Charles muttered. "Chills."

Areli stopped in front of them. "May I see your sword?"

Rolland wondered how the prophet knew about the sword, but he figured General Garth must have said something. Grasping the scabbard in his left hand, he gave it a shake. The sword slid upward, halfway out of its place. He pulled it out and held it horizontally before the prophet.

Areli laid the crook of his cane over his arm and took the blade in both of his wrinkled hands. He studied the entwining vines and the white wings edged in gold, then turned his attention to the jewels in the pommel and hilt. He seemed lost in thought for several minutes.

Finally he said, "This sword is older than you think. Older than the kings of Rygia. Older than Rygia itself."

"Older than Rygia? How did it come to my ancestors, then?"

"I cannot answer that for you." After more study, Areli said, "This sword has caused the dividing of many—race against race, kin against kin. It has seen the destruction of kingdoms and the severing of brethren."

He drew his finger along the etchings on the blade, a quizzical look on his face. Rolland was just about to tell him about the lettering when Areli brought the blade up to view the flat of it at eye level.

He's a smart old coot, Rolland thought.

Areli said, "There are letters hidden among the vines."

"I knew it! I mean, I thought they might be letters, but I didn't recognize them."

"They are in the ancient language, which has its own alphabet."

"What do they say?"

"Netish Machaira."

"What does that mean?"

"Vining Sword. It is the sword's name."

"Huh. That's appropriate, I guess."

Areli turned the blade over and gazed down the length of it for some time before saying, "The words on the other side are different. Shalosh Melek, Eva Keir. It means, Three Kings, One Hand."

"Three kings, one hand? What does that mean?"

"I know not." Areli turned his attention to the jewels in the hilt.

Rolland said, "There are words there too, by each gem."

"Indeed." Areli pointed to the diamond. "Saraph, meaning forged." He pointed to the sapphire. "Nasa, meaning borne or carried." He pointed to the ruby. "Galah, revealed."

"What does it all mean?"

Areli touched each gem again, slowly, deep in thought. "By Elán!" He put a finger on the ruby. "Red for Elyon." He pointed to the sapphire. "Blue... could it be Volon, perhaps?" He pointed to the diamond in the pommel. "That means this would be Kaion. But why a diamond for Kaion?"

"What the deuce? What are those words you're saying? Volon? El... what?"

"They are the three original races of mankind. Thus, what the sword is saying is, 'Forged by Kaion, borne by Volon, revealed by Elyon. Three kings, one hand.' Three kings, one of each different race. But one hand? How can you have three kings in one hand?"

"I don't know what you're talking about," Rolland said.

"You are not meant to know, for you are not the true owner of this sword."

A bit incensed, Rolland said, "Not the true owner? This sword's been passed down through the Longsword family line for generations."

"None of them were the true owners. They were only the guardians, as you are now its guardian. A sword-bearer, if you will."

"Sword-bearer for whom?"

"For one who is to come."

"Who is that?"

Areli only shook his head.

Since the prophet seemed to be finished, Rolland reached for the sword. But the moment he touched the hilt, Areli grasped his hand. Rolland jumped.

"You are not the last guardian of this sword," Areli said. "There will be another, perhaps two."

"Who are they?"

"Those who come after you."

"You mean like heirs?"

"Yes, your heirs."

"But I have no heirs."

Areli did not respond. Instead, he released the sword and turned a darkened expression to Charles. "I have a message for you as well, but you may not have the heart to hear it."

Charles crossed his arms over his chest and stared at the prophet.

Areli said, "Two paths are placed before you. One leads to darkness, the other to light. You must choose."

Charles said nothing.

Areli said, "One of your companions has chosen light. The other has chosen darkness. You remain in the middle. You have reached a crossroads and must make a choice. If you reject the light, darkness will steal your soul and devour your heart. Your time is short. Choose wisely."

With that, Areli took his cane in hand and departed.

"Spooky old ghost," Charles said when the prophet disappeared around a corner. "Prophet, ha! Just the ramblings of a daft old man."

"Why do you say that?" Rolland asked, still staring at the letters on the blade.

"Didn't you hear that gibberish he said about your sword? And he said you had an heir. Can't be any more wrong than that."

Rolland tossed that thought around in his mind.

"Well, one thing's for certain," Charles said.

"What's that?"

"I'm never coming back to this place. That's a promise."

34

When King Arkelaus' party returned to the southern plains of Rygia, they were met with news of the Gargon attack on the western border. King Arkelaus sent Rolland to join Captain Corden, then continued on his way to Archella, where he immediately sent for Demas.

"You called for me, Your Majesty?" Demas said as he arrived at the king's private chamber.

"Ah, Castellan," Arkelaus said. "I wish to send a message to all the barons of Rygia to meet with me at the earliest possible date."

"I'll see to it."

Arkelaus spread the Temanite documents on the table before him and sat down before noticing that Demas was still standing there, looking very worried.

"Yes, Castellan, what is it?"

"A certain, um… matter arose while you were gone, Sire."

"Yes?"

"It's about Prince Medan."

"What about the prince?"

"He went to Baron Alton's manor. He said it was for safekeeping during the Gargon attack."

"I see nothing wrong with that. Alton is a highly respected man."

"Yes, Your Majesty, but…"

"But what?"

"While he was there, he met a maiden."

"When you say *met*, what exactly do you mean?"

"You know very well what I mean."

"I see," Arkelaus said. "The indiscretions of youth. How I wish I could curtail such things in this realm."

Demas said, "This is not a good thing in light of his betrothal to Rolanda Godfrey."

"Unfortunately, he has broken no laws, unless there's more you haven't told me."

"No, that was all, except that he seems to be acting, well, differently."

"In what way?"

"He's been rather reclusive since returning. And I must add that he was very unhappy with your choice of his bride-to-be."

"I expected that. He will get over it."

"If you say so, Sire."

"Perhaps it will help if I speak to him. Send for him, will you?"

"Yes, Sire."

"Oh, Demas, before you go."

"Yes, Your Majesty?"

"King Eliada of Teman presented me with a mystery. I'll need your help in trying to find the answer."

"What is it?"

"Have you ever heard of anything called the Golden Leaves of Light?"

"No, Sire, I have not. What are they?"

"I don't know for certain, only that it was a gift given by Teman to the first king of Rygia, King Malchus Arkelaus. No one knows what happened to the gift after that."

"What would you like me to do, Your Majesty?"

"Search the archives. Especially look in the records during the time of the first king. See if there are any references to it."

"I will do that straightaway."

"After you bring Medan to me," Arkelaus said.

"Yes, of course."

"A servant girl?" King Arkelaus said when Medan came and told him what happened. "You had a dalliance with a servant girl? You're the prince! You're betrothed to marry the daughter of a baron!"

"I have broken no laws," Medan said. "And why shouldn't I have any maiden I choose, servant or otherwise?"

King Arkelaus couldn't believe his ears. "What are you saying?"

"I'm saying that Rygia has the most beautiful women in the world. Why should a prince of Rygia have to settle for anything less?"

"Rolanda is rather comely. She can make you quite happy."

Medan said, "I've seen Rolanda. Eva is much prettier."

"Eva? Is that your servant girl trollop?"

"Don't call her that!"

"She's not your wife, not even your betrothed. That makes her a trollop."

"Any commoner can have whatever woman he wants. Why should I be forced to marry someone I don't want? I'm the prince! I deserve whatever maiden catches my eye."

"Did Baron Alton put these thoughts in your head?"

"He didn't have to. But if he did, what's the harm? I should know my rights and privileges."

"Oh, my son, marriage is the greatest right and privilege a man can have. Do not sully such a beautiful thing with extraneous affairs."

"*I* have not sullied the marriage bed. *You* have done that for me by choosing Rolanda Godfrey." With that, Medan stormed out.

Arkelaus sat at his table and let his breath out heavily. As his eyes fell upon the documents from Teman, he felt despair rise in his heart. *How can we ever find light with this kind of attitude among my people? I fear for the realm if Medan should have control. Perhaps he can yet change.*

Demas knocked on the open door, holding a very large book.

"Come in, Demas! What have you found?"

"This is the history of Rygia at the time of the first king, King Malchus Alethos Arkelaus."

Arkelaus pushed the Temanite documents aside. "Set it here. Let's see what it says."

Demas set the book down and unclasped the hinge. As he began perusing the first pages, he said, "It tells here of how the barons of Rygia warred against each other for a thousand years, ever since they first set foot on this soil."

"First set foot on this soil? Does it say where they came from? Where they lived before that?"

"It says that they came in great ships from across the sea. They called their new land Rygia, for it was a rich land, filled with trees and rivers and fertile ground. Oh, here it is. They came from a land called Degar and had called themselves the Degarron, which means 'the lost ones.'"

"The lost ones? Intriguing. I wonder what made them lost? Does it say?"

"Let's see," Demas said. "It says that their homeland was overrun and they alone escaped—six tribes of the Degarron, each in their own ship. They traveled the seas in their six great ships, without a homeland, for many years, keeping to the vast ocean where their persecutors could not find them, with only brief excursions on small islands when needed."

"Persecutors? Who was persecuting them? And why?"

"That information isn't given. It goes on to say that the leader of the Degarron was Prince Arketos Aëtos."

"Prince Arketos Aëtos?" Arkelaus asked. "Interesting. Is there more about him?"

"Yes, it says that Prince Arketos Aëtos founded the royal city of Archella in Rygia and set himself up as king. But the heads of the other five tribes would not stand for that. Since this was a new land, they thought they should have a new king and did not need to hold to the first line. And so they no longer called themselves Degarron but began to refer to themselves as Rygian."

"But this Arketos," Arkelaus said. "He must be my ancestor."

"It stands to reason." Demas continued to read. "'The six tribal leaders set up their own territories and became powerful barons, building great cities and great stone castles. They built weapons of warfare to war against their kinsmen, fighting over borders and ultimate control of the realm.'"

"Yes, I am aware of that part. One thousand years of inner struggle before uniting under one king. Find that part, the part about the first king."

Demas turned a few pages. "Here it is. It says, 'One thousand years after settling in Rygia, a man of the line of Arkelia, Malchus Alethos Arkelaus...'" He looked up. "You were right, Sire."

"Indeed. Our first king was Malchus Alethos Arkelaus, of the line of Arkelia. That must be the line of Prince Arketos Aëtos. The prince must have altered his name later on."

"Or one of his descendants did."

"Yes, of course. Please, continue."

"Malchus Alethos Arkelaus rose up and brought peace to the land. He created a great army under the leadership of...' Hmm, that's odd. The name here has been blotted out."

Arkelaus rose and leaned in close to look. "Very odd."

Demas said, "Apparently this man whose name is blotted out worked together with Malchus Arkelaus to bring a solution to the strife."

"Ah, yes," King Arkelaus said. "The formation of the Rygian council."

"Yes, the council, where each baron was permitted to have a vote on an equal level with the king's. It says, 'At the very first meeting of the new Rygian council, they created a new flag under which they would unite—a silver eagle on a blue field.'"

"A new flag?" Arkelaus asked. "I wonder what the old flag was."

"It doesn't seem to be mentioned," Demas said.

"And we still haven't read anything about a gift from Teman. Read on, Demas."

Demas scanned the pages. "No, nothing. Nothing at all. Oh, here is an edict. Interesting."

"What?"

"It says, 'Immediately after the death of King Malchus Alethos Arkelaus, his son Mattan became king, after Malchus had reigned only four years. And Mattan decreed that never shall a Rygian set foot in Teman, nor will any Temanite be welcome in our land, for they are tricksters and deceivers, having brought death upon King Malchus."

"Oh my," King Arkelaus said. "I certainly hope the king's death had nothing to do with Teman's gift."

"There seems to be no other mention of Teman at all." Demas turned another page. "Ah! Look at this."

Arkelaus saw a familiar image drawn upon the page. "Oh yes, I have seen this picture before. It's a sarcophagus—the sarcophagus of our first king, King Malchus Alethos Arkelaus."

The picture was of a rectangular stone on which was etched the image of the king himself. He wore chainmail and a tunic, with a sword and belt, and a crown on his head. Above the king was a shield with an eagle emblazoned on it.

The king stood in front of a throne which sat on a dais with three steps. Behind the steps, to the left, was a doorway. Above the throne, to the right, was a window with light shining onto the king.

"Certainly is intricate," Demas said.

"Yes," Arkelaus said. "Each of these items has a meaning. I was taught this as a lad. The king's arms are crossed, signifying his humble yet brave spirit. He is dressed in mail and bears his sword, showing he was mighty in battle. The light from the window shines upon him, showing that he was enlightened with great wisdom."

"Very nice. I should like to see this sarcophagus myself."

"You cannot," the king said.

"Why not?"

"No one knows where it is."

"No one knows where King Malchus is buried?" Demas asked.

Arkelaus shook his head. "And that makes me wonder all the more if his death had something to do with the gift from Teman."

"How so?"

"Think of it, Demas. Rygia crowns its first king. Teman brings that king a gift. Shortly afterward, the king dies. His son becomes king and blames Teman for the death of his father. He rules that no Rygian shall ever set foot in Teman, and no Temanite will be welcome in Rygia. But no mention of the gift that caused the trouble, and someone's name is blotted out. Someone wanted to hide something."

"Maybe they wanted to hide the gift," Demas said.

"You know, you may be on to something. Perhaps the fact that the king's sarcophagus is hidden has something to do with it. Both the gift and the king's grave are hidden. Perhaps they are hidden together."

"It does seem possible," Demas said.

A knock on the open door revealed Baron Alton standing there. "Your Majesty, may I speak with you?"

"Yes, of course. Demas, would you excuse us?"

Demas bowed and left.

Alton stepped in and bowed his head. "My lord, I have heard some disturbing news, and I feel I must make amends immediately."

"Does this have something to do with my son?"

"Indeed, Your Majesty."

"Yes, well, I must say I am quite incensed at his behavior."

"I know, and if I was in any way responsible, I give my most humble apologies."

"Why would you be responsible? Did you fill his head with all that nonsense?"

"Of course not! I just felt that since it happened at my castle, with one of my maidservants, I should have known better. I should not have allowed it to happen. But, well, he is a young man, after all. A young man sees a pretty lady, and it was bound to happen."

"Hmpf."

"As soon as I learned what had happened, I immediately brought him back here, to remove him from temptation, as it were."

"Very wise, Alton. Well, as long as you weren't the one to put those irreverent thoughts in his head, I suppose I cannot hold you responsible. Thank you for your concern."

As Alton was about to leave, his eyes fell upon the open book on the table. "What is this, my lord?"

"It's an image of the sarcophagus of the first king of Rygia."

"It's beautiful. Are you studying it for some reason?"

King Arkelaus sat down. "Yes, and now that you mention it, you might be of help."

"Sire, you honor me."

"I know that you are a well-traveled man, Alton. Perhaps you've learned things on your journeys."

"What do you wish to know?"

"Have you ever heard of an item called the Golden Leaves of Light?"

"No, I can't say that I have. What are they?"

"Apparently, it was a gift given to the first king of Rygia."

"Given by whom?" Alton asked.

"By the people of Teman."

"Teman?" Alton suddenly looked very worried. "How do you know this?"

"I've met with the king of Teman."

"You what?"

"I've just returned from there."

"From Teman? You went to Teman?"

"Yes, I went to Teman. That seems to concern you."

"Oh, not at all. I'm just surprised. We all thought you were visiting Baron Vance."

"I was. From there, I went on to Teman."

"What were you doing there?"

"Merely making acquaintance. The Temanite king told me about this gift, this Golden Leaves of Light. He said that from it, one could obtain the knowledge of eternal life."

"Eternal life?"

"Yes. The gift was given to our first king, King Malchus Arkelaus." He motioned to the image on the page. "But the odd thing is, no one knows what happened to it. The king of Teman asked me about it, but I had never heard of it. Have you?"

"No, Sire, I have not."

"That's a shame. Such a mystery."

Alton stared at the book, a curious look on his face. "But, Sire, a visit to Teman? This is unprecedented. Why did you go there?"

"I intend to explain it all to the council at the next meeting, after General Rolland returns."

35

By the time Rolland reached Rygia's western lands, Captain Corden had already returned from Gargon and made camp in Falliwell's territory. Rolland found Justus inside his tent.

"Corden!"

"General, you're back."

"Yes, I'm back. Give me a report. Falliwell's men tell me you took the battle to the desert."

"I did," Justus said. "It only took a few days to drive them out of Falliwell's lands, but I wasn't about to let that son of a jackal get away from me again."

"Son of a jackal?"

"The Gargon leader, Barak."

"So that's his name," Rolland said. "I hope you gave him a sound thrashing."

"You bet I did. He'll never again speak the name of Corden without feeling a chill down his spine."

"So he's still alive."

"He is, but the same can't be said for his army. We annihilated them. I'm only sorry I couldn't take him out as well."

"Maybe you'll have another chance."

"I hope so. But at least I left him with a really bad taste in his mouth. One thing you have to know, though. If you ever fight on the western desert, don't take your chainmail. Once we took the battle into their territory, things started looking bleak for us until I had the men shed their armor. I lost more soldiers to the heat than to Gargon arrows."

"Hmmm. Speaking of arrows..." Rolland left the tent, grabbed his saddle pack from the back of his horse, and returned. He rummaged in the pack and pulled out the arrow General Garth had given him.

"What's that?" Justus asked.

"A Temanite arrow."

"Temanite? Where'd you get it?"

"From the general of the Temanite army."

"What? When did you—?"

"Listen, Corden. Don't breathe a word of this to anyone until King Arkelaus speaks to the council. He'll tell everyone then."

"Breathe a word of what?"

"That we were in Teman."

"You went to Teman and didn't tell me?"

"We didn't want the council to catch wind of it."

"Didn't you trust me?"

Rolland put a hand on Justus' shoulder. "I know I can trust you, and so does the king. But you were needed here, so there was no need to tell you. In fact, King Arkelaus never would've taken this trip if he didn't feel he was leaving the country in the best hands possible."

"I see," Justus said. "So what did you think of the Temanite army? What were they like?"

"Mark my words, Corden, they're not a force to take lightly. These men don't fight with mere weapons, they fight with their hearts. Rygians only fight for money."

"When's the last time Teman had a real battle?" Justus asked.

Rolland studied the look on Justus' face. "By the stars, Corden! Don't even think about testing our skills against theirs."

"Why not?"

"Why? I ask you, why? They're good people. They'll never give Rygia a reason to fight them."

"Oh yeah? Tell me about this God they believe in."

"Now that's another force to be reckoned with."

Justus raised his voice. "Don't tell me you believe it too!"

"I didn't say I believe it, I said it's a force to be reckoned with. The fact is *they* believe it. There's power in faith, even a misplaced faith."

"You don't have to tell me that," Justus said.

"What do you know about faith?" Rolland said. "What does Rygia ever put faith in? I'll tell you. Whoever puts money in their pockets, be he good or evil. And therein lies our greatest weakness."

"We have a good king on the throne," Justus said. "He's worthy of our faith."

"Let's hope that's enough."

"Enough for what?"

Rolland said, "What if Rygia had a bad king on the throne? What then?"

Justus gave no answer.

Rolland said, "You know, I once thought I saw something different in you, something better than everyone else. That's why I singled you out from the other squires."

"I thought it was because I was good with a sword."

"Sure, you were good. But you were good in more ways than with a sword. I could see that in you. But now I'm not so sure."

"Yeah, well, I've learned a few things along the way."

"Like what?"

"Like you don't put your trust in any sort of unseen God!"

Rolland stared at Justus long and hard. He knew what Justus was referring to. He knew what had made him so bitter.

He shook the Temanite arrow at him. "King Arkelaus will be speaking with the council about forming an alliance with Teman."

"What!"

"Don't plan on attending unless you'll stand in support of the king. Because if you speak a word against this alliance, I'll throw you out of the hall myself!"

Seeing the anger on Justus' face, Rolland turned his attention to the arrow in his hand. "The Temanite general gave me this as a gesture of peace. He said it shows that their trust isn't in weapons but in their God."

"I hope you haven't fallen for this idea of an unseen, all-powerful God in Teman."

"Not just in Teman, Corden. He's everywhere."

Justus' mouth dropped open. "Don't tell me you're a believer already!"

Rolland shook his head. "No, Corden. Like you, I'm not so easily convinced. But I do find it interesting. And there's something about being there, meeting the people, that makes it... I don't know. There's just something about it."

Justus poked a finger at Rolland. "I'll tell you this, General. If there *is* a God in Teman, it's he who took my wife from me. I have no respect for people who believe in a God like that."

Rolland tapped the arrow against one hand. "As I told you, this was given to me as a gesture of peace." He handed it to Justus. "Now I'm giving it to you. I think it's long past time you let your heart have peace."

~~~

Justus spent his entire journey home thinking about what Rolland had said. When he reached his cottage he found it empty, so he sat down on a bench and leaned back against the wall, holding the Temanite arrow.

Good people, huh? Power in faith? Katrina said the same thing. But it wasn't enough for her. It didn't save her.

He stared at the arrow, rolling it between his fingers. *A gesture of peace, he said. Oh, blast it all, it's been six years. Why can't I let it go?*

A cry of delight interrupted his thoughts. Six-year-old Anna bounded into the cottage and leapt into his arms. "Papa!" She smothered him with kisses.

Bett came panting. "You're home, Master Corden!"

"All right, that's enough, Anna." Justus set her on the floor.

Anna looked at the object in his hand. "What's that, Papa?"

"An arrow."

"Where'd you get it?"

"General Rolland gave it to me. It's from Teman."

Her face lit up, and she scurried off toward the bedroom, returning with a little black book. "This is from Teman too!"

Justus frowned. "Where'd you get that?"

"Bett said it was Mama's. Was it Mama's, Papa?"

Justus stared at the book, turmoil churning in his gut.

"Read to me, Papa."

"No, Anna, put that away."

Bett tried to bustle Anna into the bedroom. "Come, now, don't you be bothering your father with that."

Anna struggled out of Bett's grasp and held the book toward her father. "Please, Papa?"

Justus snatched the book from her and thrust it toward Bett. "Put this away. I never want to see it again."

"I'm sorry, sir. She found it last week and asked me what it was."

"Did you read to her from it?"

Bett lowered her eyes. "Yes, sir. When she learned it was her mother's, she begged and begged until I gave in."

"Don't be filling my daughter's head with that kind of nonsense. Put it somewhere where she won't find it."

"But why, Papa?" Anna said. "Why won't you read it to me?"

"Do as I said, Bett." Justus stuck the arrow into his belt and took Anna's hand, leading her out of the house so Bett could do as she was told beyond the gaze of curious eyes.

"Why, Papa?" Anna asked as they walked down the path. "Is it a bad book?"

Justus didn't answer.

"Was it Mama's book, Papa?"

He heaved a sigh. "Yes, it was Mama's book."

"Would Mama have a bad book, Papa? Would she?"

He stopped and gazed down at her innocent, pleading blue eyes. Now he understood what difficulty Bett faced when Anna wanted something. He didn't have the heart to say no.

Maybe Rolland's right. Maybe I have *become too hard.* He pulled the arrow from his belt and gazed at it. *All right, Rolland, you win. Time to make peace.*

"Would she, Papa?" Anna asked again.

"No, Mama would not have a bad book."

"Can Bett read it to me?"

"Yes, Bett can read it to you."

36

On the day of the council meeting, Rolland stood in the doorway, watching Justus arrive. He squared his frame to block him from entering.

"What're you doing here, Corden?"

"I've come to stand by my king."

"Are you certain?"

Justus said, "King Arkelaus charged me with protecting the royal line. If that means standing by him in whatever he undertakes, so be it."

After a thoughtful pause, he added, "He once did something for me, more than I can ever repay. He deserves my complete allegiance, and he shall have it."

Smiling, Rolland slapped Justus on the back and they entered the room together, taking their places behind King Arkelaus and Queen Estrella. The councilmen were already seated at the high table and were poring over several documents that King Arkelaus had brought.

The discussion did not go well. Not only were the councilmen incensed that the king had gone to Teman without their knowledge, but most were not of a mind to form an alliance with Teman.

"Just look at these demands," Drake said. "They want to know what we'll do to provide for orphans and widows. What business is it of the Rygian council what happens to orphans and widows?"

"It's a humanitarian concern," Arkelaus said. "The Temanites are concerned for the good of our people."

Alton leaned forward. "Why is the good of our people of such concern to them?"

"Baron Alton, not you too," Arkelaus said. "I would've thought that a man as well-traveled as you would see the benefits here."

"Benefits?" Alton said. "As I read these documents, I get the impression we're being fattened up for the kill."

Baron Vance said, "I disagree. It looks to me like Teman has a great deal to offer. Look at this list of trade items. Teman is indeed a wealthy country."

Baron Erskin said, "You only say that because your territory is close to theirs."

Baron Falliwell said, "I agree with Vance."

"Your territory borders Teman as well," Erskin said. "These two shouldn't be allowed to sway the rest of us just because of where they're located."

Carlin said, "If they're already wealthy, what do they want from us in return?"

Arkelaus said, "They are interested most of all in shipbuilding. They would like to enjoin the services of our sailors and shipbuilders to teach them their skills. And they would like a plot of land along the sea just to the north of the mountains where they could build and harbor their new ships."

"For what purpose?" Carlin asked. "Don't you think they might turn around and use our own skill against us? Marine navigation is the one advantage we have over them. I say we keep our advantages to ourselves. You never know when we might regret having given them too much power."

"Indeed, Your Majesty," Councilman Beary said, his pudgy lips forming a pucker as he spoke. "This document is full of stipulations that would put them in a position of authority over us."

"Such as?" King Arkelaus asked.

"Well, here for instance." Beary picked up a parchment and read, "'Rygia shall make no alliance with any other country without the permission of Teman's governing body.'

They seek to regulate our very existence. How can we deny trading agreements with other countries without cutting off our own means of support? Would we not endanger ourselves by—"

"Trade agreements are not the same as alliance, Lord Beary," King Arkelaus said. "This document specifically says *alliance*, not trade agreement. Teman is only doing that to protect both themselves and us."

Alton picked up another document. "They also seek to regulate the amount of ale and various tonics that come into Rygia. What right does any other country have to limit our freedoms?"

"Freedoms for what?" Arkelaus asked. "Drunkenness?"

"Anyone, man or country, who seeks to impose such stringent regulations on a man's private life will soon be taking over the entire realm," Alton said. "It looks to me like they wish to seduce us into submission by offering us gold and taking away our freedoms. Soon we'll have to go begging them for the basics of life. Do not let this list of trade items fool you, men of the council. It's nothing more than bait for the hook."

Rolland glanced to Justus and shook his head. This was not going at all well. But to his surprise, Queen Estrella rose from her seat. The room hushed.

In a soft voice, she said, "Gentlemen, you do us ill to think so little of this endeavor. Perhaps you are looking with eyes of the present, and that is your mistake. Look at this alliance with eyes of the future. You ask us to think of Rygia, of what we will become, if we were to ally ourselves with Teman. I ask you to think of what we will become if we do not."

She began to walk around the table, pausing behind Lord Carlin. "Yes, we have been strong enough to look out for ourselves, but do you really feel our strength will last? Look around you. This country is filled with hate, selfishness, greed, brutality. How much longer can a kingdom such as this stand?"

She moved to stand behind Baron Erskin. "If we continue to believe we are self-sufficient while we surround ourselves with decadence, we will crumble from within. What Rygia really needs is a guide to help us learn to strengthen ourselves with goodness that we might be able to stand in a day of trial."

As she stepped behind Lord Beary, she said, "Look again at that list of trade items. Medicines... healing skills... food crops we have never heard of... new methods of cultivation and irrigation... Are these not of untold value to us? Things such as these are for our good, not our ill."

Standing behind Lord Drake, she said, "This alliance means more to Rygia than bread and gold. It means life. If we wish to survive as a people, we must learn to care for one another. Therein will lie our strength—not in hate, not in the sword, but in compassion. Only by serving one another instead of using one another will we become as strong and united a kingdom as Teman."

Rolland saw a scowl on Alton's face as the queen moved to stand behind him.

She said, "Councilmen, do not throw away our future. If you are still uncertain as to the terms of this alliance, may I suggest an alternative? Ask for a trial period. Give the alliance one year. If you are not satisfied that Rygia has become a stronger, more unified kingdom, then pull out. We will have lost nothing. But I trust we will have gained much."

Finished with her discourse, the queen returned to her seat at the king's side.

Rolland smiled. All the men, save one, were visibly moved by her speech. It looked as though they might be won over.

Baron Alton, however, remained stone-faced. The king opened his mouth to speak, but Alton preempted him.

"Men of the council, we have heard some very powerful words from the queen. May I suggest we take time to think upon them before we make a decision? Perhaps we can reconvene at this time tomorrow."

Rolland heard Queen Estrella whisper to the king, "I believe they are near to a favorable decision. If we wait, some may change their minds."

Beary said, "Your Majesty, Baron Alton has made a good point. We've been at this for many long hours now. All of us could use some time to rest and clear our heads. You've given us much to think about, my lady, and I would like an opportunity to mull your words over."

Since the other councilmen seemed to be in agreement, the king acquiesced.

Rolland kept his eyes on Alton, whose scowl never left his face.

The next morning, Rolland stood with Captain Corden near the high table, awaiting the king's arrival. The councilmen were already there. The king was late. *Not like him to be late.*

"Corden, go to his quarters and see... Oh, here he is." Seeing a very grave expression on the king's face, Rolland whispered, "By the stars, whatever's wrong?"

Corden shrugged.

Baron Alton said, "Why, whatever is the matter, Your Majesty?"

"The queen. She has taken ill."

"Taken ill? All of a sudden? What do you suppose it is?" Alton asked.

"I don't know. She is pale and feverish and doesn't respond to me."

"That does seem serious indeed," Alton said. "Shall I send for a physician?"

"Yes, please do."

Rolland watched Alton hurry out.

The members of the council ate their breakfast in silence. When Alton returned, he brought the physician, who had bad news. "It seems to be some sort of plague, but it's not like any plague I've seen before."

"A new plague?" Alton asked. "Where could it have come from, I wonder."

The physician said, "Did you not tell me that the queen has recently returned from Teman?"

Alton said, "Why yes, you're right. Your Majesty, did you not say the queen of Teman herself had died after suffering a long illness?"

King Arkelaus glanced to Rolland. "I did."

"Oh, my," Alton said. "I do hope Queen Estrella didn't contract a plague from there."

Rolland said, "A plague from Teman? The rest of us haven't come down with anything."

Alton said, "They haven't yet. That doesn't mean they won't. I trust the queen has been confined to her chamber to keep it from spreading."

"Of course," the physician said. "Only the maidservant and I are allowed access to her."

Alton said, "In light of this, I think we ought to delay today's meeting. The king does not appear able to handle additional stress. Let us reconvene, say, in one week. Are you agreed, gentlemen?"

The council members agreed.

Rolland noted the look of despair on his king. The vigor gone from his countenance, he looked as though he were very, very tired. Frowning, Rolland knew something was strange about this whole idea of a plague, but he couldn't put his finger on it.

Alton leaned back in his seat and tapped his fingertips together. "Let us hope it is merely a plague and not foul play. You never know about those Temanites."

"How dare you suggest such a thing!" Arkelaus shouted, roused from his despondency. "Foul play, indeed!"

"One can never be too cautious, Sire," Alton said. "We must not rule out any possibility."

Rolland narrowed his gaze at Alton, a cold chill running down his spine. *Foul play, indeed.*

37

Queen Estrella remained ill the entire week.

At the end of the week, Rolland found the king in the great hall, alone. "Where's the council? I thought they were meeting today."

The king shook his head. "They've left. With Estrella still sick, they didn't want to be in the castle."

Rolland let his breath out in a huff. "What about the alliance talks?"

"Nothing I could say would convince them to consider alliance with Teman now. Not with the possibility of new plagues from that land. Only Baron Vance sided with me."

"What about Falliwell? I thought he was in favor."

"Not anymore. He changed sides."

"I'm sorry, Your Majesty."

"No more sorry than I, my friend. I believe we may never see this dream come to pass." He leaned forward on the table. "What do you think, Rolland? Do you think it's a plague from Teman?"

"Plague or no, I don't believe it came from Teman."

"Neither do I, but there is no convincing the council. I shall have to suspend any more visits with King Eliada for the time being. With threats of a plague, no one will be allowed into that country for a long time."

Rolland left the king and headed toward the soldiers' barracks, but he pulled up short when he spied Alton talking with Prince Medan. He ducked behind a hay wagon to keep out of sight but within earshot.

"I can see Your Highness is quite distressed over the

health of your mother," Alton was saying. "I think a little travel might brighten your countenance. You know, get away from all these cares and find a quiet place to relax, gather your thoughts."

"I'm not sure, Alton." Medan's voice sounded weary to Rolland. "I don't think I should be away at this time. Mother might need me."

"Oh, but even you are not allowed near her chamber, Your Highness. No one would like to see the plague befall the prince."

"Do you really think I could catch it?"

"One can never tell who might be susceptible. Perhaps putting a little distance between yourself and the palace is just what you need."

"No, I don't think that would be wise."

"Eva was asking about you."

"She was?"

"Indeed," Alton said. "I see she still catches your interest. Why not come? Just for a short visit. A day or two perhaps."

"Well, maybe a short trip wouldn't hurt."

A voice behind Rolland's ear startled him. "Taken to spying now, General?"

In one swift movement Rolland drew his sword, wheeled about, and found himself face to face with Captain Corden.

"Corden, you imbecile! I nearly sliced your head off."

"What're you doing here?" Justus asked.

"Looking for rats."

"You mean Alton?"

"Never you mind what I mean." Rolland scratched his chin. "Now why would Alton want the prince to visit his manor?"

Justus snorted. "While you were gone having your secret little visit to Teman, and I was busy defending the country from Gargons, Alton appointed himself the prince's guardian and took him to his manor. For safekeeping, he said."

"And you let him go?"

"What could I do? I may not like Alton, but there was no harm in it. If you'd been here, maybe it wouldn't have happened."

"Maybe, maybe not. So who is this Eva?"

"I'm not one of the prince's personal confidantes. However, I did overhear one of his escorts talking about it."

"What did he say?"

"Not much, just a young man's first fancy, nothing serious."

"Nothing serious? Haven't you heard that Prince Medan is betrothed to Baron Godfrey's daughter?"

Justus crossed his arms. "I heard. I also heard that Medan's not exactly pleased."

"And you don't think it's serious that he's involved with another maiden?"

"Hey, if I was betrothed to Godfrey's daughter, I might do the same thing."

Rolland grabbed Justus by the collar. "You watch your tongue."

Justus shook himself from the general's grasp. "What's with you? Do you know this daughter of Godfrey's?"

"No, but I knew her mother."

Justus glanced down at the small leather pouch hanging from Rolland's belt. "Oh, the charm! You mean Godfrey's daughter's mother was your woman?"

"Yeah, and that's enough reason for me not to hear any guff from you about her daughter."

"But you said she chose to leave you. She didn't love you."

Rolland only grumbled.

Justus said, "What I can't figure out is what made King Arkelaus choose Godfrey's daughter in the first place."

Rolland jabbed a finger in Justus' chest. "*You*, that's what."

"Me? What're you talking about?"

"Ever since you bested Godfrey in that tournament, he's carried a grudge."

"That was nine years ago!"

"Yes, and during that time he's denied all invitations to the palace, held back his royalties three times, and threatened to secede from the realm twice. Have you seen him at a council meeting lately? All because he didn't like the fact that you were made captain of the King's Guard."

"Why didn't you tell me?"

"You were dealing with enough trouble after your wife died. Besides, King Arkelaus didn't want you involved. You were much too valuable to risk getting hurt in a civil confrontation. He wanted you to concentrate on your duties, not look over your shoulder everywhere you went."

"The king did that for me?"

"Yes, he did. Didn't you ever wonder why he suddenly blotted the Joust of Death from the books? He didn't want Godfrey coming back someday seeking revenge."

"So King Arkelaus proposed this betrothal to smooth things over?"

"Actually, it was Godfrey who practically demanded it. King Arkelaus agreed in order to keep the peace. You have to admit, Godfrey's been much more congenial ever since."

"He still hasn't come to council meetings."

"But he's started paying back his lapsed royalties." Rolland leaned against the hay wagon. "If Medan refuses to marry Godfrey's daughter, it could create a national incident. That's why I don't like the idea of him going off to Alton's manor, especially if it involves some scullery maid."

"Do you think we should try to keep Medan away from Alton?"

"How do you propose to do that? He's a snake, that one." Rolland pointed with his thumb to where Alton had been standing earlier.

"We ought to at least tell the king what Medan's up to."

Rolland shook his head. "Not now. You should've seen him in there. He's taking this illness of the queen's pretty seriously, not to mention the effect it's having on the alliance talks. We better let it go for now. Just keep a look out."

~~~

Throughout the winter Queen Estrella remained bedridden, although she did experience occasional respite from her illness. On days she chose to fast, she found a measure of strength returning, but whenever she ate she would fall sick again, sometimes worse than before she fasted. Despite this, the physician discouraged fasting, saying in this weak state she must take sustenance whenever she could.

Winter finally passed. The fresh spring breezes wafting into Estrella's chamber made her feel a little better, a little stronger. One day she insisted King Arkelaus take her for a short walk to the window, where she sat and prayed. She fasted all that day and the next and began to feel stronger yet, until she felt able to walk even farther.

On the third day of her fast, the king took her to the roof of the palace where she could sit in the sunlight. That day she told Arkelaus she felt strong enough to attend a council meeting.

"Are you certain?" Arkelaus asked. "This is the first time you've left your room."

"Not only am I certain, I am adamant," she said. "I've not been happy the alliance talks came to a halt because of me. And we were so close, too. Now that winter is over, I'd like to see you return to Teman, hopefully with the news that we will accept their terms of alliance. I think if I can show the council that I am better, and remind them that no one else has fallen ill from this mysterious *plague*," she said the word with disgust, "I may convince them to give it a try. If not, I had another idea in mind."

"What is that, my dear?"

"Perhaps you could go to Teman and bring King Eliada here. Once the councilmen meet him, they are sure to like him and to consider the alliance."

Arkelaus played with his golden beard. "Now that is an idea. I like it, Estrella. Such a wise woman I've been given for a wife and queen." He placed a tender kiss on her forehead and helped her return to her room.

Later that afternoon, the king sent messages to Rygia's councilmen, telling them to gather in one week and informing them that the queen would attend.

The next morning King Arkelaus walked cheerily through the corridor toward Estrella's room. He was looking forward to seeing her smiling face as he had the day before. And he was especially hopeful about the council meeting that was to convene in just six days.

Surely they'll listen to Estrella, he thought as he opened the door to her chamber. *She has such a way of convincing people that—*

He halted. All the life drained from his body.

The queen lay sprawled on the floor, her skin a ghostly blue. He rushed to her side, but it was long over.

She had been dead for hours.

Every woman in the castle wore a veil over her face to mourn the beautiful Queen Estrella who would grace the palace no more. Rolland stood next to Justus as the body was carried out of the castle on a pallet, covered with regal robes of red, blue, purple, and gold.

~~~

Rolland couldn't remember the last time he felt like crying. He certainly did now.

As the body passed in front of them, Justus said, "You really think Teman had nothing to do with this? Looks like foul play to me."

"Give me one good reason why!" Rolland said, sadness roused to anger. "If you know so much about Teman, tell me why they'd do such a thing. They're *good* people, Corden. Don't you forget that."

He quieted his voice. "But you're right about one thing.

This does look like foul play. Someone's willing to go to extreme measures to prevent this alliance, and I intend to find out who. And why."

Justus said, "The council's forbidden any further discourse with or about Teman."

"Yeah, I know. That concerns me almost as much as the queen's death. We have to inform Teman."

"You'd dare send someone there?"

"I don't dare not to." Rolland scratched his stubbly beard. "It'd have to be someone I trust."

Justus shook his head. "Don't look at me."

"I wasn't thinking of you. You'd be too easily missed."

"Who then?"

"Charles Iscuro. He can ride fast."

"But does he have the heart for it? I heard he didn't like it there at all."

"We'll see." Rolland sent a squire to bring Charles to him.

When Charles arrived and Rolland told him the assignment, Charles responded with, "Over my dead body!"

"Shh! Not so loud."

Charles whispered harshly, "I'm not going back to that place, especially not alone. What about the plague?"

"There is no plague," Rolland said.

"That's not what I heard. Face it, Rolland, the queen died from a Teman plague, and I don't want to catch it."

"Look, if you really don't want to go, I'll send Ironfist instead. But I'd rather send you. You can ride faster."

"The only way I'll go back to Teman is if someone drags my dead body over."

"You don't have to go all the way in, just deliver the message to the garrison at the pass."

Charles narrowed one eye at the general.

Rolland said, "I'll be paying you from my own pocket."

That convinced him. "All right, I'll go."

"Thanks. And listen, Iscuro." Rolland lowered his voice yet further. "Watch your back."

Charles never made it to Teman.

When a week passed and Charles didn't return, Rolland sent a small party to search for him. They found his riderless horse in the foothills of Teman's mountains, but no sign of Charles was ever uncovered.

Rolland considered going into Teman himself to follow up on the search, but in the state King Arkelaus was in, he didn't want to leave him. Nor did he want anyone else to catch wind of Charles' disappearance so close to Teman. That would only deepen their suspicions about plagues and foul play.

But from that day on, Rolland gave greater consideration to the words the prophet of Teman had spoken to Charles. *"Your time is short. Choose wisely."*

"Oh, Charles, I'm sorry," Rolland said aloud to himself. "I should never have sent you." Charles' own words now seemed prophetic. *"I'm never coming back to this place."*

"No, you never did, did you? That old prophet was right. Your time *was* short."

Prophet? Rolland pulled out his engraved sword and ran his fingers over the ivy carvings on the blade. *If he was right about Charles, could he have been right about this?*

But he could only shake his head. He had no heir. The prophet must have been mistaken.

38

After a year of mourning for the queen had passed, spring returned to Rygia. With it came the promise of a brighter future, for it was time for Prince Medan to be married. Rolland found that even King Arkelaus was happier.

When the week of the wedding arrived, the entire palace was grandly decorated with bright banners. Everyone living in the city of Archella, and even in cities beyond, turned out for the feasting on the first day of celebration.

The next few days were filled with games, including a tournament. Rolland didn't waste his time making any challenges, and neither did Justus. The two sat together, waiting for challenges to come to them rather than expending their strength on challenges of their own.

More challenges came to Justus than to Rolland, which made Rolland happy. As he watched Justus win every joust in fairly short order, he felt a sense of relief, knowing there was someone in Rygia who could fill his shoes.

On the final day of the week came the wedding ceremony itself. The only dull spot in the grand affair was where Prince Medan stood next to Lady Rolanda Godfrey with a glum expression.

Both fathers stood nearby, beaming proudly.

Rolland had never met Rolanda before, so he took a moment to study her. Aside from looking a lot like her mother, she appeared stately and serene, with a somber look on her face. He wondered how she'd fit in at the castle and whether she'd one day make a good queen. Of course, anyone would have a very hard time filling Queen Estrella's shoes.

Giles Godfrey's nephew Gregor stood next to Rolanda. While Rolland wasn't surprised that she had brought her own champion, he was surprised at her choice—the heir to Giles Godfrey's fortune.

When the ceremony was finally over, another great banquet began in the courtyard of the castle. Rolland couldn't help but notice how quickly Medan rushed through his meal and hurried away from the table, away from his new wife, preferring to stand with Baron Alton.

Baron Godfrey kept near to King Arkelaus, talking and laughing loudly as though the two were lifelong friends. Rolanda remained at the table, Gregor at her side. Both sat in silence.

This has got to be the gloomiest wedding I've ever seen, Rolland thought.

Justus approached him. "I'm heading home."

"What? Not staying for the dance?"

Justus chuckled. "Me?"

"You dance the galliard quite well. I've seen you."

"There's no one here I care to dance with."

"You'll be leaving plenty of broken hearts, I'm sure."

Justus snorted.

Rolland slapped him on the shoulder. "Go on home, then. You're not needed here. I'm sure your daughter would like to see her papa."

"Now there's an idea," Justus said. "She'll make a nice dance partner."

As night fell and musicians struck up a dance tune, Rolland decided he'd just as soon get home as well. He headed toward the king to take his leave, but as he walked past the main table and glanced at Rolanda, something caught his attention. He stopped short, stunned.

Rolanda had pulled a pendant from around her neck and sat twirling the chain in her fingers. Firelight danced off the charm—half of a golden heart covered in fine filigree, identical to the ivy on his sword.

And identical to the half heart in his belt pouch.

Great stars! How did she get that? Great stars!

He didn't realize he was staring until Rolanda said indignantly, "Do you want something, General Longsword?"

Rolland shook himself back to reality. "I, um..." He cleared his throat. "I was just admiring your pendant. Excellent craftsmanship. Where'd you get it?"

"It was my mother's. She gave it to me the day she died."

Great stars! Juliana. She kept it. She kept it until she died. But why give it to Godfrey's daughter?

The truth struck him like a javelin. *Rolanda? Great stars! She named her after me!* His knees went weak and he nearly toppled over backward. As he stumbled away from the table, he heard Gregor mutter, "He's drunk."

Rolland barely made his way into the palace. Finding a bench in the great hall, he plopped onto it, alone in the shadows of the large room.

She's mine. Rolanda's my *daughter, not Godfrey's.*

A jumble of thoughts crowded his mind. *How much does she know? How much does Godfrey know? No, Godfrey doesn't know, I'm sure. He never would've kept her if he knew. He wouldn't have kept Juliana either.*

He opened his belt pouch and dropped the broken charm into his hand, sitting mesmerized, staring at it under the dim light of a dying fireplace.

No, no, no, it's not possible. Godfrey would've found out by now. I would've found out. I must be dreaming. Maybe that's not my pendant.

Deep in thought, he hadn't noticed when someone approached. A shadow passed over him and he looked up to see Rolanda standing there, staring open-mouthed at the broken pendant in his hand.

Silently she removed the chain from around her neck and dropped her pendant into Rolland's hand, next to its other half.

A lump stuck in Rolland's throat. "Did you know?"

Rolanda shook her head, eyes glistening.

"She never told you?"

Rolanda said softly, "Just before she died, she gave this to me and said, 'The man I love gave me a part of himself when he gave me this. And when he gave me you.' That's all she said. I never knew it was you."

Rolland's eyes brimmed. "Does anyone else know that you aren't Godfrey's daughter?"

"No one but Gregor."

"You're a wise woman."

"Perhaps I get that from... my father."

Tears spilled down the mighty general's cheeks at the sound of those words.

Rolanda sat down next to him. "Tell me about her. About the two of you."

"Juliana," he said, barely finding his voice. "I wanted to marry her, but her father wouldn't allow it. I was only a mercenary back then, a sword for hire."

He cleared his throat, sad memories halting his speech. "I thought she loved me. I thought we'd be together forever, even if we couldn't marry. I gave her this," he indicated the charm, "as a promise of..." Again his voice caught.

Rolanda said, "It has the same engravings as your emblem. I hadn't noticed that before."

He nodded. "I had it made special, just for her. But the morning I gave her this, she told me the news."

"What news?"

"Her father had pledged her to marry Godfrey. She'd known for some time, but she put off telling me until the last. Until she had to leave the city."

"I'm so sorry."

"When she told me that, I threw this against the wall. That's how it broke. She took one half and left me the other." He looked into Rolanda's eyes. "I thought she didn't love me anymore. I thought that was why she left."

Rolanda squeezed his hand. "She never stopped loving you. I often saw her holding this in her hand, crying."

"Blast it all. Was Godfrey good to her?"

Rolanda gave him a look that told him the truth.

"Blast it all! I should've come for her. I should've taken her away from him. I was a fool."

"You're not a fool. I couldn't be happier if the sun itself claimed to be my father. I must say, I'm proud to be a Longsword, if only in my heart."

She drew her arms around his neck, and he returned the embrace. When he looked up, he saw Gregor standing in the doorway, staring at them with an open mouth. Rolland quickly pulled away.

Rolanda said, "It's all right. Gregor keeps my secrets."

Rolland looked from her to Gregor and back again. "Oh, great stars. Prince Medan isn't the only one unhappy with this marriage."

She shook her head. "No, he's not. At least Gregor's promised to stay with me as my champion. I won't be alone here."

Rolland squeezed her hand. "You'll never be alone. Not as long as I'm here."

She smiled.

39

Summer passed. Rolland was pleased to keep watch over his daughter each and every day. And each time Rolanda looked at him, she gave him the brightest smile. They never spoke openly together, but volumes were shared in simple glances.

Gregor was always there too. Always at her side. Except when she was in the prince's chamber, which wasn't very often.

Rolland also noticed how Rolanda and King Arkelaus were growing close. It was good for the king, he could tell. Arkelaus seemed to enjoy having a woman in the palace again. Rolanda treated him with great respect and love, doting over him as though she were his own daughter.

She's a wise one, Rolland thought.

By the time autumn arrived, King Arkelaus was much more like his old self again. Rolanda's presence had dispelled the gloom of Queen Estrella's death. When the king told Rolland he was ready to make another visit to Teman, Rolland was glad to hear it.

On the day they were to leave, he called for Captain Corden to meet him in the stables. After seeing to it that the king's carriage was being made ready, he began to saddle his own horse.

Justus arrived and said, "You wanted me?"

"Yeah." Rolland looked left and right. Seeing they were alone, he said in a quiet voice, "The king and I are making another trip to Teman."

"What?"

"Don't tell anyone. Let everyone think we're going to Vance's."

"No one will believe you after what happened last time."

"Doesn't matter. You know, you can come with us this time, if you had half a mind to."

"You won't catch me going there."

"That's what I thought. That's why I'm putting you in charge of the soldiers while we're gone."

"Who's going with you?" Justus asked.

"Geoffrey Ironfist."

"Only the two of you and the king?"

Rolland nodded. "Brody didn't want to go, and I didn't want anyone else. Ironfist likes Teman. All the other soldiers think there's plague there."

"Yeah, well, so do I," Justus said.

"Don't be an idiot, Corden. Plague, my eye. No one else came down with it."

"Not yet. We'll see what happens when you get back."

Rolland glared at him but let it drop. "Listen, I want you to keep a close eye on Medan. He's married now. He shouldn't be traipsing off for secret dalliances."

"All right."

"And Corden, do me a special favor."

"What's that?"

"Keep watch over Rolanda for me."

"Why? She has her own champion."

"Just do it, for my sake. I told her if she needed anything, to see you."

"Why'd you tell her that?"

"Because I trust you, all right? Now don't ask me any more questions."

Justus shrugged. "If you say so. But what about you? Don't forget, Charles never returned from there. How will I know when to send a search party after you?"

"We don't even know whether Charles made it *into* Teman. His horse was on our side of the mountains, remember? We never did find his body."

"Did you ask Teman for it?" Justus said angrily.

"When will you listen to me? Teman wouldn't have taken him. I tell you, there's something amiss here. *Here*, in Rygia. There's a snake in the house, Corden, and I think I know who it is."

"Who?"

Rolland looked over each shoulder, then tightened the girth on his horse's saddle. "I don't want to endanger this journey by saying anything prematurely. What we're doing is too important. But when I return, I intend to find the snake and put it out of my misery.

He leaned closer to Justus. "I'll tell you one thing. I don't want to be next on the casualty list."

Justus crossed his arms. "Like I said, how long before I send a search party?"

"Give us a fortnight. If we're not back by then, you better come looking. But if it's foul play you're looking for, I suggest you start right here."

~~~

King Arkelaus sat at the table in his antechamber, studying the large book of Rygia's history. Opening to the page with the image of King Malchus Arkelaus' sarcophagus, he wished he had good news to bring to the king of Teman—that he had found the gift called the Golden Leaves of Light, or at least a clue to its whereabouts. But he had found nothing.

He called to one of the king's guardsmen standing outside his chamber door. "Brody! Fetch Rolanda for me!"

Brody left and returned shortly with Rolanda. He stepped into the room and bowed. "Lady Rolanda, Your Majesty." When he lifted his head, his gaze fell to the open book on the table.

Arkelaus said, "Thank you, Brody, you're dismissed." Brody stepped out.

Rolanda curtseyed. "You wished to see me, Your Majesty?"

"Yes, my dear. I'm leaving today to go visit Baron Vance. I wished to take my leave of you."

"I shall miss you and eagerly await your return."

He smiled. "And I you. I trust all will be well while I'm gone. Rolland's coming with me, so if you have need of anything, ask Captain Corden. I put him at your disposal. He is very trustworthy."

"I will. Thank you, Your Majesty."

~~~

Sometime after the king had left the city, Baron Alton heard a quiet knock on the door of his personal chamber within the Rygian castle. "Who is it?"

"Brody."

When Alton opened the door, Brody stepped in carrying a large leather satchel. "I have something for you."

"Show me." Alton motioned to a table in his antechamber.

Brody set the satchel on the table and pulled out a large book.

"The historical book," Alton said, breathless. "You got it."

"Just like you said."

"Are you sure the king was well away before you took it?"

"Watched his carriage till it was out of sight."

"Oh, Brody, you have done very well." Alton sat at the table and caressed the book with his hands. "Very well, indeed."

He leaned back in his chair and grinned. "Of all the sons I've fathered with my maidservants, you have proved yourself the most worthy. Getting a position in the King's Guard, going to Teman, now bringing me this. Keep it up, and you'll be the one I choose to inherit all my holdings."

"Thank you, Father."

"Never call me that!" Alton said through his teeth.

"I beg yer pardon, my lord."

Alton caressed the book's cover again before opening it and finding the page with the image of the sarcophagus. "The Golden Leaves of Light, that's what the king had said. The secret to eternal life, he said. Given to the first king of Rygia. The mystery must be revealed somewhere. It *has* to be."

"Uh, my lord?"

"Yes, what is it?" Alton said without looking up.

"It's about King Arkelaus. He ain't going to Vance's. He's going to Teman again."

Alton stared at him. "You sure about that?"

"Course I'm sure. Rolland asked me if I wanted to go along again. I said no."

"We need to tell Prince Medan immediately, and then make sure the rest of the people hear about it."

~~~

Rolanda raced through the palace entry and burst into the armory. "There you are, Gregor. Did you hear what's happening?"

"No. What's the matter?"

"Prince Medan is decrying his father in the streets. He's rallying the people against their king, claiming the king has gone to Teman again."

"You think it's true?"

"That doesn't matter. What the king does is his right, and whom he tells is his right. What does matter is the prince is speaking treason. Against his own father!"

"What should we do about it?"

"I don't know." She began to pace. "I am loath to hear him say such things against King Arkelaus. I myself would shut his mouth if I could."

"You don't dare. You have to keep your hands clean, as do I."

"You're right. We must find someone else." She stopped pacing. "Captain Corden! He's our man. Go find him."

~~~

Justus couldn't quite believe what Gregor told him until he headed toward the city and found that a large crowd had gathered. Prince Medan stood in the center of the crowd, having just finished his discourse. As Justus made his way through, he could hear the people speaking against King Arkelaus.

"Prince Medan's right. We ought not to make alliances with those strange people."

"They're wicked people, I heard. Just want to take over our land."

"I hear they have dark eyes. People with dark eyes ought not to be trusted."

"Why would the king go back there?"

"He must be enchanted. They cast a spell on him, I'm sure."

"Someone oughta deliver him."

Justus shoved his way through the crowd and approached Prince Medan, but was nearly taken aback by the fire he saw in Medan's eyes.

"What do you want, Captain?" Medan said angrily.

"You're speaking treasonous words, Your Highness. Your father doesn't deserve this from you."

"My father no longer sees reason. He's been bewitched by Teman. It's my responsibility to do what must be done for the good of the realm."

"Neither your father nor Teman has done anything against Rygia," Justus said.

Alton said, "Really, Captain? Is that what you truly believe? Tell me, where exactly do you stand? Are you for this alliance or against it?"

Justus had to think on that one. He wasn't sure what he thought about Teman, but he knew what he thought about King Arkelaus, the man who had once rescued him from himself.

He said, "I'm loyal to the Arkelian line, first and foremost to King Arkelaus. Where he leads, I follow."

Prince Medan squared his shoulders, defying Justus'

words by his stance. No doubt, Justus thought, because Alton was standing behind him.

"Teman killed my mother, Corden, either by plague or by poison. I will not stand with my father if he insists on allying with a country that will destroy us."

Justus hesitated. Medan had a point. If Teman truly did have something to do with Queen Estrella's death, then an alliance would surely be a mistake. But since neither King Arkelaus nor General Rolland believed Teman was at fault, Justus was left in a quandary.

He spoke in a gentler tone. "Your Highness, if you have anything against your father's behavior, you should've taken it to him first, not brought it before the people."

Now it was Medan's turn to hesitate. Justus also had a point.

Alton's eyes darted from Medan to Justus and back, a worried look on his face. "Your Highness, perhaps we should consider the captain's words. Maybe we've been too hasty. I have a suggestion. Why not wait for your father to return? See if he comes back safe and whole, with no hint of plague or foul play. If that happens, I think we should all be willing to hear what he has to say about alliance."

Medan said, "Perhaps that is worth considering."

"But if anything happens to suggest otherwise," Alton pointed at Justus, "I think *you* ought to reconsider where to place your loyalties."

~~~

Later that evening, Rolanda stood before a very angry Prince Medan in the prince's private chamber.

"You were the one who sent for Corden, weren't you?" Medan said.

"I was," she answered defiantly.

"You dared to set yourself above me?"

"You dared to set yourself above your father the king. You dared to speak against him."

"You're as insolent as your father! You're trying to

undermine my authority, aren't you? What are you after? Or perhaps I should ask, what is your father after? He's been a thorn in the king's side for years. It was because of your father this marriage was forced upon me. He must be trying to wrench the kingdom from my hands. Do you know what the penalty is for sedition?"

Rolanda said, "If Godfrey had wanted to commit treason, he would have done it years ago. On the contrary, it is you who seek to undermine the king, not him!"

Medan reached his hand back to slap her but stopped himself. His gaze grew darker. "You had better watch your step, my lady. We shall see who is the real traitor around here. Now get out."

Rolanda raised her chin and stood tall as she exited the room. Once the door was shut behind her, she let her breath out in relief, then went to find Gregor.

Gregor advised her to send for Godfrey immediately, which she did.

40

Rolland, Geoffrey Ironfist, and King Arkelaus were welcomed with open arms by the king of Teman. When King James Eliada heard the news of Queen Estrella's death, he expressed his deepest condolences.

"I do hope this doesn't put a stain on our relationship, Magnus," King Eliada said. "Between your realm and mine, I mean."

"I'm afraid it does. My council will have no dealings with Teman for fear of strange new plagues."

"I am so sorry. Is there anything I can do?"

"There might be."

"Let's talk about it at dinner this evening. My servants will show you to rooms where you can rest and freshen up."

"Thank you, James."

As Rolland and Geoffrey began to follow King Arkelaus and King Eliada through a corridor, a Temanite servant came running up to the Rygians.

"Sirs! Sirs!"

King Arkelaus said, "Yes? Something I can do for you?"

"Not you, my lord. General Rolland Longsword."

"Me?" Rolland asked.

"Yes, sir. Prophet Areli has asked to see you."

Rolland gulped. "To see me?"

King Eliada said, "Best not keep him waiting, Longsword. Areli is one hundred nine years old. He's confined himself to his room during his last days. It's highly unusual for anyone to be called to see him."

Rolland followed the servant to the prophet's room.

When the door opened and he stepped in, he expected to find a decrepit old man in a bed. Instead, he found the prophet sitting at a table with parchments, quills, and ink bottles. He wore the same long brown robe with the hood down, and his gnarled wooden cane leaned against the table near where he sat.

Areli waved a wrinkled hand. "Ah, Longsword, do come in. Shut that door, will you?"

Rolland shut the door, leaving himself alone with the prophet.

"Come, come, sit." Areli motioned to a chair on the other side of the table. "One moment, please."

As Rolland pulled up a chair, he watched Areli dip a quill into an ink bottle and write on a parchment. He studied the old prophet's face. He looked very much older than two years ago, as though he had aged a decade. His hand shook a little as he wrote. But for his great age, he didn't seem as foreboding as last time. He looked more like an ordinary old man.

"There." Areli set down his quill, picked up the parchment, and blew on the wet ink. "I am the last, you know. The last of the line of Areli. The last prophet of Teman. It wasn't supposed to be this way, but here it is. Teman will be left without a prophet for the first time since our Dark Time over two thousand years ago. For us, that is almost as bad as being without a king."

Rolland stared silently at the prophet, who stared back with brown eyes in a bed of wrinkles.

"But I'm sure you know nothing about that. And why should you? But this..." Areli waved a hand over a pile of parchments, all filled with his writing. "This is for posterity. Everything I have learned, everything I have said, it's all here. There is just one more entry I wish to make."

He leaned back. "May I see your sword once again?"

"What for?" Rolland asked.

"I wish to draw it."

"Draw it?"

"Yes, to record it for posterity."

"Why would Teman's posterity care about a Rygian sword?"

"It is not a Rygian sword. It belongs to all the races—Elyon, Volon, and Kaion. Please, allow me to see it."

Rolland pulled the sword from its sheath and laid it across the table.

"Ah, Netish Machaira, the Vining Sword." Areli spoke with awe in his voice, old eyes lighting up, fingers brushing along the vines on the blade. "So beautiful. And so mysterious."

He dipped his quill into an ink bottle and began to draw on a new parchment. Without looking up, he said, "Have you thought about the words I said to you the last time you were here?"

"Lots of times. Mostly about how I'm not the last one to carry this sword. I've since learned that I have a daughter."

"Ah, the next sword-bearer. You must give this sword to her and tell her everything I have told you."

"You said there could be another. Who comes after her?"

"That would be her child, I suppose."

"She doesn't have any children."

"Not yet."

Rolland's eyes grew wide. "Great stars! She's married to the king's son!"

Areli looked up. "Ah! So if they have a child, he would be heir to the throne of Rygia. A proper sword-bearer indeed."

"But you said no one in my line was the true owner."

"That is correct. Even if your heir becomes king or queen of Rygia, he or she would still not be the sword's true owner."

"Who's the true owner, then?"

Areli tapped the blade. "Three kings, one hand. When you find the person who fits that description, you will have found the sword's true owner."

"Three kings?" Rolland looked to each of the three gems. "How can there be three kings in one hand?"

Returning to his work, Areli said, "Let me answer your

question with a question. Do you know what race you are, Rolland Longsword?"

"I'm Rygian."

"That is your nationality. But what race are you?"

"What do you mean?"

Areli looked up. "I see. You don't know."

"How do you know I don't know?"

"If you knew, you wouldn't have asked what I mean." He returned to his drawing. "Where did you come from, Rolland Longsword?"

"Um... Archella."

"No, not you personally. Your family line. Where did they come from, originally?"

"I don't know. Across the sea somewhere."

"Did they come along with the rest of your people? When your people first settled in the northern land twelve hundred years ago?"

Rolland sat back and thought for some time.

Areli said, "Did your father ever tell you? Did he pass down any knowledge at all about the sword or about your line?"

"I was young when he died. He tried to tell me a few things on his death bed, but he was gone too quickly."

"Ah. He probably thought he'd have more time. Thought he could wait until you were older. But death has a way of taking people by surprise." Areli looked up with a twinkle in his eye. "Not me, of course. At my age, I won't be surprised when it comes."

Rolland chuckled. Surprisingly, he found himself actually liking the old prophet.

Again Areli returned to his work, keeping his eyes on the parchment while he talked. "What did your father tell you on his deathbed?"

"Not much. Just that this sword's been passed down through the family and that there might be a message in it."

As he watched the prophet work, he saw the image was nearly half done already. For an old man, he had worked rather quickly and accurately. The picture looked just like the real thing.

Areli said, "Is it that your father didn't tell you much, or that you don't remember much?"

Rolland had to think on that one. "I don't know."

Areli set the quill down. "Take my hand."

Rolland looked at the prophet's extended hand quizzically.

"Take it. It won't hurt."

When Rolland grasped the weathered hand as in a handshake, Areli closed his eyes and stayed silent for several moments, not moving except for the rising and falling of his chest.

Finally he said, "Yes, it is dim. You were filled with grief. Not listening closely. Not hearing. Only seeing. Seeing your father die before your eyes."

"What? How are you—?"

"Shh. It is old, your father said. The sword comes from across the sea, he said. The secret is in Addir, he said."

"What's Addir?"

"Shh." Areli laid his free hand on the hilt of the sword. "The sword came late to Rygia. It came during Rygia's civil strife. One thousand years of war on Rygia's soil. No one listened. No one heard the sword's message."

After a long pause, Areli released Rolland's hand and opened his eyes.

"How did you do that?" Rolland asked. "Have you done that before?"

"No. First time."

"Then how did you know to do it?"

"I was told to do it, and so I did."

"Told?"

"By Eloah."

"What's it all mean?"

"The meaning was not given to me, only the revealing." He pointed to the ruby in the hilt. "Revealed by Elyon. The meaning, however, will have to be a task for others."

"Others?"

Areli tapped the blade with a gnarled finger. "Three kings, one hand. And look here, this flower. Three petals, again signifying three kings in one."

"You are so frustrating. You're just making the mystery deeper, you know."

"Yes." Areli pointed to the sapphire. "But this... this may be the deepest mystery of all. Borne by Volon. Are you certain you have never heard that word before I spoke it to you?"

"No, never."

"That is the question, then. The sword came late to Rygia. It did not come with the others when they first settled that land. But did it come with Kaion or with..." his voice trailed off to a whisper, "...Volon? Did it come 'borne by Volon'? If it did, that would mean the Volon weren't completely destroyed by the Kaion. Could some have survived?" He shook himself. "Seems impossible, doesn't it?"

"What? What's impossible?"

"I must look into this further. Eloah grant me the strength. And the time."

When Areli had finished the drawing, Rolland joined King Arkelaus and Geoffrey Ironfist in the banquet hall. Most of the tables sat empty this time. Only a few were laid out with white linens and table settings. King Arkelaus sat at the high table with King Eliada.

Rolland and Ironfist were directed to sit at one of the lower tables with Prince Josephus and Stephen Elkanah, as last time. Josephus and his friend were sixteen years old now, with eyes full of mischief. The prince wore the same thin golden circlet on his head, mostly hidden among his thick brown curls, and the same golden medallion around his neck.

General Garth came to Rolland with a hand extended. "Good to see you again, Rolland."

"And you, Jed." Rolland clasped his forearm.

Garth tousled Stephen's light brown hair. "I just heard what you two did. You are in so much trouble."

Stephen ducked away, obviously not caring to have his head tousled. His long bangs fell into his eyes, so he flicked them away with a shake of his head.

"What did they do?" Rolland asked.

Garth teased, "Yes, Stephen, what did you do? Tell us."

"Aw, come on," Stephen said, flushing.

But Josephus burst out laughing. "It was so great! We should do that again!"

"Oh no, you don't," King Eliada said loudly from the high table. "No more cliff diving."

"But, Father!" Josephus said.

"I'll hear no more about it."

Josephus settled back in his seat. At first he looked disappointed, but then he cast a sideways glance and smile to Stephen.

Rolland said, "Cliff diving, huh? How high was it?"

"A hundred and fifty feet!" Josephus said proudly.

"Great stars!" Rolland said.

Stephen tried to hold in his laughter and wound up making some kind of stifled snorting sound, which only made him and Josephus laugh out loud. Rolland couldn't help but laugh along with them.

An announcement from the doorman distracted them. "Her Royal Highness, Princess Mariya Eliada."

Princess Mariya walked in wearing a white and gold dress and a lavender robe. Now twenty years old, she was quite a beautiful young lady, with thick, dark brown hair wound in braids all around her circlet of gold.

She stopped in front of Rolland. "It's good to see you again, General Longsword. And you, Geoffrey Ironfist."

"And you, Your Highness," Rolland said.

She took a seat next to her father at the high table, while the seven black-robed elders gathered together at one of the lower tables.

As servants began to bring the meal, King Eliada said, "I

wished to make this dinner a bit more private than last time, so you can feel free to talk while we eat."

Rolland listened as King Arkelaus told about the Rygian council's unwillingness to consider alliance and about Queen Estrella's mysterious illness and death.

Arkelaus ended by saying, "I was hoping I might convince you to come to Rygia, James. Perhaps by meeting you themselves, my people will be more open about continuing a relationship."

"An excellent idea!" King Eliada said.

Head Elder Sospater said, "Your Majesty, this is unprecedented. You ought to give it a good deal of thought before making a decision."

Elder Reuben said, "More thought? What is there to think about? A king of Teman has no business going to Rygia under any circumstances."

King Eliada said, "I am certain that if King Arkelaus agrees to ensure my safe passage, all will be well."

"No!" Elder Laban said. "Send someone else. A high official of some sort."

Princess Mariya said, "Send me, Father."

Elder Nathaniel said, "Now that might be a good idea."

"No!" Elder Reuben said. "No member of the royal line should ever set foot there. Not in Rygia, not on any foreign soil."

King Eliada said, "It won't be Mari nor any other official. I wish to go myself."

"We will not allow it," Reuben said.

As Rolland listened to the discourse between the Temanite king and his elders, he realized that King Eliada was having just as much difficulty over this alliance as King Arkelaus had with the Rygian council.

He whispered to Garth, "This alliance is never going to happen."

"More's the shame," Garth said.

Amid the crescendoing conversation, Rolland gradually became aware of a sound in the corridor. Faint at first, it slowly grew louder. First a tap, then an echo, then a moment of silence. Another tap, an echo, and a moment of silence.

As the sound came closer to the banquet hall, the room stilled. The men quieted so quickly that Rolland could hardly believe they had just been arguing loudly.

Prophet Areli stepped in and slowly walked through the room, past empty tables and toward the table where Rolland sat, coming to a halt right behind Rolland.

Rolland craned his neck to look up into the prophet's face. To his amazement, he could see a green star nearly glowing within the prophet's brown irises. This was not the pleasant old man he had just been with—this was someone altogether different. He shivered, goosebumps dotting his skin.

Areli looked first at Rolland, then at King Arkelaus, and lastly at King Eliada. "Each of you must find one thing before your quest is finished."

Facing Rolland, he said, "Your quest is for the sword's true owner. You come from a line of faithful sword-bearers, all guarding Netish Machaira until its true owner is revealed. Remember the message—three kings, one hand." Areli turned his gaze away, and Rolland breathed again.

The prophet looked to King Arkelaus. "Your quest is light for your dark realm. You must find the light in justice. Through the light of justice will you find the true king who will lead your realm to righteousness."

Lastly, he looked to King Eliada. "Your quest is mercy. A dark moment will come to you—a moment where you will be faced with a dreadful task. You must find the light of mercy in the darkness, for only mercy and forgiveness will bring peace. The cost will be great, but you must find that mercy within your own heart."

He began to leave, but he stopped and looked again at Rolland. "Work quickly, for your time is short." With that, he continued on his way toward the door.

Rolland felt the blood drain from his face. "Wait!" He jumped to his feet, Garth right behind him. Catching the prophet just outside the door, he said, "What do you mean, my time is short?"

The green star in the prophet's eyes burned right into his soul, and immediately he regretted having asked the question.

But the prophet softened his expression and said, "Do not fear. If you cannot complete the task, the sword's last bearer will." Areli turned and walked away, leaving Rolland standing agape.

He felt Garth's hand on his shoulder. "You all right? You look rather pale."

"I don't know. I need some air."

Garth took Rolland through a corridor and out onto the stone courtyard. "What happened?" he asked. "You look like someone just walked over your grave."

"Those words. He said the same thing to Charles Iscuro. He said to choose wisely for his time was short. And then Charles died.

"Perhaps if he *had* chosen wisely, he'd still be here."

"I want to choose wisely," Rolland said. "I want to choose the light, like Geoffrey has. How do I do that, Jed?"

Garth smiled. "It's easy."

~~~

King Eliada sat in confusion for a few moments after Areli left the room. Finally he excused himself from the table and caught up to Areli in the corridor. The two walked in silence for a time.

When they reached the prophet's chamber, Areli said, "Why are you following me, James?"

"I... I just wanted to be with you. I'm afraid..."

"Afraid of what?"

"I'm afraid I don't understand. I'm afraid of the dreadful task you said I'd face."

As Areli turned to look at him, King Eliada saw that his eyes were moist. The look on his face made him think perhaps Areli knew much more than he was saying.

The prophet's countenance softened, and he gripped the king's hands tightly in his own gnarled hands. "I shall see you again soon."

James smiled. "I'm glad to hear that."

Areli opened his mouth to speak, then seemed to think better of it. Turning away, he muttered, "How little you understand, my friend."

The next morning King Eliada escorted the Rygians to the pass and bade them farewell, leaving them with a promise that by spring he would convince the elders to allow him to visit Rygia. But upon his return to his palace, hope once again fled from his spirit.

The prophet Areli had died.

When it came time for the burial, the king stood with Mari and Josephus on a grassy hillside covered with white gravestones, his aching heart a lead weight on his chest.

"I've known Areli Beth-Birei since my earliest days," he said to no one in particular. "He had stood beside my father and my grandfather during their reigns. He was already an old man when I took the throne. I cannot imagine a kingdom without him in it."

Looking at Josephus, he wondered, *How can this happen in Teman? Being left without the line of prophets. My son... What kind of realm will he inherit without an Areli at his side?*

By the look on Josephus' face, the king knew his son was thinking the same thing.

"I don't understand," the king said. "He told me I would see him again soon. Those were his last words to me. What could he have meant?"

41

As King Arkelaus and his two soldiers emerged from the woods of the foothills, he gazed, unfocused, across the Rygian plain. He rode in silence, thinking on the words the prophet had told him. *"You must find the light in justice. Through the light of justice will you find the true king."*

"True king? I wonder what he meant by that."

Rolland remained silent, evidently deep in his own thoughts.

Arkelaus said, "And that prophecy for you, yet another mystery. A line of sword bearers? Netish Ma... what were those words he said?"

Rolland pulled his sword from its sheath and laid it across the saddle, running his finger along the ivy on the blade. "Netish Machaira. I need to tell her. I need to tell her everything."

"Tell who?"

"You're not going to believe this, but—"

Rolland's voice was cut off sharply. At the same time, King Arkelaus heard a sharp whizzing sound and a dull thud. Rolland slumped forward, an arrow protruding from his back.

"Rolland! Rolland!"

Geoffrey placed his horse between the king's and the area where the arrow had come from. But all was silent again in the wooded foothills. No more arrows came. No sounds of soldiers. Nothing.

Rolland began to slide off his horse.

"Rolland!" Arkelaus sprung from the saddle and

managed to catch the body just before it hit the ground. "Rolland!"

No response.

"Help me, Geoffrey!"

Geoffrey dismounted and helped the king lay Rolland's body down. "Sire, we should leave. Now!"

"He's not breathing. He's dead. By Elán, he's dead!"

"Sire, we must move!"

"We need to go back to Teman," the king said.

"No!" Geoffrey said. "That killer's still there somewhere! We need to get you away now!"

The two hefted Rolland's body up and laid it over the horse's saddle, then rode as quickly as they could to Ravenhill, the nearest village. From there, they sent a messenger to get Captain Corden.

~~~

Justus beat his horse mercilessly until it was near collapse. Pulling into a village, he took the first horse he could find. He rode all through the night, changing horses as often as he could.

By the dim light of morning, he reached Baron Vance's lands. Ahead on the plains, he sighted the king traveling toward him, surrounded by several of Vance's men-at-arms. Beside them, a wagon lumbered along. The sight of the wagon made Justus' heart sink deep into his stomach.

As he neared, he could see by the look on King Arkelaus' face that Rolland was indeed dead, as the messenger had told him. The body lay on the bed of the wagon, covered with the general's long blue cloak bearing the image of the ivy-covered sword.

Justus leapt from his horse and bounded toward the wagon, muscles tense, jaw set. He reached toward the cloak but hesitated, his hand hovering just above the blue fabric. Forcing himself to continue, he threw the cloak aside.

"Rolland! Great stars, Rolland!" Feeling the king's hand on his shoulder, he said, "What happened, Sire? Who did it?"

"I don't know. I am so sorry, Captain."

One of Vance's soldiers held out two halves of a broken arrow. "This is what killed him, Captain. Looks pretty strange to me. Can't say as I recognize it. It's not one of ours."

Justus snatched the arrow from the soldier. "Temanite," he said through his teeth.

"Pardon me, sir?" the soldier asked.

Justus shook the arrow at the king. "This is a Temanite arrow, Sire."

"But... how can that be?" King Arkelaus asked.

"I think I can guess!"

"How do you know it's from Teman?"

Justus pointed to the shaft. "This wood. We don't have this kind of tree in Rygia. And the way the fletches are attached to the shaft. This is Temanite craftsmanship."

"No!" Arkelaus said. "It's not as you think."

Justus asked the soldier, "Did you look for the killer?"

"Yes, sir. We combed the woods but found nothing. Whoever it was could easily have gotten away before we arrived there."

"So it came from the woods in the foothills?"

Geoffrey said, "Yes, Captain, just after we left Temanite territory."

"Did anyone go into Teman to ask about it?"

Geoffrey said, "I took the king away from there quickly. Didn't want anything to happen to him. It was only him and me, after all."

King Arkelaus said, "I was ready to return with Vance's men, but they prevented me."

Vance's soldier said, "You know we're right, Your Majesty. Who knows what might be waiting for you back there. You need to gather your full forces before you even think about setting foot in Teman again."

"I agree," Justus said. "Sire, send me to Teman with a contingent. I can question them and learn the truth about—"

"No! I refuse to send an opposing force there. I don't want them to feel threatened."

"*They* threatened *us*!" Justus waved a hand over Rolland's body.

Arkelaus said, "Going to Teman in full force will accomplish nothing. I do not believe a Temanite did this."

"Why not?"

"It's not their way. They're good people... noble people."

"That's what Rolland thought, and look what happened to him!"

"That's just what they want us to think."

"They who?"

"Whoever did this. Listen to me, Corden. Do not succumb to anger. And do not turn on Teman. Someone wants this alliance stopped, and they were willing to kill to do it."

Rolland's words rushed into Justus' mind. *"There's a snake in the house, Corden, and I think I know who it is. I'll tell you one thing... I don't want to be next on the casualty list."*

He slammed his fist into the wagon.

King Arkelaus laid a hand on his shoulder. "Don't give up on this alliance, Captain. I need you to stand by me in this. Don't let Rolland's sacrifice be for nothing."

"Sacrifice! Sacrifice for what? For whom? Why does there have to be a sacrifice? Rolland didn't deserve this!"

Arkelaus spoke quietly, but his gaze penetrated deep into Justus' memory. "And what would this world be like if we all got what we deserved?"

The words brought to Justus' mind something the king had said to him long ago.

"I don't deserve mercy by your hand," Justus said.

"And what would this world be like if we all got what we deserved? Nevertheless, mercy is what you shall have."

Justus' anger began to subside, only to be replaced by unbearable grief. "What do we do now?"

King Arkelaus stepped close to Justus and spoke so only he would hear. "The subversives may very well be among our own people. I no longer know who to trust, therefore I cannot send a contingent to Teman. But would *you* go... alone?"

"No!"

"Not even for me?"

Justus' shoulders slumped. "Yes, Sire. For you, I would."

"Good. I need time to think on this, but sending you may be the best thing we can do. Let us tend to Rolland's body, and then we shall decide."

Justus held Rolland's ivy-engraved sword as he stood in the pasture behind Rolland's cottage. Before him, Rolland's body lay in a pine box. Next to it, workers finished digging the grave.

A crowd had gathered. An angry crowd.

King Arkelaus somehow managed to calm them. He had made Justus and Geoffrey swear not to tell anyone that the weapon was a Temanite arrow, but the rumor was already spreading.

Prince Medan called for an immediate attack on Teman. King Arkelaus put a quick end to that, saying they must first send communication to try to discover the truth.

Fortunately, a heavy rain began to fall. Cold and wet, the people hurried back to their homes before the pine box was lowered.

Justus remained, rain dripping from his hair into his eyes. When he wiped it away, he saw that King Arkelaus was still there, as well as Rolanda and Gregor. Rolanda's face was streaked with rain and tears.

The workers picked up the lid for the box and looked to Justus. Solemnly, reluctantly, Justus laid the beautiful sword in Rolland's cold hands.

"Seems a pity we'll never see that sword again," the king said.

Justus said nothing.

The king opened a small leather pouch and dropped its contents into his hand, showing the golden heart to Justus. "I found this on his belt. Looks expensive. Too bad it's broken. What do you think we should do with it?"

Rolanda spoke up. Gripping a pendant at her neck, she said, "I think... I think he'd want it with him."

"I agree." King Arkelaus dropped the heart into the pouch and laid the pouch gently on Rolland's chest.

The lid was nailed on and the casket lowered into the ground. When Justus finally left the scene, Rolanda still remained.

4
DARKNESS

42

On the evening after Rolland's burial, Justus stood outside the closed door to King Arkelaus' chamber, hearing a tempestuous exchange inside. Prince Medan stormed from the room, a cloud of anger on his face.

Justus rapped on the open door. "You called for me, Sire?"

"Yes, Captain, come in."

As he stepped in, he could see the worry on the king's face. "Forgive me, I don't mean to intrude. Shall I come back later?"

"No, Captain, stay. I wish to speak with you."

"About what, Sire?"

"I've been reconsidering whom to send into Teman to learn the truth about Rolland's death. Assuming the truth is to be found there and not here."

"Sire, I've already accepted that task."

"I know you have. I just want to make certain that *you* are the right person to send."

"I don't fear for my life."

"That's not what concerns me."

"Then what is it?"

The king paused for several moments. "You know of my search to bring light to this dark land, do you not?"

"Yes, Sire, Rolland told me a little."

"Well, now my son knows it too. As you have seen, he did not take it well." He shook his head. "I will not live forever, you know. My son must lay hold of the same vision I have, for it will be up to him to carry it out when I am gone. And yet his heart is already filled with darkness. He will not listen to me."

"What did you say to him?"

"I told him I have come to believe in the God of Teman, as did his mother. He became rather agitated by that. He has this idea in his head that Teman will bring us danger. I no longer know how to reach him, Justus."

Justus had no answer for the king, for he struggled with his own feelings regarding Teman. All he could say was, "He might also fear the plague that—" He stopped himself.

"That what? That killed his mother? My wife? Do not be afraid to say it. I have come to terms with the death of my wife and found the peace my spirit needed. You must also find that peace."

Justus frowned. "I was willing to be open-minded about this alliance with Teman until Rolland was killed."

"You are bitter against them," Arkelaus said.

"Why shouldn't I be?"

"I cannot send a bitter man to Teman."

"Sire, the truth must be discovered—"

"And it will be. But I don't think you are ready."

"But, Sire—"

"Look at me, Captain. Do I not have the same cause to be bitter? I lost a wife, as did you. I lost my dearest friend, as did you. Yet I do not blame Teman. In fact, I found my healing there."

"But Rolland was killed by a Temanite arrow."

The king's voice became stern. "You must understand something, Captain. The people of Teman are not to blame for any of this. Teman offers us hope and light. If dark things are happening in Rygia, do not blame the light. You must *find* the light, Justus, not shun it."

Arkelaus gave a start at his own words. "Find the light in justice!"

"Pardon me, Sire?"

A look of awe spread across the king's face. "It's *you*."

"What is?"

"'Through the light of justice will the true king be found.' The light is in you."

"What true king? What're you talking about?"

"Through you, not through my son, will the light be brought to this realm." The king's awe was replaced by relief. "Ah yes, the prophet was right. My quest is over, just as he said, for I have found the one through whom the light will come."

"What light?" Justus asked.

"You do not see it, but it is there, in you. I had seen it before, when you were younger. After your wife died, I thought you had lost it. But it's still there, deep inside, asleep, waiting to be awakened."

"Sire, I don't understand what you're saying."

"You have a noble heart, Justus. You curse the darkness in this land, as do I. Yet even you do not understand the reason you are the way you are. What makes you noble? What makes you honest? What makes you steadfast? It is the light within you. You have been made the way you are for a reason."

Now Justus gave a start. The words Katrina spoke many years ago echoed the king's statement. *"Eloah has made you the way you are because he has destined you for greatness."* He stood silent and still, wanting to fight the reality of a strange and haunting presence in his spirit, but finding he could not.

The king stared out the window. "I sought help from Teman to bring the light into Rygia. Rolland stood at my side from the beginning. He believed in me when none others would. Now I must depend on you, Captain. The light is the one thing that can bring hope for our people. I need you to help me win the council. Honor the memory of General Rolland by standing with me, as he would have."

"My duty is to stand with my king, but..."

"You have doubts. I understand. And yet, I now believe that you truly are the one to deliver the message. Perhaps a trip to Teman is just what you need."

The king picked up a parchment that lay on a table. "I've prepared a letter for King Eliada. I need you to deliver it, and I need you to go alone. One man alone will pose no threat to them."

"Of course, Sire."

"Very good. There are still some finishing touches I need to add to the letter. Come to me first thing tomorrow morning, and I'll send you on your way."

"Yes, Sire."

"When you arrive there, you are to go straight to King James Eliada and give the letter only to him."

"As you wish, Sire."

King Arkelaus studied Justus' face. "Your grief for Rolland runs deep, I can see that. Please understand, Captain, we will get to the bottom of this. But you must not blame Teman."

"I've heard that more times than I care to remember."

The king put his hand on Justus' shoulder. "I do not understand Rolland's death any more than you. But I do know this—there's an evil at work here much greater than you or I could fathom. Still, I think victory is near at hand."

"Victory, Sire?"

"The king of Teman has promised me that by spring he will be able to come here, to Rygia. All I need do is convince my council to allow him entrance and be willing to listen to him. It may take me all winter, but by Eloah, I will do it! But I need your help, Justus. Not only must you deliver this letter for me, you must stand beside me in this wholeheartedly."

Justus could give no answer. While he did not entirely agree with the king, he could not deny the presence of a great and powerful force drawing him. As he looked into the eyes of his king, he began to see a deeper peace, a deeper understanding, than he could comprehend.

He needed time to think it over.

~~~

Prince Medan stormed into Alton's chamber. "I don't believe it! I just don't believe it!"

Alton motioned for his servants and soldiers to leave. When the door was shut, he said, "Believe what?"

"The things my father told me. The worst of it is, he doesn't believe that Teman had anything to do with Rolland's death."

"How can that be?"

"I don't know. Well, at any rate, at least he's sending Corden to investigate."

Alton's eyes grew wide. "Sending Corden where?"

"To Teman. He's to go alone and—"

"What! No, you can't let him do it."

"Why not?"

"Don't you think they'll just kill him too? Begging your pardon, Your Highness, but your father is not thinking rationally."

"Perhaps you're right. After the things I heard him say, he truly does seem bewitched. What do you suggest, Alton?"

"If anyone goes to Teman at all, it ought to be with a mighty force, just as a precaution."

"Would they not think we're attacking them?"

"Perhaps that is exactly what we ought to be doing."

~~~

Rolanda stood with Gregor at the gate of the castle as Baron Giles Godfrey approached, surrounded by a score of his best men-at-arms.

"Why did you summon me?" Godfrey asked.

Gregor said, "I feared for Rolanda's safety."

"If that prince has dared harm you—"

Rolanda said, "No, he has not harmed me, but he has threatened me."

"How dare he," Godfrey said through clenched teeth.

"Wait, there's more," Rolanda said. "Prince Medan has been speaking openly against King Arkelaus."

"Yes, I know. I received a sealed letter from him shortly

before getting your message. What's going on?"

Gregor said, "We don't know, but I didn't want Rolanda to be without protection here. Especially not after what happened to General Rolland."

"Rolland? What happened to him?"

"He's dead. He was killed on the road to Teman. No one knows who did it."

Godfrey scratched his scraggly golden beard. "You were wise to call for me. I'll get a room at the inn and report to the king in the morning."

~~~

The next morning, Justus arrived at the castle fully intending to back the king wholeheartedly. But as he passed through the gate, he came upon a great commotion in the courtyard. People ran about haphazardly, like children who had lost their way.

He grabbed the first boy who came near. "What's going on here?"

"Haven't ya heard, sir? The king! The king's got the plague!"

Justus stood in shock. A few moments passed before he could gather himself, but when he did, he raced into the palace and headed straight to the king's chamber. There he found the physician with a grave expression on his face.

"Oh, there you are, Captain Corden. The king has been asking for you."

Justus stepped toward the bed and halted at the sight of his king's ashen face.

"Justus..." the king rasped.

Justus leaned over the bed. "I'm here, Sire."

"Justus..."

He laid a hand on the king's shoulder. "I'm right here, Sire."

"Jus... tus..."

Seeing the glazed look in Arkelaus' eyes, Justus realized the king was not fully conscious.

The king continued to rasp, "Jus... tus..." but his voice became weaker and quieter each time.

Once again a storm raged in Justus' spirit. Why was it every time he felt he might give in to the tug in his heart, something like this happened? First Katrina, then Rolland. Would King Arkelaus be next?

43

Rolanda jumped at the sound of her door slamming and frowned when she saw Prince Medan standing inside her room. She was alone with him, for she had sent Gregor into the city to tell Giles Godfrey about the king's condition.

Medan looked very angry.

Bravely, she said, "How dare you enter my private chamber without knocking."

He grabbed her arm. "What've you done?"

She tried to wrench her arm from his grasp. "What are you talking about? Unhand me! You're hurting me!"

Medan gripped tighter. "What have you done to my father?"

"Me? Why do you think I had anything to do with it?"

"The porter informed me that Baron Godfrey arrived in Archella yesterday evening."

"What if he did?"

"Why did he not report his arrival to the palace?"

"Godfrey doesn't have to tell the palace of his every move."

"It's customary for a baron to inform the palace of his presence in the city. Your father neglected to do so."

"It was late. He was coming here yet this morning."

"How convenient of him. And suspicious! According to the porter, he arrived shortly after sundown. My father was still well at that time. The porter also says you and Gregor were there to meet him. You had quite a long conversation. What were you discussing?"

"I can discuss private matters with him if I choose."

"Really? When those private matters might have something to do with the health of the king? I think not!"

"What are you saying?"

"After you met with Godfrey, you went into the king's chamber, did you not?"

"Yes, I did. I am accustomed to bidding your father good night, as you well know. And if you were wondering, the king was in perfect health when I left his chamber."

"Did you bother to inform the king of your father's arrival?"

"There was no need for me to do Godfrey's business when he would have attended to it in the morning himself." With her free hand, she tried to pry the prince's hand off her arm, but Medan yanked her toward himself.

"You were the last person in my father's chambers last night. After your father arrived—secretly, I might add—you spoke to him, then went straight to the king's chamber. No one else was seen coming or going from there all night. In the morning we found him ill, perhaps near death."

"Release me!" Rolanda said.

To her relief, the door slammed open and Gregor burst in. "Unhand her!" He squared off with the prince but wisely kept his hands off. He did, however, stand to his full height and snarl down at the younger, smaller man.

Medan released Rolanda, but he said, "You were the last one with the king. If you ask me, that makes you and your father the prime suspects."

Rolanda rubbed her sore arm. "You're insane! I have no reason to wish the king ill."

"Godfrey's been a grievance to the king for years. He has reason to see the king suffer."

"Godfrey got all he wanted when I was pledged to marry you. He may be a harsh man, but he would not have done this. If it's blame you seek, I suggest you look elsewhere."

With a glance toward Gregor's scowling face, Medan pointed a finger at Rolanda. "If my father dies, you'll die too." He left, slamming the door.

Gregor said, "That's it, we're leaving tonight. Medan's given you all the reason you need."

Rolanda plopped onto her bed and burst into tears.

Gregor knelt in front of her, taking hold of her trembling hands. "What is it? What else has he done to you?"

"It's not that." She wiped away one tear only to let others out. "Oh, Gregor, do you love me?"

"More than anything. And now that you've got reason to leave, we can finally be together."

"Do you mean it? Even if I tell you—"

He caressed her hair. "Tell me what you will, I'll still love you."

In a burst of bravery, Rolanda said, "I'm carrying Prince Medan's child!"

Gregor's mouth dropped open, but the shock soon passed and he said, "Do you think I didn't know this could happen? It doesn't change the way I feel. Wait a minute." He rose and began to pace. "Your child is heir to the throne. Have you told Medan yet?"

She shook her head.

In one long stride, he bounded to her, took her head in his hands, and kissed her on the forehead. "Such a wise woman. Come home with me, Rolanda. Uncle Giles won't argue your leaving, not after what Medan just said. Leave this place and be mine at last. I won't wait another day."

~~~

No one in Archella could be convinced the king's illness wasn't a plague from Teman, except for those who believed it was more than a plague. Rumors spread rampantly about foul play on the part of Teman, perhaps poison.

Even Justus was affected by the rumors. All the evidence pointed to Teman. Everything was fine in Rygia until King Arkelaus had gone there. Justus found himself listening to the words Alton had said to Medan in the market square.

"See if your father comes back safe and whole, with no hint of plague or foul play."

Alton's words seemed almost prophetic. And yet there were so many more questions that needed answers. Finding the letter that King Arkelaus had wanted him to take to Teman, he went to see Prince Medan.

"Your Highness, allow me to take the king's letter to Teman. I promise you, I'll get to the bottom of this."

Prince Medan snatched the letter from him and tossed it into the fireplace. "My father was not himself when he wrote this. It's full of nonsense."

Justus watched the parchment curl in the flames, slowly turning to ashes. "Do you believe Teman's at fault?"

"Of course I do."

"Then we should either investigate or attack. Those are the only options I see," Justus said.

"Believe me, Captain, my best people are working on what is to be our next move."

As Justus left the castle that day, he came to a sad realization. King Arkelaus' dream was dead. And the sadder truth was that he himself was willing to let it die.

Over the next several days, Justus learned that Rolanda had left and that Medan was happy about it. Medan had the castle scribes draw up divorce papers to make it official. The next thing Justus heard was that Medan's trollop Eva was summoned to the castle.

Before long, more women were brought to Medan. Maidservants, daughters of merchants and nobles, anyone who caught his eye. He was even known to ride through the city and look for someone new. Justus did not approve of the prince's behavior, but who was he to oppose him?

He also noticed changes taking place among the maidens who entered the palace. Each one would come to Medan with the same childish innocence in her eyes, then in just a few days those eyes turned hollow and lifeless. Even so, the women were quite happy with the prince's attentions and the status they held while in the palace and were never aware of what they had lost.

One cold evening as Justus returned to his cottage, he quietly entered Anna's room. His ten-year-old daughter slept peacefully, her chest slowly rising and falling with each soft breath. After stoking the fire, he approached the bed and stared at her for a long time.

Even at this young age she looked so much like her mother. In only six short years she would be the same age Katrina was when he had met her. His spirit burned to think what might happen to her if a man like Medan ever saw her.

After several minutes he left her room, quietly closing the door behind himself.

Bett looked up from her sewing. "You look troubled, sir."

"I am troubled."

"A trouble shared is a trouble lightened."

Justus stared at the gray-haired woman. He always enjoyed her light-hearted spirit and her whimsical sayings, but this time her words brought no consolation.

Bett stopped her work and let her hands drop into her lap. "What is it, sir?"

"Medan's been taking one woman after another into the palace."

She resumed her sewing and answered without looking up. "Yes, I have heard. I think it's contemptible what he's doing. Abusing his position in such a manner. And right under his father's nose! While his father lies sick!"

"I worry about Anna," Justus said.

"So do I."

He peered out the window, watching a cold November rain patter on the glass pane. "Don't take her out of the cottage anymore, at least not far. She can go to the barn or the beach, as long as you keep watch for passersby. But don't ever take her to the market, and don't allow anyone inside this house."

"Oh, Master Corden, are you certain? Do you know what you're asking of her?"

"I know exactly what I'm doing. I want people to forget I have a daughter. Then by the time she's of age, no one will ask about her."

44

The next morning as Justus ate breakfast in his own cottage, Anna came to him.

"Papa?"

"Yes, Anna?"

"Bett taught me something. Can I say it to you?"

Justus noticed Katrina's little black book in Anna's hand. He leaned toward her, elbows on the table. "Sure, go ahead."

Holding the closed book in her hands, Anna shut her eyes and said, "My justice will become a light to the nations." She opened her eyes and beamed proudly.

The words caught Justus by surprise. "Show me that."

She opened the book and handed it to him.

At first his eyes were drawn to the markings that Katrina had put in the margins. Then he saw the verse Anna had recited. It was underlined, as were all those that bore his name. Those were Katrina's favorites.

He turned his attention to the words, *"My justice will become a light to the nations."*

He felt a twinge in his heart. Not a twinge of heartache or pain but the kind of twinge an empty heart feels when the thing longed for is near.

Light in justice. Maybe King Arkelaus was right.

King Arkelaus had shown a bit of improvement the day before, so Justus resolved to try to speak with him about this. But when he arrived at the castle and stood outside the king's chamber, the physician emerged with a bad report.

"He's taken a turn for the worse."

"Worse? What do you mean? He was improving yesterday."

"It seems that he is near the end."

"The end? What are you saying?"

"The king is dying, Captain. Nothing more can be done."

Justus bolted into the king's chamber and stopped abruptly. Pain was etched across the king's face. His skin was pallid, his breath shallow. Justus stepped to the bedside and laid a hand on the king's shoulder. Immediately he drew back his hand, surprised at the intensity of the fever.

"Your Majesty, can you hear me?"

The king's eyelids fluttered.

"Who was the last person to see you, Sire? Who was in your chamber?"

Arkelaus' eyes betrayed his confusion. "My son..."

"Prince Medan? What did he say to you?"

No answer. Justus stood by the bed and waited, but the king lay still, almost lifeless. After a long time, Justus put his hand near the king's mouth to be sure he was still breathing. Feeling a faint breath, he waited yet longer, turning away to look out the window.

The king's faint voice startled him. "Darkness. Darkness approaches. Beware. It has already taken Medan."

"What do you mean?" Justus asked.

The king appeared to summon every last bit of his strength to speak. "Light. Must find light. In you."

"In me?"

"Light in you. Also darkness. They fight. They fight inside you."

"I don't understand."

"Your past. They come from deep in your past. The light and the dark, from different sources. They fight to control you. You must choose."

"Sire, I—"

"Protect my son, Justus. Protect the royal line. Through the light of justice will you find the true king."

Those were King Arkelaus' last words.

The next day, he was buried.

As the body was laid in the ground, Justus stood like a statue, gripping the Temanite arrow that Rolland had given him. He did not hear the words that were said, nor did he notice the hundreds of veiled ladies in mourning.

All he knew was the emptiness in his heart. The same emptiness as when Katrina died. And when Rolland died. Only King Arkelaus could hold back Justus' anger and grief. King Arkelaus had always been a guiding force in his life. Now he was gone.

Goodness. Light. Faith. An unseen God. *Ludicrous. The moment someone begins to have faith, everything falls to pieces.*

With every shovelful of dirt thrown on the king's grave, Justus could feel bitterness digging its roots deep into his spirit. He stared at the arrow Rolland had given him, remembering what Rolland had said at that time. But those words only angered him now.

"No, Rolland," he said at last. "It's not time to put painful memories to rest. It's time to avenge them."

~~~

When the funeral was over, Alton watched with great interest as Prince Medan paced furiously in his private chamber.

"What happened?" the prince said. "I thought he was getting better. How did he die?"

Alton said, "I've consulted with our best physicians, and they've come to the conclusion it was indeed poison."

"Teman!" Medan said. "It's Teman's doing! They killed Rolland, and now they've poisoned my father. And my mother as well! We must do something about this! They must pay for what they've done!"

"Indeed," Alton said. "But what do you propose we do? Are you saying we should go to war against them?"

"That's exactly what I'm saying. We can prepare all

winter long. Then, come spring, we'll be ready to attack in full force."

Alton hid a smile. "Be careful, Your Highness. Teman is a powerful country. I've heard they are undefeated at battle. And we have recently lost a great general. Without Rolland Longsword to lead the men, we're at a loss."

"You're right, as always," Medan said. "What do you think we should do?"

"We need to find a new leader for the army, someone who is also undefeated. Someone whose leadership is unsurpassed. Someone who hates Teman as much as you."

"Who is that?"

"Why, Captain Corden, of course."

"Make Captain Corden a general? He's barely thirty years old."

"He's the best man for the position," Alton said.

"But Kelsie's next in line. He's older and has more experience."

"Kelsie could never lead the men in something this big. You need someone the men look up to. Captain Corden's your man."

"But the people will expect *me* to lead them. I'm not quite the fighting man my father was."

"Oh no, Your Highness. The people understand you are in much too great a state of grief to be fighting at this time. Let Corden handle the war. You can join him on occasion, just enough to let the men see you and be inspired with vengeance for your father's death."

Prince Medan opened the door and called to a servant, "Bring Captain Corden to me at once!"

~~~

Anna watched intently as her father scraped a whetstone across his sword. Again and again she heard the terrible rasping of the stone against the metal blade. When he finished, he brushed a rag up and down the shiny silver weapon.

Finally she could bear the curiosity no longer. "What are you doing, Father?"

He didn't answer. His face was colder than she had ever seen before.

In a small voice, she said again, "Father?"

Justus held his sword up to the light. The gleam along the smooth blade seemed to satisfy him. "Mark my words, Anna, this is the only thing to put your trust in." His voice became hollow as he added, "I expect to be gone a very long time for this. Bett will take care of you."

Anna's eyes stung as they filled with tears. "Where are you going, Father?"

He placed the tip of his sword into the scabbard hanging from his belt, then paused. With a hardened expression, he said, "A lot of Temanites are about to meet their God."

With that, he slammed his sword into its sheath.

That sound would ring for the next seven years.

APPENDIX

from the annals of Teman

THE FOUNDING OF RYGIA

After the three Calandrian Wars, the Elyon lived in peace with themselves and walked in righteousness with their God, Eloah. They kept to the Three Mandates that Eloah had given them, and Eloah blessed them.

In those days, the Elyon of the land of Teman would occasionally travel across a rich but unpopulated land to the north, all the way across a wide river, where they found a primitive people who called themselves the Xulon. These people had fair skin and ashy white hair, but their eyes were dark like charcoal.

The Temanites tried to share their knowledge with the Xulon people—knowledge of farming and of healing plants and of reading and writing, but most of all, knowledge of Eloah. But the Xuloners, being quite primitive, were afraid of them and would not listen. In their fear, they killed many of the Temanites.

So it was that as the remaining Temanites returned southward through the rich land, they spied several very large ships approaching. This was the year 4350 since the dawn of creation.

The Temanites saw that the new people looked similar to the Xuloners in that they had fair skin and light hair, but their hair was golden rather than ashy. Even more amazing to the Temanites was that the eyes of the newcomers were blue. This was something never before seen.

When the new people came ashore, the Temanites discovered that they were much more advanced than the people of Xulon, for their ships were large and stout, and they possessed tools and weapons and the ability to read and write. They had also brought with them everything they needed to begin new lives, including farming implements and livestock.

The newcomers asked the Temanites if that land was settled, and the Temanites said it was open land and they were welcome to settle there. And so the newcomers settled in the land north of Teman, and they called it Rygia, for it was a rich land full of forests and rivers and tillable soil.

The Temanites attempted to extend the hand of friendship to the newcomers, but they quickly learned that these fair people, who now called themselves Rygian, were a proud and contentious race, even taken to warring among themselves. For a thousand years, the Rygians were unable to form a unified realm, instead living as separate kingdoms within the land, each owned by a powerful lord called a baron.

After many attempts to befriend the Rygians, resulting in the deaths of many Temanites, the people of Teman no longer sent expeditions to Rygia, leaving them alone to war among themselves.

In the year 5350 since the dawn of creation, the Rygians at last united under one king, King Malchus Alethos Arkelaus. Since Rygia was now at peace with itself, the people of Teman sent another expedition to try to open relations with them.

The Temanites brought a great and valuable gift with them—the Golden Leaves of Light, which contained the knowledge of eternal life. King Malchus accepted the gift and seemed anxious to open relations.

When one year had passed, the Temanites returned to Rygia to see what the Rygians had done with gift, and they brought with them the son of the Temanite king.

But they found that the people of Rygia had spurned the gift and that King Malchus had been slain, leaving his son Mattan as king. King Mattan and his soldiers slew the

Temanites, even to the slaying of the Temanite prince, and swore that no Temanites would ever again be welcome in Rygia.

Why the Rygians spurned the gift and the givers remained a mystery to Teman. And the Temanites were unable to learn what had happened to the Golden Leaves of Light.

THE TEMAN-RYGIAN WAR

Two hundred years after the days of the first king of Rygia, in the year 5580 by the Temanite calendar (1230 by the Rygian calendar), during the reign of King James Eliada the Vigilant, the people of Rygia came to war against Teman.

The Rygians, under the leadership of General Justus Corden, known as the Conqueror, attacked without warning or provocation on the day of the summer solstice. Thus did Teman face what was to become a long and terrible war.

Teman suffered most greatly that first year, having been caught unaware. In subsequent years, however, Teman regained control of the Pass of Mount Paran, which is the only entry point into the land, and were able to drive the Rygians back.

Throughout the seven-year war, the people of Teman called out to Eloah for help, and he answered them. Rygia's ships were dashed to pieces upon the coastal waters, and Rygia's army was driven back time and again by hailstorms, landslides, and harsh winters, as well as by the sword. With the help of Eloah, Teman was able to keep the Rygians from passing beyond the Velan Mountains.

But during the seventh year of the war, the Rygians began to reclaim the Velan Mountains and pressed forward farther than they had in the past. More Temanites died that year than any other.

The war had taken such a terrible turn that the Rygians may have been close to marching on the royal city itself had not King James Eliada taken matters into his own hands. As was discovered later, he had gone unarmed to express mercy to General Corden.

Although King Eliada was killed by the hand of General Corden, the war did come to an end and the realm was spared.

THE ALLIANCE

In the Palace of Rygia
A woman in danger, a man at a crossroads, and a greater threat looms on the horizon. Only an act of extreme sacrifice can change one man's heart and save an entire realm.

On the Isle of Caledron
An ancient evil threatens to destroy the people of faith, and the princess is to be their first victim. Facing death, she must learn some hard lessons in forgiveness.

On the Road to Teman
Events in both Rygia and Teman lead to a meeting of the two kings, but a simmering darkness threatens to disrupt the burgeoning alliance. Will one man's search for light bring salvation to his realm or cause the very darkness he seeks to avoid?

In the Eyes of the King
A young maid's abusive father amasses a great debt. An entire nation is indebted to a greater power. Only the righteous king can offer atonement to both. But pride and intolerance stand in the way.

In the Heart of a Princess
A lowly orphan girl feels unworthy of the king's love, but with the arrival of a mysterious princess from another land, the fate of the king and of the realm may be up to her alone.

In the Shadow of Caledron
With a price on both their heads, Justus Corden and Squire Fox must return to Rygia to find the true prince and bring him to safety. Threatened by the darkness themselves, their friends in Teman are unable to come to their aid.

On the Throne of Rygia
All his life has led to this one goal—to put the true prince of Rygia on the throne. But he may have to sacrifice people dear to him in order to see it accomplished. In doing so, he could lose the allegiance of his people.

ALLEGIANCE

Read about all your favorite characters from *The Alliance* as their adventures begin to span the entire globe.

Song of Petros
As Teman and Rygia join the fight to reclaim the realm of Petros, the true test of allegiance comes down to one mysterious Caledronian.

Son of Caledron
His mysterious beginnings lead him down an ever darker path. Only the prayers of a few believers can save him from himself.

Land of Fire
When Captain Fox turns up missing, only Therion and his untrained crew can attempt to find him, but it means sailing to the last place anyone would wish to go—

Shacor, the land of fire. On their way, they meet a strange man who can either help them or betray them. Either way, no one trusts him.

Gates of Orella
As Therion begins to fulfill his dream of rescuing boys from the Calandrian training grounds, he runs into some very mysterious beings in a land long forgotten. Watch for the return of an equally mysterious friend.

Race to Rhakos
With bonus short story: Attack at Orella
It's long past time for King Malchus of Rygia to consider marriage, and he finds a woman who instantly captures his heart. But the people of Rhakos have their own plans for both him and his beloved.

Return to Caledron
The son of Justus Corden is finally of the age to be knighted. But under a ruse, he winds up on the isle of Caledron and becomes witness to a foreboding prophecy given by Prince Joram of Teman years ago.

Eye of the Dragon
With bonus short story: Sky Devil
In the wake of the death of a champion and the betrayal of a baron, Rygia tries to pull itself back together. Meanwhile in Petros, Kaion children have gone missing, and an underground kaion movement is on the rise. Someone close to Alexander Corden is also missing, so he must join in the search and attempt to save the very people he had come to despise.

Rise of the Gryphagon, Vol. 1: Hope Falls

As the Meketi people of Shacor face ever-growing hardships under their Kaion masters, one slave girl struggles with the concept of a coming gryphagon who could save them. Just as her life begins to turn around, hope is again snatched away.

Rise of the Gryphagon, Vol. 2: Hope Rises

As Alexander Corden's destiny begins to unfold, he makes plans to strike at the center of Caledron's strength. But an enemy within his ranks and a horrible new weapon of the Kaion threaten to subvert his efforts.

Return of the Volon

Rygia and Teman face their greatest threat yet, as the powers of Caledron discover who the Rygians truly are and send all their forces to utterly destroy them. Taken away from his homeland at Rygia's time of greatest need, Alexander Corden discovers where the Volon have been living and what they've been planning. Now he must find a way to return home and warn his people of a new threat.

THE HUNT OF THE UNICORN

In allegorical fashion reminiscent of The Chronicles of Narnia, "The Hunt of the Unicorn" tells of the fall and redemption of mankind.

An evil threatens the beautiful realm called Castle Garden. By an act of disobedience, the child princess falls victim to the Dark Land, unwittingly bringing its destructive forces into her father's realm. The only key to her survival and the future of Castle Garden is the capture of a beast that most believe is mere myth—a unicorn.

As the best hunters of the realm gather to seek the mythical beast, a young commoner named John finds himself thrust into their world. In medieval times, hunting was a pastime reserved for nobility, yet John is a mere gardener who spends his life with his knees to the ground and his head in the clouds.

Disdained by the noble hunters, John is uncertain of his own worth and struggles with the purpose for his being included among them.

Through the grueling months of the hunt, John learns that more is at stake than the princess' life, more even than the survival of Castle Garden, and the unicorn's purpose greater than anyone could have imagined.

This novel is inspired by the seven tapestries called The Hunt of the Unicorn, circa 14th century, which themselves tell of the fall and redemption of mankind and use the unicorn as a symbol for Christ. Many scenes, characters, and symbolisms in this novel can be found in each of the tapestries. The hunt itself is based on an actual medieval-style hunt as depicted in 14th century illustrations.

This stand-alone book is great for ages 12 through adult. Available at Amazon.com in Kindle and paperback format. The Kindle version is full of color photos of the tapestries on which the story is based.

PRONUNCIATION GUIDE

Addir: ah-DEER
Areli: ah-RELL-ee
Arkelaus: ark-uh-LAY-us
Avalee: AH-vah-lee
Aven: Ā-vehn (like haven)
Aviur: AH-vee-ur
Degar: DAY-gar
Degarron: dah-GAIR-un
Elaad: EE-lahd
Elán: ee-LAHN
Elan: EE-lahn
Eliada: el-ee-AH-dah
Elkanah: el-KAH-nah
Eloah: ee-LOH-ah
Elyon: ELL-yahn
Eshana: ee-SHAH-nah
Iscuro: ISS-kur-oh
Josephus: joh-SEE-fuss
Kaion: KYE-yahn
Kolan: KOH-lahn
Mari, Mariya: MAH-ree, MAH-ree-ah
Nakar: nah-KARR
Netish Machaira: neh-TISH mah-KYE-rah
Rolanda: roh-LAHN-dah
Rolland: RAHL-und
Rygia: RYE-jee-ah
Skotos: SKOH-tohs
Sospater: SAHS-pah-ter
Teman: TEE-mun
Temana: tee-MAH-nah
Velan: VEE-lahn
Volon: VOH-lahn

CPSIA information can be obtained
at www.ICGtesting.com
Printed in the USA
LVHW081754280922
729507LV00001B/31